white guys

ANTHONY GIARDINA

WILLIAM HEINEMANN : LONDON

Published in the United Kingdom by William Heinemann, 2006

1 3 5 7 9 10 8 6 4 2

First published in the United States by Farrar, Strauss & Giroux, New York 2006

William Heinemann
The Random House Group Limited
20 Vauxhall Bridge Road, London, SW1V 2SA

Random House Australia (Pty) Limited
20 Alfred Street, Milsons Point, Sydney,
New South Wales 2061, Australia

Random House New Zealand Limited
18 Poland Road, Glenfield
Auckland 10, New Zealand

Random House (Pty) Limited
Isle of Houghton, Corner of Boundary Road & Carse O'Gowrie,
Houghton 2198, South Africa

Random House Publishers India Private Limited
301 World Trade Tower, Hotel Intercontinental Grand Complex
Barakhamba Lane, New Delhi 110 001, India

The Random House Group Limited Reg. No. 954009

www.randomhouse.co.uk

A CIP catalogue record for this book
is available from the British Library

Papers used by Random House
are natural, recyclable products made from wood grown in
sustainable forests. The manufacturing processes conform to
the environmental regulations of the country of origin

ISBN: 0 434 01605 5
ISBN 13: 978 0 434 01605 1

Printed and bound in Great Britain by Clays Ltd, St Ives plc

For
Barry Kennedy
(1950–2003)

And for
Sloan Harris

. . . Terrible were his crimes—
but if you wish to blackguard the Great King,
think how mean, obscure and dull you are,
your labors lowly and your merits less—
—Robert Lowell,
"Death of Alexander"

part one

Billy Mogavero was my friend from the age of about eight, or whatever age it is that boys separate from their mothers, begin their forays outside the tight circle of skirts and family gatherings, and form their own, even tighter circles on playgrounds, or, in our case, on the long, broken strip of beach stretching from Boston Harbor all the way up to Gloucester. We were located in Winship, somewhere in the middle of those two points. There are boys who, at eight or ten, are more than normally handsome, well built, instinctive leaders, and I have noticed such boys nearly always have a streak of meanness in them. That was true of Billy, but we followed him anyway, because we had no innate leadership qualities ourselves, not Johnny Lombardi or Freddie Tortolla or Kenny DiGiovanni, or me, the only Irish kid in the group, the ethnic runt.

We all followed Billy, but Billy followed just one person, and that person only sometimes. That was his father. Mr. Mogavero was a tall, skinny man who had married late. He wore glasses, and he was the butcher for the Star Market. When we went there to meet him—when Billy needed money for the movies or to get a cut of meat his mother had asked him to bring home—his father would come out the door that led into the frosty inner harbor of the Star Market meat department and wipe his hands slowly and carefully on the blood-smeared apron he wore and look us all over. With the glasses on, he might have been a schoolteacher. He said our names carefully, one by one, as if he owed us all the respect he would give to men who had come on business.

It is odd that it begins this way, this story I have to tell, with us following Mr. Mogavero on the boardwalk on a series of warm summer evenings in the late sixties. There was, at that time, along the boardwalk, the three-quarters-empty shell of a once-great amusement park, Fantasia. Its memory still hovered over the town of Winship. The park had been built in the 1920s, a huge pleasure dome, a "city by the sea" imposed on the marshland that spread back and fanned outward from the beach. It had put us on the map. A train had once carried immigrant workers out of Boston on Sundays (The Fantasia Special, it was called) to pay their ten cents and ride the flume cars into the Great Lagoon, or to sit coupled in the scooped boats of Love's Journey and emerge, after a trip through the tunnel, under a shower of confetti. Or else to visit Dark Town, where Negroes played Dixieland music and staged mock alligator hunts. All that was left by the time we were kids were the roller coaster and the kiddie rides, the Dodge 'Em cars and the Caterpillar, and a sometimes-working Wild Mouse. Mr. Mogavero used to take us boys Sunday nights into what was left of the park, to dispense quarters so that we could play Skee-Ball, to stand and watch us on the Dodge 'Ems. He did not participate. He stood and watched, and when we were tired, he made us follow him in a direction opposite to home.

He led us to deserted places, places where the marsh had broken through the territory of the old park, other places where stores and warehouses had taken up residence. Some nights Mr. Mogavero would make a halfhearted attempt to explain what had once been here, what a ride like Tragic Honeymoon had looked like in its heyday, and how it had worked. "The couple would stand up there, and there was a mechanical illusion, made them look like skeletons." His hands would go up to describe the scene in the air, but he would give up halfway, as though exact communication was less important than pure suggestion. What we were left with was how strangely beautiful and spectral the old park remained for this quiet man.

There is nothing more to say about those nights except for the anger with which Billy endured his father's wanderings. No boy wants to see his father as in any way out of the ordinary. The rest of us were lucky: the Italian boys' fathers were big, hairy, energetic lugs, deliverers of oil, night watchmen in factories, bus drivers. My own father was a teller in a bank. They listened to baseball games on transistor radios; they sat on the stoops of their small, packed-together beach-town houses on summer nights and drank beer; they put down Negroes and insulted hippies and fags and asserted an American regularity we all deeply prized. We knew how to throw baseballs and catch footballs, they took the time to make sure of that, though it was not like now: they rarely came to the organized games we played in Little League or Babe Ruth. They took us to church and afterward scoffed a little at what the priest had said, so that we should know certain sins were not to be taken seriously. It was an easy life, without large expectations, and it probably surprised these guys to see the incomes their sons managed to achieve when, in the nineties, the economy picked us up on that high, curling wave we miraculously knew how to ride. One by one, Mr. Mogavero would return us to these waiting fathers, and they always exchanged words, but you knew right away from the way they looked at Billy's father that he was not a member of their club.

On those nights, I'm convinced, something started in Billy, an attitude toward the world essentially hard, as though his father's dreaminess were a strop he was sharpening his blade on. For me, it had another effect. I'd lie in bed after those walks and look out my window, which had a view beyond the houses and the TV antennas and the row of stores on the next block to the marsh where the great, dormant Fantasia now lay. Nobody wants to believe that there had once been a world better than the one you were born into, but if that is the information fed into your young consciousness, it tends to stay there.

One of the ways I have learned to accommodate the past—or maybe it's truer to say, one of the ways I have learned to fight its pull—is in the work I do now. I am a salesman for the textbook division of Endicott Press. Endicott has branched out in the last couple of decades to include historical survey books, and three years ago we launched a foreign languages division, which shows signs of doing very well. Our reputation, however, was made on the literary anthologies we began publishing in the early 1960s, when the market for literature began to boom on American campuses, and we have remained a leader ever since. We now publish anthologies of African American and Native American and Asian American literature; our selection of Chicano writings, published just two years ago, has done spectacularly well, particularly in the West, and a gay-and-lesbian anthology has just been published. Our bread and butter, though, is and always has been the book we refer to in-house as "White Guys." "White Guys" sells in the hundreds of thousands annually. It is the text of choice at community colleges and for the less-imaginative graduate assistants at the big state universities. It begins with an excerpt from Charles Brockden Brown and his eighteenth-century religious maniacs and ends with a story about a lovesick football coach in late-twentieth-century Albuquerque. Though it is not, of course, literally comprised of stories written only by white males, the bulk is still there: it is a testicular view of America, unquestionably.

Never a reader in high school or college, and having fallen into this job by benign accident (the father of a college buddy set me up), I took to the road as a very young man with a briefcase full of books and, finding time and a little energy on my hands, began to read from beginning to end the stories in our cash cow. I thought I was probably the only one of the young salesmen doing this, that it might give me some sort of leg up. Mostly what I felt, though, reading these stories in motel rooms in Utica or Wilkes-Barre, was how depressing most of them were, Henry James and Willa Cather and Sherwood Anderson chronicling lives that started out hopeful and then fell into some hole. After reading one of these stories, I would put the book down, go to the window of whatever motel I happened to be staying in, and, looking outside, feel something begin to shift for me; an easy and basically innocent take on the world that had served me well up to this point began to seem too weak an instrument of defense.

You have to understand who I was then: a young guy who had done little in the past four years except get drunk and half sleep through his classes, party, and watch a criminal amount of sports on TV. Nothing at all had happened to me except for one thing, and I had basically swept that under the rug. Nothing existed to stand in my way except that old affinity of mine for getting caught up in the dregs and eddies of the past. But now, gazing out into the light of the motel's commercial surround, I began to detect another light at the edge of my vision. It seemed the light of the stories I'd been reading. As old as many of those stories were, it felt like it was still out there, exerting a familiar pull—the light in which people failed.

I remember one such night in particular. It was early November in western Pennsylvania, and I'd been sitting in my motel room before dinner, reading a story by John Cheever called "The Country Husband." By the time I went out for dinner, the story's effect hadn't really gotten to me. But I found as I sat in this family restaurant, empty at this late hour except for a couple of solitary guys like me, other salesmen or divorced guys, and a couple who sat in morose silence in a booth near mine, that whatever it was I'd been pushing away in my first months on the road, whatever mood of fear and trepidation had been nursed through my reading of the stories in "White Guys," that mood was now squarely, frighteningly in front of me. I can't say it was "The Country Husband" alone that did it to me. But Cheever's story, with its emphatic suggestion of the emptiness of suburban marriage, of lives like my own hanging by a thread of misplaced hope, had reached me at a point where my ducks were all in a row. Cheever's well-chosen words had knocked them all down.

When do boys decide who they're going to be? I don't have the answer to that one, but I know I *had* decided by that point. I wanted something soft and ever-present in the life I saw around me. I wanted husbandhood and fatherhood and a certain kind of woman who attached to those concepts in my mind. I wanted, in a very basic, unashamed way, the life I saw in the movies, in advertisements, in which a couple, still young, sit in a car full of kids. I wanted the whole package that went along with that image: sofas and large-screen TVs, and a small boat, a Boston Whaler. It had not yet occurred to me that those dreams might be in any way insufficient.

I had little appetite that night. Things I had hardly noticed before suddenly seemed inescapable. Who were the lonely guys sitting in this restaurant with me tonight, and how had their loneliness been arrived at? Why weren't the couple in the next booth speaking?

I paid quickly and went back to the motel and lay under the covers, and here is what happened to me: I knew then that I did not merely want the Life—the wife and kids and dog and boat—I wanted it fiercely. I wanted this dream so badly it did not even require individuals to fulfill it: a *specific* wife, *specific* kids. I wanted to cling to forms. Almost anyone would do, as long as I could prove John Cheever wrong. Give me those beautiful forms, I promised myself in the way of young men, and I will love them to death.

The next day, I found myself wandering down the hallway of a small private college in western Pennsylvania. There is a light to the hallways of such third-tier institutions that is like the color of food that's been poorly wrapped. There is old dust and, always, a discarded book left outside a professor's office, a book that the professor in question has left there on purpose, secretly hoping someone will take it.

I had determined to make several cold calls, calls to men who had received sample copies of the newest revised "White Guys." But as soon as I found myself in that hallway, I began to wonder if it was possible anymore for me to *do* this job, never mind generate new revenue from it. I knocked on the door of a man to whom I had sent the book, a man named Professor Bill Adamcik, and listened to his gruff voice, inside, say, "Come in."

I took a seat in Professor Adamcik's office before I was invited to. He started to lift a hand in protest, then thought better of it. He told me he was busy before I'd even gotten a chance to tell him I was from Endicott. I asked if he'd had an opportunity to look over the sample copy. He scowled. No, he hadn't had time. Then, after a pause, he said, "Besides, that volume is too stodgy. I haven't used it in years."

I knew then that I had two choices: leave the room or go for broke. I chose the latter. I asked him the simplest, most naked question I could think to ask: Had he ever read "The Country Husband"?

For a long moment he gazed at me with a reluctant sense of curiosity. "I have, yes," he said, and shifted in his chair. "Why do you ask?"

"Well, when you call this volume *stodgy*, I don't know." I shook my head. "I'm going to take a guess I'm a lot like your students. I mean, we're all just trying to figure it out." I let out a very small laugh, to show him I could poke a little fun at myself while remaining, in essence, deadly earnest. "These stories, especially this one—I'm not ashamed to say they *get* to me."

Professor Adamcik's eyes narrowed slightly. Beyond him, outside his oversize windows, at the edge of the brown and yellow November grounds of the college, lay the athletic fields. Boys in maroon and black soccer uniforms stood in clumps. He saw me looking at them and settled lower in his chair.

"What—*got* to you?" he asked, and I could tell that he was testing me, to see if I'd really read it.

"Well, like I say, I'm a young guy, with it all sort of in front of me. And here's a story about a guy who's got it all, everything I want—" I leaned forward slightly. "Wife, kids, great house. And then he nearly dies in a plane crash, and he can't get his wife to listen to him. It's like the *things* in his life have taken over."

I shook my head, aware now that I was doing everything for effect, and marveling at my own newfound ability to lampoon, for the sake of a sale, things that had kept me awake the night before. "So what's Cheever saying?" I asked in the same breathless, highly charged mode. "That it's all *meaningless*?"

Professor Adamcik smiled at that. But then, after smiling, he turned and faced out his window. Beyond him, at the edge of our vision, the soccer players spread into formation. I considered his days on this patch of Pennsylvania devoted to sports, this man with his sparse dark hair and trimmed gray beard and eyes that seemed to have begun a steady retreat into that place where things mattered to him less and less.

"I know there are fancier volumes," I said. "I think we're aware—at Endicott—that what we put out isn't exactly cutting edge, but—"

"It's just one view," Professor Adamcik said, turning to me. "Cheever's. It's just one view of marriage, of . . . the life you want."

I didn't respond immediately. I sat and waited, watching him as he looked me over. In my training in sales, I had been taught always to maintain dominance, to never let the buyer get ahead of me. It occurred to me now that that strategy might work with the dumb, but not with the smart, and professors were, of course, among the smartest. But what they also were was lonely.

So I allowed him to talk. I did no more than listen. He seemed reluctant to say too much, aware that I might be laying some subtle trap for him. But when I made no move toward bringing him to the point of sale, when the whole notion of my wanting anything at all from him (save to listen) seemed to have evaporated, I saw something begin to happen to him that I have since seen happen in a hundred other academic offices. I watched him fall into his need for me.

Things are never so simple that I can say Professor Adamcik ordered "White Guys" from me that time, or the next. But I kept coming, and eventually he did. "For my freshmen," he said, as if to excuse this lapse in his judgment. But really it was to keep me coming, to know that once or twice a year I would arrive and sit in his office and engage him with an idea or ask a question to which I believed he might offer some illumination. This is my life now. This is what I do: knock on doors and offer my stirred-up soul to men who have stopped believing that people like me exist—thinking men, questing men, readers. I am not really any of those things, of course, at least not in the way these men assume. What I am is something much simpler: a man who had a momentary perception of one of the ways the past wants to pull you under, and until very recently, at least, managed to stay afloat.

By the time this incident happened, Billy was no longer really a part of my life. I believed at that time that his effect on me had been a function of adolescence and was slowly evaporating. If asked, I might even have said I barely remembered the night Billy's power got to me in a new way, a way that was more difficult to outgrow, on the night of our senior prom, in 1978.

Disco reigned that year. We were desperate to escape all that— Kenny, Johnny, Freddie, Billy, and I. We were cooler, or at least considered ourselves to be (Devo was our band of choice), so as soon as we could cut out from the prom, we took our dates down to the beach and Freddie brought out some of the dope he bought regularly from a cousin who worked in Boston. Freddie was already full of himself, with an oversize head and an air of knowing all the angles. He loved to rub whatever connections he had in our faces.

The girls who were with us that night were girls we'd each been with for a while, but there was nothing serious going on. The one exception was Billy's date, Carol Casella.

Carol had transferred from a parochial school to Winship High in her junior year, a blond girl with a face of that extraordinary peach-fuzz quality that made every boy in the high school want to touch her, while knowing instinctively that it was more than we deserved. This modesty she'd brought out in all of us resulted in her going dateless for most of junior year, until Billy walked up to her one day in the cafeteria and asked her out.

They were legendary in the world of Winship High School. Billy had already come fully into his looks. His big, pouty, roundish face had matured without passing through any of the debilitating stages of adolescence. He had the look of sexual readiness before any of the rest of us. I was more than half in love with the sight of them together, his dark frame against the soft blondness of her, and on this night, as on many others, I found myself staring at them.

It was not something Billy ever failed to notice, my staring. In a way, he could be said to have thrived on it. What was strange was that the first thing I noticed as I stared at Billy that night was a hint of uncertainty in his eyes. He covered it with a big, mouthy smile, as if it were him, not me, who'd caught the other at something. I knew by that smile that a change was coming.

Billy stood up. He dusted off the seat of his tuxedo pants, which were wet from the sand. Carol helped him, her gesture spontaneous enough to make it seem like they were attached to the same set of impulses. Then Billy started walking away from us, toward the boardwalk, where our cars were parked, Carol following at a distance.

We all decided to get up and go after him. Johnny was the only one of us to balk; there was a prematurely aged part of him that always kicked in at such moments and tried to hold us back from our wilder impulses. Billy's car was gone, so we all got into our own and for ten or fifteen minutes searched the streets of Winship, streets quiet on this May night before the beach season had officially started. If any of us were annoyed at Billy's disappearance, we sat on it. It was unthinkable that the evening should continue without him.

Finally we spotted Billy's car parked alongside the alley behind the train station. The trunk was open and Billy was leaning into it, removing something. Carol was in the front seat.

"What's going on, Billy?" someone shouted.

He didn't answer us. Billy's earlier uncertainty had given way to a darker mood. Changes in him always happened quickly; we were never quite prepared for them. It might have been disgust written across his face now as he hoisted a gas can out of the trunk.

I thought I could guess what had sparked his new mood: the four of us in our cars, with our ties still in place, and our air of placid acceptance of whatever tepid pleasures the night ahead of us might bring, the parties and the drinking and the bonfire on the beach, and afterward the sacking of the layers of taffeta. He turned away from us, started down the alley, carrying the heavy gas can. We could follow him or not, it was all the same to him.

I knew where he was headed. The alley was bordered on one side by a chain-link fence protecting the train tracks; the T stopped here on its way into Boston. On the other side was a large wooden wall with the words FANTASIA BALLROOM — DANCING NITELY barely decipherable. The wall had faded over time, gone from white to gray, and in certain places the paint had completely worn off and the wooden planks had taken on a sickly green tinge. It had been left up long after its time because the urge still existed in our town—

Mr. Mogavero was not the only one to feel it—to honor what we had once been.

We watched Billy carry the gas can to the place where the sign's wording was, and then we all got out of our cars, though none of us—not even Carol—came close.

"I told you you didn't have to come," Billy said, and he splashed gas liberally onto the sign, stepping back when some came back against him. He took out a box of matches, and he might have gone ahead and set fire to the gas if a car hadn't pulled up just then.

It was a Winship police car. Billy lit a match and thought a second, then blew it out.

We all recognized the cop inside. He was Charlie Porto, a cop in his early sixties, round, and with one of those genial, sad faces of older men who want to be liked. We'd known him for years. He'd even coached some of us in Little League. The patience we all remembered was there in the way he sat in the car, just making us aware of his presence, as if that should be enough to temper or even halt whatever marginally illegal thing we might be up to.

But we were not so far from him, and the scent must have reached him.

"Is that gasoline I smell, Billy?"

He had never coached Billy, but he couldn't help knowing him. There were previous small brushes with the law, and there was also the football team Billy had played on, prominently but unspectacularly, for three years.

Billy's response was to sniff hard. "I don't know, Officer Charlie. Is it?" He had a little smile on his face.

Charlie Porto looked at the rest of us, his way of gauging the seriousness of what was going on, of deciding whether he needed to step out of the car. Our faces must have been blank—at least unhelpful—because he did get out. He walked up to us in that rolling movement of an unhurried fat man.

"Tell you what," he said as he got closer to Billy. "You just bring me that gas can and those matches in your hand, and we'll forget this. You can go on to your parties, or whatever." He turned around and glanced at the rest of us, and there was something mildly heartbreaking in the way that glance asked us to remember the diamonds of certain municipal parks. He was calling to an old agreement, one he couldn't see had been superceded.

When he turned back to Billy, it was to see him kick the can a few inches toward him.

Charlie Porto didn't know what to say then. For a moment or two he simply rocked back and forth on his hips.

"Come on, Billy, before this gets serious, it's time to cut it out."

Billy turned away from him and looked up at the sign. I caught the look of offense on his face at being referred to so intimately, so familiarly. With a quick motion he lit a match.

We all stepped away immediately, and when the match hit the pool of gas, everyone made a run for it, the girls making disgusted noises and Johnny leading the way back to the cars. I'd had the same reaction at first, but I turned around after a few steps to see Charlie Porto making a broken run toward the burning pool at Billy's feet. Billy was waiting for him. Even from a distance I could see the savagery with which Billy hit the policeman. He laid him on the ground too quickly, in a way that seemed unfair, as if they'd been poorly matched. Charlie Porto kept trying to get up, and Billy kept hitting him until the older man lay there motionless. It was over sickeningly fast. I ignored my girlfriend's halfhearted beckoning and stayed after the others were gone.

"What the hell are you doing, Billy?" I shouted.

He ignored me; I doubt he even heard me. He was in another place.

Carol, all this time, had said nothing. But I was aware of her stillness there, almost her expectation of this kind of behavior coming from Billy. An unconscious police officer lay at her feet, she was wearing an expensive gown whose pale tangerine folds scraped against the dirty alley he had brought her to, and this was the night of nights, her senior prom. Yet all this she took in some sort of stride.

Billy hoisted Charlie Porto under the arms, but the man's weight was too much even for him. It was then that he looked up and acknowledged me.

"Come on, Tim. Let's move this guy."

At first I didn't respond. Billy hoisted Charlie Porto under the arms and started dragging him. To save the man this indignity, I went forward and took his legs. I was relieved to see that he was alive. He was still hard to move, though. All the time we were carrying Charlie Porto to his car, I made noises to let Billy know how disgusted I was, but he didn't seem to hear them. He was still in his own quiet place.

We laid Charlie Porto out on the backseat of his car, his fatness making it hard to arrange the body properly. I decided I should stay there until he awoke, to do something at least to make up for Billy's cruelty.

Billy unlatched Charlie's holster and removed the gun.

"Jesus, Billy," I said, and started to reach for the gun to keep him from using it.

"Oh, relax, Tim. I'm not going to shoot him. What do you think I am?"

With surprising expertise Billy dropped the bullets out of the chamber, then jingled them in his hands and threw them as far as he could. He glanced back once at the toppled policeman and started moving toward Carol.

It was then that I realized how much I didn't want to be there. In some domesticated part of me, I hungered for the night as it was supposed to have gone. The sign itself worked its way into my sudden nostalgia. I wanted things left as they were.

Billy was nearly at the sign, reaching into his pocket for the matches, when I shouted, "Don't do it!" Part of me hated him now.

He turned and looked at me, surprised that I had spoken, surprised maybe, in some deeper part of him, that I was still there.

"Why?" he asked.

"He's right," Carol said. Her head had been lowered up till now in patience. She lifted it and said, "You don't have to burn the goddamn sign."

"No, I don't have to," he said, and splashed more gas over the wood, "but I'm going to. Shit, yes. I'm going to."

He placed the lit match against the wood at the lowest point where the gasoline had spilled, and it went up.

Carol shielded her eyes. The flame, initially quite large and dramatic, died down so that only the gas was burning. The wood, soaked with water and salt for more than fifty years, wouldn't take. Billy looked at it with curiosity now.

I moved a little closer toward him. "It means something to people," I said.

"Thank you, Tim, for your Rotary Club take on our little expedition here."

Carol turned to me then for the first time, as if she were just now distinguishing me from the pack. It was a look of approval I was receiving, and it made me beam.

Billy splashed more gas onto the sign. This time some got on Carol's dress, she uttered a small cry and stepped back. Billy didn't light the match, but looked at her a moment as if he was taking in her vulnerability, her *girlness*. It wasn't exactly compassion on his face now, but something else. In dumb show, it looked as if she was pretending to be angry, maybe even *was* angry. She mimed pushing him away, hitting him, and all he did was touch her bare shoulder, look at it with what seemed a kind of wonder. She watched him looking at it.

I could see then, very suddenly, that a change had come over Billy and Carol. Billy placed his hand against her back, and in the next moment they were moving toward me, Carol gazing slightly downward, her hand bunching the spot where her gown had been soiled. I knew they didn't even see me. Something had just been decided between them, and they were moving off as if all that was left for them to do was to obey it.

In the aftermath, everything that was tawdry about the scene— the alley itself, the abandoned gas can, the police car in which I could see the first signs of Charlie Porto stirring—came forward in a way that their being there had at least partially obscured. I was hit by the stupidity of my being there at all, the fall guy for Billy's stunt. So I ran down the alley in the opposite direction from the police cruiser, crossed the street, and sat on the seawall, far enough away so that I knew no one could see me.

I sat there and wondered what the end of this might be. Was it too late to rejoin my friends, to make the evening yield up the simple high school pleasures it had promised earlier? I knew I should be worrying about Charlie Porto, but I wasn't. Though I was trying to push it away, the thing that was still with me was the way Billy and Carol had looked as they passed me.

I was still waiting in my life then for the consummate fuck, the act that would take me out of myself and onto some higher plane. Sometimes you can know things exist without actually experiencing them, and tonight, in the look Billy and Carol had given each other, I knew I'd come close to some central, powerful source. In all his sordidness and violence, Billy was also a guardian of the world's special rooms, the holder of the key. He seemed to need the violence sometimes just to tap into his own tenderness, but having reached it, it was like he was able to open that room to me. To say, Look, Tim, look what's inside. I could see Charlie Porto stepping out of his car and calling for backup, but it was not the reality of this or even the possible danger that affected me now. It was Billy and Carol's sex. I could taste it as I sat there. I could taste the way it would feel to bite Carol's lips and hear her gasp against your ear and to watch her neck stretch as you pushed in a little farther. I could feel, too, what it would be like to do that pushing, to feel the wetness of her and her resistance, too, and the way that wetness would spread deliciously against your thighs.

Though the sign suffered no real damage that night, Billy would go to jail for his assault on Charlie Porto. The rest of us he would refuse to implicate, even going so far as to swear we'd tried to stop him. So we all went to college, while Billy did six months. Always, he gave the sense that whatever had happened between him and Carol that night had been worth it. "My semester abroad," he liked to call it afterward, and smiled.

two

We didn't see Billy again until we came home for our Christmas breaks. We all knew he would be out by then, so we made sure to gather at his house.

Christmas night in an Italian house has a certain feeling. I don't know what it is about these people, but it was always different in my friends' houses from the way it was in the O'Kane home, where my mother made sure to wrap up the uneaten turkey early and my father sat in front of the TV puffing on a cigarette with a kind of relief as soon as it was five o'clock and the day could be officially declared over.

I was glad when I was old enough to visit my friends' houses on Christmas night. There were always uncles around in those houses, big guys with close-cropped hair and enormous cheeks, for whom, after they'd drunk enough, it ceased to matter that we boys had a perpetually stoned look. All that fell away, and they tried very hard to assert a brotherhood-of-man feeling by taking us aside and, with dark, deeply sincere eyes, asking, "Listen, if there's ever anybody's legs you need broken, I'm the guy to call, you hear me? I'm the guy."

We decided to smoke some pot in Freddie's car before we went in, the four of us quiet and a little strange with one another. Freddie and I had gone to UMass together. Kenny and Johnny were commuters—Kenny to Suffolk, Johnny to Northeastern—and I think the relative secrecy of our college lives made Freddie and me want to lord it over them. We were full of our college pranks, girls we had slept with. I'd believed, coming home, that those experiences had changed me in important ways, but sitting in the cannabis haze of Freddie's car, I wasn't sure it was true. Freddie had grown a beard, so his big, blockish face looked even more square than usual. Kenny tried to wear his wispy hair in a David Cassidy style that didn't suit him at all, and we made fun of it. Only Johnny, straight-shooting Johnny, hadn't altered his looks.

When we went inside, the crowd in Billy's house made loud noises of greeting. Billy was sitting at the end of the long Mogavero table between his father and Carol Casella. He was wearing a faded yellow cotton shirt, and his hair was short. The shirt set off the paleness that prison had brought to his skin. But he'd worked out in jail; he looked fit.

He smiled at us, but he didn't get up. He was drinking a beer, and beside him, Carol was drinking one, too. She had been at Simmons for a semester, and she was wearing a black dress and gold earrings, an outfit far too elegant for this gathering. A change was visible in Carol, not so much in her face itself as in the pose and visible hunger that can reshape a face and alter how you take in the features. I felt, in that first instant, that in spite of her elegant costume, Carol Casella had become, over the course of the last six months, very slightly cheapened.

"So how was it in the joint?" Kenny asked, and we all knew right away that was a stupid question, though we were glad Kenny had broken the ice.

Billy didn't answer at first, just swigged from his beer.

"I survived," he said.

"That's all that matters," one of the uncles said, as if to seal the solemnity of the moment.

In the car, Kenny had asked the rest of us, "So you think Billy got fucked up the ass in there?" and we had all hooted in response, but now Kenny asked that question in silence. I could feel it being asked, and Billy, knowing what we would be thinking, just smiled in a sly manner and took another swig of beer.

Carol kept looking at him, and I couldn't take my eyes off her, because I was trying to define the exact thing that had happened to her while Billy was inside, the thing that had chipped away at her elegance.

Though it was winter, it was a warm night, and toward the end, we all sat out on Billy's stoop and drank beer.

"You guys all smelled like weed when you came in," Billy said. "You reeked of it."

We laughed. A few months before, it would have been a joke we all shared, but now Billy wasn't laughing.

"No weed in there, in the joint?" Kenny asked, and Billy's small, dismissive laugh was less an answer than a comment on the way Kenny had said "joint."

We all sat on the stoop, and Billy stood on the sidewalk. We were set up to be his audience, except there seemed to be nothing he wanted to display to us.

"What are you gonna do now?" Freddie asked. "Go to school, or what?"

Billy turned and looked down the street, at the end of which was the beach. This was the Italian section—one of the Italian sections—so there were multicolored light displays, some of them flashing on and off. Billy had put off applying to college while the rest of us had been filling out our applications. This had made him seem cool at the time, but now I saw how it might limit him, making him this strictly *local* being.

Carol came out and sat in our midst. She'd been doing the dishes with Billy's mother, and she had a film of sweat on her. She said, "Whew, hot in there," and took a swallow of Billy's beer.

Six months before, this degree of proximity to Carol would have had an enormous effect on me. Looking at her skin and taking in that indefinable scent of a girl at a certain acute stage of ripening would have made me antsy, and I would have shifted on the stoop. But there was none of that now. She wiped the sweat off that perfect skin with the back of her hand, and it was only then that I got what I hadn't gotten inside the house: that flawless, unapproachable skin had added a layer. Carol Casella had started to take on, unbelievably, a little fat.

I wanted to go home then. There was something too sad about

the cheap shirt on Billy's back and the infinitesimal slackening of Carol's beauty, something that made me want to run ten miles down the boardwalk so I would be too tired to think about it, and I decided that's what I would do as soon as I could get away.

Billy's little brother, Ronnie, came out and joined us, too. Ronnie was a dark, quiet, strange kid—he might have been fourteen then—who had some vague sort of trouble at school. There had been nights when we would come over to Billy's and find Ronnie and Mr. Mogavero at the kitchen table, going over math or English homework, and Ronnie would look up at us from under his dark, curly mop of hair as if he would give anything in the world to escape the patient manner with which his father tried to direct his attention away from us, back to the work sheet. But it wasn't just a kid needing help with his homework, and we all knew that.

We made room for him to sit with us, and there were all kinds of Joe College remarks about how Ronnie might be doing with the girls. Somebody handed Ronnie a beer, and he was drinking it when Mr. Mogavero came out.

He came out and cleaned his eyeglasses. One by one, he took us in, the way he used to when we'd gone to visit him at the Star Market. He might almost have been wearing a smile, until he saw Ronnie with the beer. Then his face seemed to tighten back into itself, very quickly and scarily, as if someone had pulled the skin hard at the back of his head.

He had the beer out of Ronnie's hand in a second. Ronnie seemed poised for a blow that didn't come. Mr. Mogavero put the beer down; that was all. He composed himself.

"You come inside now, Ronnie," he said with a gentleness that seemed more like him. "You let these boys have their beers."

Ronnie didn't get up at first but looked to Billy.

"Let him stay out," Billy said. "We won't give him any beer if you don't want."

"No, he's coming in," Mr. Mogavero said.

Ronnie looked at Billy again, and this time Billy turned away. Mr. Mogavero reached down and put his hand on Ronnie's shoulder until Ronnie stood up. They stood in the doorway, framed by the light coming from inside. It was a pose of intense protectiveness. Mr. Mogavero had his hands on Ronnie's shoulders. Then they went inside, and beside me, I could feel Carol let out a breath, her gaze fixed on Billy as Billy lowered his eyes to the sidewalk, humbled for the first time in front of us.

My father got me a job the next summer as a teller-in-training at his bank, First Winship Trust.

He had remained a teller there since first starting at the bank twenty years earlier, when my two older sisters were six and five and my mother was about to become pregnant with me. It was to have been the beginning of my father's career as a "banker." He had done two years of college on the GI Bill, and the understanding was that all he'd have to do in order to climb up the ladder at First Winship was to go back, at night, for two more years. That was the plan in the old days of my parents' marriage, but my father had never done those two years. He hadn't become a branch manager or an assistant vice president or any of the other things he was supposed to become, the things he had promised my mother he had every intention of becoming on those nights when they'd sat on the boardwalk with their two little girls and he had begged her to let him in her pants one more time, so that he could conceive the boy of his dreams, his Timmy, the last, third child she didn't really want.

That part is mythology, the little glimpses into their marriage parents leave around the house in the form of asides and offhand remarks. The first part, though, is true. My father promised and then reneged on his promise because, apparently, he never wanted to be anything but a teller, a man without large responsibilities. He wanted to square life off to a neat, grassy plot he could mow without breaking a sweat, then wipe his hands and settle in for a Budweiser in the salty Winship dusk.

The woman who trained me that summer was a short, dark-haired, unmarried thirty-five-year-old named Maureen Feeney. Maureen was known to us in the house the way certain women on

TV were known to us—the way, for instance, the Ruth Buzzi character on *Laugh-In* was known to us, or Edith Bunker—as a dependable entity whose eccentricities have been well established. What "Maureen" had said at work would be relayed to us over the supper table, and we would all, my mother first among us, laugh.

Maureen Feeney was one of those single women who existed at that time, slimmer and slightly more stylish than their married cohorts, yet with all this going for them, they carried on themselves a blunted matrimonial edge, one that led you to know—and more importantly, I think, led *them* to know—it would never happen. What it made of Maureen, according to my father, was a "loudmouth," a maker of sexual cracks he loved to repeat. These may have been some of my parents' best moments, this laughing over what Maureen had said, because the quality of their laughter let the rest of us know that however strong my mother's disappointments, sex, at least, was still alive between them.

I paid close attention to the way Maureen looked at things, the precise manner of her sighs, the times when she would suddenly announce, "I just have to have a cigarette," and how, after lighting it and taking the first puff, her small, tight body would seem to descend into itself, as if it had been held until that moment just a little too high by an invisible string. Like so many adults, she seemed to be listening to a monologue going on in her head, and I tried to listen to it, too.

You have to imagine, maybe, in order to understand what happened next, the way I looked in those days. I only know it because of the pictures my mother still keeps around the house, but I remember how I felt, the confidence that comes from being a tall redheaded kid with a face that was once described to me by a girl as "virginal." I wasn't one, not then, though of course there are levels of male virginity, and I suppose by the stricter standards, you could say I still was one. I'd been inside girls, but it had only been a kind of advanced masturbation; no one had ever gotten inside me. I weighed about 150 pounds, but in my own mind, in the way I bounced through the world, I weighed a good deal less, and it was not an enormous surprise—though a small one, yes—when Maureen Feeney, in the course of the second week of my training, began rubbing against me, seemingly accidentally but for too long to be strictly that, as she leaned forward to point something out to me.

Walking home with my father at the end of the workday, it was all I could do to keep from blurting out this new information, as if it were a simple addition to our file of Maureen Feeney sex jokes, to be shared over the dinner table, to regale my mother with. That I couldn't do this put me at a distance from them maybe for the first time in my life.

It was in the third week that Maureen asked me to her apartment for dinner. She had skillfully slipped the invitation into a conversation we were having about a restaurant on the boardwalk, a highly regarded place called the Blue Grotto, where Billy happened to be working as a prep cook that summer. "I hate the way they do langostinos there," Maureen said. Her speech had a kind of worldliness to it that I knew she wanted to show off. That and "my apartment" were her ways of showing me she lived a life of independence, though I also knew, from what my father had told us, that Maureen's "apartment" was located on the top floor of her mother's house.

I arrived at her house on time, but it turned out to be the wrong time. Her mother was just coming up from the basement when Maureen came down the stairs to greet me. Maureen had an apron on, and a light summer dress that showed her bare armpits, and she was wearing scent. The mother was gray and heavy, darkly wary of me. At the appearance of her mother, the girlish smile Maureen had put on to greet me turned hard and they exchanged a couple of words that only pretended to be friendly. The mother passed into the house, and Maureen led me upstairs, but it wasn't easy for her to return to any kind of lightness.

The first thing she told me was that she'd decided against the langostinos in favor of a scampi recipe I would "die for." She stood at the stove as she said this. On the table she'd placed, in welcome, an open bottle of beer.

It all began to feel a little like playacting. At the bank, Maureen carried herself with a certain authority, but here, right away, I had seen where the authority in this house lay. As I sat drinking my beer and listening to her chatter at the stove, I saw in another light the worldliness with which she'd painted her nights as a discerning customer of the Blue Grotto. There is an age—I was nineteen that summer—where you begin to see people's lives in their actual dimensions, and you can't stand it, you really can't.

But I have to say, too, that the scampi was delicious, and Maureen introduced me to wine, and after a while, sitting at her table in the candlelight, eating her truly good food, and getting a little loaded on Bolla valpolicella, I was able to forget the sour notes struck at the beginning of the evening.

When dinner was over, Maureen lit a cigarette with one of the candles. She sat back from the table and tapped the ashes from her cigarette into her empty scampi plate.

"Your father's a funny one, isn't he?" she asked.

I wondered if she wanted to trash my father or if this was leading up to some intimacy about him, and I guarded myself against both those possibilities.

"How so?"

"Oh, all these years at his teller's booth. He hardly says anything. Quiet. Polite. What's he thinking? Still waters, you know? What's he like at home?" She took a long drag and plucked at her eyelashes before blinking and staring intently at me.

"He likes to drink beer, mostly," I said.

"That's a revealing comment, that is," she said, and I had the feeling, for the first time, that she might be laughing at me. "You're at the age where you don't want to look too hard, aren't you?" She smiled as if she had my number.

"What's that supposed to mean?"

"Relax, Timothy. I should get these dishes in the sink." But she didn't move. "Except I don't want to. I'm too tired. Let Rome in Tiber melt."

I had no awareness of how things were supposed to proceed. At school, it was understood that if a girl agreed to come up to your room or invited you into hers, you would fuck her. The preludes were raw and tacit. But Maureen staring at me made me understand something was supposed to come from me. I didn't want to lean forward and kiss her, because I was so aware, within this silence, that she was Maureen Feeney, and in spite of the hard, straight tits, something preceded her sexuality—a large, vague obstacle I needed to figure out a way to get around.

She puffed again on the cigarette, and I was certain that the next thing that would happen would be her politely dismissing me. I would find myself within the next five minutes walking home with a full belly and too much wine in me, and a kind of self-disappointment that I had failed to measure up to some adult standard.

She saved me from this agony by saying, as if she had made the decision *in spite of* who she had decided I was, "Oh, come here, for God's sake."

"Oh, come here" turned out to be an invitation to kiss in the little kitchen alcove where Maureen had cooked the scampi. We each carried our dish and placed it in the sink, and then Maureen lifted her arms to either side of her so that I could see what I was supposed to do, embrace her and draw her near, and we stood like that, kissing, for maybe five minutes.

And then we went to bed.

Maureen took charge immediately. She pushed me down, and that was where I stayed while she lowered herself onto me and executed a series of motions that got her what she wanted, and no more. She was all business about it. I can't say that at that point I was sexually excited by *Maureen*; when you're nineteen, sex is mostly inspired friction, and you'll fuck anything. But I was excited by *something*. Maybe it was the strange and unusual feeling of being under her, like a girl, watching the closed-eyed, isolated pleasure she took in the act. When it was over, Maureen lay back with her eyes half closed and asked me to get her a cigarette.

I had to return to her kitchenette to fetch one, and when I came back into the bedroom, she looked at me and closed her eyes and said, "I can't stand it."

I was going to say, Can't stand what? but something of the authority with which she said things kept me silent. She sat up and lit the cigarette. I got into bed next to her.

She smoked without looking at me, and she covered herself with the sheet. I wasn't sure why, but Maureen seemed embarrassed now, and after a time I guessed this meant she wanted me to leave. But the only word I could say was, "Well."

She looked at me, nervous and tight.

"Listen," she said finally.

"What?"

I placed my hand against her back and rubbed gently and felt her stiffening rather than softening under my touch. She let out a couple of tense breaths.

"What?" I asked again.

She leaned forward, and I thought she was going to cry or something, so I sat up and put my arm fully around her and pulled her toward me and felt her small head lower itself against my chest and her muscles finally began to relax, and with the onset of these things, some kind of feeling for Maureen Feeney came over me. I kissed her with more tenderness than I would, until then, have believed myself capable of. Her lips opened, and she looked surprised. She looked, in fact, terrified. It was as if the woman who had climbed on top of me with such manly expertise had disappeared and we were just beginning the delicate dance of seduction. When I entered her this time, she kept her eyes wide open. The words "My God" escaped her lips, but I had heard those words before from girls, and I knew, without knowing how I knew, that Maureen did not mean them the way those girls had, but in some other, more deeply private way. It was the funniest thing, really, because we were fucking, that was all, but something else was happening, too. It was as though that Maureen Feeney moment I'd been so intrigued by in the bank—that moment when she'd narrowed her eyes at an unseen object and seemed to be internally piercing it— as though that moment had opened up and expanded so that it was me she was piercing, fully taking me in.

I didn't quite know afterward, or in the weeks that followed, just what happened to me that night. My bank teller training was over by then, and Maureen would only come to my station every once in a while to see if I was sorting things properly or if I had any questions. At slow moments I watched my father at his station, his head cocked thoughtfully, as if he were ticking off the moments until five o'clock. As for me, I was ticking off the hours, too, because I was now seeing Maureen four nights a week, and all I could think about was the feeling of being inside her, the way it felt in the midst of the act, like things were crawling up inside me, little beings that reached parts of my insides and then burst, like some sort of internal Paintball game was going on, and within the fucking wanting to lick off Maureen's makeup so that I could strip away all the put-on parts of her and get down to the simpler and more entirely beautiful being I was discovering her to be.

After sex, Maureen always smoked, and her voice took on a lower register. Honest things came out of her. "I've never loved anyone," she said once. "It's the funniest thing, isn't it, because all around me, all my life, people have been 'falling in love.' So it seemed this inevitable thing. Of *course* it would happen. But it never did." Then she would lean in against my chest. Who was this person she was telling such things to, this non-boy she deemed capable of receiving them? After opening herself up to me, she would sit up and stare ahead, though not in despair. A sense of extreme luckiness would come over both of us.

At one or two in the morning I would leave Maureen in bed. "I've gotta go. My parents think I'm out with the guys."

She liked to chide me, say things like "No, they don't," but it was a fiction I persisted in believing, and I would dress and go out into the street and breathe in the 2:00 a.m. salt air and walk home by way of the beach, feeling the way you can feel only at nineteen, like the most powerful sexual being on earth.

Two in the morning was about the time the staff of the Blue

Grotto got off. I always knew if I walked that way, there was a good chance I would find Billy lined up with the others on the sand, all of them smoking. Most nights I avoided them. I didn't want to expose what I was doing—my late nights with Maureen—to Billy. But things with Maureen had gotten to the point where I no longer felt Billy could spoil them, and one night I walked to where I knew I would find him.

Billy's trademark that summer was a greasy red bandanna he wore on his head. He generally wore it with a T-shirt and an old pair of khakis that had started, by midsummer, to reek of clams. It was as if jail had taken all the desire for style out of him, another of the ways I thought Billy wanted to meld with this town, become indivisible with it.

"I can smell it on you" was the first thing he said to me that night.

I looked out at the water, embarrassed for myself but feeling an intense sort of post-sex romanticism that made me feel I was only half there. The waves broke far out, and the land that jutted out at either end of the beach was in silhouette. I knew the houses at either end. They were not great houses, but the way I felt tonight, they could have been castles.

"Who is she? What's so special?" Billy lifted one sweaty hand and wiped off his lips. He took a long drag on his cigarette and looked deeply into me. "Timmy," he said, and chuckled lightly, as if he was remembering something about me. In a tight group, boys gauge each other sexually early on.

For a while then, we stood in silence, listening to the waves. I wanted to resist that lessening that Billy's laughter made me feel, to tell him that things had happened to me to alter whatever sexual judgment he may have reached.

"Maybe I'm in love," I said.

Billy ignored that. He took a last puff and then stamped his cigarette in the sand. "You want to go for a swim, Timmy?" He'd already begun unbuttoning his shirt. "This is what I do at night. To get the smell of the clams off me."

He started on his pants, stepped out of them. He wasn't wearing underwear, and behind us, the crowd he had been smoking with applauded.

"Come on," he said, holding his clothes bunched in his hand and walking down to the water. "Get the smell of clams off you, too." He turned to me and smiled.

I stripped down and walked to the water with him. We left our clothes at a distance from the farthest reach of the incoming waves.

The water was freezing at two in the morning, but Billy didn't hesitate. He stepped in until he was up to his waist, then began splashing water under his armpits. He dived in, and for a while I couldn't see him. I took my time about following, but eventually I dived into the cold water, and when my head came up, I hoped profoundly that this would be a short swim, that Billy wouldn't stretch it out. I watched his head and shoulders rise ahead of me in a convulsive, brilliant breaststroke. I stayed in the crawl and looked up at the houses on the point. They didn't look so romantic to me now. All I could think of was my bed and my house and my parents asleep inside it.

Billy finally rose and shouted to me, "Good, isn't it?"

"It's all right," I shouted back.

He looked out at the dark horizon and back to me. "Who is she?"

"She works in the bank."

"No! She works in the bank? Which one is she?"

I stayed quiet. I knew he'd make fun of Maureen if he knew it was her.

"Billy, how long do you stay out here?"

He went under and then came up. "How big are your balls now, Timmy? Walnuts, right? No, worse. Little acorns. 'Cause of the cold, right?"

"What are we, out here to discuss the size of my balls?"

He laughed. "You want to go back in?"

"Yes!" I shouted very loud. "Yes!"

"But it's beautiful. It's so fucking beautiful. This is where we live. This shitty little town. But there's the *ocean*. Sometimes I can't stand it. Like, am I ever going to be able to leave?" He swam in place. "Carol's pregnant, Timmy."

It arrived and landed on me like a diving bird that had taken a chunk out of my skull.

"Christ, Billy."

"Yeah, Christ."

His head turned sideways, as if he was contemplating the long Winship shore.

"How long?"

"We don't know. We're careless. Couple of months."

He was close enough now that I could see his face. It was a classic Billy expression. Nothing was written on it. You could project whatever you wanted.

"What will you do? Have it, or . . ."

He wasn't answering, just looking at me, as if this moment was not about him at all, but about my reaction. He was studying my reaction. Then he came upon me very quickly and put his hands on my shoulders and dunked me.

He held me down long enough that I started to become frightened. I pushed against his arms and neck until he released me. I came up within inches of his face.

"Son of a bitch, what are you doing?"

"Trying to drown you."

"Why?"

"I don't know. I had this impulse. You out here with your stupid face. This is just a stupid pregnancy, Timmy. Don't make it so big." He looked at me in an intense, challenging way. His hands were on my shoulders again, and he held me down before I could stop him. I pushed and tried to grab his neck.

"Billy," I shouted when I was finally up, and water poured out of my lungs.

"Don't fucking make it so big, okay?"

"Okay. Don't fucking drown me."

We were suddenly quiet, and I pushed away as far as I could and wound up hitting him on the side of the face. He recoiled. Then he laughed.

"Okay," he said. "I deserved that."

"So what are you going to do?"

"Ask her."

"I'm not going to ask her."

He looked at me another long moment and then started swimming in.

When we were coming out of the water, Billy did what I knew he'd do: grabbed both sets of clothes and ran up the beach with them. There was nothing to do but follow him and hope that the group he'd been smoking with had dispersed.

He was standing pretty much where I'd met him. He'd left my clothes in a neat pile for me.

"Thanks," I said.

"Remember when I did that to—what was that girl's name?"

"You know that girl's name, Billy. It was Angie Capaldi."

The story of Billy and Angie Capaldi had become a Winship High School legend a few years before. Billy had abandoned the girl naked in the water, taken off with her clothes.

"Aren't you getting dressed?" I asked.

"In *these*? What would be the point? Carol's meeting me here. She brings me dry clothes."

"I guess I'll go, then," I said. "I've got about eighteen gallons of seawater in my lungs, thanks to you."

"Wait for her. She'd like to see you."

I don't know why I waited. No, I do. The sight of them together was still too much for me to resist.

Carol drove up about ten minutes later. She was wearing a pair of jeans and one of Billy's shirts, the flaps hanging outside the jeans, and I wondered whether this wasn't to cover the beginnings of a belly. Her hair was pulled back into a ponytail. She looked housewifely as she came down the sand with Billy's clothes, but not in a bad way. The pregnancy had given her, for me, a renewed charge.

When she saw me, she smiled. "Timmy, what are you doing here? I mean, it's like two in the morning."

"He's got a girlfriend." Billy was pulling on his pants. "She keeps him out late."

When he was finished dressing, he smoothed back his hair, and the two of them stood looking at me, for all the world like a settled couple, a couple with a baby on the way.

"Can we give you a ride?" Carol asked.

"Sure. I mean, no, it's really close. I can walk."

"We'll give him a ride," Billy said.

"He got you to swim with him, hmm?" she asked when we were in the car. "I hate it when he wants me to. I won't go out there."

"She's afraid," Billy said. "She's afraid what happened to—what was her name, Timmy?"

At first I couldn't imagine why he was asking me to repeat a story we had just talked about on the beach.

I didn't answer.

"Who? What happened to her?" Carol looked first at Billy, then at me.

"Tell her," Billy said.

"No. It's not my place."

He lay his head against the top of the seat in exasperation. "Timmy's my biographer, but he wants to tell the cleaned-up story of my life."

"I want to know."

I was silent for a minute. A police car passed us, slowed down, went on. Billy looked at it carefully.

"He left this girl in the water and took off with her bathing suit," I said.

Carol looked at Billy with great, perhaps exaggerated seriousness, but the kind that can give way, at any moment, to laughter.

"You didn't do that."

Billy shrugged.

She hit him, the way a girl hits.

"Hey, don't. I am getting hit too much tonight. Timmy was hitting me, and he *hurt*."

"What did the girl do, Billy?"

Again, he shrugged.

"She called her sister," I said. "Word had it, anyway. She walked to the boardwalk."

"*Naked?*"

Neither of us said anything.

"You are a shit, Billy."

"You not going to speak to me? You going to break up with me?"

"Why did you do that?"

"Because I didn't like the sounds she made. When we did it. In the waves. These porno girl sounds. Like she'd . . ."

He glanced at Carol, stopped a second, gauging her reaction or maybe something else, speaking to her in that secret code they had, and it was then I saw that Billy had his reason for bringing this up again.

"Like she'd been watching too many porn movies," he went on, "and she thought, Oh, this is the sound you make when you're really, really excited."

He mimicked some of the sounds for us. Carol didn't laugh, but went on looking at him with renewed interest. She scratched the back of the seat.

"Where do you live, Timmy?"

"Winthrop Street."

It was a short drive to the little house where, I was surprised to see, a light was still on in the front window. Someone was waiting up.

"They got the light burning for you, Timmy," Billy said when we were stopped. He started to pull Carol toward him. She was resistant.

"What?" he asked.

"I don't like thinking of you that way."

He pulled her to him so that the back of her head rested against his collarbone.

"Yes, you do," he said.

They both looked at me then.

"Do you believe he did that?" Carol asked.

"Yes, I do," I said, and opened the door.

"Good night, Timmy," Carol said.

Before I went inside, they arranged themselves in the front seat, performing a series of light, deft motions, easeful and unconsciously aware of each other's bodies. Watching them, I couldn't help offering a look that must have given away all my feelings. For a long moment Carol stared up at me as if she wanted to ask what was wrong.

In the living room of our house, my father was watching television. He had the overhead light on, and the room was bathed in a fluorescence that made all our belongings look cheap.

The movie he was watching was *Flight of the Phoenix*, a particular favorite of ours. We'd watched it three or four times together, and as he studied my face recognizing the movie—the grizzled faces of James Stewart and Richard Attenborough and Hardy Krüger, the unmistakable studio desert imagery—his own face lit up.

"Will they make it, Timmy? Will the *Phoenix* lift off? I'm glued to my seat."

He had a glass of milk beside him and some sort of biscuit on a plate.

"What are you doing up so late?"

"Not waiting for my errant son, that's for sure. There's no telling when you'll get in these days."

I sat on the hassock, ready to fend off any potential question about Maureen.

"Really—what are you doing up?"

"It doesn't happen often, but every once in a while I suffer from the old insomnia."

He took a bite of the biscuit. He had a long, close-to-rugged face, and his hair curled upward into a stiff, woolly crest that tilted to the right.

"Is your stomach all right?"

"Right as rain."

"What's with the biscuit?"

He shrugged at me, his grin returning. "I thought you'd be more excited," he said, pointing to the TV screen. "These are our boys."

I nodded, as if to demonstrate some comradely feeling.

"You look wet, by the way."

"I've been swimming."

"No? In the altogether? It must be freezing." He looked me

over, some question hovering at the back of his mind. If I'd been swimming "in the altogether," then with who?

When a commercial came on, he disappeared and came back with a towel. Standing behind me, he toweled off my head vigorously and happily. "There you go."

He sat with the towel in his lap. The movie came back on.

"I think I'll go up to bed, Dad. As much as I'm on the edge of my seat to see whether the *Phoenix* takes off."

He smiled. "Well, I won't tell you."

"No, you've got to. In the morning, you've got to tell me."

There was a silence in which our joke settled on his face like a benediction.

"But I've got to get up tomorrow morning and be a teller," I said.

"Oh, the bank won't wait. Oh yes, people must make their deposits. Money must accrue."

He seemed to have become tired all of a sudden. We told each other good night.

At the top of the stairs, I opened the door to my room and heard my mother shifting in hers. We had a tiny upstairs, three small bedrooms and the one bathroom all backed into one another, so that it was impossible to have true privacy. When my sisters still lived at home and shared a room, I was always seeing them in their bras and underwear, and when I started masturbating, I knew I could never do it in bed when anybody else was upstairs, because of the groaning of the springs. My parents, too, I suspected, had to keep things quiet in their bedroom. It was that kind of house, physically open and physically secret, and I think we all liked it that way. I tapped on my mother's door, just to let her know I was home, which she'd asked me to do that summer. Then I went into my own, undressed, and sat on the edge of my bed, facing the window.

I knew as I sat there that Billy would make Carol get rid of that baby. It appeared to me as a certainty that he would fight all the softness in life that appeared before him, as if out of an old allegiance to something else. And just as he rejected all that softness, I felt a huge desire for it opening in myself. I couldn't help wanting what he already had.

I saw, too, how the awakening of this dream doomed Maureen Feeney. She could never be the girl beside me in the car, could never have a baby, could not be brought home to my parents to sit with us on Christmas nights and fit in the way Carol had at the Mogaveros'. Underneath all that would be the suppression of my parents' laughter at the folly of their son. "Maureen Feeney, oh, Lord," they would say to each other, in private, and roll their eyes.

three

It was not until eight summers later that the dream of that night, the abiding dream of my young manhood, came to fruition.

By then it was the late-middle 1980s, the time of the Iran-Contra hearings, the summer of *Full Metal Jacket*. I was deeply ensconced in Boston. My home office was Endicott's corporate headquarters on Stuart Street. I shared an apartment with two other guys in a renovated harborfront warehouse in Charlestown, and at night I used to meet my old Winship friends at a bar located just off the Public Gardens and named after a popular television series. Our hair was shorter then, Reagan-era short, and we were off pot and into shots of Stoli. Our faces had begun to take on some of the weight of larger salaries and single-guy takeout and seats in the tenth row behind the visitors' dugout at Fenway. We were deeply Republican in our thinking, though registered and hereditary Democrats. We would never openly admit it, but we liked Reagan. We loved, anyway, the world he'd made possible for us, that feeling in America then of having been released into something, as if a gun had gone off and someone shouted *Run*. We did, we ran, and we liked it.

Somewhere on the other side of the newly complicated Boston skyline, Winship lay entrenched in its marshy, salt-encrusted cove, a place that would not change, the place of our fathers and our youth. Though we had moved less than ten miles south, when we thought of Winship, it was as though our lives were taking place now in another, richer century.

Sometimes, on those nights at Cheers, we would step outside to drink on the sidewalk and get away from the crowd. On the street, minivans whizzed by, and in them were attractive women who had kept their bodies trim even though the backseats of those vans had one or two toddler car seats and the de rigueur child-friendly sun-filter was pasted to the back window. They occasionally glanced our way. We were what their husbands had looked like five or six years before, before the kids, before the early battles and the settling of a marriage. We were the thick-thighed young guys they had looked at once and said, All right, yes, that one, *him*. In their sneaked side-long glances, which vastly amused us when we caught them on summer nights, was all the regret over a too-easy choice that a woman in her thirties is capable of, as well as an inescapable acknowledgment of the lust that had driven that choice in the first place. Some nights we hooted in recognition of this complicated look, and we shouted "Yes!" and "Take me!" until the minivan drove out of sight.

We had begun our ascent—Kenny toward a spot in the D.A.'s office, Freddie in the inner circle of a big developer, and Johnny in the corporate headhunting office of his wife's father. I'd begun to grow as crude and hungry as any of the other young men at the bar in Cheers. A young man looking for a wife, if he has escaped the early romantic traps, becomes a kind of cattle breeder, alert to flank and rump and thigh, as if he knows, in the first sight of these, what the yield might be. That was me on those nights.

It was not always Kenny and Freddie and Johnny who joined me in Cheers, but it was never Billy. The eighties were not Billy's decade. He had disappeared, more or less, into Winship, as I'd known he would. After the summer of her pregnancy, he had dropped Carol. For the next few years, word of him filtered back to us: he'd been in and out of school, had gone to California, had come home when his mother died unexpectedly. His life felt diminished, and some nights at Cheers we could feel our own triumph over Billy. We had been right not to go at life full throttle early, the way he had. We had bided our time and escaped into something better.

On the night I met my wife, I found myself standing behind her at the bar. There was a small, fuzzy mirror over the line of beer bottles, just enough to see yourself in. I liked the fact that I was growing into a heftier version of myself. The time I'd put in at the gym had yielded a guy who looked like he'd spent years throwing his shoulders against opposing tackles. I remember lifting one hand to rub my chin—a small, stupid gesture of self-appreciation, unforgivable in anyone over the age of twenty-seven—and found her looking at me doing this, a tiny, caught-you smile on her face as she reached for her gin and tonic.

She had short hair and the kind of big, smart eyes that have always made me sit up straighter. I was an idiot, she was thinking, but a cute idiot. She took her drink to her friends' table, the waiting girls, buyers for Saks, or teachers, or nurses with their masters', girls with frosted hair and big, pouty lips covered with lipsticks that emulated the shades of the more-sophisticated colors of Life-Savers.

Oh, the girls of those years. Their knees under the table and the spilled gin and their hands with long fingers and their slim waists and the delicate sight of a thin gold chain falling into the clove-scented passage between two serious breasts. And the weight of breath itself and the strong negotiatory feel of the initial conversation, which will go this far and no further, or else further, until her hand goes to her throat or somewhere else it has no business going, and you know she is in the initial stages of losing control. An opening will soon appear in her eyes, a place you will dive into, all your genetic drives geared toward a specific leap, as if you are saying, Continue the race with me! Propagate! while you ask if you can fetch her a second Bellini.

I followed this girl to her table, the cute idiot whom she might have dismissed forever simply by offering a sullen enough look. Instead, she looked as though she barely knew I was there. The other girls—the Amys and Jills and Sharis—seemed more keyed into me.

I said, "Listen, I hate getting caught like that."

"Like what?" She fingered her gold chain, but only to free it, and took a sip of her drink. She wore, I remember, a dress with wide black-and-white stripes. And a belt. Everything she did, every move called toward an alert part of myself, as if every gesture were saying, Don't miss this; this is important.

I smiled in as charming and self-deprecatory a way as I knew how. Her expression didn't change, but a little give appeared in her eyes.

It was then that I caught a glimpse of some quality in her beyond her sheer attractiveness, a deeply settled inner territory that halted all the foolishness in me. Not that words like that ever come to your mind when you're in the moment. What you do instead is you rub the hair on the back of your hands and decide that this is where you dig your trench: you are not moving from this place until you get what you want. Don't let her go, that's all you're thinking.

And it is this complicated set of instinctual messages that allows her to look at her friends and laugh. The others offer unspoken encouragement. There are worse-looking men at the bar. He seems harmless, and his wallet is probably thick. *Go ahead.*

"I—" And then nothing. Nothing follows. "This is stupid. I'd like to talk to you outside."

"I'm with my friends."

"Oh, don't be like that," Amy says. "We're big girls."

"Talk to us all," Shari adds.

"I'm not good at that."

"He's shy," Jill says.

"Right."

"What's outside?" she asks finally, leaning slightly back.

The answer is obvious, but it comes out sounding like the cleverest thing you could possibly say: "Boston."

There is a silent murmur around the table. John Fogerty's "The Old Man Down the Road" is on the sound system, the bass line like a finger running along some internal vein leading directly to your liver. It makes you deliriously happy. At last she picks up her drink. You follow her, then lead her up the steps. Outside is where the boys who hoot stand, the ones you are frequently among. She looks uncomfortable near them, so you try to guide her across the street.

At first she is hesitant to get too far away from the bar, her friends.

"I'm not going into the park," she says, and you see her—childhood, adolescence, the Peter Frampton posters she used to hang on her bedroom wall, the swimming medal she won, and the fact that, the summer after high school, she lost her virginity to a boy she misjudged. And has outgrown all these things. What you love about her is the mature stance: I don't have to have this experience. Or you. I don't have to have *you*.

"No. Okay. But I'm safe. I just wanted to get away from . . ." You tip your chin toward the drunk account execs, the planners, the chino-clad thugs who are pulling down sixty G's and are not yet thirty. "But we don't have to."

And then she crosses the street. You are careful with her, careful with the traffic, careful to stand at a distance, the two of you with your drinks, the newly safe Public Gardens, and as you look at her, you realize something you didn't know five minutes before, when you were simply being attracted to her. It is her life there, as she stands before you, the thing she bites down on, the thing present in the muscles of her neck. It is that life you want, not merely the girl. A jet soars past, blinking red in the summer night. A couple—too well dressed merely to be out for a walk in the Public Gardens— disappears behind a tree. All of these details have a vitality you do not quite understand, until an hour has gone by, an hour in which you have talked, and made her laugh, and watched the way she holds her head, and felt that deep and compelling draw to her become like a shock inside you, a raw nerve in the tooth you keep pressing your tongue against, until she tells you she has to go back to her friends. Then something in you leaps to keep her there, something says, put on any show, find any means to not let her slip away. So you get down on your knees, not knowing why you are doing this except to offer worship, while she laughs easily and says, "Get up." And you have to laugh, too. You cannot overwhelm this woman with your desire, though all you want to say is, No, no, you don't understand a *thing*. So you rise and take her hand and lead her back in with no intention of ever letting go—you will ride in the trunk of her car, you will strap yourself to the side door—and as you clutch the hand of this woman you'd neither seen nor heard of until an hour ago, this woman who is the bodily impression of all the things you have so deeply longed for, you feel that you are finally and definitively overcoming Billy and all he represented.

Nothing can hold you back now. Nothing.

four

I hadn't known, not at the beginning, that I was marrying into money. Teresa DiNardi lived with her parents in the suburban city of Graymore. She was a schoolteacher. When she first brought me home to meet her father, he seemed of a piece with the ruddy-faced Italian guys with whom I'd grown up in Winship. He had one eye missing, but there was no great symbolic portent to this. He'd lost the eye, it was explained to me, not on any foreign battlefield, but in a gruesome and clumsy fishing accident near Egg Rock, in Nahant. He was in the insurance business.

I didn't know Graymore at all. I knew the north shore and a little of the south, but the knotted cluster of inland suburbs was unknown territory. I learned about it while sitting in Tony DiNardi's suburban kitchen, waiting for Teresa to emerge for our dates. While he peeled an orange or kept one eye on the evening news, Tony made sure I became educated about the town and about the attendant familial drama into which I was trying to insert myself.

Graymore had been built and settled by Italians in the first decades of the century, but in order to thrive there, those early masons and bricklayers and the entrepreneurial landowners among them had had to build big houses on the choicest lots and sell them to wealthy outsiders. Well before the 1950s, when Tony DiNardi began his climb to prominence (from selling insurance to brokering it), it had become the favored Boston suburb of Jewish professionals who moved into those houses and began occupying the offices of the old stone downtown buildings, bringing with them stethoscopes and dentists' drills and copies of *Blackstone's Commentaries*. By the time I appeared on the scene, the Italians had managed to grasp power in Graymore (they were principals of schools, heads of the police and fire departments, and one of them had recently been elected mayor), but I was made to understand that power was always a nebulous thing. Where others saw a prosperous, quiet suburb, a place of minivans and soccer tournaments, Tony DiNardi managed to evoke, in these kitchen tutorials, a plain on which turbaned horsemen, scimitars drawn, might at any moment swoop in to reclaim territory they only seemed to have given over.

When you marry into a family, you marry a mythology as well, a dense forest out of which the girl emerges, seemingly unencumbered, at the bar of Cheers. There was another forest we had to hack our way out of—a sexual forest—but I don't believe that difficulty had nearly the effect on our future lives as the legacy Tony DiNardi imposed on us almost from our first date.

To take care of the sexual business first: before meeting me, Teresa had found herself engaged to a young man, also a teacher in the Graymore school system, who left her sexually unsatisfied. Her experience was not vast, but she knew enough to know what she was not getting, and she had broken things off at the last possible moment, on the night before she and her mother were to meet with the lithographer who was to design the wedding invitations. The look on her face I'd recognized and been drawn to in Cheers was, it turned out, the residue of Teresa's romantic disappointment in the year since she'd canceled her engagement to Peter Graceffa. No suitors had arrived who were superior to him—and no sex, good or bad. She'd begun to think she'd missed her moment. In my bed in the converted Charlestown warehouse, I tried to coerce her into falling in love with me, and I discovered that maybe the sexual disappointment she'd experienced hadn't been all Peter Graceffa's fault. She had never been awakened in any significant way, and she expected magic. For months, I conducted a siege, held a crying Teresa in my arms, attempting to convince her that she need not be resigned to failure. I came to know her body in ways I hadn't known anyone's since Maureen Feeney's. The siege finally ended in victory. We celebrated Teresa's first orgasms with an expensive meal at Locke-Ober, and we immediately began drawing up wedding plans. At that moment, I remember feeling the onset of a surprising nostalgia for the months of exploration.

We were married, and two years later, two reasonably happy years spent in the top floor of a two-family in Belmont, Teresa became pregnant. When I say "reasonably happy," I don't mean that as a put-down. We were cautious. We dipped our toes in the waters of marriage. I think it was because of how intense those first months had been. Sometimes, on those exploratory nights, Teresa's eyes had opened very wide, as if she could not quite believe she was allowing a man to say certain things to her, to draw her so far out of her father's house and away from the things she'd grown accustomed to thinking were normal and safe. As soon as she'd achieved what she felt she needed to achieve, she tried to domesticate sex, to give it borders. I, not wanting to rock the boat, went along with this. But maybe there was a part of me, too, that wanted to keep it safe.

After we'd announced the pregnancy, Tony and Katie DiNardi began dropping by more often, on surprise visits. They'd always regarded our second-floor rental as a kind of playhouse, something built deliberately smaller than life-size, in which we were practicing for our future, real lives. Our intention had been that we stay there until we could afford the down payment on a house, but the DiNardis wouldn't hear of it. We stood firm, or tried to. It was initially only as an attempt to humor them that we began taking Sunday drives into "the country."

"The country" was what opened up beyond Weston and Concord. We visited Acton, Littleton, Sudbury, Ayer, those outposts, intensely green, where land was still bordered by stone walls dating from the eighteenth century and where the last of the farmers and the big landowners had begun to parcel out their holdings. Lots of varying sizes were available the farther out we traveled, for prices that were still not prohibitive.

I remember the Sunday the Realtor first took us to Bradford, a small, lesser-known hamlet that was, in her words, "on the way up." Bradford had recently instituted its own school system after years of busing its older students to the regional middle and high schools. We stopped beside a large, recently cleared indentation in the woods near Bradford's main road, large enough for a super-market to be built, or a small mall. "Here's the baseball field they're building. For Little League and such," the woman said, and brushed back her soft-looking blond hair with one hand. She was of a piece with many of the women I'd noted in these towns. She wore a brown tweed jacket and brown leg-hugging pants, and she made it seem we were a distraction in her day and soon she'd be back where she properly belonged, on top of a horse. There was also an air of detachment about her, a measure of condescension in the way she referred to the "night lights" the good citizens of Bradford in-tended to put up over the field, as though such things were myste-riously important to some people, if not to her. She had the same quality I'd noticed in women buying bread, or lightbulbs, in the market in Bradford's tiny center where we'd stopped, or those wait-ing for gas to be pumped in the filling station just off Route 2. There was a bruised and postromantic aspect to these women. It gave the town the feel of a place such women came to after they'd discovered the deep flaw in their marriages. They came in Volvos and Saabs, in coats purchased on Newbury Street in Boston. They came with blond, pressed-looking children who rode in the backs of the Volvos, children who stared out the windows of those cars. Their fathers would take such children down to the new field and work them hard through the paces of youth baseball, and at night (we saw this as we were leaving Bradford), the lights would come on in their houses, seen through the trees at a distance from the road, and a warmth would emanate, and you would feel that what was here was the most desirable quality in the world. I could feel this; it had the effect of a hand gently squeezing my heart.

Tony DiNardi fell head over heels in love with the place. Walk-ing over the felled branches of a lot in the midst of being cleared, he'd exclaim, "Now this is it! Nothing's happened here yet. You've got your own school system, and I'll bet it's going to be a good one, because these people here aren't pikers. And look at the space you've got, look at the land."

The words that stood out for me were "Nothing's happened here yet." Lying in bed together on Sunday nights after those drives, Teresa and I entertained ourselves by envisioning the house we might build, the child who would live there, the perfect lives now possible for us. Somewhere in those Sunday night speculations I imagine we each must have felt the force of the wave her father represented. It had picked us up and was carrying us—it would be useless to fight—but weren't we enjoying it just a bit too much?

When the architect's drawings came in and we saw the house proposed for the lot Tony had bought us in Bradford (one and a half acres, with the ten acres bordering us to the west owned and protected by a trust), they literally took our breath away. Then the figure attached to the house came in, and I immediately assumed we'd have to make compromises. I mentioned this to Tony one night at dinner and then made the further mistake of pretending I planned to pay for it. He was in a bad mood, and when I made my comment about the house no longer being quite affordable, he snapped, "You're a book salesman, what *can* you afford?" Through the rest of the meal I could sense Teresa deliberately not looking at me.

By the time the house was finished, such moments were forgotten. We moved through the large light-filled rooms in the full understanding that living here would change our lives, enlarge them in ways we couldn't yet understand. We'd had the baby by then, a girl, Gabrielle Rose, and during the weekend afternoons of that first fall—dry, with brilliant oranges on the maples and yellows on the birches—we would strap Gabrielle in the Snugli and explore the dimensions of our property. The old rock walls still stood, heavy with lichen. At our boundaries we could see no other houses, just endless woods. We felt both alone and protected, and the notion that all this was ours affected me physically, gave me sudden pecking erections in the woods. I wanted to take Teresa down into the soft leaf mulch; I was still unused to the barrier of an infant. Sometimes we would hustle back to the house and, if we were lucky, be able to put Gabrielle down for a nap while we tested each piece of furniture and every burnished floor. They were wild sessions, fed by the power of having been handed a life as expansive as our property itself. Afterward, cleaning up, I would linger while we waited for the DiNardis to make their regular Sunday visit. I would linger naked, is what I mean, while Teresa straightened up and chastened me. "They're going to be here any minute, Tim." There were times when I remained naked, standing at the window even as the Town Car pulled up and Teresa's parents, present-laden, emerged from the car, as if they might look up at me and—what, exactly? And how would it change anything? By the time the Di-Nardis got to the door, I'd be fully dressed, my hair smoothed in place, waiting with an affectionate, welcoming grin.

In those early years of marriage and fathering and wandering around an enormous house wondering how my name had ever possibly come to appear—even if only as a cosigner—on the mortgage, I had a standing date, the first Monday night of every month, to meet Freddie and Kenny and Johnny at the Branding Iron, a massive steak house perched at the edge of the Massachusetts Turnpike, just outside Boston, where that fat cross-state highway becomes a sleek city artery. We had a regular table—a booth, actually, done in red leather in which no creases had yet appeared, plush and sweet-smelling red leather that always seemed slightly warmed in anticipation of our ambitious young asses.

The dining room of the Branding Iron was as vast as the main saloon of a casino. Over each table hung a heavy oak chandelier with candles burning in red glass globes. At the far end of the room was a wall-size window overlooking the pike, and on the other side of the highway some of the skyline was visible.

We all wore suits to these dinners. Greeting each other, Freddie, Johnny, and I would make a fetish of checking out the condition of one another's suits; we would chide Kenny for the off-the-rack specials he went for; we would argue, briefly, about design. Nobody took this seriously: it was great, gleeful fun. We would hold the big menus in our hands, though we always ordered the same things, and staring over the tops of them, we'd scan the crowd. It was predominantly male, chiefly of the hunter-gatherer sort, guys who after a couple of drinks start to get a certain flushed, combustible look that strips away the business-class veneer and reveals the raw ethnic material underneath. Late into the night, this roomful of guys in suits began to resemble a rugby club at an away game. It was not a place you'd want to bring a date, not because she wouldn't be welcome, but because, being in this place, you wanted to be with men, you wanted to slouch down in your seat with your legs far apart, you wanted to loosen your tie and get a little sweaty. And besides that, there were the small, meaningless flirtations. The Branding Iron was known for hiring waitresses with enormous breasts—Irish and Italian girls who had left a couple of kids at home with the babysitter—and they would kid and flatter you and subtly insinuate that if you weren't married (and she knew you were; hey, you had that look), endless vistas might open.

Vodka was the drink then of young men on the make, young men learning manners, but Scotch was the drink of a man who had arrived or, anyway, of a man who felt he had arrived—single malts, the lesser known the glen the better. Scotch was what arrived at the table, a pair of them each consumed before dinner arrived. We always talked first about Kenny's cases. He was in the D.A.'s office, angling for manslaughter convictions, and he usually had a story to tell. There wasn't much to say about my work at Endicott, and Johnny was circumspect when it came to what went on at the head-hunter's.

Freddie now worked for a man named Edwin Winerip who made a fortune in the 1980s gussying up a few second-rank cities, cities in serious decline whose "marketability," as Freddie put it, had been vastly improved by the development of in-city upscale retail outlets, malls built into the infrastructure, occupying old armories, abandoned docks, that sort of thing. For a long time, Boston thought it was too good for the kind of suburbanization that Winerip represented, but "Look," as Freddie told it, "when's the last time you saw a white face shopping on Washington Street?" So Boston had finally fallen. Freddie had been hired in the late eighties. His job was to scout locations, talk up retailers. Did Lands' End fancy a store on the Charlestown piers in a mock-nautical outlet to be called Seven Bells? Would Waterstone's bookstore like to put a flagship store in North End Clearing? If some part of us wanted to make fun of Freddie's new marketing voice, that part had to coexist with the fact that he had become the first of us to make more than a hundred thousand dollars a year.

We were impressed enough with all our fortunes, though, to call these our "bigdick lives." It became an in-joke that evolved out of a comment Kenny made one night describing some of the assistant D.A.s he worked with. "There are bigdick lawyers and littledick lawyers," Kenny had said, and Johnny's Scotch had gone down the wrong way, it was such an uncharacteristic, mock-tough thing for Kenny to say. But we loved it. We began applying the adjective to just about everything. Some nights I'd call Teresa from the road and ask if she was cooking a bigdick dinner for the night I came home, or if the shit she was cleaning off Gabrielle at the time was a bigdick poop or a littledick poop. She was, of course, never as amused by this as we all were at the Branding Iron.

We'd all except Freddie had our first children by then. Kenny and I had girls (Gabrielle was now a year old), Johnny a little boy. Freddie tolerated our proud-daddy stories, the showing around of pictures, and since he was married to another Winerip executive, we assumed they were just waiting a few years. But one night Freddie and I were in the men's room at the Branding Iron at adjoining urinals, and he asked me if I'd ever had to get my sperm tested. I told him no, I hadn't, and waited for him to tell me the next thing. He just shrugged and smiled, and we shook off. That was as far as we penetrated into each other's marriages, or into the littledick problems of life.

One night we happened to get drunker than usual. We were kicking back, the smoke from our cigars making a kind of nimbus around us. Freddie provided us all with cigars from a store he knew in the North End. Edwin Winerip (who looked like a third-generation Kennedy and dressed in suits from a London tailor) tipped him off as to who imported the best cigars. "Dominican," Freddie would announce with that air of special knowledge he'd picked up, cutting the ends with the cigar cutter he always carried.

"So I'm talking to my father the other night," Freddie said. "Guess who he ran into?" He blew out a long stream of smoke while he waited for us. "Billy Mogavero," he said, giving up. "And guess where? In the paint store. You know Goff's old store? Only it's not Goff's. It's a Sherwin-Williams outlet, something. And Billy's behind the counter, mixing paint."

There was no immediate comment.

"You guys have an opinion about that?" Freddie asked.

The mention of Billy made things feel briefly, weirdly strained, as if Freddie were willfully imposing some value on us other than the one we'd all agreed to honor at this table.

Kenny said finally, "He's lucky he's not in jail. Employment must be some kind of triumph for him."

Another pause. I could sense invisible things bouncing in the air, a whole welter of unspoken thoughts colliding. We were all trying hard to act like it was a minor matter, Billy Mogavero's fate.

Johnny shook his head.

"What?" Kenny asked.

"I don't think so," Johnny said. "I don't think jail was ever any kind of destination for Billy. He was a very controlled hoodlum." After he spoke, Johnny slowly turned the ring on his finger. Johnny's inherent caution—the thing that had made him such a dull companion in adolescence—had matured into a form of coolness. Some part of him seemed freed up by the certainty of his future success.

"How so?" Kenny asked.

Johnny shrugged.

"No, I know what you mean," Freddie said. "I don't know how I know what you mean, but I do. He's fucking somebody really good."

"Who's good in Winship?" Kenny asked, and laughed, as usual, by himself.

"She doesn't have to be in Winship," Freddie said. "He's biding his time. He's going to surprise us. He doesn't follow our clock."

"What's our clock?" Johnny asked.

"What do you mean, what's our clock?" Freddie answered. "We

got a clock we're all listening to. Otherwise we wouldn't all be thirty-one years old and married and saddled with kids and earning—well, some of us are earning money."

"Yeah, fuck you," Kenny said. "And you're not saddled with a kid, either."

"No, but I might as well be. I hear the clock ticking." He moved his finger in a slow half circle.

"Timmy's not saying anything," Kenny said.

"He's thinking of Carol Casella."

Something felt a little effortful in Freddie's tone, as if he was trying to get us back to an old way of talking, a sexual unhiddenness that belonged to a past time. "If Carol Casella walked into this room now, you'd throw it all away for one—"

"Only if she was seventeen," Kenny said, and showed his teeth in a funny way. "I would, too. If she was seventeen and walked in here." He grabbed his empty Scotch glass with both hands.

Maybe it was only the ensuing five-second silence, but our worlds seemed a lot thinner than they had half an hour before.

"You want to know the joke?" Freddie asked. "We go back to Winship, they're all still there. The kids we went to high school with, they're all there, Saturday nights at the Blue Grotto. They hang out together. They have sleazy little affairs. The girls Billy wouldn't give a hello to in high school, they've all developed a sudden need for paint."

"Why are we thinking about him?" Kenny asked, and made a face, as if the drift of the conversation had become distasteful to him.

For a few moments we all puffed on our cigars.

"How often do you guys go back?" Freddie asked.

"Once a month maybe," Johnny said, and took a last sip from his Scotch glass.

"You bring the Club for the car?" Freddie asked. "When you park outside your parents' house? The last white town in greater Boston, and I always check to see if the tires are slashed. I always worry, I'm in my parents' house, is somebody going to bust the car window?"

After Freddie had spoken, Kenny nodded a couple of times.

"You worried about your Festiva, Ken? Your Geo? What is it you drive these days?"

"Fuck off. I'm just more energy conscious than you guys."

We all laughed at that. He had always been cheap. He still was.

"It's the land that time forgot, that's all," Kenny said.

Again, we could have settled up, driven home to our wives, lowered our Scotch-soaked heads over the babies' cribs to fawn. Instead we all stayed, and I could feel the tension among us.

"We should all go back. Together, sometime," Freddie said.

Nobody picked up on it.

"What do you say, O'Kane?"

"What, to show off?" I asked.

"Shit, yes."

"I'm not into that."

"Not into that. The guy who lives in the best house of us all."

"Come on, Johnny's house is as good as mine."

"The boys who were made by their fathers-in-law."

I could see Johnny bristling at that. "How much do we each owe?" he asked.

"Wait. Wait. Wait. Wait." Freddie put his hand over the bill. "No shit. We all go. Together. We pay a visit to our parents and we see our friend."

After giving an appearance of considering it, Johnny shook his head slowly. "Count me out. Saturdays I spend with the family."

"Oh, fuck the family, " Freddie said. "You guys are all going soft on family. We got Monday nights at the Iron every month, and the rest of your nights, what do you do? Push a shopping cart around, read stories to the kids?"

"Wait'll it happens to you," Kenny said. "It's kind of fun. I go through the whole day, I can't wait to see her."

"Oh, you disgust me, DiGiovanni."

"Come on," Johnny said, "let's take care of this bill. Sixty-six dollars each, and then let's leave her a bigdick tip."

While we were digging for cash, Johnny sat back. "You can go, Freddie. You want to see him, you go."

"Look, all right, we don't see him. We just take a trip, the four of us. We go just for fun. We bowl, for Chrissake."

There was a brief silence at the table.

"We *bowl?*" Kenny and Johnny asked at the same time.

"O'Kane's not saying anything."

I shrugged.

"What do you do on Saturdays?" Freddie asked.

"Actually, I think we're scheduled to make a birdhouse this Saturday."

"No kidding?"

"From a kit."

"No kidding? *Scheduled?* A birdhouse. I can't wait to have kids."

I smiled and glanced at Kenny and Johnny for some corroboration. They both were staring quizzically at me.

"Maybe it's all gone too far," Kenny said, "when we're looking forward to building a birdhouse."

Two weeks later, on a Saturday, I waited on my front porch for Freddie to pick me up. Whether or not it was the birdhouse that had done it, he had finally convinced us. We all owed our parents a visit, and our wives were glad enough not to have to accompany us. Then there was also the other thing, the unspoken desire to see what had happened to Billy.

My house is angled so that it faces the road. To get to it, you drive past five hundred feet of woods, a birch grove our back windows face out on. A stone wall separates our property from the road, and a thin strand of birches guards us there as well.

There are things about my town that have sometimes troubled me since moving here. On the cover of one of the books I sell for Endicott, an anthology of early New England writing, is a painting of a railroad cutting through virgin wilderness while a boy sits on a hill gazing down at it. It's a painting I can't help thinking about at certain moments. As more people have moved here, more of the woods have been cut back to make room not just for houses but for those little retail outlets you see in small, elegant towns. Each of the three mini-malls in Bradford is cut to a uniform design; shingled roofs, single stories, faux gaslights. The effect, surprisingly successful on a rainy fall night, is of stepping inside the eighteenth century. You half-expect fires to be burning inside each of the stores, and a plump-cheeked, bonneted proprietress to appear at the counter. We have three separate stores specializing in flowers and assorted froufrou, two women's clothing stores, a Café Metropole specializing in "coffee confections," and, for the hipper crowd, Ellen's Java. We have Clara's Home-Cooked (assorted takeout, very popular with the O'Kanes), a Video a Go Go (with an extensive foreign section), and four different haircutting and nail and facial salons, as well as a Brooks and Butterfield Spa. Our two bakeries are Four and Twenty Blackbirds and the Crustee. Though we are a town that prides itself in not allowing in any chain stores (except for a single Dunkin' Donuts, here before any of the others moved in), there is another element we have let in—nothing so huge, but still something that makes me feel like the young boy in that painting, sitting on a hill and watching a force arrive that is eventually going to change everything.

I don't have these thoughts all the time—or even, as time goes by, all that frequently. That morning, for instance, while I waited for my friends, I very much wanted them to drive up and notice me in this scene. I happened to be wearing a dark blue J.Crew sweater and a fairly new pair of washed khakis. It was late October, and some of the maples surrounding the birches still held on to their leaves. In my good clothes, in front of my beautiful house, I could easily have been a model for J.Crew or L.L.Bean, this whole scene I was in the midst of could have been an image of the desirable life pictured within their catalogs, and if Teresa and Gabrielle and Scooter (the golden retriever we'd gotten soon after moving into the house) came out, that would have finished the image off perfectly. I wanted my friends to drive up now. I wanted, I'm a little embarrassed to say, their jealousy. So I stepped inside to get the others to join me.

Morning light comes into the house in a solid wave as soon as the sun lifts above the trees. There was a wash of it just then, illuminating half the central staircase and the entirety of the big, open living room. At the far end of the hall, facing me, was the kitchen, and I could see Teresa in a bathrobe, not new, standing over Gabrielle, who was hooked onto our kitchen counter in her baby seat, eating her breakfast. Scooter was nearby, alert for any stray food that might drop his way.

I walked down the hall and touched Teresa's arm. There was a patch, on the arm of her robe, of caked food. Gabrielle must have spit up there at some point. I scratched at it and looked at Teresa in what I thought of as a gently beckoning way.

"Want to come out?" I asked.

She looked at me as if I had used a tone of seduction, and out of habit she made a face of resistance. We had come to that juncture of our marriage—that post-baby time, when the sexual rhythms change—where she felt that every time I wanted her for something, it was some sort of sneaky prelude to sex.

"I'm feeding her," Teresa said, not unkindly but without much warmth.

Gabrielle picked up a slice of banana and mashed it in her hands.

"She's making kind of a mess, isn't she?" I asked.

Teresa looked at me as if trying to figure out if this last comment contained some veiled criticism of her. She'd gone back to teaching this fall. There were dark circles starting under her eyes. As a gesture of conciliation—to show her I meant no criticism at all—I touched them.

"What are you doing?" Now there was a tone of genuine annoyance in her voice.

"Nothing."

"You keep touching me. What's the matter, you don't like the way I look?"

"No. I like the way you look. I just wanted you to come outside and wait with me."

"I'm feeding her. And I'm not dressed."

I moved in to embrace her, but she still felt resistant; nothing in her body came toward me. Gabrielle made a sound, and Teresa looked down at her and broke away from me, so that my hands fell. Teresa went to the sink and wet a facecloth and washed Gabrielle's face off, and she may have been a little rough, because Gabrielle started to cry. When Teresa lifted her up, the baby's foot caught in the hooked seat, and that set her wailing even more. I stepped forward to try to free her, but in order to do that, I had to pull her down, which hurt her. The cry she sent up was unearthly. Teresa took Gabrielle and went with her to a corner of the kitchen to console her, and Gabrielle, still crying loudly, sent me a look of utter betrayal.

"I had to pull her down," I said.

"I know. Shhh," she said, the last word spoken to Gabrielle. "It's all right."

"No. I'm going for the day now, and I feel shitty."

"Don't," she said, and continued to rock Gabrielle, and I knew that the two of them had already moved past me, that beyond the fact that I was going away for the day, there would be this further separation.

It was on the tail end of this that I realized the guys were at the door.

They were framed there, dressed like me, in new jeans or chinos, looking expectantly through the open door in a way that made me wonder how much of the preceding scene they'd witnessed.

"Hey," I called.

"You ready?" Freddie asked.

"Sure. Yes. Saying goodbye."

Teresa smoothed her hair and moved into view, smiled at them in a way that seemed false to me and made me more than a little angry at her.

"Big day out, huh?" Teresa said, and moved down the hallway to the door. I followed her, and we both stepped out onto the porch. She closed her robe against her.

"So we'll keep him out all day. You can call the boyfriend," Freddie said, and rolled his eyes back and stuck his tongue out to suggest sexual release.

"Oh, yeah. You sure I'm safe?" Teresa's smile was really bothering me now, not so much because she hadn't found it in herself to smile at me all morning, but because it seemed so phony. "So what are you boys going to *do* in Winship?" she asked.

"Just what we used to," Freddie answered, "before you knew us. Smoke some pot on the beach, burn down a sign or two."

"I hear you guys were real studs," Teresa said.

Her joking was driving me crazy now. (Where did she get off, using the word "stud" like that, like she used it all the time?) I wanted to grab her by the wrist and take her back into the kitchen and demand that we finish whatever we'd started there.

"Oh, yeah," Kenny said, and the three of them laughed.

Johnny looked at his watch. "Well, we should get going." We had promised him an early return.

"Okay, don't get into too much trouble."

I bent forward to kiss Teresa. She didn't quite offer me her lips, but I managed to connect with the side of them. We piled into Freddie's van, Kenny and I taking the backseat.

"So where's the birdcage?" Freddie asked as were driving away.

"Shut up," I said. "And it's a bird*house*."

"Rough morning?" Kenny, beside me, asked, in a way that made me think they'd all seen too much. But it was good that Kenny was the one to bring it up, because his face was more generous than the others', like he'd known a few rough marital mornings himself.

"I hate the silly, stupid fights," I said.

They were all quiet. We were passing woods, with occasional houses peeking through, and Freddie was slowing down so as to notice the houses.

"They're *all* silly, stupid fights," Johnny said from the front seat.

"Punctuated by fucking," Freddie said.

"*Occa*sionally punctuated by fucking," Kenny said.

"Which is punctuated by a baby waking up," Johnny said. "And you say to your wife, let him cry, five more minutes, please. And she bolts out of bed. And that's it for another week."

"Or month," Kenny said.

"Thank you," I said. "This is making me feel tremendously better."

"We're here to help," Kenny said.

The marriage discussion was over. I could practically feel us burying it before anything dangerous appeared. I caught Freddie looking at me in the rearview mirror.

"You happy?" I asked. "Here we all are, headed back to Winship."

"I'm happy. I just want to know, who lives here? Who lives in these houses, in this town that looks like Benjamin Franklin's going to step out to take a leak?"

"Kennedys," I answered. "Lesser-known Kennedys. Sargents. Welds."

I had started listing the names of the more patrician governors of Massachusetts.

"Volpes," Kenny added, bringing in the one Italian in the group, the tough-looking ex-construction guy who was governor when we were kids.

"Volpe doesn't live in a place like Bradford," Freddie said, and lifted his little finger in an exaggerated manner. "Volpe doesn't drink tea like this."

Route 2 cut through Bradford, and from there it was a straight shot to Cambridge, past Fresh Pond, after which we connected to Storrow Drive and crossed the Tobin Bridge. Nobody was saying much of anything. There were comments about the downtown construction, the coming Big Dig, the new bridge that had been proposed to run alongside the Tobin. As we were crossing the bridge, Freddie tried to entertain us with his knowledge of city politics and his theory of power. "See, it's never one guy. People think there are these guys who are all-powerful, but I'll tell you who's got power: the guy who can bring together eleven other powerful guys, all of whose desires can be brought to bear on one thing. That's how things get done in this city."

Beside me, at the tail end of this comment and in reaction to it, Kenny mimed masturbation, and Freddie picked up on it.

"What the fuck you doing, DiGiovanni?"

"What's it look like I'm doing?"

"Save it 'til we get to your parents'. Your mother gonna cook meatballs today?"

Freddie was referring to one of the great rituals of our adolescence: masturbating together in the DiGiovannis' basement while the smell of Kenny's mother's meatballs wafted down.

The old highway that crossed through Winship was essentially a peninsular highway running close to the coast, with marsh on one side and beach on the other for about ten miles. Just before you got to this highway, at the point where the land thinned out, what seemed like a dozen smaller roads converged into the main one. Traffic came from all directions, and businesses sprouted up at crazy angles: auto parts stores, fish wholesalers, mason supply. Driving through this chute, you had to look in about seven directions at once.

"I *hate* this," Freddie said, negotiating it, while the rest of us stared out the windows. Already we could sense the presence of the beach. Freddie turned off the highway, and we were in one of those neighborhoods that Winship had given over to the new immigrant class. It was Kenny's neighborhood, his parents holding on as it shifted around them.

"We're in the 'hood'" was how Freddie put it.

"This is not the hood," Kenny said, annoyed enough to slam the door when he'd stepped out. Our agreement was that we were all going to visit our parents, then meet up for an early lunch.

Though they knew I was coming, there was no one waiting on the porch of my parents' house when we got there. I found my father in the kitchen with Brendan, the five-year-old son of my sister Sharon. They were watching cartoons. My father was leaning forward, smoking, fixed on the moving figure of a pig who was being chased through one of those lunar cartoon landscapes where identical green outcroppings appear every five seconds or so. Of the two of them watching, he was the one who appeared more intent.

"It's nice to see you're challenging yourself mentally, Dad," I said.

He turned to me, smiled briefly, tipped some ashes into a saucer.

"Oh, this is a very interesting pig," my father said. "Uncatchable, though fat."

I pulled up a chair and winked at Brendan, who looked at me without changing his expression.

"Is Grandpa corrupting you, Brendan?"

My father's eyebrows lifted. "Well, it's only because I missed all this stuff when you children were little," he said. "Working as hard as I did. Breaking my back so we could keep up the payments on this castle."

"Every Saturday morning this guy would drag me out of bed, Brendan, to watch cartoons. Don't believe a word he says."

Brendan looked from one to the other of us.

"It seems to me they weren't as good then," my father said. "I don't recall anything quite as entertaining as this pig."

"I see all this stuff that's been coming out about the harmful effects of secondhand smoke has gone right over your head, huh, Dad?"

I tried to fan some of the smoke away from Brendan. My father raised his eyes to the heavens.

"Dad, he's what, five?"

"We all grew up in houses full of smoke, Tim," my father said gently, with an undercurrent of seriousness. "And lived to tell the tale. They love to scare us, that's all. It's their business, the scare business."

"Maybe we'll take Brendan down to the beach and play some ball, what do you think?"

"I think we're pretty happy right here, Tim. Good to see you, by the way."

"Where's Mom?"

He pointed upstairs, seeming glad to be left to appreciate his cartoon pig.

I found my mother at work cleaning what was still the single bathroom in the house. She had aged in the Irish way, her skin collapsing into a fretwork of creases. The last of her vanity had gone into her hair, which she dyed close to its original red. She had dressed for the job in a bright pink sweatshirt and gray sweatpants.

"You dressed for me, Ma."

"Yeah, I always like to look beautiful for this chore."

We shared a perfunctory hug; then she leaned against the doorframe, crossed her arms, and studied me.

"Well, you look prosperous."

It was never a very warm look I received from her. There always seemed something a little wary in it, as if some part of her old un-happiness, her long disappointment with my father, had had an ef-fect on our relations as well. I thought what probably happened was that one day, long ago, she had said *Enough*, and pushed both me and my father away and retreated to that narrow channel where her affections could run toward her daughters.

"I guess I'm prosperous enough," I said. "You never come visit us in our prosperous house, though."

"Oh, that house scares me," she said, and mock shivered, though I suspected that being in my house filled her with jealousy of Teresa for gaining so effortlessly that material splendor that had always eluded her. I suspected that when she and my father drove home from visiting us, she was particularly cold to him.

"What scares you?"

"Too big. And all those woods. In my old age I need to know there's people around."

I nodded. Beyond her, I could see through the open door into my old room. The bed was unmade, and what looked like Brendan's pajamas were thrown half onto the floor. I experienced a strong urge to lie there.

"You don't mind if I have a little lie-down on the old bed, do you?" I asked.

"Help yourself."

She went into the bathroom and closed the door, happy enough, I supposed, to have an excuse to finish her job.

The bed held the damp smell of a five-year-old boy. I listened to my mother, a room away, going through her chores. The late morn-ing light came in through the bedroom window, but the window looked as if it hadn't been washed in years, and I thought of going into the garage and getting a ladder and doing the job myself. But part of me didn't want to get up, wanted merely to lie there, and I realized that for all its problems, this had always been a happy enough house, that its very lacks had constituted a thickness all its own, that it had managed—just in the way we'd all congested in this small space—to fill up in a way my own house never quite did. Half consciously I picked up the top of Brendan's pajamas and sniffed them and allowed the warm child-scent to linger in my nostrils.

Finally, though, I realized that this retreat into childhood was not what I'd come for, so I got up and moved past the closed door of the bathroom and went downstairs. My father was just where I'd left him.

"Want to take a walk to the beach?" I asked.

"You're too damn healthy, that's your problem. I bet you *jog*."

"In fact I do. Come on."

I managed to coerce him outside, though he made a great old man's fuss about finding and putting on his jacket. Brendan stayed planted in front of the TV.

"You should do something about this porch, Dad," I said when we stepped outside.

"Suggest something."

"How about rockers? Christmas is coming up. I can get you and Mom a nice pair."

"I bet you can." He stepped down onto the street. Always skinny, he looked even frailer now. The ass of his chinos fell into large folds from not being filled. The gray hair sprouting on the back of his neck looked almost wild, and I could imagine him in the barber's chair, waving away the extras—the shaving of the neck, the trimming of the ear hairs—staring himself down in the mirror with his particular insistence, even in matters of personal grooming, on the unflattering truth.

"So what are your plans for retirement, Dad?"

He glanced sideways at me and seemed to be suppressing a groan. "Is that one of the questions from the handbook? *What the Caring Son Asks His Decrepit Father?*"

"Right. I keep it in the glove compartment."

"Sounds that way. You're almost another daughter, Tim. You tell me not to smoke; you worry about my retirement."

"Yeah, well, I do. I was in my old bedroom. The window's got dust on it from the year one."

Again he looked askance at me, huddled deeper in his jacket.

But there was also a suppressed smile. He was enjoying being ornery.

"Tell me—what do you think of old Winship?"

We had reached the beach highway, which was not a highway at all, just a main drag. Even in the years of the amusement park's long decline, there had been a solid row of stores here, a kind of kids' paradise, saltwater taffy and caramel popcorn and Skee-Ball and Fascination. Now there were condos, six stories high, brutal blocks of concrete.

"Who lives in those monstrosities?"

"Two types of people, Tim. The old and the very old. Oh, and you'll be amused by this. Seems we have our own little gay ghetto. Their own bar, the works. Just down the way."

We chose a bench on the boardwalk, and sitting, he lit up. He looked up and down the beach, a mild suspicion coming over his face as he surveyed girls pushing strollers, young Hispanic guys rollerblading, the old and the very old walking slowly or being pushed by Caribbean nurses.

"So what brings you here without the family, Tim?"

"Maybe I just wanted to see you," I said.

"Well, here I am in all my glory."

"Why don't you and Mom ever come to my house when I invite you?"

"We came. Remember? How long ago was it?"

"Christmas Eve, last year."

"There you go. Seems like yesterday to me."

He smiled cagily, and I remembered how uncomfortable the night had been. Teresa's parents had been there, too. It was Gabrielle's first Christmas, and we were making a big do out of everything. The evening had started off well enough, but at a certain point politics had come up. Tony DiNardi was a classic Reagan Democrat, one of those men who assumed every man of his generation must feel as he did. When he asked my father where he came down on a certain issue, my father answered, "Well, I'm a bit of a contrarian, Tony. That's my political party, I guess. The Contrarian Party." Tony had not known how to take it. For a long, uncomfortable moment, he seemed to believe that such a party existed, and when my father laughed, it made him feel stupid. For Tony Di-Nardi to be made to feel stupid cast a pall over any gathering. When we started opening presents, the DiNardi offerings were lavish, and I knew my mother, who had bought a few modest things, was embarrassed. She sat on the edge of her chair making elaborate noises as each DiNardi gift was unwrapped, and then she went into the kitchen, where I found her doing dishes.

After I'd walked my parents out to their car that night, I watched them take off, my mother with her careful hair turning to make sure my father could successfully navigate backing their small Datsun down the driveway. I wanted to help them, and I found myself patting my pockets, as if there were something there I could give them. And then it occurred to me there was nothing, because nothing I owned was really mine. I turned and looked at the big house, a vision illuminated by hundreds of tiny white Christmas lights, and thought to myself, You make forty-five thousand dollars a year as a book salesman. This isn't yours. What was mine was driving away in the Datsun.

"You didn't have a good time," I said to my father now, as if he shared my memory.

"Oh, they're nice people, those Italians you've married into."

"Dad, don't say anything anti-Italian, okay? We grew up around these people."

He leaned back, took a short drag on his cigarette, and shot me an appraising glance. "You enjoying your life, Tim?"

The question was unusual for him, and I wondered what was behind it. Had he noticed something?

"Am I en*joy*ing it?"

"Yes. An uncomplicated question if ever there was one."

"Some parts of it I do."

"Which parts?"

"Gabrielle. My friends." I paused. "Parts of my job."

I had left out, deliberately, anything about Teresa. Our morning was still too much with me, her resistance to me and the way she had said "I bet you guys were real studs." Sitting on the boardwalk with my father, my whole morning with Teresa began to seem doubly false.

My father nodded, saying nothing.

"Did you enjoy your life? I mean, when you were my age?"

"Well, your mother will tell you I was selfish. That's what she'd say. We all know what a man's job is, don't we? But I think I took things as I found them. And I suppose that's my sense of the job."

He took one final puff of the cigarette and then put it out. When I glanced up at him, he was looking hard into my face. The occasions when a father shows his love are really very odd and confused moments. Because men, most men, are not expressive, and I don't trust the ones who are. This was just a very basic hard perusal of my face, but in it I felt the intensity of his unspoken feeling. He couldn't hold it any longer than I could.

"So," he said, to close off the sentimentality of a moment that hadn't been sentimental at all. He stood, and I did with him.

"Do you ever run into Billy Mogavero?" I asked.

"Billy Mogavero? Tim, I'm a recluse. I see my wife, my daughters, my grandchildren, occasionally you." He pursed his lips, as if he was thinking what to add to this. "And television, I see television."

The others were already waiting outside my house when we got back. Johnny was eager to return home, and he wanted to know right away where we planned to eat.

"Relax," Freddie said. "Let's take a little decompression ride. Everybody's parents doing great? Anybody else have to listen to prostate problems? Raise your hands."

We were passing the place where the old Fantasia Ballroom sign had been. It was gone, in its place a large, cheerful mural-like painting of a roller coaster with several of the old lesser rides surrounding it.

"What happened to the sign?" I asked.

"They're building a museum, my father said," Johnny announced. "They tore down the sign, and they're keeping it in storage until they get the thing built."

Freddie turned his van off the highway in a place we hadn't expected him to. We were in front of Goff's old paint store.

"No," Johnny said. "Tortolla, no. No fucking way."

"A quiet visit."

"You promised we'd be home by one."

"This'll take five minutes," Freddie said, and stepped out of the car.

"The deal was lunch," Johnny half shouted, but Freddie had already gone inside.

Goff's had been a dusty store overseen by a crabby old guy; this new store was lighter and airier, and testified to the presence of a new, upscale market. There were two guys behind the counter, one of them a young blond guy in a crew cut. Billy, waiting on a tall young woman who held a list in her hand, was standing over the machine that shook up cans of paint.

When the blond guy lifted his hand to ask us what we needed, Freddie just pointed to Billy. It took thirty seconds or so before Billy looked up, and a few seconds more for him to display recognition of us.

He had the beginnings of a gut, his hair had receded some, and his arms—he was wearing a faded blue T-shirt—were more thickly muscled. He moved differently now, from the hips, the way men do who've performed manual labor all their lives. Although these changes weren't profound, some change in Billy was. The effect he had on us immediately was to make us more aware of our bodies, as if he might be about to throw something to us that we'd have to be ready to catch.

"The next is Oriental Silk," his customer said after Billy had handed her the mixed can of paint.

"Gallon?" he asked, and while he went to fetch it, he nodded to us.

"Welcome to Winship," he said.

It was five minutes, while he mixed the paint, that we stood there. Johnny made a series of unhappy noises and went to look at the color samples hanging on the wall. Kenny was smiling, as though he was enjoying the very difficulty of this scene, while Freddie leaned into the counter, as if he was making an intense study of Billy.

"You want me to take care of this?" the blond crew cut asked Billy, referring to the customer.

"No, it's all right," Billy said, and smiled just slightly. "These guys have got nothing to do."

"In fact we do," Johnny said. "Some of us have got families waiting."

Billy looked at Johnny, a very cool, appraising, slightly amused look. "How big's your family, John?"

Johnny waited a moment before saying, "I've got a kid."

Billy nodded, trying to look like he was impressed. The Oriental Silk was mixed and placed on the counter before his customer, who had been looking at us all curiously, trying to figure out this scene.

"Is this going to be enough?" she asked. "It's an awfully big room." She shook her head. Her blond hair was held by a scrunchie in the back, and she touched it, started to pull it out.

"You can always come back," Billy said.

He had a good tone for a salesman. He wasn't hurried, and there was something easy about him. After he'd reassured the woman, he and the blond crew cut carried the cans of paint out to her car.

As soon as we were alone in the store, waiting, Johnny said, "He's thrilled to see us."

Then Billy came back and stood behind the counter and folded his arms on his chest and took us in. Kenny was the only one to rouse a smile from him.

"Somebody told me this—I know this can't be true—that Di-Giovanni's a lawyer."

Kenny's smile was so wide that he nearly blushed.

"In the D.A.'s office, somebody told me. No less."

Kenny turned to me as if to comment on this hilarious guy. As if to say how nothing had changed. Same old Billy.

"And the rest of you, I've heard nothing about. I'm clueless. Except that Johnny's got a kid."

"Hey, Billy," Freddie said.

"Who's that behind the sunglasses?"

Freddie took them off, offered the kind of smile that's called for when two business acquaintances want to pretend to great warmth.

Then he put out his hand. Billy registered the awkwardness of it but took Freddie's hand anyway.

"What time do you get off, Bill?" Freddie asked.

"*Fred*die," Johnny said.

"What's Johnny pissed about?" Billy asked.

"He wants to go home."

"Three. I get off at three," Billy said.

Freddie glanced at Kenny and me, as if to check on our availability, while Johnny steamed behind him.

"I'm taking the fucking train," Johnny said.

"No, we can't stay until three," I said, coming forward to save things. "We just came by to say hello."

Billy looked at me then, as if for the first time that day, taking in what had changed about me. Behind his eyes a little light seemed to go on, and I felt flattered.

"No, that's not enough," Freddie said. "Lunch at the Grotto. We take you out. Do you get lunch, Bill?"

"On Saturdays I bring a sandwich. We close too early to take lunch."

I loved how unembarrassed he was by the details of his life.

"You like it here, Bill?" Freddie asked.

"Well enough," he answered, clearly unoffended.

"Well, do you get a *break*?" Freddie asked.

"I do get a break," Billy said. "I go out back and smoke a cigarette." He hesitated a moment and held his face as if there would be a little wit in what he was about to say. "Would you like to join me?"

"Of course," Freddie said before turning to Johnny. "That is, if Mr. Lombardi will spare us a few minutes."

Billy led us around to a garagelike door in the back, and lifted it. There were boxes loaded with paint cans, and he took a seat on one of them. He had brought out a pack of cigarettes, but he didn't offer them around.

"*Merits?*" Freddie asked. "*Merits*, Bill?"

"What do you smoke, Fred?"

Freddie opened his jacket and displayed a couple of cigars. He wore a large shit-eating grin.

Billy raised his eyebrows, pretending to be impressed. "Whoa," he said.

I prayed Freddie wouldn't be asshole enough to offer him one, and I was hugely relieved when he closed his jacket. "I work for a guy, Bill, who takes me to places, these little cigar stores you wouldn't believe. Places the tourists don't see."

Billy, dragging on his cigarette, nodded as if he was interested. I kept waiting for the little eye motion that would give away his game.

"Still selling books, Timmy?" he asked suddenly, as if he'd been picking up on my thoughts.

I nodded, remembering that our last conversation had taken place my first year out of college, when I'd been living at home, just starting this job. "Good memory, Bill."

"And Johnny, how do you support your little family?"

"Johnny got lucky," Freddie answered for him. "He married Carol Auletta, whose father is Auletta Manpower. Which you've heard of."

"Can't say I have."

"Well, Johnny'll run it one day."

Billy paused for a second. "I guess I am feeling distinctly out-classed." The words didn't correspond to his physical movements. His body retained an easy looseness as he spoke. "Overwhelmed, even, by all this success."

"Actually," Kenny said, "Fred's the only one of us who's making money."

"How's that?" Billy asked. "The cigar man?"

Freddie seemed pleased that the attention was back on him. "That's right. Edwin Winerip. You've heard of him?"

"I've heard of nobody. You guys are making me feel like a rube."

"Okay. Relax. You've heard of Seven Bells in Charlestown? North End Clearing?"

Billy shrugged. "These are what? Restaurants?"

"*Bill*. Do you never leave Winship?"

For a moment Billy looked offended. It seemed to give the lie to my theory that he was putting us all on.

"I do occasionally, yeah."

"Do you *shop?*"

Billy turned away from Freddie and looked at me. He scanned my face for something.

"If I *shopped*," Billy said finally, "how would I know these places?"

"They're retail outlets. Malls," Freddie said, soft-pedaling the last word, as if saying it outright represented a kind of defeat.

"And you build them?"

"I don't build them. I build them up."

Billy sat back on one of the stacks and opened his legs and leaned against another, higher stack. "Well, that must be interesting work."

Freddie tried to do the same thing Billy had just done, but his stack was lower than Billy's, and as soon as he recognized the position this put him in, he stood up. "It is."

Billy had watched Freddie as he awkwardly maneuvered himself out of the inferior position, and this time he couldn't help himself; a smile crossed his features. "Well, I should get back," he said, and hopped down off the stack. He ground his cigarette on the floor. "But hey, I mean it. Thanks for stopping by."

"Hey, Bill, give us a couple of minutes," Freddie said.

Billy stood with his hands on his hips, as if that was exactly what he was willing to give us. It was clear now, to me anyway, exactly how unimpressed he was with our bigdick lives.

"We've heard you've turned into a good guy," Freddie said.

Billy looked as though he wasn't sure how to take that.

"My father tells me he's seen you walking with your father on the boardwalk. And such. He told me you coach Little League." Freddie nodded appreciatively. "Model citizen."

Billy looked suddenly suspicious of Freddie's tone, which had changed, though not so definitively that I could put my finger on exactly how.

"Listen, I'd like to talk to you in private for five minutes, Bill.

Could you gentlemen spare us five minutes? Bill, have you got five?"

Billy laughed, as if Freddie's proposal was slightly ridiculous.

"I'm asking for a purpose, Bill," Freddie said, a new seriousness in his voice. "I'm not just being a jerk."

"You want to see me in private?" The disbelieving smile was still on Billy's face. "Step into my office."

"What the fuck do you suppose is going on?" Kenny asked after the two of them had gone inside.

"Freddie's asking him if he can see his dick," Johnny said.

"That's what it seemed like. Like *love*," Kenny said, and looked from one to the other of us and laughed.

"Don't you feel like the biggest idiot that ever walked the earth?" Johnny said, looking at me. "Don't you?"

"I don't know."

It was true. I didn't. I couldn't tell him exactly what I was thinking, but it wasn't that we were wasting our time. In fact, I'd noticed in all of us, with the exception of Johnny, an uncertainty in our manner when we were in Billy's presence, as though what was new about our lives—the money, the smooth way we ordered at the Branding Iron—was being called into question. Without being able to say exactly how, I think we each understood that in going home tonight, our lives would feel slightly different.

When Billy and Freddie emerged from the store, Freddie had placed one hand, lightly, on Billy's shoulder and was gesturing with the other. We could not quite hear what Freddie was saying, but his head was moving in jerks as he spoke, as if his words required extra emphasis. Billy, a few inches taller, was looking down on Freddie's jerking head with a combination of superiority and undisguised interest.

By the time they reached us, Freddie's face looked big and goofy in its pleasure with himself. He lifted his wallet out of his pants pocket, removed one of his cards, and handed it to Billy. "I'll be calling you, Bill. But meanwhile, any questions, you call me."

Billy studied the card. I hoped he might rip it up. Instead, he pocketed it and said, "Okay." To the rest of us, he nodded. "See you boys. My break's up." He tapped the surface of a box of paint, a light and gentle tap like you'd give a child's head, and went inside. We followed Freddie to his 4Runner.

"What'd, you give him a blow job?" Kenny asked when we were inside.

"Yes," Freddie said, and maneuvered us onto the street. "Delicious."

"Don't even think about lunch," Johnny said. "You have used up our lunch time. But I seriously want to know what that was about."

"Seriously? I offered him a job."

"No you didn't."

"Yes I did."

There was a silence in which none of us knew what to say. Johnny shook his head several times.

"And he said—" Kenny asked.

"Yes. He said yes. What would you say if you were mixing paint forty hours a week for ten bucks an hour and somebody offers you almost twice that?"

"Twice?" Johnny was incredulous

"To schmooze. Essentially to schmooze. You'd say yes. He said yes."

"I don't fucking believe you," Johnny said.

"You guys live sheltered lives." Freddie's voice was now very low, very controlled, the exact antithesis of what it had been with Billy. "Johnny, you have to produce nothing—with the exception of children for Carol Auletta—and you're made. Tim, you sell books—a tough field, especially given that they've bought the same books the year before and they're going to need them the next year."

"You are such a—" Johnny started to say.

"And me?" Kenny asked.

Freddie released a big, gassy smile. "You think you're in the real world, Kenny. Hookers get killed, lowlifes get killed, you deal with some sleazy types. But who pays your salary? The state. You get a conviction, the state pays you; you get a no bill, the state pays you anyway."

"And you, Mr. Real World—"

Freddie's index finger, cutting Johnny off, stabbed the air as if he were pointing to the words he was saying, as if they existed in the air. "Has to invent what's going to happen. Out of whole cloth. Out of nothing. Out of pure desire." He paused a second. "Why does anybody do anything? Answer me that. What do any of us need? Money? Yes. Of course. But something else. We all need a *person* in our life. We all need to wake up with a boner, and our wives sometimes don't do that for us anymore. There's got to be somebody out there in the world we can't wait to *see*. We get up in the morning, we are dying to *get* to that person, even if it's only to talk, to have coffee . . ."

"So?" Kenny asked.

"So? Billy."

After a moment's pause, as if to allow us time to put things together, Freddie continued. "I could tell inside of five minutes what the guy's still got. You see him with that woman, the customer? You see the way she was flirting? He will do very well for Winerip. And that's my job, to do very well for Winerip. To bring *in*—"

"To bring in what?" Johnny asked. "Trouble?"

"John, in your work, in your very complicated work at Auletta Manpower, has the word 'fuckable' ever come up? Do you have familiarity with the word 'fuckable'?"

Johnny laid his head back against the headrest of his seat.

"I take it you haven't. It doesn't mean what it sounds like, exactly. We're *all* fuckable. Literally. But to be fuckable is to incite a desire. That's all. To incite a fanciful . . ." He waved his free hand around. "Desire. Three-quarters of the potential clients I talk to are women. Does the Gap *need* another store? Do any of these—Pottery Barn, Victoria's Secret—*need*? No. But do these women potentially need Billy?"

He paused.

"You think I'm being crude? He's not going to fuck them; it's not that blatant. Some of them he will, but not all. But he's going to incite the desire to fuck in ways you and I can't. Or don't."

He looked around at the two of us in the backseat. "Pens will meet paper," Freddie went on, "on the bottom line. Because Billy schmoozed the client. Because of a game of *golf*."

"How do you know Billy plays golf?" Kenny asked, and Freddie, turning again in the driver's seat, laid on him a look of such intellectual superiority, of Kenny's so having missed the point of Freddie's subtle exegesis of how business was done at Winerip, and this look lingered for so long that he missed entirely the fact that we were approaching the dreaded Winship bottleneck. Freddie turned around in time to swerve out of the path of one car, only to be broadsided—toward the rear, on Kenny's side—by another.

I was wearing a seat belt, but I still managed to hit my head against the window glass. Maybe I was out for fifteen seconds or so, but I still heard things. I heard Kenny shout "Oh Jesus" while outside the car Hispanic voices cursed us. Coming out of this brief unconsciousness was like waking up at the beach, that sun-dazzled absorption of every sound for miles around. A pair of Hispanic men were approaching the car, and Freddie, sounding frightened, said, "We gotta get out of here," but the car wouldn't move. I realized that I could see the Hispanic men without the filter of glass. All the glass in the van's side window seemed to have broken against Kenny's head. Johnny blinked, trying to make the shift from his concentration on how this accident affected him personally to some sense of what he ought to be doing for us in the backseat. "I'm okay," I remember saying, though nobody had asked me. Kenny was covering his face with his hands, and the two Hispanic men, looking through the shattered glass at Kenny, seemed to drop their hostility.

I was still in a daze when the ambulance came. By then Freddie had managed to yank open the side door of the van, after which the door fell off. It may have fallen on the foot of one of the Hispanic men, I don't remember, but there was a fair amount of yelling after that event. Johnny by then was trying to figure out what to do about the blood on Kenny's head, and I stepped forward, out of the seat, or tried to, because as soon as I was half standing, I fell and laughed, embarrassed, and Johnny looked at me, too. "You okay?" he asked. Kenny was crying, still covering his face.

Then we were in the ambulance, we were parting traffic, Johnny and I sitting next to Kenny, who was still crying, though not covering his face anymore, because the medics had told him not to.

The blood that covered Kenny's features looked like a clay mask that hadn't set, as if he had dipped his head quickly and carelessly into a vat of blood, so that his eyes, staring out of it, had the look of a whole fish that is set before you on your plate—that frozen, astonished stare.

"Don't touch yourself," one of the medics said.

We were headed toward some hospital in Boston; nobody had bothered to tell us which. Johnny told me to put my head between my knees. I shook my head and stayed intent on Kenny, as he swallowed with what seemed great, forced pain and stared through us at the roof of the ambulance, looking very, very scared.

five

Teresa learned something about the male body—or maybe about her own power—the night I came home from the hospital, having been diagnosed with a mild concussion.

Kenny had had to stay, of course. There was no question but that he would live. The glass had broken against him in such a way that most of his face had been cut, but not as deeply as had first appeared. Still, his face would change, extensive plastic surgery required. We were not allowed to see him until after his wife arrived; he was awake only long enough to acknowledge us, though he looked deeply embarrassed by the whole incident. It was dusk by the time the rest of us took separate cabs home. My driver, dark-skinned, of mysterious ethnicity, stared at the woods and the occasional houses of Bradford and appeared more frightened than impressed. We caught a glimpse of each other in the rearview mirror: he was looking at me as though I must be a creature of enormous wealth, while I wanted to say to him, No, no, listen, you've got it all wrong, I'm from *Winship*.

The house was ablaze as the driver pulled in where I'd directed him. Some primary sense of economy hit me when I saw the lights illuminating the tall cathedral space that reached to the small third floor. This would someday become a playroom for Gabrielle and any new DiNardi-O'Kanes who happened to come along, but for now it was completely empty.

My clothes stained with some of Kenny's blood, I stood at the door and watched through the beveled glass Teresa approaching, holding Gabrielle. Teresa scowled at my clothes—I thought it was an odd way of showing concern, if not entirely unexpected—and as she did, I turned to watch the driver, who was having trouble backing down our steeply angled driveway. With his leaving, my last connection to the day's weird logic would be severed. At that moment I felt a strange nostalgia.

"Get out of those clothes," Teresa said right off. "We should wash them right away."

So I stood in my underwear, submitting to her, holding Gabrielle in the washroom while she poured solvent over the bloodstains on my pants.

"It's not that big a deal," I said.

"No? Blood, not a big deal? How's your concussion?"

"I feel like this whole day has been a puzzle and I've lost a couple of the pieces."

She smiled at that, finally letting down some of her guard. "I made something good, too. Lamb."

"I could eat lamb."

Teresa lit candles, wanting to make this as much like our traditional festive Saturday nights as she could. I thought I understood why she professed so little interest in the events of the day. They represented, for her, an impediment, as if she had some plan in mind for the evening other than nursing me. I found, maybe in reaction to this, that I wanted very much to sleep, and later I did doze in front of the fire Teresa had made. After putting Gabrielle to bed, she came down and joined me, pouring herself a glass of wine first, nuzzling up to my body, and asking me if I wanted any.

"If I drink wine now, I'll sleep forever," I said.

Dimly, I recalled our morning's difficulties, now light-years away.

"If I were you, I'd want a bath," Teresa said. "I'd want to make sure somebody's blood wasn't still on me."

Our second-floor bathroom has an arched window over the tub. It's actually pretty splendid. Lying there, you can look out into the woods, and at night you can presumably be seen. Teresa and I, when we bathed there together, had stoked our vanity by imagin-

ing phantom hunters or lost Bradford husbands getting a glimpse
of us. That night it was me alone in the tub, Teresa sitting on the
lip. She'd been careful with me, helping me in. There were more
candles, and she had turned off the overhead light, and it was only
my awareness of her attempt to create a romantic ambience that
made me feel at a distance, as if there were something else more important, something I had to tell her.

I wanted to tell her about the day I'd just had. But every time I
tried to bring something up, she'd just nod and push the wet hair
off my forehead, and between these affectionate ministrations of
hers and the sips of wine she offered, I found myself simultaneously
aroused and being lulled into a kind of stupor.

The next morning, she was amused. "Do you remember anything from last night?" The truth was, I did and I didn't. I knew
we'd made love, and I knew I'd been only partly awake for the act,
but the fact that a penis could more or less function while its owner
slept had clearly given Teresa an idea. Several weeks later I awoke
in the middle of the night to find her on top of me, and not many
weeks after that, we sat on the edge of our bed gazing fixedly at the
home pregnancy test, watching it turn blue. "Yes!" Teresa shouted,
and reached over to hug me, expecting that I would match her reaction. It seemed not to have occurred to her that I might feel different. We had discussed having a second child, and I had argued
for waiting, not because I didn't want another kid, but because I
thought Teresa was too determined, plowing straight ahead as
though that clock Freddie had referred to in the Branding Iron
were ticking away in her head.

There are always, I suppose, compensations. The little girl who
arrived at the end of this second pregnancy had my red hair—mine
and my mother's. I'd suggested we name her Irene, after my
mother. Teresa, though touched by the idea, pooh-poohed it. "Irene
is a name for an old lady, Tim. That's not a name you give a baby."
We decided to name her Nina, though that name—Teresa's
choice—never seemed a perfect fit. The baby had that pale roseate
coloring, Irish to the bone, a translucency to her high brow where
the veins show through.

Of course it was a disappointment not to have a son, but that sort of disappointment belonged more to the world of the Branding Iron, where the birth of a boy gave you bragging rights, than it did to the hospital. The sight of this new daughter in the little pink hat they put on her to keep her head warm was enough to make me half want to die. Soon after her birth I followed her into the nursery, where they bathed her and left her in a warming tray. I lowered my fingers so she could grasp them, feeling the strength of her pull, leaned in close, and whispered the name Irene low enough so that the nurse behind me wouldn't hear.

After the accident, Kenny's wife refused to allow him to attend our Monday night sessions at the Branding Iron—we had become, in her eyes, too dangerous—and his place was soon taken over by Billy.

Billy was newly employed by the Winerip Company, and though presumably he had to dress for work, he always managed to arrive at the restaurant in jeans and a sweatshirt, sometimes wearing a jacket and sometimes not. He pulled up in the late 1970s Pontiac Le Mans he drove, a nondescript brown car with large patches where the paint was entirely worn off. He met us in the lobby and always cased the dining room with a look comprised of equal parts curiosity and surliness. Because, in Billy's presence, we had lost the first of our rituals, that of checking out one another's suits, our greetings took on a new awkwardness.

The waitresses, since Billy had joined us, grew more attentive. When they brought our drinks, they always sent him a hairbreadth lick of attention that contained in it something profoundly serious. Billy acknowledged it, that was all, the waitress went away, but we'd all seen it and were again back in high school, the old distinctions asserted in this new field we'd formerly considered our own.

Freddie had known inside of five minutes at Winship Paint what Billy still possessed. He had set Billy up in a fairly low-level position as an assistant marketing director at the Seven Bells Mall in Charlestown. He wanted Billy to learn "from the ground up," so what Billy spent seven days a week doing was decorating the mall, writing press releases, draping promotional tables. We learned all this from Freddie. Billy was characteristically silent about his work, though he didn't seem embarrassed by whatever diminishment might have existed in the words "draping tables." On weekends, Freddie relieved Billy of his chores, allowing Billy to accompany him to his "out of the box" marketing sessions, which took place on golf links, primarily. The inference was that Billy was staying in the background, learning how things were done, watching, refining himself.

"He's the only straight assistant marketing guy we have." Freddie laughed, and Billy made no comment, took a sip of his Scotch, stared out at the blue Boston landscape that seemed to hold a special interest for him, and then turned to one or the other of us to ask a question about our lives. He wanted to know all about Johnny's business, for instance, the stealth required to know who at one company might be open to an offer from another. Sometimes, after our third Scotch, Billy would single me out and ask me about family life, what it was like to have two kids, two girls, and then he'd sit back to listen in that recessed, not particularly welcoming, but still intently interested way of his.

One Monday night, when we were alone in the parking lot after Johnny and Freddie had taken off, Billy lingered, his hands in his pockets. Again it was fall, a year after the last fall, when we'd rediscovered him in Winship.

"Freddie says that house of yours is really something," Billy said.

"It's big." I laughed, maybe a little falsely, not wanting to give away too much of my complicated attitude toward my house.

"Yeah, that's what I hear." Billy spit through his two top teeth, an old neat trick of his. "*How* big," he asked, "exactly?"

I looked around for something to compare it with. The buildings bordering the Branding Iron were all city dwellings, tripledeckers and industrial buildings. "I guess you'd have to see it."

"I'd like that," Billy said.

I hesitated, surprised. I could not immediately put these two parts of my life—Billy's presence, my domestic scene—into the same frame. But I was flattered.

So it was arranged, a Saturday night, dinner. I asked if he wanted to bring someone, and he said no, he'd be coming alone. Teresa balked at the idea. Irene-Nina was still in her infancy; the milk from Teresa's breasts had a way of leaking out and staining whatever dress she wore; she didn't like the small amount of weight she hadn't been able to shake off after the birth. I tried to reassure her and told her I would cook.

Bradford must have taken note of Billy as he'd come off Route 2 and plowed through the pristine, Volvo-friendly center of town in his Le Mans. He had dressed for the occasion, a crisp white shirt and a sport jacket. He brought a bottle of wine.

I had done the main part of the cooking by the time Billy arrived—a simple chicken dish I remembered from my Charlestown days—but there was still the warming to do and the last ingredients to be added. Teresa's absence was explained by the fact that she wanted to get Nina and Gabrielle to bed before coming down, but I knew the real reason was that she wanted to gussy herself up before she met Billy. We opened the wine, and Billy looked around the kitchen with that new interest of his that couldn't exactly be called appreciation. This part of my life was all a mystery to him.

"How'd this *happen*?" He lifted his arms and shook his head, unembarrassed to display his wonderment. "I mean, what'd this house cost, half a million?"

"Not quite. Maybe three hundred and fifty thousand."

He took a second before asking the next question, as if he wasn't practiced in certain social niceties and needed to consider before asking. "And—you've got it?"

"Hell no, hell no." I laughed. "If it was all up to me, we'd live in some hole." He looked at me as if he was catching me in a lie, or if not a lie, a pose I thought might be more acceptable to him. "My father-in-law paid for most of this."

He went on looking around the kitchen, feeling the burnished wood of the cabinets gleaming in the recessed light. Then Teresa came down in a black dress I hadn't seen her wear since the night, a year before, when we had to attend a ceremony honoring her father at the Graymore Lions Club.

During dinner Billy spent a lot of time looking at Teresa, not staring but looking, and not looking sexually but in some other manner. He seemed almost shy of her, or shy of the questions he wanted to ask, and I wondered whether in all his knowledge of women, he had somehow missed out on the knowledge of women who came from money. Teresa stepped into the silences and tried to nudge us into our old relationship, as if she wanted not simply to know about it but to see it in action.

"Timmy tells me things," she said at one point, "about the old days."

Billy seemed embarrassed by the reminder. His face tightened a little. He sipped his wine.

The girls would not go to sleep easily that night. While Teresa went upstairs to attend to Nina, Billy and I stepped out onto the back deck. It was just warm enough to stand outside. From his inside jacket pocket Billy removed two fat cigars.

"These things are fucking ridiculous," he said, "but Freddie says I've got to smoke them."

I waited a second before asking, "Do you have to do everything Freddie tells you to?" Billy looked at me, then at my clothes. He seemed to be taking in the quality of my shirt, my pants, as if he were feeling the material, sniffing it. Expensive clothes like the ones I was wearing are soft, and it was that softness Billy seemed drawn to. Then he put one of the cigars in his mouth, wet it, and bit off the end.

"I'm supposed to have a cigar cutter." He spit the end into my yard and licked the shardy bits off what was left and handed the other to me before lighting his own. He blew a big plume into the air.

"Here's what he wants," Billy said after a moment, now that it had been made clear he had no intention of answering my question. "He wants me to fuck women for him." He pulled a bit of cigar off his lower lip and shifted against the deck railing. "Amazing, huh? That he can't do that for himself?" He turned to me. "You met this guy Winerip, Timmy?"

"No."

"They're so fucking impressed by themselves. Silver hair. These clothes. The way they move. The *offices*. Freddie, too. And then, underneath, *some*thing. I don't get it. Something." He shook his head.

"What?" I smiled, I thought cunningly, to try to draw him out.

"It's like you guys never grew up." He paused a second, watching what my face did in reaction. "I'm sorry. I don't want to offend you. Here I am, sitting in your beautiful house, eating your beautiful meal. And what have I got? But . . ."

He scratched his lower lip with the smallest of his fingers. I could see he was trying to soften what he'd just said, smiling slightly at me, but the damage was still there.

He blew another long plume into the black air. "I saw it the day you all came to the paint store. In these clothes that were like . . . how much do you have to pay for a *sweatshirt*? For *chinos*? I thought I was looking at four guys who had signed up for the Asshole of the Month Club." He laughed a little.

"But you took the bait, Billy."

"Sure I did. Yes." He nodded. No more explanation.

Teresa came down then with Nina. We saw her through the glass doors leading into the dining room, balancing the baby on one side. Billy opened the door for her.

"She's going nowhere," Teresa said, "least of all to sleep. I figured I might as well join you."

"She's beautiful," Billy said, and reached out to run the back of a finger up and down one of Nina's cheeks. She had been crying, and her skin was flushed.

"Doesn't she look Irish, Billy?" I asked, but Billy didn't answer.

"Jesus, I wonder sometimes what's taking me so long," he said instead.

"You've got to find the right woman, that's all," Teresa said, and looked at him in a way that was not so unlike the way the waitresses at the Branding Iron looked at him. Because I thought I knew Teresa, I wasn't so scared, though I was a little surprised.

"It's too cold for her out here," Teresa said. "Why don't you guys bring those cigars inside? I don't mind."

"It's all right," Billy said, and put his out. "I've gotta go anyway. I've got a date waiting."

"Why didn't you bring her?" Teresa asked.

Billy didn't answer.

"What about dessert?" Teresa asked, anxious to hold on to a little of the evening for herself.

Billy looked at his watch. "No, really," he said without apology.

I walked Billy out to his car. I ran my hand along it. "Freddie's going to want you to replace this," I said.

"Nah. Never. Here's where I draw the line." He leaned against the car a moment, his arms crossed, as if he wanted to talk some more. "There's got to be one thing," he said. "One thing they don't get about you. One place that's impregnable." He lifted his eyebrows. "You didn't know I knew such words, did you?" he asked slyly. "Impregnable."

I shook my head, not knowing how to respond. "Good. You keep one thing to yourself."

He got into his car and drove away. Sometimes I thought it was so *odd* that he was back in my life, one of life's strange jokes. But I also thought, at moments like this one, that it was inevitable. I watched the lights of his big, gangly car disappear. Then I called Scooter, and we went for a long walk.

Several months after Nina's birth I was called into the front office at Endicott and told I was being given a new assignment. Endicott was gifting me with a long swath of new territory, beginning in New Haven with Yale, running up the Connecticut River through a group of tony mid-Massachusetts colleges like Amherst, Smith, and Mount Holyoke, reaching west to Williams and north to Dartmouth. This valuable territory had always belonged to a man named Jack Goshgarian, but Jack Goshgarian was taking steps toward retirement. It was assumed that with my growing family, I'd appreciate not having to be on the road overnight quite so much.

I was given a company car for these trips. Jack Goshgarian

traveled with me at first, introducing me to his contacts at the bookstores and to the occasional professor. It was a return to the fields of my college years (the territory included UMass), the scents and the particular feelings of those years, the memory of girls, of all those nipped-in-the-bud relationships, and sometimes, walking on the main street of Amherst, I felt a wish to run into one of those girls. It seemed to me now a rich world I had run through like a dog, impatient for the far-off scent of a girl I wouldn't meet for years. Why had I been so eager for those specific things I'd associated with Teresa? There were one or two girls at UMass who I believed—had I taken things further with them—could have revealed things to me about sex, and about myself. What if I had slowed down, allowed things to develop, been braver? In my mind sometimes I played out imaginative scenarios that had never happened. In the car driving home with Jack Goshgarian, it was never money I thought of, not the increased amount this new territory might provide. I had become far more interested in sexual memory.

I developed a new set of habits after Jack Goshgarian relinquished his prize territory to me. Route 2, as it runs east from the junction of Route 91, must be the loneliest highway in the world. There's a bridge called the French King; then for long patches the trees form a kind of roof over the road, the land on either side just a density of vegetation with an occasional glimpse of water or an abandoned-looking house to break the monotony. These houses, even the ones with lights on, possessed a chill, as if nothing good could be going on inside. When small restaurants appeared at the side of the road—tiny, houselike establishments with names like Country Living or Starlite or Boxcar—they arrived with such a keen sense of welcome that I found it irresistible to stop and order a fried haddock sandwich or a meatloaf special. The women inside these restaurants all had terrible hair—either those tight curls worn by old women who visit the hairdresser regularly or that overly streaked near-death experience that is the favored hairdo of down-on-their-luck women. But I always felt at home in these restaurants; there was a flat-out sense of lived life there that was the exact antithesis of Bradford.

Full-bellied, with that sense of well-being that only hot third-rate food can give you, I penetrated the outer dark, drove through Wendell, Leominster, Lancaster, Lunenburg. The company car had a tape deck, but I chose instead to drive with one finger poised against the radio's SEEK button. I sought out the oldies stations, the mix stations, and one particular program I could get for only about twenty minutes of the drive, in which a husky-voiced female DJ fielded calls from brokenhearted listeners, in response to which she played an only occasionally appropriate brokenhearted love song. I had taken to talking back to the radio on these long drives, and once when—in response to a particularly affecting listener's sob story—she played Lionel Richie's "Stuck on You," I found myself shouting "*That?* You're going to play the poor woman *that?*" More often, though, I would find myself singing along at the top of my lungs. More often than I cared to admit, "Stuck on You" was exactly the kind of song I wanted to hear.

In the mood that these long night drives sent me into, even pathetic songs like "Afternoon Delight" and "Magnet and Steel" were enough to get me excited, and Peter Frampton's "Baby I Love Your Way" or almost any high-grade Elton John or Bryan Adams could lift me into the stratosphere. I learned something that those who don't do long distances can't possibly learn: great music never corresponds as closely to the heart's crude longings as lesser music does. Sheathed in my car, encased within my own personal karaoke, I would have given you all of the Beatles for three minutes of Harold Melvin and the Blue Notes' "If You Don't Know Me By Now," the entire canon of Bob Dylan for thirty seconds of the Chi Lites' "Oh Girl."

The drive home from Northampton or Amherst was ninety minutes, from New Haven or Hanover considerably longer. All that time, I rode the radio dial. It was often the case that after suffering through a musical desert in the middle portion of my ride, I'd hit pay dirt closer to home. Roy Orbison's "Not Alone Anymore" would come on just as I reached the Bradford exit, and I'd find myself circling the town, prolonging the ride just to stay with the song's emotional high. Finally I would pull into the driveway, shut off the car, and feel myself emptying out, life flattening. In this mood I found I didn't want to go into the house, didn't want to submit to the constrictions of family life, the limits of who I was to the three people inside.

It was around this time that I began going back to Winship on a regular basis. The reason was simple: Billy invited me. He made it seem as if there was something he needed. We always lingered after the others had left in the parking lot of the Branding Iron.

It was easy enough to take him up on his first offer to come to Winship and meet his girlfriend. With my new territory, I no longer had to get up the next morning and catch my regular seven-o'clock flight to Pittsburgh. So I followed him over the Tobin. The house Billy finally pulled up in front of was on the other side of Winship from where we'd all lived, and it was a step down from our parents' houses, located in one of those squeezed-in neighborhoods that had been built to accommodate a swath of solid ground in the surrounding marsh. I followed him inside and saw from the look of the woman sitting at her kitchen table how unexpected I was.

"Paula, this is Timmy." Billy went directly to the refrigerator, found a bottle of seltzer, and drank from the bottle.

I was a given a warm, if uncertain, smile. Paula stood and rubbed her hands against her tight jeans before shaking mine. The crust of what must have been a genuine former beauty—maintained through makeup and jewelry and frosted hair—looked fragile. For a moment I thought I recognized her.

"Did we go to school together?" I asked.

"Oh, no. No," she said, as if I had some minor fame she needed to humble herself before. "No, I went to St. Mary's."

She looked at Billy before asking what she could get me. There was an embarrassed quality to her, as though the house itself had been unprepared for my coming. The kitchen was paneled, with little framed samplers and generic paintings on the walls, the sort of kitchen that always reeks to me of an attempt on the part of the formerly wild and reckless to assume the postures of middle-class life. It could all have been purchased, a model of the acceptable, in a cheap store.

"Nothing, thanks," I said. "We just had one of our enormous unhealthy dinners."

I was trying hard to loosen things up. She smiled at me but kept looking at Billy.

"I wanted him to meet you," Billy said in response to that look, and he shrugged and leaned back against the refrigerator.

"You live here alone?" I asked, just to get something going.

"Why don't you at least sit down?" she said, and pulled out a chair. When I'd done as she'd asked, she said, "No, I've got a son, Ryan. He's ten." She looked more comfortable sitting. "He's asleep, of course. Only time I get to pay these." She gestured to the bills she'd been paying when we'd come in. "After he goes to bed. And when Bill's out working. Which is a lot lately."

Billy had told me nothing about her except that she existed, and nothing at all about a boy, ten years old.

"Well, that's great. Your son's ten, huh?"

Billy brought over a framed picture, handed it to me. It was a team photo, a group of nine- and ten-year-olds, the conventional poses, the baseball caps, the way little boys look everywhere. WINSHIP PAINT 1992 LITTLE LEAGUE EASTERN DIVISION SUFFOLK COUNTY CHAMPIONS. Billy stood to one side of them, looking a bit bulkier than he did now, one hand in the pocket of his team jacket, the other leaning on a bat. On his face was a slightly crooked smile. Billy pointed to a small, unexceptional-looking boy in the front row.

"That's your son," I said to Paula with oversized enthusiasm, as if to fill the vacuum in the room. "And you're the goddamn coach, Bill."

Billy sent me a curious look, as though "goddamn" was the wrong word. He took the picture and placed it back where it had been.

"Are you sure I can't get you a beer?" Paula asked.

I placed my hands on my belly and made a face to indicate sat-
edness. She pretended to think I was funnier than I was.

The whole scene had begun to make me uncomfortable, so I
said, "Listen, it's late. I should be getting back."

"You came all the way here, we can't even give you anything?"
Paula asked.

"He's got kids, Paula. He's got little kids."

Her glance went too quickly from Billy to me.

"You're the one with the girls, right?"

"Right."

Billy had talked about me. It was a mild surprise. The word
"girls" elicited from her the same reaction it did from everyone: say
the word "boys" and people looked at you with a certain rough appreciation, but "girls" made you appear, I knew, only sweet and unthreatening.

"And Billy's right. I've got to get home to them."

He did not see me out. In my car, warming it up in front of
Paula's house, I looked up and felt for an instant the echo of what it
had been to be outside of Billy's sex in the old days, to be sitting on
a seawall knowing he was down the beach with Carol Casella. I
opened the windows and smelled the beach in winter. On the way
out, I chose to drive past my house, where I saw a light on, my father suffering gamely through one of his insomniac evenings.
Which of the movies of my childhood was he watching tonight?
Not wanting to draw attention to my presence here, I drove
quickly past, not slowing down long enough to see.

The next time Billy asked me to Winship, a few weeks later, it was
to see his father and his brother, Ronnie. "They're up this late?" I
asked in the parking lot of the Branding Iron, by way of an excuse.
I had thought afterward about the way it felt after he'd introduced
me to Paula, the return to those old adolescent feelings, and I wasn't
sure I wanted to repeat it.

Billy's father and brother were watching Jay Leno that night
when we stepped in. Billy's father was in a maroon bathrobe, very

thin and faded. His leatherette slippers were cracked, and the piping around the toes had discolored. He had taken on the gray, unfocused aura I've noticed in old priests. To the change—Billy bringing a friend home rather than arriving alone—he reacted with initial discomfort.

"Of course I remember you," he said, and shook my hand in the old Italian manner, taking my hand in one of his and covering it with the other. "How's your father?"

Ronnie was in his late twenties now, but his face looked undeveloped, permanently blurred. He was dark, and he wore a mustache that was like an adolescent's, wispy and resembling a layer of coal dust. The TV they watched was a portable, placed directly atop the kitchen table. The kitchen had a masculine sobriety that wasn't the same thing as a lack of care. Someone cared. Things were stacked neatly, and everything was clean, but there wasn't much of anything.

"He's got Eddie Murphy on," Ronnie said to Billy, as if, having acknowledged me, he was freed to reassert the comfortable normalcy of their habits.

After a silence in which everyone had turned for a full minute to Leno, Mr. Mogavero seemed to remember the forms of courtesy. "Billy tells me you go out for some pretty fabulous meals," he said.

"I don't know if fabulous is the word for those meals," I laughed. "They're certainly heavy on the meat."

I watched Mr. Mogavero's reaction, recessed like his son's, the two of them having mastered the art of never letting you know what they thought. Stupid of me not to remember he'd been a butcher.

"So," Mr. Mogavero said, turning to Billy and adjusting his glasses, "you're not seeing Paula tonight."

Billy drew a glass of water from the tap. "I've gotta give my dick a rest sometime, Dad." He lifted his eyebrows to the old man. Ronnie let out a yelp of delight. "If you don't give it a rest, the skin gets raw and you go around all day dying to scratch it."

Ronnie yelped again. Billy was doing this for him, but not entirely for him. Mr. Mogavero swallowed and looked at me, like one of the old comedians—George Burns or Jack Benny—who had perfected the art of the double disappearance, hiding a blank stare behind a pair of thick glasses. Yet nothing in him seemed particularly offended. This was their house; these were their rituals. Welcome.

"Like the end part, right?" Ronnie said, pointing to his own crotch.

"Right. The end part."

They all three went back to the TV. End of sore dick discussion.

After a few minutes Ronnie turned back to me, as if responding out of delayed curiosity. "Where do you live now, Tim?"

I told him, and watched his small, wary eyes close around the foreignness of the word "Bradford." Billy had gotten all the looks in the family. They had skipped Ronnie entirely.

But he worshipped Billy. It was evident in the way that, while he waited for Eddie Murphy to come on, he glanced at Billy at intervals, something mildly expectant on his face each time.

From time to time I saw Billy looking at me as if he was monitoring my reaction. He would never let me know exactly what he wanted me to see, but that there were specific things he wanted me to know was clear.

Then, at a certain point, Billy seemed to decide I had seen enough. He signaled to me and gestured to the door.

"So, the family," he said when we were outside. He still held the glass of tap water.

"Ronnie. He—" There was no easy way to ask the question.

"He bags groceries at the Star Market. Where my father's the butcher emeritus." He raised his eyebrows. Another of his surprising words. "Problem is, he talks to people. He doesn't know when to stop. So the manager, Chickie Malone—you remember him?"

"From high school. Yes."

"He takes him aside. He calms him down."

"You have a diagnosis?" It was the boldest question I knew how to ask.

Billy blew out his cheeks, as if a burp might be coming.

"We don't do diagnoses in Winship, Tim. We do—he drives, he can bag groceries, and as long as Chickie Malone's manager, we're probably all right."

A silence followed the words "all right." It let me know that it was important for Billy to do well at Winerip in ways the rest of us couldn't understand, another in the string of carefully released impressions he was forcing on me.

I wanted then to soften whatever pain might exist around the problem of Ronnie. "I could never joke about a sore dick with my father."

Billy swigged the last of the tap water. "No? Maybe that's because you never get one."

The look he sent me then was only seconds long. Teresa was contained in it. It was as if he had seen everything the night of the dinner. I had been getting close to him. Now I felt myself pulling back.

"So tell me," he said, forcing the burp down again. "Confirm something for me. Paula. She'll never make it in this world, right?"

I knew right away what he meant by "this world."

"Oh come on," I said. "Don't ask me that."

"No. I am asking you. And I don't want a bullshit answer, either."

"Why don't you ask Freddie?"

"Because I am never going to ask Freddie a question like this. Because I wouldn't show Freddie that much respect. That's why I'm asking you."

"I don't know what you mean."

"Bullshit." After a pause, he said "Bullshit" again. Then he laughed lightly. "Fucking coward. You know exactly what I mean. I am soon to be invited to parties, Tim." He rolled the glass between his hands as he spoke. "At the Prudential. Very posh affairs. Who do I bring?"

He seemed to be answering the question for himself. It was an exquisitely uncomfortable moment.

"You could try bringing her," I said. "See how it works."

Billy looked sideways at me, his eyes shifting a little, as if he had nothing but contempt for my answer. Also, as if he heard the truth in it.

"I don't think you know the first thing about business," he said. As soon as the words were out of his mouth, he shook his head, as though he couldn't believe he'd said them.

Then he looked up at the houses opposite us. "You think I could throw this glass up on top of Ferlazzo's roof so it crashes up there?"

It was not a compelling question, so I waited for him to ask the next one.

"Not so it crashes against the house, and not in their backyard, but on the roof. What do you think?"

"I think you could probably do that, if you wanted."

He stepped back and threw the glass up. We listened to the splintering on the roof. In the silence afterward, Billy ran his hands up and down his arms, as if warding off cold, and he stared, with an indecipherable look, at the roof he had successfully reached.

"Good night, Tim."

Billy began dating, officially, women from Winerip's affiliates—the greater Boston world of commerce—soon after. There began a parade of them: Ellen Swerdlow from I. Magnin, Jane Mendelsohn from Copley Place, Vivien Patchett from John Hancock Financial. We learned about them first from Freddie, and then we met them, it was inevitable; there were gatherings as our lives expanded, and Billy became a part of the larger circle. When Johnny's second son was born, Billy was there at the baptismal party, Jane Mendelsohn beside him.

Jane Mendelsohn was blond, with intense blue eyes and a slightly hooked nose and a mouth that had hunger and curiosity in it. Like most of Billy's girlfriends, she came on strong; she cowed me. I could never be interesting enough for her, with my simple life, my house in Bradford, my daughters. She would ask questions and then nod her head too eagerly, as if the answers I gave her were more compelling than I knew them to be.

They were retail women, Billy's girlfriends. He liked to make fun of them, in their presence, for their hawkish interest in the materials of others' homes, in other women's dresses. Their conversations were peppered with insider information on real estate deals, on slick movers in city government, and hearing these things, Billy rolled his eyes. This only amused them and egged them on.

Billy wore suits now to these gatherings. Two years after starting at Seven Bells, he had done sufficiently well to be moved into corporate marketing, where much of his time was spent traveling with Freddie. Winerip was considering moves into places like Denver, St. Louis, Cincinnati. Freddie and Billy flew out to study the competition. Their strategies—Freddie always acted as if major, major deals were going on—were kept secret. When Freddie used words like "positioning"—as in, "We're figuring out how to position ourselves"—the rest of us saw the world of developers for what it was, a bunch of undereducated guys with strong testosterone, but Freddie wanted us to see it as a secret society whose rituals required a heightened language, a kind of commercial poetry.

A degree of secretiveness had crept into all our lives by then. The evenings at the Branding Iron lost even the shadow of their former raucousness. Maybe it came down to the increased prominence of money in our lives. Freddie had started aping Edwin Winerip and having his measurements sent to his boss's London tailor. Johnny refused, ever, to deal in cash. These were small things, but when I remarked on them, I was sent a look that told me that if I needed to remark—if I hadn't understood intuitively—I had missed some seismic change in the social climate.

Even Kenny rose. At the party given at the State House to celebrate Kenny's promotion to chief of homicide, his wife was pregnant. Among his cronies at the Suffolk D.A.'s office, a legend had arisen concerning the plastic surgery Kenny received after the accident. We heard about it in offhand remarks. Kenny was reputed to have had a run-in with mobsters, his old Winship connections. "They sliced his face," Freddie heard one assistant D.A. tell another over a plate of Stilton cheese. Freddie couldn't wait to relay this to me. "He's got a reputation as a hard guy," Freddie said, laughing. "A bigdick." As soon as he'd resurrected the old word, his eyes sought out Billy in the crowd, to be sure Billy hadn't been close enough to hear.

Vivien Patchett was Billy's date for the event, the one less-than-beautiful girl Billy dated in those years, and the one we had him

pegged to marry. We spotted them on the balcony, Billy pointing
out something below them.

"You believe it?" Freddie asked me as we studied from a distance the elegant figure Billy cut. "Three years ago the guy was
selling paint. And screwing bims in Winship." He shook his head
and chuckled. "But I guess if Kenny DiGiovanni can become the
hard guy of the D.A.'s office, anything can happen."

Freddie had, in those days, a barely masked sorrow of his own.
There were still no Tortolla offspring, seven and then eight years
into the marriage.

"I've got frozen embryos up the wazoo," Freddie told us. "They
live in these little holding pens. I jerk off into a cup, and then they
travel to the egg in these petri dishes so the poor little things don't
have to swim too hard. And then they put the fertilized eggs into
Ilena. But none of them attach."

Sometimes I felt as though the emotional secrets we shared were
all smoke screens, sent up to distract us from having to talk about
the truly secretive parts of our lives, those having to do with money.
Nonetheless, we shared: Freddie his petri dishes, Johnny the breast
cancer scare his wife underwent when their second baby was still an
infant. All I had to offer was my resistance to the vasectomy Teresa
had started after me about. Even Billy, after a time, came to share
in this ritual of the personal. He'd had to hire a woman to come in
during the day because his father, increasingly dependent on help,
refused to go into a nursing home and abandon Ronnie to his own
devices.

Still, whatever the personal gloom we proposed to one another
over the sixteen-ounce rib eye and the horseradish mashed potatoes
at the Branding Iron, we took our bodies out to immensely better
cars, BMWs and Lexuses, sleek and dark-colored, with little lights
running along the dashboard like the lights that line the landing
strips of airports. Billy's Le Mans had died sometime in the mid-
nineties, but he refused to graduate very far. He picked up a Monte
Carlo, "pre-owned." He got a kick out of the way that phrase, in the
new, slicked-up retail world in which he prospered, had come to
replace the word "used."

In those years, Teresa and I never had to pay for a vacation. Tony DiNardi owned two vacation houses, one on a private stretch of Good Harbor Beach in Gloucester, the other on Lake Sebago. We always did a week in each, and those were the best weeks of the year, the ones I looked forward to. At Good Harbor, as soon as she was old enough, I'd take Nina down to the beach and teach her Wiffle ball. When you have two girls, I think one of them becomes the boy. You can't help imposing certain things on them. Gabrielle had gravitated almost from birth toward the feminine, but Nina was different. She had a great swing from the age of three. I had high hopes for her.

Toward the end of our weeks there and at Sebago, the DiNardis always joined us. Even this didn't spoil things, because at his vacation homes Tony was able to let go of his need to expand and dominate. He became just another Italian grandfather in a fishing cap, humbler and more easily pleased. Sometimes, holding one of the girls on his knee, he would break into a rousing chorus of "The Gang's All Here," and on the line, "What the hell do we care?" I saw hints of an anger and tiredness underneath his habitual striving.

At home, I started to assistant coach T-ball as soon as Nina was old enough. If we still knew few people in Bradford, we were at least starting to meet them. Teresa surprised me by opting for public school for the girls, so at the ice-cream socials and the open school nights we got to know the people who lived, like us, in big houses nestled deep in the woods, people whose lives were hidden, as ours were, by sleek cars and soaring property values. At Saturday morning T-ball practices I got to know guys with names like Chip Holmes and Neil Sennott, Bradford men with kids my daughters' ages. Vague moves were made to try to become more friendly. I was sensitive to the initial steps in a dance that would lead, weeks later, to an invitation to one or the other of our houses, the result of which would be an awkward evening in which at most one beer would be drunk and the visiting couple's eyes would scan, with a raptor's precision, the details of home furnishings. The game seemed to be to reveal as little about yourself as possible while showing the most teeth and pretending to hipness (there was always very classy jazz playing, Miles Davis or John Coltrane) and the serenity of a Buddhist. Everything was always wonderful with everyone's kids; they were headed to Harvard, to lives of creativity and wealth. No doubt about it. When we heard through teachers at the school about the prevalence of Ritalin in the student body, it always had to be other children, not the children of Chip Holmes or Neil Sennott or us, or indeed of anyone we knew.

Though my income had pretty much plateaued around fifty thousand dollars, we were okay, though just barely, because Teresa made the same, and I got a nice bonus every Christmas, and on each of our birthdays Tony DiNardi wrote us a check for ten thousand, and on each of the children's birthdays a hefty check was deposited in their accounts. In my encounters with professors, I rarely brought up "The Country Husband" anymore. In seducing a professor, I stressed now some of the things that had become important in 1990s education, which Endicott had learned to capitalize on. "There are anthologies that have more diversity," I might find myself saying. "That's for sure. But I think you're probably finding that diversity, all by itself, is getting old." Here I'd smile and pause, testing the waters. More often than not, I received a return smile that, however condescending, betrayed agreement. Endicott had picked up in its market research a distaste, among the deeply tenured, with the word "diversity" itself. We were to pounce on it.

Sometime in my middle thirties I stopped driving with my finger on the SEEK button and started listening to Books on Tape. This was Teresa's suggestion, and I took it up: popular histories, detective novels, self-help. I took them out of the new, beautifully appointed Bradford Library. There was something virtuous about descending the library steps with the two little girls clasping their oversize picture books and me clutching *The Seven Habits of Highly Effective Families* (a book I had to wait weeks for, incidentally, because the waiting list was so long).

It was a pleasant enough life to live day by day, with growing social calendars and lots of activities for the girls. In the fall, when the colors changed, I would sometimes feel, driving home in the car, a burgeoning sense of excitement at how simply and beautifully *packed* middle-class life could be. I sometimes wonder if, had things gone differently, I might have been able to live this life all the way to old age, to be as satisfied by it as any other man. It's a question, that's all. I'll never know. Because in the spring of 1997 Billy began dating Patty Shaughnessy.

six

She was, in a way, the least likely serious girlfriend we could ever have imagined for Billy, even less likely than Vivien Patchett. She had a round Irish face with freckles on it, nondescript brown hair that she kept simple, and an overbite that her mother hadn't had the money to fix with braces. Her prettiness came less from conventional means than from an abundance of confidence. She'd grown up in Dorchester and in the South Boston projects, one of seven children, and she seemed, at first, as unimpressed by Billy as she was by anything else in the world she'd ascended to as a senior loan officer at BayBank. In Dorchester she'd been neighbors with Mark Wahlberg and his brother Donnie, and once, when Teresa and I were double-dating with her and Billy and the suggestion was made that we all go to see the movie *Boogie Nights*, Patty scoffed. "Why should I pay to see Mark Wahlberg take out his dick? He was always doing that in the projects, and I didn't have to pay seven fifty to see it."

Billy always looked at her when she spoke that way with an amused pride. The fact that we double-dated, something that had never happened with his other girlfriends, we took as a sign that Billy intended to bring Patty into our circle in a more official capacity. Teresa had another idea. "He's watching us," she would say when we drove home after those dates. "Do you see him? He studies us when he thinks we're not looking. It's like he wants to know how we do it." When I asked her why she thought he might be doing this, she was silent for several seconds before shaking her head. "I'll let you know when I figure it out."

What was strange about these evenings were the places Billy insisted we go. Boston was then enjoying a great run on new restaurants. Every week, it seemed, one would open, and the consumer magazines and the food section of the *Globe* would run praising articles. But Billy wanted no part of the upscale. "Raise your hand if you know what lemongrass is," Billy said as we drove in the Monte Carlo to a restaurant of his choosing. "Raise your hand if you dream at night of lemongrass. Or warm chocolate cake. Who's had enough warm chocolate cake to last a lifetime?"

When he got no reaction from us, he turned to the barely amused Patty Shaughnessy. "Or how about some farm-raised catfish in a chipotle-cumin roux? That's really what I'm in the mood for tonight. Or some spit-roasted lamb. And God, just let me take a look at the spit."

Hugely amused by himself, he would turn to Teresa and me in the backseat. "Tim, what's a *spit*? Do any of us even know? We're paying for our own ignorance."

So we would find ourselves, courtesy of Billy, in some ancient downscale establishment, no wait on a Saturday night, water damage on the ceiling. "I love this place," Billy announced in one such restaurant, holding up the big laminated menu. "My parents used to come here; this was their big date. Or when my father was feeling flush, this was where he'd take us. For fish."

"They've probably got the same fish in the refrigerator," Patty said. "They've been waiting for you to come back so they can unload the '75 catch."

"Ha ha. Very funny."

"Is that Dinty Moore beef stew I smell?" She made an exaggerated show of sniffing. At the other tables were old couples, barely speaking to each other. For some reason this, too, always pleased Billy.

Their bantering made it worth putting up with the oversauced lasagna and the bland and undersauced fish that were the staples of

Billy's favorite restaurants, which Patty had her own names for. "Tonight we're eating at the Last Legs." Or, "Where is it tonight, Bill, the Over the Hill Inn or the Hold-Your-Nose-and-You'll-Have-a-Good-Time Arms?"

"We'll get out for under thirty bucks a couple," he answered, and mock-swatted her. "Thirty bucks. That'll get you an appetizer the size of my fingernail at L'Espalier."

Billy had never seemed funny to any of his girlfriends before. All the rest had been too much in awe of him, or else trying to fix him up. But Patty Shaughnessy's way was to behave as though the two of them had just been strapped together into the seats of a creaky and not terrifically safe-looking roller coaster, as if they had just handed their tickets to an unsavory attendant and the chain had already begun to pull them forward.

One Saturday night Billy drove us out to the woods in the middle of the state, to a restaurant Patty had warned us about by saying, "This place, they had to get a broom to get rid of the cobwebs when Billy called. They had to bring the waiters back from the dead. They didn't know what a reservation was. Billy had to spell it for them." It was a restaurant called Romeo's Ten Acres, in which the tables were arrayed around a dance floor. An ancient band, fronted by a white-haired singer, played standards. Many of the tables were empty, and Patty looked up from her menu and said, "Do you feel like you just walked into *The Shining?*" Then she looked at Billy, as if her patience had finally reached its end. *"Why,* Billy?"

Billy glanced at her, then around the place. It was as though he was picking up a scent he liked, the way someone who likes to be around horses feels when he enters a stable.

That night, when the band went into a song called "The Talk of the Town," Billy took Patty's hand and led her to the dance floor. He had taken off his jacket, and under the blue and red lights shining on the dance floor his white shirt looked iridescent. He held Patty so that one hand was just above her buttocks, and he drew one of her hands toward him so that their clasped hands pressed against his chest. He looked down at her with an intensity of pleasure that made something rise in my own chest, that sharing of another's sexual excitement—as if the feelings occurring in another person's body are actually occurring in your own—that I have experienced maybe half a dozen times in my life.

Something else lingers from that night. Billy drove us home. Bradford was closer to Romeo's Ten Acres than Winship was, so it had made sense for them to pick us up. We drove under the broad arms of the Bradford maples, and Patty Shaughnessy, looking up at them, murmured, "Should we live in a place like this, Bill?" She didn't turn to him right away for an answer. "Quiet," she said.

Billy gazed down at her. At first he seemed to be studying her with the familiar detachment with which he sometimes studied our faces at the Branding Iron, except on the end of this look was a smile. "Too fucking quiet, don't you think?"

"No," Patty said. I'd say she said it dreamily, except that conventional dreaminess wasn't a part of her repertoire. If somebody could muse with hardheadedness, she could.

"How many kids are we going to have?" Billy wanted to know.

"Dozen," Patty said. Then she cut out the jokey tone. "Or two. The usual number. Boy and a girl. How's that?"

"Very neat," Billy said, and nodded his head a couple of times. In their breathing quiet afterward, the fallout of their humor with each other, was yet another whiff of the sensual. I wanted to be with them in the making of the boy and the girl.

"And we'll be happy, happy, happy," Billy said. "Right?" He pulled into my driveway and stopped in front of the house. "You guys don't mind us being sappy, do you?"

Billy sent me a wide-grinning look that contained in it an eradication of all the other looks I'd ever received from him. In that moment, it was just possible to believe that every dark part of him had been released by this new thing, this simple happiness.

There were still Monday nights, though fewer of them now, when I followed Billy to Winship. What he liked to have me do was meet him at his house, then the two of us get into his Monte Carlo and drive up the beach highway toward Gloucester, where there was a particular place he liked to park, a place where we could sit and watch the waves crash against rocks.

Once there, he would take out a pint bottle of whiskey and drink directly from it and offer it to me.

"Bill, you know I don't do that," I would say.

"Drink? You don't drink?"

"Hell, I drink. I just don't drink out of bottles after I've already put away three or four at the Iron."

"The Iron," he repeated. "I like that. The *Iron*. The way we always want to make places ours. We give them cute little nicknames. The *Grotto*. The *Iron*. We want to be so fucking comfortable in the world. Like nothing's ever not us."

I sat back and smiled. There was an element of performance in these little sayings of Billy's, as if he were playing a version of himself he knew I enjoyed.

"Oh, you're so amused by me, aren't you, Tim?"

"Always have been."

"When you should be home. When you really should be home."

I had an answer ready, because I felt I had to. "Here's the rule," I said. "We don't talk about home. We don't talk about where I should be."

"Right. I'm your little excursion into the world."

Billy mostly obeyed my limits. Though all we did was talk while Billy drank, these nights still left me with a sense of acceptable transgression. Just being there with him did that. It was as though I were taking the word "home" and attaching it to a long line, then casting it far out over the water to see if anything leaped and bit. Whatever came up here, I knew the next morning I would be at the breakfast table, feeding Nina and Gabrielle before taking them to school. Those mornings were the order to which I had lashed myself. I did not really feel I was risking anything on those nights with Billy.

And he, too, seemed to be moving toward order, toward marriage.

"Think I could do it?" he asked one night, and turned to look at me.

"Do what?"

"Be married? Like you? I mean, do you look at me and say this is definitely, definitely somebody who should never, ever, walk down the aisle?"

"No, I don't say that."

It was a lie, actually. I knew it at the moment I said it, though never at other times. When he and Patty Shaughnessy were together, I believed in them.

"You know what was the closest I ever came? I mean, before now. You remember that girl—girl, woman—Paula, I introduced you to?"

"Sure."

"The one with the kid? Her. I could have married her. And I would have, probably, if you guys hadn't shown up that day."

"I always wondered, Billy. That kid wasn't yours, was he?"

"No. *No.* You think I could abandon a kid like that if it was mine?"

"No. I just . . ."

"That's one of the things that scares me. As a matter of fact. While we're talking."

"What?"

"What do you do when things start really belonging to you?"

It was his earnestness that got to me sometimes. That night, after asking that soft question, he shook his head, pulled his shirt— an expensive one—away from his skin, and glanced behind him at the road with a hungry, edgy look in his eyes, as though he'd welcome some kind of trouble, if only as a distraction.

When it was time to go, I insisted that I be the one to drive. I had him move over to the passenger seat, and I drove us back to Winship. Billy snoozed most of the way, waking only to stare at me and blink and say something like "Good man." To make sure he was safely delivered home, I walked him up the steps to his house. Inside, at the kitchen table, we could see Ronnie sitting with the woman Billy had hired, the woman who took care of Mr. Mogavero and cooked for him and Ronnie. Billy, in his drunkenness, appeared troubled to see her still there. He glanced at the clock.

"The fuck you still doing here?" Billy asked.

"My husband, he come and pick me up." She had the placid, un-hurried, slightly melodious voice of the Caribbean.

"Husband," Billy said in a scoffing way, and put one finger down on the kitchen table. He looked from Ronnie to the woman and back. Then he squinted at the clock. "I pay you 'til ten."

She shrugged. The TV was not on. It was unclear what she and Ronnie had been doing to entertain themselves. Beside the TV, the table was empty except for a plate that had some crumbs on it, a pile of napkins, and a *TV Guide*.

"It's okay. I'll take the bus," the woman said. Billy had yet to in-troduce us.

"The bus. The bus doesn't run this late," Billy said. Then, to stress the absurdity of it, "The *bus*."

"I could drive her home, Bill," I offered.

The woman looked up at me. Her eyes were slightly watery, her age indecipherable, though my guess was she was in her thirties. Not beautiful, a little overweight. There was a force of patience in the way she looked at me, as if I were the thing that was wrong in this room, the thing she must wait out.

Billy looked at me as well. He appeared to be on the verge of saying something, but he hesitated, stopped himself, glanced to the side before looking at me.

Ronnie stared up at me, too. He looked cowed and also afraid to let me see how little his presence mattered here.

"Her husband picks her up," Billy said, and it sounded, strangely for him, like a naked admission of guilt.

Billy and Patty were married in the fall of 1998. There had been an eighteen-month courtship, but as there was hardly any buildup to the wedding, it was rumored among us, wrongly, as it turned out, that Patty must be pregnant.

They bought a house (Billy had revealed to us, proudly, that Patty had, all on her own, saved up enough for a down payment) and began inviting us to it in the spring, after they'd had time enough to get settled. It was a modest bungalow in Waltham, for which they still had to pay more than three hundred thousand dollars. The furniture in it was more conservative—heavier, more solid than the rest of us owned. Billy always appeared happiest when he could take us out of the house into his backyard, which was long and studded with trees. "Maybe I'll cut these all down," he said. "There's hardly room to throw a ball back there."

"They're fruit trees," Freddie said. It was late March when we were first invited, and the trees hadn't yet started to bud or establish a clear identity. "Christ, Bill, these are apple trees. You don't cut them down."

Billy looked genuinely perplexed. He didn't try to hide, as he usually did, his own ignorance of something. "Yeah? I own apple trees? How do you know?"

"Because you learn these things," Freddie said.

"When do they—you know—get apples?"

Freddie looked at the rest of us and laughed in a mocking though still gentle way. "They'll come, Bill."

By late spring, there were buds on Billy's apple trees and Patty was indeed pregnant. It still troubled Billy that there was no straightaway. Where would he throw a ball to his son? He would have one or another of us stand at the end of the row of trees and throw to us, but the ball, if it went even a little bit high, was misdirected by the trees' branches.

"Relax," Freddie said, watching Billy and me throw to each other one afternoon. "Maybe it'll be a girl."

Once, after I'd thrown the ball back to him, Billy held it in his hand and looked at me for a moment in one of those instances of hiddenness he was so good at. He reached up and pulled down one of the branches of the tree above him, and the petals fell. He picked one up and sniffed it.

"Good, huh?" I asked.

He didn't answer me. His look had turned quizzical, even a little resistant.

He lived in a neighborhood of retirees and youngish working

couples like himself and Patty. I could tell he was pleased not to live in a house like the rest of us lived in. That he could see his neighbors, watch them as they got in and out of their cars or went about their yard work, seemed to make him happy. I surprised him once, on a Saturday. I was out driving with Nina—we'd gone to see a movie in Belmont—and I decided to stop by his house. I found him in the backyard, wearing a T-shirt and an old pair of khakis, pushing a wheelbarrow full of soil. He'd dug a hole out of the grass and was going to fill it. Patty wanted a flower garden. She was sitting in an Adirondack chair, her belly just starting to show.

Nina was seven then, quiet and uncertain around strangers, though willful and determined within the safety of her family. She stood between my legs, staring at these two as Patty poured us lemonade. They had been welcoming enough, though it occurred to me that we may have been intruding, forcing them to break out of their near-erotic privacy.

"What's your name?" Patty had asked Nina at the beginning.

"Irene," I'd answered for her.

She slapped me on the knee, as she always did. "It's *Nina*," she said.

This was our game. As soon as she was old enough to understand, I'd started singing "Goodnight Irene" to her in the car, and she always shrieked, half in anger, half in delight, her given name.

Watching our game, Billy and Patty looked at us with immense curiosity, as if the notion of even this complicated a relationship between parent and child was one they had not yet envisioned. It was still all potential for them, all future tense. The blossoms on Billy's trees had disappeared by then, leaving in their place thick-looking green leaves and the pale beginnings of fruit.

Patty lost that baby. In the fall she lost another. Billy, sullen in the Branding Iron, barely alluded to the details of this second miscarriage. He started to drink more heavily, but not so heavily that it was cause for worry. He stared at the Boston skyline one crisp late fall evening as if he were trying to find the one invisible but crucial thing wrong with it, the fault in the city's structure that would cause it, one day, to crumble.

"Listen," Freddie said, trying to cheer him up, "worst comes to worst, you join Ilena and me at the adoption agency."

"What are you going to get, a Chinese baby, Fred?" Billy asked. He took a long swallow of Scotch.

"If we do . . ."

"I see these couples, so fucking happy with their Chinese babies," Billy said.

The rest of us were intensely quiet then, looking out the window.

"Well, if we do, Bill," Freddie said finally in a voice of highly worked restraint, "I imagine we're going to be one of those couples. Very happy with our Chinese baby."

Billy made a circle on the table with the moisture from his drink.

Kenny was back with us by then, and he made a stab at trying to bring about a peace. "Hey, man, it's hard. It's hard to lose a kid."

Billy turned to him, and in that first instant it seemed that something was about to break in him, gratitude to Kenny for this, but I could see that impulse running squarely into its opponent, that resistance he had to giving us any kind of power. He wouldn't even nod his head in agreement.

When everyone had gone that night, when we were alone in the parking lot, Billy looked at me and tipped his head forward and seemed immensely young and vulnerable.

"It's only two, right? Plenty of people have two."

"That's right, Bill."

Still, there was that visible war in him. To have allowed me to see even this much of his frightened side was difficult for him. He hated it.

"A word of advice, Bill. Don't insult Freddie for having to adopt, all right?"

"That was not my finest moment, was it?"

"No."

"But it's still true."

"What is?"

His hand went out, as if he was trying to ward off the very thing he was about to say.

"No, it's ridiculous. I think it's ridiculous. Everybody trying to make their perfect little family, with like a Chinese kid. I'm fucking Cro-Magnon about this, I know, but there are *divisions*, aren't there? You can do it or you can't do it. Nobody wants to live in a world where there aren't divisions anymore. Like fucking Viagra. Instant boner. Nobody fails, right? Can't get a baby, get a Chinese kid, get a *black* kid, who the fuck cares?"

He kicked a can across the parking lot. His hands went out as if there was something elegant and triumphant, something game-winning about it.

"Look, you just keep trying," I said.

"Oh shut up." He looked angry now. "Shut the fuck up, because you don't know. Ever heard of an incompetent cervix, Tim? I bet you haven't." He paused a second. "Means what it says. Incompetent. Keeps opening up. Her mother took this drug when she was pregnant with Patty. Girls whose mothers took this drug have an incredibly lousy success rate. So don't give me this 'just keep trying' shit. The fuck do you know? It happened so easy for you. Right? It was easy."

I waited a moment, feeling strangely calm.

"Yes it was." Then: "I wasn't even there for the second one. Second conception."

I smiled a little, and he picked up on it immediately.

"Who was there, Tim?"

He thought he'd just learned something about me. He seized on that knowledge, not as if he enjoyed it, but because seizing on potential secrets in others was what he did.

"Me. It was me. But I was half asleep."

He smiled. "Did it in your sleep." He kept the smile. Something was turning in his mind. "Why don't you come with me, Tim?"

"No. Not out to Gloucester. I'm not going with you. Not to one of your drinking sprees. Go home."

"I'm going home. I want you to come."

I hesitated a moment. "Why?"

"You know where I live. Right? It's on the way. This will take no time at all."

It was, in fact, on the way, and there were times with Billy where you had to give in. When I drove up, his car was in the driveway, but he wasn't.

"Out here, Tim," I heard.

It was dark in the back, but I could make out the lit ash end of Billy's cigarette. He was sitting on a picnic table, a piece of furniture new to the backyard.

"Patty had me build this. You buy all the parts. Instant backyard, you know? Good thing we waited on the swing set."

He gestured to me with the pack of cigarettes. I shook my head.

"So why'd I come, Bill?"

He raised the cigarette in his hand. "You know, I much prefer these to the fifteen-buck Dominican cigars I have to smoke with Freddie and Edwin Fuckface."

Again I shook my head. I anticipated Billy's vitriol and checked my watch.

"You late for something, Tim?"

"No. I just wonder . . ."

He sucked in a long drag and looked at me, then up at his house.

"We're due to try again. She's a fighter, my wife. I mean, her sisters and brothers, half of them are dead or in jail. But she got to where she's got, and she's not going to let anything stop her."

He cupped the lit cigarette inside his hand as if he wanted to study it.

"But you're having your doubts."

He shrugged. He looked back at his yard, the stripped trees, the neighbors' houses.

"What the fuck am I doing here, Tim?"

"What are you talking about?"

He made a small, shrugging gesture. "You heard me."

"Come on."

"Come on," he mimicked me. It was as if he had alerted me to some truth about himself he'd expected I'd understand. And maybe I did. But I didn't want to. I glanced up at my car.

"You want to go, Tim? You had enough of me?"

"Billy, I know you're upset."

"Right. Right." It was as though he had decided consciously to back away from the hard truth he had just placed silently between us. "But still. Think about it. Lives like this, maybe they're for guys like you, Tim. And for Freddie, if he could just get it up."

"He can get it up. He just can't get those eggs to attach."

Billy looked up at the sky. "Are you the most innocent asshole that ever lived, Timmy?"

I didn't say anything.

"Do you—*believe* everything anybody tells you? There are no— what does he call them?—floating embryos. I could tell you stories about what it was like when I started at the Fuckface Corporation, but I'm not going to do that, because I want to protect your innocence, all right? And now, because of this sick fuck Freddie Tortolla, I am in this life." He pushed himself off the picnic table and took a flask out of his pocket.

"Come on, Billy."

"Come on what? Come on what, Tim? You let me numb myself, all right? I go in there and fuck her and she gets pregnant, and what, four months from now she loses it? And then what? *Again*, because she's a fighter, and all so we can live this life I have no *business* in."

He took a swig, then surveyed his yard before turning back to me. It was as if he was gauging the next thing he'd say, holding back on something on my account.

"It's beautiful, though. Isn't it? Apple trees. The neighbors. Smells like cider in the fall. Burning leaves. Goddamn paradise."

A light came on over the back porch. The door opened, and Patty came out. She was belting her bathrobe.

"You should talk louder, Bill," she said.

"I know," he answered. "Let everybody hear."

They were silent, looking at each other, fifty feet separating them. Some beseechment was in this look, as if each were asking the other a difficult question.

"Who's that? Tim?" she asked.

"It's Tim," I answered, and raised my hand.

"Okay," she said. "I'm goin' to bed, Bill. Just, whatever complaints you got, why don't you not let the neighbors hear them?"

After she'd gone inside, Billy laughed appreciatively. "You see?" he asked. "You see what I'm up against?"

He threw the flask so that it landed in a corner of his backyard. Then it seemed he would go in.

"You want to drive to Gloucester?"

"No, Bill."

"No? We can't, right? Too late. Shit." He smiled at me while clenching and relaxing his fists.

"I'm gonna go now, Bill."

"Right. Okay." He smiled. "Go back to your mansion, where you can do it in your sleep and cute little—girls—come out, one after the other. Lucky life."

Billy stopped talking and allowed something else in, a quiet, a pause, and all the things that fill a pause. Again, he looked around his yard.

"Go ahead in," I said.

He scratched the picnic table with one fingernail.

"You know you want this, Billy."

He looked at me then as if I'd surprised him. But whether I'd hit on the truth or not, that much he wouldn't let me know. For a second, though, in his eyes, I believed I saw something. I thought I'd gotten him right.

"Go ahead and want it, Billy. It's not going to kill you."

Whatever I thought I'd seen before, it had ducked under now. In its place was a moment's pure hatred of me.

"Sure. Yes. You're fucking brilliant, Tim. You should write the book."

He headed into the house then. On his way, he pointed back at me, a long, direct, accusing finger laid against my witnessing presence. He repeated the words "Want it" as if he was lampooning some old football locker-room chant.

For her next pregnancy, Patty elected to have her cervix tied up, a procedure they told her would up the chances exponentially of her being able to carry a baby to term. But several months in, she developed an infection, and when her cervix was untied, the baby came with it. That was number three.

On the trail of the loss of Billy and Patty's third baby came another, lesser loss. We stopped going to the Branding Iron on our regular Monday nights. The third miscarriage had released a pocket of venom in Billy more lethal than anything we'd seen before, so we weaned ourselves from those dinners.

In place of the Monday nights at the Branding Iron, I now had extra nights at home. At some point I remember there being a suggestion—one or the other of us made it—that we make something of those freed-up nights, go out on regular dates or get the kids to bed a little early so that we could have time together in the house. But we never did.

Some nights after the kids were in bed and Teresa had fallen asleep in front of the TV, I took Scooter out for longer walks than even he wanted. We'd walk, me carrying a flashlight, into the woods, usually ending at the clearing where the DiNardis had begun pouring a foundation after years of delay.

Tony had surprised us one day, a few years before, by telling us he had wrested a three-acre parcel adjoining our own lot from the trust that had been holding it for decades. It was his stated intention to build a new house, for what he called his twilight years.

Something new was coming out of Tony in those years. At those gatherings—the dinners given, in increasing numbers, to honor him—he would sometimes take me aside late in the evening and point out one crony after another. "That guy—Cincotta—I wanted him to hire me for his landscaping business. I was a kid, fifteen, sixteen. Called me a greenhorn. Refused to hire me." The contempt in his voice was as undigested as something he'd eaten ten minutes before. One after another he knocked down the master builders of

the Graymore Italian community and then gestured that it was all
to be kept secret, this side of him. On Sundays, when he came and
we walked over to examine the builders' progress, I found myself
encouraging him in his foraging of the past, as if in some way his
doing this served me as well.

People—Billy—called me innocent, but I knew that wasn't entirely true. It was not an accident that Billy got me to drive with
him on those trips up to Gloucester, or that Tony decided to make
me his late-life, tell-all biographer. I played a game with darkness,
opening my net wide. I suppose I always believed I could escape if
the actual thing came too near.

It was on a casual Sunday visit to my parents' house that I discovered, by mistake, what Billy was hiding in Winship. But first I discovered something else.

I had brought Nina to visit my parents this particular Sunday.
By now—she was eight—she was the only one besides me who
could stand the closed, smoky odor of the old house. At a certain
point the two of us always had to make a break, practically gasping
for air, to the beach. But before we got to that moment on this particular Sunday, I found myself for a few moments in their kitchen
alone, and I picked up the local newspaper. There, just to the right
of a fold in the paper, was Maureen Feeney's picture.

It's probably not possible that in looking at that picture, I didn't
simultaneously see the brief headline above it, which read, simply,
MAUREEN FEENEY, 55, with the subheading LONGTIME FLEET
BRANCH MANAGER. But it felt as though it took several seconds.

The photograph had been taken in these later years, and it managed to iron out entirely the sensual element that was, in my
knowledge of Maureen, the core of her. Her hair looked submissive.
It flew back from her face in tightly controlled crested waves, and
she was wearing a suit, with a shirt that looked as if it was made
from one of those sheer, cheap fabrics beloved by lower-echelon
businesswomen. It was buttoned to the neck. From the look of her
skin, I could guess at a degree of makeup, but there were folds that

hadn't been there—of course they hadn't been there—on the nights when I went to the upstairs apartment for langostinos, for beer, for the steady immersion in one another that was the defining event of my twentieth year.

Longtime Fleet branch manager. I remembered that she had become, toward the end of his working life, my father's boss. Fleet had absorbed First Winship Trust, and Maureen had ascended some, not much. She had left a mother (the old crone still alive), four nieces, and a nephew. Gifts in her name were to be sent to North Shore Hospice. My father had left the newspaper open, the crease worn along the edge. "Oh, that Maureen," he would say at the supper table, the windows open on a summer night, my parents then impossibly, criminally young, and laughing. "What she said today!"

I couldn't stay in the house after reading this, so I grabbed Nina and led her outside, under my father's gaze. He knew I'd seen, though I didn't think I could speak to him about it yet. I took Nina to a bench on the boardwalk and then just sat there, breathing hard.

It is the great blessing of the company of eight-year-olds that they never ask "What's the matter?" So we sat there until my breathing returned to normal, with me just rubbing her shoulders and her allowing it. Then we did what we always did, wandered Winship.

It was an aimless walk (I only knew that I didn't want to go anywhere near Maureen's house) that found us eventually on Billy's street. I was not looking very hard at Billy's house as we passed it, but something inside caught my eye. It may have been no more than a flash of white rushing past the window, but it suggested a certain kind of activity inside. Were Billy and Patty visiting? I couldn't see his car anywhere, but that might only mean he'd parked it down the block.

It was a crazy idea to see Billy while I was in this state. Nonetheless, I knocked, and after several moments Ronnie answered. He seemed at first confused by my presence, checked behind me for his brother, looked disappointed. There was weight on him now, a fuller, rounder, older face. It struck me all over again how dark he was. His hair had started to recede.

"Hey, Ron," I said. "We were taking a walk. I thought maybe your brother might be here."

I became aware then that my voice was breaking—grief, or shock, still had a hold on me—and that I'd better stop talking if I didn't want to embarrass myself.

"No, he's not," Ronnie said.

"How's your father, Ron? He okay?"

Ronnie stared at me a few seconds, his eyes slightly, confusedly narrowing. It was all he offered in the way of an answer.

"Crowded today on the beach, huh?" he asked, and stepped out onto the porch.

"Yes."

He looked at me as if that would be that. I wasn't sure where it came from, my suspicion that he was hiding something from me.

"Everything okay, Ron?"

"Sure."

He went back inside. The encounter had been unsettling enough that I found I couldn't immediately leave. I said to Nina, "Wait," and I moved to the window. From there, just far enough out of sight that I believed I was hidden, I could see Ronnie step into the kitchen. A few seconds later, from out of it came the woman who watched Billy's father. In her arms she held a baby. The flash of its small white-clothed figure was what I'd seen from across the street and been arrested by. The woman rocked it. She looked large and capable, so that in rocking it, she could actually take on some other chore, though she didn't have one yet. All she did was lean against the doorway, looking inside to where Ronnie was and talking to him, while the baby's little legs kicked at her breast and she reached down to grab them and hushed it.

When Teresa and I next met them, at a fish restaurant (another of Billy's choices, an old, overbuilt harborside emporium reached through the bowels of downtown), Patty laid out her new plan.

"They tell me the best chance I have is if I spend the next pregnancy in bed." Patty was starting to look tired now, pouchy around the eyes. "So there's nine months there, give or take. And then I want to spend six months with the baby, at least. And there ain't no way in the world the bank's giving me a fifteen-month maternity leave."

Billy picked up a box of matches printed with the restaurant's insignia—an anchor around which a long fish had entwined itself—and rotated it under his fingers.

"You can tell how thrilled he is with this," Patty said.

"So it means you have to quit?" Teresa asked.

"More or less."

"More," Billy said.

"Right, I quit. And look, I'm not crazy about this. The idea was, originally, that we were going to do this without screwing up our careers. But that idea went out with the third miscarriage. And anyway, I'd be totally shocked if I couldn't get a job fifteen months from now.

"So what we do," she went on, "and Billy doesn't like this either, so anticipate the heavy sighs to come, is we rent out the house in Waltham for two years, make ourselves a little profit, and move in with his father in Winship."

In reaction to this, Billy gazed out the window, patiently studying the slight up-and-down movement of the fishing trawlers berthed nearby.

"Which solves a lot of problems, you think about it. We can live there on one salary. Billy pays through the nose for the woman who looks after his father. So I'm there, he doesn't have to do that."

"Why don't I just cut off my dick, Patty?" Billy said.

"Why don't you? Solve everything."

"Right. So we fire Hortense; we send her out on the street with her baby. What else do you want to do, cut off her welfare payments?"

"He pays her under the table," Patty offered us. "This is going on, how long, Bill, four years?"

"I can't afford to give her a dental plan."

"Ha ha. Meanwhile—hello!—you don't live there anymore, the old man is eligible for a nurse paid by Medicare. But does Billy allow that? No. He says his father's *used* to her."

"He is."

Patty had ordered a Cosmopolitan, which she hadn't touched. She ran two fingers up and down the stem of the glass. "So that's the plan. What do you think?"

Teresa shrugged encouragingly, took a healthy gulp of her own drink. "Billy, you don't sound too enthused."

"How about you two give us a baby?" Billy said, and smiled goofily.

We laughed, flattered, seeing a second or two too late the edge to it.

"No, seriously. You guys seem to have no problem doing this, just pop out another one, give it to us."

Patty, gazing down into her drink, continued the steady up-and-down movement of her fingers along the stem.

"You know what I always think when I see a woman doing that?" Billy asked. "You know what I think they really want to be doing that to?"

Patty released her fingers.

"I mean, I wish you'd just drink it."

"The thing is," Patty said, "he talks this way when we're in public, like this. But it'd take me five minutes to get him to jump me. Less. Five *seconds*. He wants this as much as I do." Her chin hardened in a way that let me see how formidable she must have been on the playgrounds of Dorchester. "But I'll admit it. This is what I want. If there's a way I can get this, I'm going to go after it."

It was chilling, in the moment, to hear that, because while she spoke, it was as if Billy didn't exist in any important way.

"Listen," Teresa said, breaking the silence. "I think it's a good plan. Really. You don't lose the house; you just rent it."

"What about my apple trees?" Billy asked.

Teresa looked as if she wanted to laugh. "What about them?"

But to Billy it was not a laughing matter. "Some fucking renter comes in, does he take care of them?"

Teresa held his eyes a long moment before releasing them, flummoxed by this. "Well . . ."

"Exactly. And my wife, the pride of the Mary McCormack projects, she thinks nothing of taking this poor black woman and her baby and throwing them out."

"Look," Patty said, "you don't look to me to provide a safety net for these people. I came up from where I came up, which makes me like somewhere to the right of Jesse Helms on these issues. She'll find another job. *I'll* take care of your father and your brother. For fifteen months. Then, if she wants, she can come back."

"But if you're supposed to stay in bed . . ." Teresa gestured with her hand to finish the sentence.

"I'll get somebody in for the heavy lifting. Somebody we can pay by the hour. Once Ronnie comes home from work, I mean the kid is not helpless. I'll be the queen, shouting orders from my bed."

That seemed to end the discussion, and we were all at odds for a moment.

"You said she had a baby, Bill?" I asked. "The woman?" I had never told him about my surprise visit.

Billy leaned back in his chair, took the plastic prong on which his martini olives had been impaled, and jabbed it gently into his own forehead. "Little Charles." He smiled slightly. "He's almost a year. Cute kid."

"She lives *in* now," Patty said. "They've taken her *in*. Do you believe it?"

Billy looked at me a second, as if checking on something in my face. When I returned his look, he glanced away.

He made a gesture toward Patty, tried to put his arms around her. "Hey, we're going to be okay."

It was unconvincing to all of us. Patty did not loosen her posture.

"You know what I think?" Billy asked. "We do like Freddie and Ilena. Where's their baby coming from?"

"Romania," Teresa offered. "Do you believe it?"

"There you go. Romania. There's the ticket." Billy finished off his martini. "Hey, I gotta pee. Timmy, come with me."

"What's he going to do, hold your dick for you?" In Patty's face, after she spoke, was the sense of having made a mistake. There was something a little off about Patty now, as if her determination, the set of internal instructions she was following, had set her apart from us. She had lost her easy ability to banter with Billy, the hallmark of their early days.

"You know," Billy began, "I tried to take this girl out of Dorchester, to give her some class."

Patty made a hooting sound. "Right. Where was I gonna get class from you? From *Winship*? From the king of the paint store?" There was again a sense of misjudgment in the way they looked at each other, a confusion as to how they had so managed to lose their way. Everything cut, it seemed. Every offhand thing.

"Come on, Timmy," Billy said, to end it. "Come hold my dick."

Instead, he led me to the cocktail lounge. He ordered us both martinis, his third, my second, and brought me to a table. There were vestiges here of this restaurant's 1960s heyday, when it was a favorite of Boston's power brokers. Their pictures covered the walls of the cocktail lounge: Cardinal Cushing, Edward Brooke, Jack and Teddy Kennedy, and men of more local renown—Edwin Logue, Kevin White. All were pictured shaking hands with the restaurant's Greek owner, their mouths half open, their eyes watchful even in the midst of their own self-celebration.

Billy stared up at these with his small, mysterious smile. "Cardinal Cushing used to drink here, Timmy," he said. "In these very chairs, His Eminence warmed his ass. Cocktail waitresses used to come and sit on his lap."

He smiled devilishly, trying to get a rise out of me. "His Eminence, the cardinal. Imagine it."

From our table inside the restaurant we had faced the harbor, but the high glass wall of the lounge faced downtown. The skyline rose over a tiny inlet full of boats. On this fall evening the new buildings were lit in an orange glow, and that glow repeated itself on the water of the inlet.

"Up there. That's where I am. You see that building? Seventeenth floor."

"I see, Billy."

He was alert to whatever might be condescending about me; he took in my small remark, mulled it over, chose to let it go. Our new drinks came, and he lifted his to take a large swallow and looked again at the pictures lining the walls.

"Look at these guys," he said. "I got a lot of respect for these old dead guys."

"They're not all dead, Bill."

"What'd they want? They wanted power, right? They wanted . . ." He moved his hands so his outstretched fingers were touching one another. "To *build*, you know? And they lived in this imperfect world, but that was all right. They understood the imperfections; they accepted them. They had mistresses. They had houses that were normal houses. They went to church, and then they sinned, and big fucking deal." He took a big, pleasurable sip of his drink. "So it's a fucked-up world, but it's still solid, and that's the world we grew up in, you and me." He studied my face a moment. "Right?"

"Right." I covered the top of his drink with my hand.

"What are you doing?"

"Trying to prevent you from getting any drunker before dinner. Not that I'm not enjoying this ode to the old world."

"Leave it, okay?"

He grabbed the drink away. There was hostility in his face, but he did not sip any more. He seemed to be trying to work his way back to a comfortable intimacy with me.

"And now what have we got? We're not half the men they were, and we think we're so *good*, we make our kids wear *seat belts*, and everything's, you know, for the *kids*, but we're not *good*. We're the greediest people on the face of the earth. *Us*. All us good guys. We're so greedy we make these guys on the wall look like altar boys. You know why? Because they wanted power. Simple—*power*. But we want—perfection."

He made the word pop out of his mouth like a bubble.

"We've got some vision in our heads, Tim. Of a perfect world. Big houses and big yards and our kids in big, enormous vans, and we drive them to their perfect schools, and all of it's about *us*.

About us having perfect lives, and we don't care anymore one shit about anyone else's life. Not one *shit*, Tim."

"You've been drinking too much."

He grabbed my wrist. "Listen, I love that girl in there. You question that for a second?"

His question had come very suddenly, and he looked angry, as if he'd hit me if I gave him the wrong answer.

"No."

"Okay. Don't. 'Cause it's true. And here we are with a problem. We can't have kids. So big fucking deal. Once upon a time, you would have accepted that, that was your fate. We all have aunts and uncles like that, right? You heard it all the time. 'Uncle Joe and Aunt Mary, they can't have kids.' Boom. End of story. But that's not enough for us. We don't stop until we get it perfect." He sat back, paused for a few seconds. "Patty and me, we got it good now. We got a nice small house. We love each other."

For a moment then, while he was speaking, I wondered what he might be leaving out of this scenario.

"So things should be okay. Only they're not. Things are fucked; things are terrible—do you see her now? Do you see what she's starting to look like? All—greedy. I can't stand it sometimes. She's looking, like—*piggish*. Because of this vision that's out there. This vision that *you* put out. *Your* fucking life, Tim. Are you so happy in your life?"

I hesitated before speaking. I looked at Boston, the orange lights reflected in the cold-looking water. I heard a noise coming out of my throat. It might have been the beginning of laughter at Billy's bold, absurd question.

"Truth to tell, Billy . . ."

"You're not." He lifted his drink. He stared hard at me. He took a sip and laid his hand flat on the table. "Don't try and hide it, because frankly, you're not good at hiding things. I want you to do me a favor, Tim."

"What?"

"I want you to go in there, lay it out for her. Tell Patty. Tell Patty you're unhappy."

"I can't do that, Bill."

"Why not? Tell her the whole fucking story of life in the burbs, Tim. Tell her how fucking bored you are."

There was a silence. He took another sip of his drink.

"I can't do it, Bill."

"Why not?"

"It'd hurt Teresa, for one thing."

He looked over my face for a second, his old heat-seeking stare.

"What, you two pretend with one another? She thinks you're happy?"

"I don't know what she thinks. Come on, let's go back."

Billy put his hand on my wrist, holding me there. "You're telling me you're not honest with your wife, Tim? You pretend?"

I didn't answer.

Billy made a face of put-on shock. "I guess we all have to lie sometimes, don't we, Timmy? To keep things going. Don't we?"

"I don't know."

His fingers tightened on the stem of his drink until I thought it would break. Finally he released it.

"Do you believe I have to go back to Winship? I have to live in my *house* again? With my father? With *Ronnie?*"

"And the woman? Will she stay or will she . . ."

"Oh, she'll go. Patty will see to that."

"And the baby? What'd you say his name was?"

"Charles," he said, and in the next moment deflected it, as if he were flicking crumbs off the table. "His name is Charles."

seven

Billy and I didn't talk much to each other that winter. We relied on our wives to keep us informed of anything important. So I knew things through Teresa. I knew that Patty was pregnant again. I knew that the house in Waltham had been rented to an academic couple from Brandeis. And I knew that Patty and Billy were back in Winship.

Then, one night in early spring, he did call.

"What am I, abandoned now, Timmy?" he asked.

His voice had taken on a heavy, burdened-sounding air, as though I had hurt him by not staying in touch.

"Where you calling from, Bill?"

"Doesn't matter."

"Home?"

"How about I pick you up, we go for a drive?"

I held back from telling him I was working on the roster for the girls' softball team Chip Holmes and I had agreed to coach.

"Why don't you come over, Billy. We can open a couple of beers."

"You know what I'm doing, Tim? You know where I'm walking? I'm talking to you on a fucking *cell* phone. You remember those walks my father used to take us on? 'Here's where Hurley's Dance Hall used to be'? Like we gave a shit. I was so fucking embarrassed, but hey, what do you do when somebody's your father?"

There was a pause.

"You there, Tim?"

"I'm here."

"So what—do we all become our fathers, Tim? Here I am doing the same thing. I'm looking for the stuff that used to be here when we were kids. Where's the Wild Mouse, Timmy? Where's the goddamn Tilt-A-Whirl? Where's the fucking caramel corn?"

I chuckled lightly, assuming that was what I was supposed to do.

"Didn't this place used to have lots of marsh?"

"It did," I answered, careful now. I could hear the sounds of cars passing from his end of the line. "It always smelled, at low tide, vaguely of shit."

"That's right. Okay. Question: What happened to the marsh? There's no more marsh. They covered it over. Everything I'm looking at, it's going to sink someday, right? I mean, isn't that true?"

"Technically, yeah, I suppose."

"Everything I'm looking at now—Jesus, do you believe how much they've built this fucking place up? All these big—Jesus. Toys 'R' Us. The Winship Megastar 14. Target. Staples. *Applebee's.* This world of corporate shit. All of it. It's going to sink into the marsh." For a moment I could just hear the cars passing him. "Maybe all the old stuff'll start coming up when that happens, huh? Planet of the Apes. Up'll come Tragic Honeymoon. Coontown."

"It wasn't Coontown. It was Dark Town."

"Right. Weren't they sensitive. PC before their time." There was another pause on his end, a series of cell phone clicks. "Come on, I'll come pick you up. I can be there in twenty minutes. I gotta get out of here. I gotta stop looking at this shit."

"Billy, I've got to be at a meeting in Hanover, New Hampshire, tomorrow morning at ten o'clock. That means I hit the road at six."

"Busy boy. You staying over?"

"As a matter of fact I am."

"What do you do in those motels in Hanover, Tim? Hmm? Those lonely nights on the road. What's it like? The motel pay-per-view. *Brenda Is Randy.* You ever see that one? Out comes the pud, right? You're in Hanover. You're watching Brenda on the screen fucking some guy whose dick is like twice the size of yours. So out comes the pud. And the right hand starts flogging it. Right? You're watching Brenda come. Her tongue is rolling all over those big, collagen-stuffed lips. The remains of your pathetic McDonald's meal on the bedside table. The sandwich wrappers. The cups. There it is, Timmy. There's our lives. The big mass-market fantasy. Watching Brenda come. Am I capturing the quality of your life with some exactitude, Tim?"

On the paper in front of me I made a line connecting the name Julia Hooven with the position 2B. Then I blurred the line, doodled around it.

"Hey, Bill. That was good."

He laughed. "Have I got you?"

"To a T."

"*Brenda Is Randy*. The perfect title. The perfect pay-per-view title. Except it kinda sounds like it should be a cross-dressing fantasy, now that I think about it."

"I take it you've seen it."

"Tim, I *own* it. I own the fucking DVD. I bought it so I could get the special features. Interviews with Brenda. Off-the-cuff stuff."

Again there was a silence.

"So this is some mood you're in, Bill. How's Patty?"

"Pale as a fucking ghost. But getting big. This one looks like it's gonna take. My house is like some horror show, between the old man who won't die even though he's eighty-fucking-seven and my brother the retard, and my cow of a wife lying on the bed for nine months, screaming at us. But we're all really happy, Tim." He laughed. "No, it's working out great. We'll get the kid, we'll get out of here, we'll be back in Waltham before you know it."

I tried to figure out whether the hollowness I heard at the end of those words was something I was putting there. In the meantime, someone seemed to be yelling at Billy from a passing car.

"Who was that?"

"Nothing. Where was I?"

"Waltham."

"Right."

Freddie had hinted, in a conversation we'd had a few weeks be-

fore, that Billy might be on his way out at Winerip. Whether it
was the souring of their relationship or the downturn in the economy that was causing it, Freddie didn't care to say. I wondered now
whether Billy was going to bring this up, or whether he even knew.

"How's things at work, Billy?"

Deliberately, it seemed, he didn't answer.

"Everything okay there?"

"What are you doing right now, Tim?"

"Nothing, Bill."

"Something you're ashamed of, I bet. Where's your wife?
Where's Teresa?"

"All right, Billy. You want to know what I'm doing? I'm going
to give you a little grist for your critique of suburban life. I'm
working on the roster for the girls' softball team."

"Oh heaven. Oh shit. The Bradford Boomers. Let me guess.
How many Tiffanys?"

"None, actually."

"How many Ambers?"

"We're cooler than that, Billy, in Bradford."

"Give me the names."

"We have a Chloe. We have a Jordan."

"I bet Jordan has a tight little ass."

"Billy, come on."

"I bet Jordan makes you want to die when she runs out into left
field in her jeans. I bet you die a thousand deaths, Timmy. The little breasts poking through. But it's really the asses, isn't it?"

"All right, I'm hanging up."

He laughed. "Why? So you can go on pretending that doesn't
happen? So you can go *shopping*, Tim, and pretend you're not feeling what you're feeling? Hell, join the crowd, Tim. Listen, I was
reading about this guy—"

"Maybe I don't want to hear this."

"No, no, you've got to. This is great. You ever see the little corners of the newspaper, the police log, the court news? Here's some
gym teacher in some high school in—I don't know, Sharon or Med-
way—he loosens a couple of bricks in the wall of the boys' shower

room and inserts a fucking video camera in there and films the boys
taking showers. A married guy, needless to say. With kids. And of
course, you know, matter of time, he's found out. I mean, of *course*
he's found out. What did this guy think? Did he expect he was just
going to go on fucking the wife and living his cute little life, and
then, at night, late at night in his little secret place, watching these
movies? Or—better, *better*—did he want to be found out, just to
make something real happen in his life? Is that what we really
want, Tim, just a hit of the real? Even if we have to be punished for
it? What do you think, Tim?"

At first I didn't answer. "I don't know, Billy."

"No, come on come on come on come on come on. You gotta say."

"Aren't you the guy who wanted to go back to the world of lies,
Billy?"

"Yeah, but honest lies. Lies where everybody knows you're lying. Not like now, where we all pretend our lives are so goddamned
squeaky-clean."

"All right, Bill. You know what I think? We're not all as pure
as you. Sometimes people want two things. Sometimes they're
weak, they want . . . That gym teacher, maybe he really loved his
kids. Or maybe he just had a great backyard, and sometimes—just
sitting there, drinking a beer in the spring—maybe it all seemed
perfect for a moment. Just perfect, the way it can seem. And maybe
he thought, Yeah, I'm fucked up, but I need this."

He waited. He gave me his attention.

"I think maybe all we really want, Billy, is some kind of balance. You listening?"

"Yeah, Tim, I'm listening. Balance." He allowed a soft laugh.
"You know what that word makes me think? It makes me believe
we can find excuses for anything. For anything. Balance. It's like
there are these words around, and if you jump, you can catch one to
justify whatever the fuck you're doing. Balance. That's a good one.
That's one you hear on TV commercials. Good enough. It'll do."

"Okay. What is it really, Billy? You want this kid so badly. You
both do. So you're back in Winship, and Winship's gone, and that
hurts."

"Right, Tim, you've got it. You've got it exactly."

"Billy, listen. Just hold on, okay? Just see this through. It's going to end, this part of things."

"No it isn't, Tim. No, hell no, it isn't. It's gonna go on, Timmy." He paused then, and I could feel him winding up for the next thing. "It's fucking never going to end."

He didn't hang up. But I could tell in the next second that he was gone.

I heard about the shooting the night it happened only because Johnny called me.

"You got the news on, Tim?" Johnny asked.

"No."

"Turn it on. Hang on with me. I got Channel Five."

On the screen was a four- or five-story brick building, with what looked like searchlights focused on it. I could see after a moment that they were just the reflections of a number of police cruisers with their flashers going full tilt. People were out, milling and excited, and the words on the bottom of the screen read MARY ELLEN McCORMACK PROJECTS, SOUTH BOSTON.

"What is this, John?" I asked.

"You're not going to like it. Keep watching."

A female reporter, Asian, was interviewing a white woman with a round, fat face and terrible hair, a woman wearing an old blue parka.

"It was a black car, looked to me like a hatchback, with one of those wings on the back," the woman in the parka said, with that overeager look those who are rarely listened to get when they become sources of important information.

"Johnny, fill me in."

"This is Billy and Patty they're talking about, Tim. They've been shot. Both of them. They were visiting Patty's mother, I guess."

"Jesus."

I had an impulse to go and wake Teresa, but I couldn't believe Johnny had it right.

"How can that be? Patty's not supposed to be out of bed."

"This is real, Tim. They're not saying how bad. It looked pretty dicey, the way they were both taken into the ambulances. I guess it took fifteen minutes for one to come. That's a lot of blood lost."

We were interrupted by Johnny's call-waiting—it turned out to be Freddie calling—and by the time he was back, the reporter was recapping the story before breaking away.

"A suburban couple from Waltham, pregnant with their first child, were apparently visiting the wife's mother here in the Mc-Cormack project in South Boston, when an assailant appeared out of a car, reportedly a hatchback with a spoiler on the trunk" ("No," Johnny couldn't help but say, "one of those *wings*") "shot both of them and then escaped. No motive of course is yet known, but the shootings have disturbed the seeming quiet that has descended in the past few years on this racially mixed section of South Boston."

"They've got to do that," Johnny said. "Say 'racially mixed.' There's like ten fucking black families in there, so that makes it 'racially mixed.' Why not just say a nigger did it. Be more honest."

"Which hospital did they take him to?"

"I can imagine. Some hospital in South Boston. Tim, I got a sick wife and two kids to get ready for school in the morning."

I waited for Johnny to come through. His pause was two seconds long.

"Right. I'll meet you."

We were told, after a couple of phone calls back and forth, that Billy had been taken to Carney Hospital in Dorchester. It was too late to wake the DiNardis to watch the girls, so I went alone. Storrow Drive to the Southeast Expressway, over to the other side of Boston, the less river-softened side, the side graced not by Harvard and MIT but by huge natural-gas containers and wrecking yards.

Off the exit, I followed my written directions but must have missed an important turn. Middle-class Dorchester gave way to a world of triple deckers and businesses with names like Chanique's Hair Salon and Pit Stop Barbecue.

In front of one of the triple-deckers, I found a group of Hispanic girls hanging out on a stoop. I pulled up next to them and asked directions to the hospital.

One girl broke away from the others and looked with a challenging form of curiosity into my car. I was driving the Lexus, Tony DiNardi's gift to Teresa on her thirty-ninth birthday. Had I thought twice, I would have brought the Explorer, but what difference would it have made? She would assume that I was here to buy drugs.

"You lookin' for what, the hospital?"

"Yes."

She continued looking into my car and then at me. I kept expecting some compatriot of hers to leap out from behind a building. Instead, she gave me detailed directions and at the end said, "Nice car, mister," and went back to her friends.

In the emergency room at Carney, where every instruction was written in four or five languages, they told me Billy was not there. It was an orderly who figured out who I was looking for. "You talking about the shooting?" he asked. "They brought them to Tufts Medical." His voice reminded me of the woman Billy had hired, the mother of Charles: the same island lilt. I had the sense then that such people as he and the young girl who had given me directions here were my natural allies at this moment; that someone like them—a black or Hispanic man—had likely shot Billy and Patty, but it would be another black or Hispanic who might right now be swabbing their wounds and putting catheters in them, and this, in my highly charged state, felt like a major insight into race. I thought I'd really nailed it. I was wild with gratitude for the kind ones in this underworld; I was going to remember this; I was going to talk everyone out of the instant racism that would inevitably shoot up in reaction to this attack. I believed all this as I darted through the streets approaching Chinatown.

Tufts was slick and efficient, more of a white person's hospital than Carney had been. At the desk they told me, essentially, that they could tell me nothing, and that the place to wait, if I wanted information, was the emergency-room waiting area.

My friends had all arrived ahead of me. Freddie and Johnny were talking to reporters, with whom the small room swarmed, while outside, three TV trucks had pulled up. Kenny was trying to make himself scarce. He'd been to the crime scene. As soon as he found out it was Billy, he'd driven there and was now, as a result of his office's inevitable prosecution of the case, trying not to talk to the press or to let himself be too easily identifiable as an interested party. Among the many fascinations of the night, this was not the least: watching Kenny go into reverse action, the deeply professional side of him coming to the fore.

Freddie and Johnny were keeping the reporters busy, telling the story that would be spun into myth by morning, when Billy would become the beloved Little League coach, the high school football hero, the dogged and ambitious young executive, the householder so devoted to the ideal of family life that he had moved his pregnant wife into his "aged" father's house (every newspaper used that strange word "aged"), where a "semiretarded" brother (Freddie's unfortunate phrase, picked up by one of the papers) had been "practically brought up" by Billy. It was an amazing thing to watch these two guys, coerced by the presence of reporters' pads into becoming mythmakers, pumping the story of Billy so high that when it appeared the next morning, he was virtually unrecognizable.

I could barely break into the conversations they were having, and I did not choose to introduce myself as yet another "friend from Winship." Instead, I sat and, when I was approached by a reporter, said I was waiting for someone else entirely. It may have been because I was alone, and not caught up in one of these tale-weaving conversations, that I was the first to hear that Patty had been confirmed dead. It came to me on the face of a female reporter speaking into a cell phone. I knew it because of the way her face changed, hardened and set for three or four seconds in the way a face does when it's receiving information both troubling and useful, before she stepped off into relative privacy to make another call.

———

When morning light came into the waiting room several hours later, we were all still there. Kenny and Johnny had fallen asleep, sprawled in the uncomfortable chairs; Freddie was doing the crossword puzzle in a day-old *Herald* ("Who played Aunt Bee in *Andy of Mayberry?*" he asked me just before dawn). Only Kenny was in a suit. A few reporters were still there, flipping notebooks open, sleeping.

"Who wants coffee?" Freddie asked when the sun came up. "Gotta be someplace open, right?" He looked around at Kenny and Johnny. "Wake 'em or let 'em sleep?"

"Let them sleep," I said, and volunteered to go out and look for coffee myself.

Of course nothing was open yet. It was a raw early May morning, the light unflattering to the stone architecture of the theater district bordering the hospital. Traffic hadn't started yet in any appreciable way. A few pedestrians were on their way to work.

No open coffee place showed up by the time I reached the Common, and there was none in sight beyond. The light made a broad assault against the buildings on Boylston Street, against the high glazed windows and the ancient stone. Seeing it this way was like seeing the city awakening with a drawn face, before it had time to put its makeup on. There were two Bostons, everybody knew that, the old Brahmin city and the new creation, the flashy place that had grown up in the eighties and nineties, a hybrid of Reaganomics and the input of companies like Winerip, which tried so hard to strip cities of the grimy layers that made them what they were and turn them into sparkling theme parks. But on seeing the city now, so near sleep, you could see how deeply it fell back on its Brahmin genes.

There was no coffee until I was nearly at the State House. A small bagel café carried the early *Herald*. A photo of Billy was on the cover. It was a picture of him at the end of a victorious Little League game, a game that he apparently had to attend in a suit. He was captured with his tie undone, his shirt soiled with sweat, a uniformed boy who must have been Ryan under his left arm, his right arm lifted in a victory punch. Beside it was Patty's official BayBank photo. Her death was confirmed there, but I was ahead of the game in other ways: I knew Billy's condition remained critical even now, eight hours after the shootings. I bought four coffees, knowing they'd be cold by the time I got back to the hospital. I took them to a bench on the rise of Beacon Hill, sipped from one, and, looking at Patty's picture, started to weep in a way I hadn't allowed myself to all night. A woman on her way to work looked at me curiously. I realized my cell phone was ringing.

"I heard," Teresa said. She waited a moment. "Oh my God." She started to cry, which dried up my own tears. "I can't believe it, Tim," and in the way she said "Tim," I felt her relying on me in a way I hadn't felt in years.

"When are you coming home?" she asked.

"I don't know. I'm supposed to be in Williamstown. I've got a million calls to make."

"I'm taking the day off," she said. "I can't face the monsters today. Where will you be?"

I told her to meet me in the waiting room.

"The morning news said they're trying to save the baby," she said.

"That's more than I knew."

"It's twenty-four weeks," she said. "A boy."

As soon as I'd returned to the hospital, I saw that the coffees I'd brought were unnecessary. TV crews had returned and supplied Kenny and Johnny and Freddie with hot cups. There was one more with them now. Ronnie had arrived, looking even more blurred and unfinished than he habitually did, his hair matted and one eye looking as if it wouldn't open all the way. They were trying to calm him.

"I woulda been here last night," he said. There were tears in his voice. "Nobody was there to stay with my father. I called that bitch, but she wouldn't come."

None of us asked who he was referring to by "that bitch," though I knew.

"I'm the brother. Maybe they'll let me see him."

"Nobody gets to see him until he's out of Intensive Care," Freddie said. "Listen, maybe we can get one of the nurses to give Ronnie a Valium," he said to the rest of us.

At the sound of that, Ronnie's face did what it had been doing most of his life: expressed helplessness. It was as though the thing that had always been missing in him, and maybe the only important thing, was the faculty of saying how things should go. I put my hand on his shoulder to comfort him. "Nobody's giving you a Valium, Ron. Don't worry."

We waited all that morning, with much of our energy spent keeping Ronnie calm. We read both papers. The *Globe* was more circumspect in its coverage. Billy and Patty were on the front page, but in an insert, their wedding photo, where they looked less like suburban royalty than they had on the cover of the *Herald*. In her wedding picture, Patty's beaming red face set her if not directly in then at least close to Dorchester, and Billy needed a shave. The larger photo on the cover of the *Globe* was of the ambulances in front of the McCormack project, while the bodies were being loaded in. In the *Globe*, it started out at least as a city story, a crime story, where the *Herald* played it up from the beginning as a yuppie tragedy.

Our wives began arriving late in the morning, and they brought things to us. It was touching to see how they had dressed up. Teresa carried a bag of muffins and Kenny's wife, Lynn, brought croissants. Only Carol, Johnny's wife, was absent. She had just begun a new round of chemotherapy for a recurrence of her breast cancer and was too weak to make the trip.

The women were better at communicating with the emergency-room staff, who'd gotten prickly from dealing with reporters. It was Teresa who learned that Patty's mother was upstairs with her daughter's body and that there was no definite word on the baby, and it was Lynn who told us that Billy's wounds were in the groin.

Freddie grimaced. "Jesus, of all the places to get him,"

Our cell phones were in action all morning. Freddie and Johnny both had business to conduct in absentia, and Kenny kept checking in with his office, disappearing for an hour or so. By late morning a

kind of graveside humor had developed among us. We were punchy
from waiting and from lack of sleep. We stared out at the foot traffic on Washington Street, people in the midst of a day, unaffected
by this. Ronnie slept, blessedly, with his mouth open. From time to
time Teresa laid her head in her arms and cried, and I held her,
ashamed of feeling that this was going to be good for our marriage.

"My father wants to come," Teresa said after calling him.

"There's no place for him here," I said.

"That's not the point. He wants to be with me."

"Teresa, this shouldn't be a family party. It should be just us. *I'm*
here for you, okay?"

She surprised me by accepting that, surprised me even more by
approaching Ronnie—when he woke up and stared blearily into
the early afternoon light, his face as empty as a newborn's—and
placing her hand on his shoulder while she offered him some of her
leftover muffin.

By midafternoon it was announced that Billy was out of danger,
but the police were the first to be allowed to see him. By the time
we got to go up, there were only four of us left. The women had all
gone home to attend to children's schedules, and Johnny had
reached his limit. "You can see him for five minutes," the nurse told
us. "But I've got to warn you, he was only conscious long enough
to talk to the police, and he's probably not going to wake up again
for a while."

So "seeing" Billy meant standing in the doorway, watching him
lie there, his eyes closed, a body under layers of sheets. Even though
he was buried underneath all this, I had a strong sense of Billy's
core animality, a life force rising through the hairs of his chest as
they sprouted from the hospital johnny. His breathing sounded
harsh and troubled.

Ronnie started crying as soon as he saw his brother, and the
nurse who had led us in, sizing up the situation, asked us to restrain
him and then took me aside. Of the four of us, I must have looked
the least disheveled.

"As soon as he's conscious again, there's something we have to
do," she said.

She was young. As she spoke, her eyes kept slipping beyond me toward what else might be going on on the floor. "There's the matter of the baby."

"Is he alive?"

"A decision's being made."

"What kind of decision?"

"He's on life support, but it doesn't look good."

"So who makes the decision?"

"Well." She looked at me briefly, as though I should know such things. "With him in this condition, that'd be his wife's mother."

"Listen, he'd want this kid. I know he would."

"We don't know if he's going to be in any shape to take care of it. And frankly," she chipped at her nail, "the doctors wouldn't even be asking this question if it wasn't already hopeless. They'd just go ahead and save it."

She let me take that in. "The policy is, if a child is going to die or is already dead, the surviving parent gets to say goodbye to it."

I didn't say anything.

"We dress it up like it's alive."

"Jesus."

"No, it's okay," she assured me. "You want to be here in case he wakes up?"

"Yes."

"Okay, but your friends have to go downstairs. Especially the brother."

After they all left, I stood by Billy's bedside. He remained asleep. An hour or so later they wheeled the baby in. Patty's mother accompanied it. Her gray hair spun outward from her scalp with the thinness of cotton candy. She wore a pair of sweatpants and walked with a sideways hobble. Her face looked wrenched around her sealed, gray-lipped mouth, like wood that starts to give around a too tightly turned screw.

"I can't stay and watch this," she said.

"It's okay," the nurse said. "We've got—" She looked at me, questioning.

"Tim," I said.

"We've got Tim."

Patty's mother left. The nurse wheeled the baby in its mobile bassinet to a place beside Billy's bed and listened to its heart with a stethoscope. This was a different nurse, taller, in her late thirties, with short, severe hair and glasses, and, I could see in her manner, kindness.

"Do you know, had they picked a name?" she asked with careful surface pleasantness, as if what we were discussing was everyday.

"I don't know."

"That's too bad." I knew she had another place to go, but she stood there and touched the baby's forehead.

"Is he alive?"

"His heart is beating very slowly now. Twenty beats a minute. The decision's been made to take him off life support. So basically what that means is that he's going to die sometime here, in this room. Are you all right with that?"

"Yes."

She looked at me, to be sure.

"If your friend wakes up, he may want to hold him. You can call one of us."

"I could do it, couldn't I? I wouldn't hurt him."

"Of course you can do it. But if you need help, call one of us. We'll be in to check his heart rate. Umm . . ." She puffed her cheeks out slightly, hesitant to say the next thing. "The grandmother didn't ask for a priest. Are you sure—"

"They weren't religious."

"All right then. Don't be embarrassed to call us if you need any help. If I'm not here, ask for one of the others. One of us should be available. And this could take some time."

Forty-five minutes went by with no movement from either of them except for a couple of shuddering movements from Billy—an attempt, I thought, to move the leg on his wounded side. The infant was maybe nine inches long, swaddled, his skin a dark ruddiness verging on blue, the lids of his eyes sealed shut, the mouth . . . What can I say about the mouth, except that its smallness and tenderness were the source of everything for me. He had one of those little caps on, ineffectually warming the dying head. I moved close to try to hear some breathing, but of course there was none, only the heart, which announced itself in slow thuds against the tiny chest.

I wanted Billy to wake up so he could name him. I wanted Billy to claim him, because it was me who was bonding with him there, with his smallness and his helplessness and the way he was making me feel, as I had felt with my own newborns, the inherent unfairness of being thrust into this uncomfortable world, of being asked to breathe, to swallow, to clench and unclench tiny fists. This boy did none of these things, only lay in a profound silence. I placed my hand lightly against his chest and felt the heart.

"You a friend?" I heard behind me.

A young man held a camera, one of those large, old models, with a strap around his neck.

"Who are you?"

"From the *Herald*. The hospital is letting us take one picture. When your friend wakes up."

He was blank-faced, focused entirely on his business.

"Why don't you wait outside, okay?"

The baby took forever to die. Billy woke up late in the afternoon, stared at me with an expression I had seen before only in wounded animals, that primal lack of understanding of pain.

I said, "Hey, Bill, your son's here," and lifted the baby—he weighed almost nothing—but by the time I'd gotten him into Billy's arms, Billy had passed again into unconsciousness. Another hour went by before he woke for longer than a few seconds. He blinked a couple of times and looked at me in a questioning way.

"Billy, do you know what happened to you?"

He tried to form the ghost of a smile. "I think I was shot."

"I got your son here."

His eyes shifted slightly in the baby's direction, but moving his head looked difficult.

"You want to see him?"

"He okay?"

"Why don't you hold him."

"With what?"

Both his arms had IVs connected to them.

I lifted the baby. "I think I can make this work," I said, and laid him across Billy's chest, where he took up no room at all.

"He okay?"

"Yeah, he's fine."

Billy looked down at him. Something happened with Billy's lips, a motion I couldn't read.

"You got a name for him, Bill?"

"No."

"How about one?"

Billy didn't say anything. The baby lay there, no motion at all.

"They want to take a picture, Bill."

"Who does?"

"The *Herald*."

"Fuck 'em."

"Good. Fuck 'em." Then I waited. "Listen, you're supposed to say goodbye."

Billy closed his eyes. "To who?"

I paused. "To him."

"Where's he going?"

I didn't answer, but tucked the swaddling clothes a little tighter around the infant's body, and I knew as I did it, as I touched him, that he was gone.

"Okay, maybe I should put him back now, Bill."

He didn't say anything, looked as if he might be headed back to sleep.

I lifted the weightless infant, lowered him into the bassinet. I put my hand on his forehead, as the nurse had done. It felt as if he was already in a room somewhere else, wherever they would take him next, remove the hat, remove the swaddling, these little vestiges of his brief importance.

I went out and found the nurse. The photographer, waiting, looked angry.

"He never woke up?" he asked me.

"No."

He came in, and after the nurse listened with her stethoscope, he took a photograph anyway, asking the nurse to move them closer together so that he could get father and son in the same tight shot.

After he left, the nurse looked at me. "Did he ever wake up?" she asked.

"Yes."

"And a name? Did we give this baby a name?"

"Yes. William. Call him William."

That night Teresa and I held each other as we hadn't in a long time, though, out of some instinctual sense of the limitations of the moment, we refrained from sex. Teresa asked me to describe the baby's death scene, and I did. She got up to get herself a glass of water, and I looked at her naked body as it passed across the shaft of moonlight coming in through our bedroom window. I realized I hadn't looked at her in a long time.

"Come back to bed," I said.

"I'm getting water."

She knew she was being appreciated, desired. I noticed how she had retained her thinness, worked hard at it, and as this had been done in privacy—almost out of my seeing—it led me to a consideration of all the other privacies, all the things we do by ourselves and don't tell each other about, how life tends more and more that way.

I visited Billy as often as I could, saw him through his slow recovery, his first walk to the bathroom. We never talked much. He stared out the window at another building's wall, and he watched television. At night together, we tried to become millionaires.

"What is an aspidistra?" Regis Philbin asked, and Billy said, right away, "B. An Asiatic herb."

"Good, Bill, shall we sign you up? See if you can get on the show?"

He didn't answer, kept watching, seemed to want no engagement at all.

Just once I managed to ask the question that had been bothering me since I'd first heard about the shooting. "What was Patty doing out of bed, Bill? I thought she was supposed to stay in bed."

"She was feeling good," he said, but that was all.

Sometimes Ronnie was there. Once or twice, when the TV was on and a black actress happened to appear on the screen, Ronnie said, not quite under his breath, "Fucking bitch. Fucking black bitch." There was no comment from Billy, but the particular quality of his silence made it seem like a code passing between them.

In the *Herald*, two days after the shootings, a female columnist known for her lack of sentimentality (the photograph above her column had her wearing a "Don't fuck with me" smirk) ran a page-one piece titled THEY KILLED ONE OF THEIR OWN. In it, Patty's lifelong battle to educate herself and then bring her siblings out of the projects received a kind of hard-boiled sanctification. Two of Patty's brothers had died drug-related deaths. Many of those who left the projects and seemed to be making it in the outside world were drawn "inexorably back," according to the columnist. The inference was that someone from the projects had killed Patty. The name that was prominently mentioned, in this and other columns, was Whitey Bulger, the white drug lord who, even after his supposed disappearance, still hovered over Southie.

In this, as in much of the reporting about the shootings, a number of signals felt uncomfortably mixed. It was as if Patty's murder became a beaker into which the city was able to pour whatever gripe came to mind. There were writers who pounced on Southie as the last section of Boston that hadn't ascended (had "refused to ascend," according to one local scribe) but remained enmeshed in racial and tribal loyalties that would always spill over into violence. There were others who saw in Patty's murder a kind of punishment inflicted on good, rich Boston by some agent of the dark side. Forget the new economy, was the inference. Forget what we'd all believed Boston had become. The primitive had resurfaced.

All of this could come about because the facts were so few. They had not been robbed. Patty's pocketbook had contained fifty-seven dollars in it, Billy's wallet thirty-two.

"Will you have the woman come back? Hortense, I mean," I asked. "To take care of you?"

Ronnie shot Billy a quick look, then lifted his eyebrows unbelievingly as he glanced at me.

"Oh, sure, Tim. Sure. Who do you think did it?" Ronnie asked.

I looked to Billy, but he was staring straight ahead, saying nothing.

"All we got to do is say the car," Ronnie said. "The kind of car."

The air felt charged—this was their first admission of any-thing—so I was careful when I asked, "Well, why don't you?"

"Shut up, Tim," Billy said.

"Why? I mean, isn't this something—"

"Shh," he said.

Ronnie said, "It's complicated. Right, Bill?"

Billy said, "Right."

When it was time for Billy to go home, a nurse was provided through the generous health plan Billy retained through his proud employer, the Winerip Company. From the time of the shootings, Winerip had insisted that Billy was one of their most valued em-ployees. Freddie cautioned us against any mention of the old threat against Billy's job. "We love the fucking guy," Freddie said. "We couldn't live without him. Got that?"

At Patty's funeral, Jane Swift, Massachusetts governor, appeared and hugged Patty's mother and enjoyed soaring ratings for a couple of days after a speech about the mindless violence that was no longer "allowable" in our city. The *Globe* ran a long piece on Billy and Patty. The paragraph that dealt with Billy's jail time carried the heading WILD OATS and contained the information that the Mo-gavero family had contributed to the fund for the long-promised Fantasia Museum, in which the sign Billy had once tried to burn down would be enshrined.

After a number of weeks the newspapers' intense early interest began to taper off, though never more than a few days went by without some new "lead" being announced. The investigation cen-tered on the car that had been seen by several residents to approach the entrance to Patty's mother's building, then take off quickly in the aftermath of the shooting. Everyone was certain it had been a hatchback, but was it an Escort? Billy continued to tell the cops he never saw it. They had been shot inside the building's vestibule, out of sight of the street. It had been a man of color, that was all he remembered. He helped the police artist draw a composite picture, and it appeared in the papers. The eager cops of South Boston fingered a likely suspect, there was a flurry of editorial interest, and then the suspect's alibi held up and he was released.

On weekends I helped Billy exercise. We walked to the boardwalk and back, Billy holding a cane.

"Is it because you don't want people to know about the baby, Bill? About Charles? I mean, you could nail this guy. The nurse's husband, right?"

He stepped forward with intense attention to the stress of his inner thigh.

"Plenty of time for that, Tim."

Paula turned up at the house some weekends to nurse Billy. Late in the summer he ousted the renters from the Waltham house and moved back in. He was alone there. A nurse provided by Winerip came, he told me, to look in. He could walk now, unassisted. Paula sometimes cooked for him. He changed none of the pictures, changed nothing at all. He lived there and talked about going back to Winerip in the fall.

That he was sleeping with Paula again I accepted the same way I'd accepted his moving back to the house. Their manner with each other was softly deferential, hardly erotic. She smoothed his hair a lot; she put her hand on his shoulder. Billy looked old and tired after the accident, like a man growing into bitterness. You could see the lay of the future story. He and Paula would someday marry but have no children. He would walk with a limp.

My marriage changed that summer. Teresa and I started clinging to each other more than we ever had. Sometimes in the middle of the day, on the road, at work, I'd feel a sudden flaring in my chest, the onset of need. But we were both very careful of this change, not wanting to push, as if the slightest force would make it all fall apart. Once or twice we made love without protection, our gift to each other as we nosed past forty, a modest way of teasing life into doing something for us.

We had signed on, too, to the campaign of our neighbor, Chip Holmes, running for selectman in the fall. Chip and I had grown friendly through coaching girls' softball. Now, together, Teresa and I were going to work on his campaign, the first such thing we had ever done, and the first thing we had done together in ages.

On Labor Day, at the end of that long, strange summer of Billy's recovery, we hosted a cookout in our backyard. We invited the Di-Nardis and the Holmeses. I set up the volleyball net, and everyone but Katie DiNardi played. The Holmeses had two children, a girl a little younger than Gabrielle, a boy roughly Nina's age. Tony Di-Nardi knew nothing of the game but to whack the ball with all his might each time it came to him. On his side of the net, Chip Holmes politely, humorously showed Tony the niceties, how to pass off to one another, how to play as a team. During the course of the afternoon they developed a relationship. Chip, a self-made man, was "in computers." His bundle had been made early; now he consulted. On the corner of my deck, Tony conversed with him, nodding his head deferentially, clearly in awe of this much younger man's ease in a world he, Tony, knew nothing about. Chip had blond hair, worn a little long, a bodily looseness draped in expensive sports clothes, an earring in his right ear. It was only when Tony took in this earring that a more confused look crossed his face. Chip handed us a bunch of flyers before he left, invitations to a fund-raiser we were supposed to mail.

"He's an interesting young man, your friend," Tony said after the Holmeses had left.

From the front porch we could see the shadow from the far trees at the edge of the meadow start to move toward us, the end of a day on which we had played and sweated, the good endorphins moving through us. Tony DiNardi put his hands into classic volleyball position, the position Chip had showed him, and laughed.

"You'd better be careful, Daddy," Teresa said. She was sitting on the front porch glider in a yellow dress that reached midway up her thighs. "Timmy might get jealous."

"Oh no," Tony said, and barked out a laugh, and then, as a kind of chorus, made the same laugh again.

I looked at Teresa, and there was an odd moment of disjunction between us. It had been a small thing, her pointing out the jealousy I actually felt over Tony's preferential treatment of Chip. But at this moment I knew she was happier than I was. She smiled at me, and I smiled back, but I felt we were pushing it.

When it was time to leave, Tony and Katie moved across the meadow to the point where a homemade path started into the woods, leading to the house they had finally finished and moved into. Scooter followed them halfway, then abruptly stopped, started rolling in something.

"Oh God, we're going to have to hose him down," Teresa said. She came and took my hand, aglow with the pleasures of the day.

We could hear the sounds of the TV inside the house, the girls watching, the moroseness that sets in on children when they realize their vacation is over. For a moment we both thought of Patty. I knew it from the way Teresa's eyes looked. I had the feeling of wanting one more thing from the day. The girls went up to bed, and Teresa asked me when I was coming up, a sure hint that we would make love.

"In a minute," I said.

On the back deck, I lit up a joint. It was something I had taken to doing lately, with pot provided by a connection of Kenny's. Kenny had surprised us all by revealing he'd gone back to using the stuff. The pressures of his job and the birth of a third kid were his excuse. I didn't do it so often, but I thought it might give me what I was still looking for from the day. Perfection, maybe. I remembered my old conversations with Billy. Perfection was what the day had not yielded up. I had to smile at that, at how much I still wanted.

Not many cars passed our street this late at night—it was now well after nine—but one (and I had the sense that it was the same car) made a traverse, first one way, then the other. I watched it, thinking nothing. Then it came back, for a particular reason, and I felt scared. Finally it pulled into my driveway, uncertainly at first, then with greater confidence, until it was parked in front of the house. I went onto the porch to meet it.

It was Billy's Monte Carlo. He had left it behind in Winship. Ronnie stepped out of it. He reached into the passenger side and extracted a bag.

"Ronnie," I said. "This is a—"

"This your house?" he asked.

"Yes, it is."

He glanced up at it. It was hard to read his look. There was always a little suspicion in the way Ronnie looked at everything. Something was wrong here, in Ronnie's view; it was as if he didn't want to come too close to the house.

"How'd you find it, Ron?"

"Internet," he said.

I raised my eyebrows, though he could not see that.

"I didn't know you had a computer. Come on in."

"We don't have one. Billy's got one. We were there today. You can get maps."

"I know that, Ron. Come on in."

"I didn't know if it was the right house, though." He wasn't budging.

"Ron, come *in*."

He held the bag like a football, close to his body and high. Finally he moved toward me. I put my hand on his shoulder and ushered him through the house into the kitchen. Upstairs, Teresa had the TV on loud enough that she didn't know we had company.

Ronnie, still clutching the bag, gazed around the house as if the whole apparatus might suddenly spring into action, catching him unawares.

"So what do I owe the—"

He lowered the bag onto the dining-room table. It made a thud.

"Is this a present, Ron?"

"Kind of." He looked out the back window, where he could just make out the volleyball net.

"Am I supposed to open it?"

He folded his arms.

Curious and half amused, I looked into the bag. In the bottom of it was a snub revolver.

"What's that, Ron?"

"I don't want it anymore."

"Okay. But what is it?"

"Don't tell Billy."

"Don't tell Billy what?"

He shook his head. He wouldn't look at me.

"Don't tell Billy what, Ron?"

He looked at me as if he expected me to understand.

"You keep it, okay? I can't anymore."

"Ron, you've got to tell me. Is somebody going to come looking for this gun?"

He rubbed his nose back and forth. I saw that he had reached the end of his ability to answer questions. He'd barricaded himself into a place all his own.

"Ronnie, whose gun is this?"

I watched the movement of his chest, a heartier echo of the chest of the infant I had watched die.

"Okay, I gotta go," he said.

"Ron."

"You take a left down at the end of your driveway, that takes you to Route Two, right?"

"Ronnie, you can't leave me with a gun and no explanation."

He started toward the door. I wanted to shout after him, but I also didn't want to make a noise loud enough to alert Teresa. I caught up with him at the car.

"Ron."

He got in and started it up.

"You want to tell me?" I asked.

The look he wore was like the old look, when he was a kid and his father had forced him to do his impossible homework.

I stepped away then, not really wanting to but understanding that Ronnie had given me something because he could no longer physically bear the burden of it. He pulled down the driveway, going backward, backed clumsily onto the lawn, straightened the car. Soon he was taillights.

"Was that someone?" Teresa asked from upstairs when I was inside.

"Chip. Looking for a . . ." I didn't have to finish. "I'll be up. I'll be right up."

I went back to the dining room, opened the bag, looked at the gun. I didn't know guns. Fat and oily, like a well-fed slug you uncover when you move wood. I closed the bag.

Then I went into the backyard. I went into the woods. I cursed myself for not bringing a flashlight, because I started tripping over things. Brush and deadwood. Rocks. Saplings. When I was far enough in, I dug a hole, bare hands, ten inches deep, and buried the gun inside its bag. I scratched my hands so as to loosen the caked dirt, most of which had bunched under my fingernails. When I stood up, the world shook slightly. I realized I'd been unconscious, or as good as, for the time it had taken me to get the gun from the dining room and bury it out here. In my mind, some bulwark had gone up to halt the slide of things. I wouldn't think of what this meant, or could mean. It was for Ronnie I was doing it, for that look he'd given me. Through the woods, I could just see the lights of my house. In the air I could smell fall, all that was coming. Chip Holmes's campaign. It was the event, I'd believed until now, that would dominate the coming season.

part two

The soccer fields of Bradford were dug deep into a section of woods a lone homesteader named Elijah Grierson had cleared and built a house on in the early 1800s. Apparently Elijah had had no descendants—or none, anyway, who survived—because when the Bradford Preservation Society made a play to have the house restored as a historical site and descendants were sought out, none had come forward. So the single-story house, which had sat in a state of abandonment and disrepair through much of the past century, was torn down in favor of a plan put forward by the Bradford Department of Recreation.

On the weekend before the land was cleared (this all took place the fall before the shootings), a demonstration had been held on the town common. It was a surprising thing to see: first, because Bradford didn't normally host demonstrations—not one had taken place in the ten years we'd lived there—and second, because these earnest citizens standing under the oaks of the common were faces I might never otherwise see. They were the other Bradford: Elijah Grierson's threatened house had brought out the gray-haired and the ruddy-faced, women in good raincoats who looked as if they had missed out somehow on having children, portly men holding coffee cups from Ellen's Java, many of them hoisting signs (SAVE ELIJAH GRIERSON'S HOUSE, FIND ANOTHER FIELD, DON'T TRASH OUR HERITAGE FOR SPORTS). The whole spectacle was so mesmerizing I had to drive by it twice to take it in.

There was something absurd in the sight of these citizens,

white-knuckled and patrician, climbing out of their burrows to in-
sist on the rights of a ramshackle dwelling over what seemed to me,
and to most others, the patently superior claims of our sons and
daughters. The Grierson land had been chosen for its flatness; up
till now our children, those who played soccer, had to be driven to
the fields of a neighboring town. I couldn't take in the sight of the
protesters without putting beside them the image of my daughter
Nina as she appeared at the beginning of a soccer match. At eight,
Nina had begun wearing her hair short. It bunched and curled and
flew out in about four different directions. Her lips had a full, nat-
urally pouting redness; she had large, freckled cheeks and fierce
eyes. Some warrior, long buried in the bloodlines of the O'Kane
family, had come charging out of the mists the night she was made.
She had a boy's haunchy buttocks, and her first move on the field
(she was a forward) was to hunch down and lift up her socks and tie
her cleats, then to remain more or less in that pose, an appetite for
action determining her body's posture. I could not watch these little pregame moves of hers without feeling that some possibility existed for her on that field that had never existed for my friends and
me on the playing fields of Winship. (For one thing, we never
played this game.) I don't think I actually envisioned life as a soccer player for Nina. It was instead that soccer—the utter seriousness and ardor with which she approached the game—seemed a
kind of spur or catapult toward a future of excellence and order, as
if an entire life could be lived that way, on a series of bracing cold
afternoons where one's color was always high and movement was
clean and sure. It was a mildly embarrassing feeling to have—too
much, I knew—and in the grip of it I always found myself turning
to the others at the edge of the field, the other parents in their good,
warm coats, some of us with open briefcases and others with cell
phones, as if to apologize.

But I couldn't help it. I treasured the ritual of soccer night. It
was never just the game. It was, afterward, the herding in. As the
light fell and the game came to an end, we the parents had to wait
while the girls formed their lineups and clapped "Good game!" to
one another. Then they had to meet their coaches for final instruc-

tions, chastisement, and praise, which Nina always received with a detached, almost dissociated look on her face, until an elbow from another player or a word from the coach brought her back. She had developed the athlete's at-rest stance—the gracefully out-slung hip—that I had never quite perfected. Then the girls were released and Nina came running toward me. Here was the night's keenest repeated surprise: that this girl, such a force on the field, should be willing to collapse into my arms or climb up onto my back, fresh-cheeked and as open to me as she'd been at four or five.

When the girls had to be driven to Concord for their games, we'd always carpooled in order to get them there early. We all attended the games, of course—it was practically a rule—but whoever was in charge of the car pool got to take the girls to the McDonald's on Route 2 afterward. All that was left, on the nights I drove, after the last girl had been dropped off, was a short car ride home. Clearing Elijah Grierson's land allowed us to change the rituals of those nights and make them more private; after the games we got to drive our daughters individually to McDonald's. Nina and I were met there by the other girls. They all piled out of their Grand Voyagers and Odysseys and dashed to the counter, a gaggle of blue uniforms and white socks, blond and dark hair sleek and well cared for, clear faces and beautiful long young legs under the glow of the McDonald's counter, on the other side of which a blotchy-faced teenager who would never come within sight of their opportunities took their orders.

The girls all sat together with their Big Macs and their fries and their tall shakes, the decibel level of the McDonald's interior raised by their shouting and laughter. The waiting parents sat at separate tables, murmuring to one another, sharing what little we felt could be released from our carefully guarded lives, until the collapse set in and one or another of the girls approached our table, long arms flapping exhaustedly at their sides, practically begging to be carried to bed.

Then came for me the best part: driving home together in the silent car. These were autumn nights. In the light of the headlamps, fallen leaves lifted and blew in that time-honored manner

that always makes a suburban guy know he is deeply in the suburbs. Yet it never felt like cliché when it happened. It always
seemed to clarify my life and give it, even if only for a very brief
time, some ungraspable meaning.

Along Bradford's sparsely populated roads, the houses, well lit
and cozy, sometimes made me feel that I had entered one of those
model railroad villages, where the stationmaster is forever caught
swinging his lantern and where, in the window of one of the snow-
topped houses, a grandmother is seen lowering a freshly baked pie
to a table. I don't think we create such scenes solely for our children; they are the world we want to live in, and Bradford, on such
nights, seemed to have attained that desired stillness.

This part of life felt like a gift. Gabrielle had been indifferent to
sports and had played for only a couple of years. So with my older
daughter I had had nothing like these nights, Nina riding beside
me in an exhausted silence, her thoughts retreating to her private
world. I allowed her to stay there, but I was always grateful when a
few words emerged: "Jesse Hirsch is such a jerk." I didn't feel compelled to ask the follow-up question—"Why is Jesse Hirsch such a
jerk?"—though when I did, her answer was usually just a shake of
the head, a large yawn. She was safe; that was all she knew. She was
going home, and she was safe.

On the day of the protest, I parked my car at the edge of the
green. My excuse for stopping was that Teresa had asked me to pick
up milk and rolls, but really I'd stopped because I wanted to stare,
and after two passes in the car I began to feel a little conspicuous.
Up close, I saw that these were not angry faces. They laughed and
joked with one another. It was stupid of me not to realize until we
were crossing the green that Nina was in her soccer uniform (I was
taking her to a practice), a dead giveaway as to which side we were
on. But the looks I received didn't seem fixed on our membership
on the opposing side of the debate. Something much more basic
was at work. It was all there on the face of one particular man as he
regarded us. He had that squint-eyed, supercilious look certain
portly Harvard boys get as they pass into their late fifties, and
everything about us seemed to add a log to the fire of his disdain.

Go away, he might have been saying to us. Just go *away*. They wanted to keep things as they had always been here, and it was only later, as I was standing at the counter of the store, paying for my groceries, that I remembered how it was not so long ago that I had thought of myself as the boy on the hill in the painting, that I had apprehended the change beginning to happen here and had resisted that change internally. All of that seemed a very early version of myself, a part of my youth, which I had left behind. Looking down at the little girl at my side made me understand just how far I had traveled from that old posture of retreat. She seemed even more real than she had before, a very concrete composition of time and also—though I had foolishly complained about her unconscious conception—of effort. Her body spoke to me that way now.

I looked out once more at the protesters, who seemed suddenly as vague and insubstantial as phantoms, wanting something that could no longer be wanted. I told Nina we'd have to hurry if we didn't want to be late for practice.

I think of that scene sometimes when I want to trace things; specifically, when I want to trace where I was, who I was, at the time of Billy's shooting.

I thought a great deal, of course, in the days and weeks afterward, about what it meant—Ronnie's bringing me the gun that night. But I didn't call Billy, not right away. I held to a scenario, the only possible one that excused Billy—and excused me as well—where the gun was one Billy had bought to kill his assailant, who was known to him. The story I'd come to believe in the hospital—the coded story Billy and Ronnie kept signaling to each other—was too strong to let go. And there was too much of life, too, ongoing life, that didn't want to be disturbed right away. So I said nothing.

I always intended to confront Billy eventually, but then things happened that fall. The attacks happened a week after Labor Day and, for a while, dominated everything. Then the habits of life intruded—the girls' activities that had to be attended, Chip

Holmes's campaign, the get-out-the-vote parties we cohosted. It became possible, even easy, to put the question off for another day.

Chip Holmes won his election handily. Given that it was an off year, and Chip's victory representative of an electoral tide that was seen to be altering the outer grid around Boston, we attracted the attention of the *Globe*. This was the first town election in which "the new Bradford," as the *Globe* called us, began to assert itself. After the ripping into the woods and the building of new houses, after the establishment of our own school system and the building of our athletic fields, we—that is, the left-leaning young professionals who had formerly clung to the towns on the lip of Boston—were now seen to be a force. The old, quiet, we're-not-really-here Bradford was thought to be crumbling, and the *Globe* documented that crumbling by running a photo of me and Chip at his election-night party, the two of us toasting each other and grinning, those grins making us look, unfortunately, a little avaricious.

Among the calls I received the day the photo and article were published was Billy's. He had left a message, and it was not until the next night that I faced up to my responsibility to call him back. Even then I found myself looking for an excuse to put it off. When I got home from work, I wandered out to my backyard and walked along the perimeter of trees, aware as I did so that my heart was beating at an irregular pace. Looking into the woods, I thought I could probably not even find the place where I had buried Billy's gun. Then I realized that was not true; it might take no more than five minutes for the police, or anyone else, to find it. I had not been careful about what I had done. It seemed essential then that I ask Billy to come and take it back.

After I decided that, I went inside to make the call.

"Well, aren't we the impressive politico these days" was Billy's first comment. Then he chuckled. "Big victory for the—what did the *Globe* call it? I got it here somewhere—"

There was the sound of a moving of objects, a kind of low animal grumbling coming from him as he searched.

"It's okay, Billy, you don't have to quote the *Globe*."

"No. No. Here it is. The 'family-first forces of Bradford.' Nice. I like that."

I was less eager now to keep the conversation going than I might have been in former years.

"How are you, Billy? It's been a while," I finally said, after what was, for me, a long silence.

"Oh, I'm . . . fine, Tim." I had the impression that while he was talking to me, he was also playing some little game with himself, flicking unlit matches into a wastebasket from a distance, that sort of thing. "For a guy who lives in a house full of ghosts."

I had no answer to that.

"Do you remember that song, when we were kids, about the guy whose wife died? 'Honey.' Remember that one?"

"Hum a few bars."

"Oh, come *on*. You remember it." He proceeded to sing. *"'See the tree how big it's grown but friend, it hasn't been so long it was a twig.'* You remember that piece of shit."

"I do. Yes."

"Well, that's where I live, Tim. I live in the Honey House."

I thought that what he wanted was small, appreciative laughter, so that was what I gave him. But in the silence afterward, which went on for quite a while, I had the feeling that he was looking straight into me.

"What is it, Bill?"

"What?" His voice had a yawning, bored flatness to it, as if he hadn't minded the silence as much as I had.

"What are we not saying here, Bill?"

I had a moment's fear after I'd said it, as though I'd invited an answer I wasn't ready for. I prayed he'd deflect it.

"Well, you never call," he said.

I almost laughed, with relief as much as anything. But there was a curtness to his breathing that stopped me.

"You're too busy with this guy Chip—what the fuck's his last name?"

"Holmes."

"I like his earring, by the way. Looks like a very hip guy."

I picked up on Billy's surprising jealousy, but chose to change the subject. "How's work, Bill? What's going on at work?"

For a moment he seemed to be deciding whether or not to answer me.

"I don't know why they keep me on. The fucking noble widower. It's not exactly sexy for them anymore. But I suppose it would be bad PR for them to let me go now."

I waited a moment, sensing he had more to say.

"The thing is, they can't figure out what to do with me. So I knock off early and come home to the Honey House. Maybe it's not a good idea. What do you think? Do you think maybe I should move, Tim? Except I like it here. I like the kitchen. I like the yard. When I wasn't here, I missed it."

Hearing those words—the tone slightly mocking, as if it were me, not him, who had chosen this life for him—made me wonder whether everything he said, this entire conversation, he'd been putting me on.

"You still seeing Paula, Bill?"

"She comes, yeah."

We each allowed the next silence.

"What, are you criticizing me for that, Tim? For not being faithful enough?"

"I'm not saying that."

"What am I supposed to do, just stare at the walls?"

"Bill, I'm not criticizing you."

"Hey, you still see your friends, Tim?" There was a slight disparaging tone to the word "friends." My mention of Paula had done something to him. "You guys still go to the *Iron?*"

"No, those nights are a thing of the past."

Suddenly he was earnest: "I hear Johnny's wife isn't doing so good."

"She'll pull through," I said.

"Listen to you. Mr. Positive. Mr. Chipper. Sometimes—let me tell you something, Tim—sometimes the worst thing happens."

"I know that, Billy."

"That's when you take off, right? 'See you guys. Gotta go see my friend *Chip*.'"

"Don't tell me I'm somebody who takes off, Billy. Who was there with you? In the hospital. Who held your son?"

He was silent. It suddenly felt stupid and small to have insisted on.

"I'm sorry," he said. "Forgive me. I was not fully present. Recovering from a gunshot wound, as I recall."

I paused a second before speaking. "Right. You're forgiven. And I'm sorry, too."

"Okay."

But from that point of softness, there seemed nowhere for us to go.

"I heard, somebody told me afterward," Billy said after the long, uncomfortable silence, "that you named him."

"Right. Yes. I did."

"That was a good thing."

I said nothing.

"What'd he look like, Tim?"

I made some vague sound, stalling, and Billy said, "Hmm?"

"You know, he was too small. Too small to live, I guess. They're very blue when they're that small."

"You've seen them before, like that."

"No. No, I didn't mean that. I guess I'm just generalizing."

"Well, don't *generalize*, Tim. Tell me what he looked like."

"Jesus, Billy," I said gently. "He didn't look like much of anything. He was a baby."

"Right. They don't look like much."

But he was hanging on for something.

"Somebody told me afterward," he said. "Maybe you can tell me if this is true, that there was a chance they might have saved him, only somebody had to say so. Somebody had to stand up and say, yeah, you know, do what you've gotta do."

I waited a moment, stifling what I might have said.

"Only I wasn't capable. I was *out*. Nobody was asking me, Tim. So this little boy dies. My son dies, Tim, because nobody asks me."

It was insanity, but it seemed as if he was on the edge of tears.
"Billy."

"Tell me, did they ask *you*, Tim?" There was a pleading tone in
his voice now.

"I think they asked Patty's mother."

"Oh shit, *her*? This woman who could barely—*her*? *She* got to
make the decision?"

"I think so, yes."

"They told me they asked you. There was a nurse, afterward; she
told me they got your okay."

"That's not true, Billy. I was told there was no hope for this
baby. Nobody ever asked me."

I let the semi-lie sit. There were sounds above me, the girls
shifting from room to room, Teresa getting after them for some in-
fraction of the house rules. I wanted to go upstairs and see what
everyone was doing, to assert some dumb fatherly being.

"Why'd the nurse tell me that? That you said it was okay to let
him go?"

"Billy, all I remember is they told me it was up to the next of
kin. Patty's mother. That's all I remember."

He waited a long moment before speaking. "Okay, Tim," he
said in a way that didn't seem quite resigned. "Okay."

"You don't believe me."

"No. I believe you. You at your window, Tim?"

"No, I'm not. I'm in the den."

"Well, is there a window in there? In the *den*?"

"Sure."

"Go to it. Okay? Look outside."

I felt resistant to getting up, to following his orders. But finally
I did.

"You looking?"

"Yes."

"Okay. So what are we both seeing? Trees, right? Bare trees. November. So what's my point? This baby was supposed to have been
born in August. He'd be—what?—three months now. Remember
we used to throw to each other under those trees in my yard?"

"Sure."

"Huh?"

"Yes. Yes I do."

"And it would worry me, the way the branches hung down?" He paused. "I had them pruned. The week before Patty died, I hired some guy to prune the trees so the ball wouldn't get caught. Do you believe that? The week before. The tree guys told me it was the wrong season. I said, fuck it. *Do* it."

I had no idea what to say to that. Finally what I came up with was, "A little premature, wasn't it?"

"Hmm?"

"It would be years before you could play catch."

"Yeah, but I couldn't *wait*. I couldn't *wait*. I wanted everything to be ready."

I was trying hard to sound Billy's voice—to press against it with all the sensing instruments I had—for the lie, the evasion, the false note. His brother had brought me a gun; it was buried in my backyard. But I could find nothing in Billy's tone to connect to that fact. I thought I knew this man. I thought I knew when he was lying.

"Well, that must—kill you. The sight of that."

"Right. Yes it does, Tim."

I could tell he hadn't liked my answer. When he spoke, it was as though he were trying to separate his own words, to make them not touch one another.

I decided to just plow right ahead into whatever I felt like saying. "They say you can tell which trees are healthy and which are sick from the way they move in the winter wind. Did you know that?"

When his words came, they arrived with the same flat sense of separation. "I didn't, Tim."

"I don't get it, Billy. Why are you talking like this?"

"Tell me more. About the health of trees."

I waited before speaking.

"If they snap—you know, like arms—that's a sign of health."

"Good. I'll watch for that."

"Okay, Billy," I said then, to let him know it really was time to go.

"What, are you trying to get off, Tim?"

"No. No, Billy, listen. If this is something you don't want to talk about, shut me up, okay? But the way you and your brother were talking in the hospital, I couldn't help putting it together. It was Hortense's husband—the nurse's husband, or whatever he is—who shot you, right?"

He didn't say anything. I wondered then if he even knew. Had Ronnie brought me the gun in secret?

"And here it is November," I went on. "Isn't it time you came through with that? *Told* somebody? Kenny's office is investigating this. I mean, you know that."

"It's better," he said, and took what sounded like a long swallow, "if they come up with that on their own, Tim."

"Why?"

"It just is. If they snoop around and discover it, it's going to have some force. I mean, they're stupid not to look there, but I guess they don't get it. They don't know which dots to connect."

"You mean about the kid? About Charles?"

Again, he didn't answer, but I took that as assent.

"You could actually help there, Tim."

"How?"

"Well, plant it in Kenny's brain somewhere."

"Kenny's had to recuse himself from the case. He can't be involved."

"What's that word?"

"What, recuse?"

He chuckled. "Oh, that's a good one. I like that. Recuse. And bullshit. Bullshit Kenny doesn't know what's going on."

"I think he's working real hard not to."

"Well, it'll soon come around. Because you know what, Tim?"

"What?"

"First they've got to get around to suspecting me."

I said nothing, just stood there a moment, partly stunned, staring out at my trees, as if I hadn't been given permission to move from that spot.

"You know how they think. They've got to get to that. They've got to be thinking it, anyway. The husband, why not? I mean, look at me. Why *wouldn't* they think that?"

"I don't know," I answered. "Because there was a car there, maybe. A car that was seen to take off."

He seemed to be listening carefully to the reverberations of my words.

"Right. But maybe there are explanations for everything, Tim. So let them think it was me. Let them sniff in all the corners of my life, Tim. Let them. And then let them come to the truth. You could help that. At the right moment."

"When?"

"I'll tell you. I'll tell you when they've gotten close."

If there was a moment to say, And about the gun your brother left me, it was now. But I was certain in that moment that he had no idea what Ronnie had done.

"So speak to me, Tim."

"What do you want me to say, Bill?"

"I can hear the fear in your voice. All I want you to do is wait, okay?"

It was not lost on me that this might be a very elaborate game Billy was playing, brilliant in its way, to work up everyone's natural suspicions of him, to draw them out into the open, then to use me, as he very well could, as his line of defense. I had seen the woman; I knew about the child. His use of a word like "fear" felt calculated. Of course it would be fear I would not want to own up to in my safe house, surrounded by my band of trees. He could use "fear" as if standing up for him, possibly protecting him, was an adventure, a playing of the edge, like our nights in Gloucester. It was his way of flattering me.

"All right, Tim. I'll let you go."

"Right."

We both allowed a brief silence before hanging up.

nine

The DiGiovannis, Kenny's parents, had always been the oldest set of parents in our group, so it was not a great surprise when Kenny's mother died the week before Thanksgiving.

On the morning of the funeral I brought the kids over to the DiNardis early to be taken to school. When I got back, Teresa was standing in our bedroom, slipping on a black dress and fastening her necklace. She asked me to hook it for her.

The top of Teresa's dresser smelled of perfume. She'd spilled some. Perhaps it was this, or the scent of the faint coating of powder on her skin, but when I approached her and began clasping the necklace, I felt that urge right away to make love. I suppose it had been a while, and the urge was just breaking through the crust of our familiarity. Teresa had started frosting her hair. Certain women in very tony places like Bradford liked to play the edge of trampiness, but Teresa managed to carry it off. She wore too much makeup usually, but looking at her in the mirror that day, I saw something close to the smart, sexy, I-can-take-care-of-myself face I remembered being so compelled by in Cheers, that face I had wanted to pace my life to. I put my arm across Teresa's breasts from behind and held her to me.

"Hey, we could, we have time," I murmured.

"We have five minutes," Teresa said, and tried to slip on an earring.

"Well, five minutes . . ."

"That'd be fun, wouldn't it?"

She smirked, but then our eyes met in the mirror. There were things we no longer talked about. Our marriage proceeded as if at a certain point we'd each decided that the things we couldn't get from it were things we could renounce. It was that simple most of the time, yet there were still moments when old demands, old needs, and old unsatisfied requests flashed across Teresa's eyes and made me want to pounce on them, glad, in a perverse way, that she still thought highly enough of me to ask for more.

I unzipped her dress.

"Hey, Tim."

"Five minutes is enough." I kissed her neck.

"No. It's not five minutes. Because then I have to start all over again, getting myself ready."

But as I lowered her dress over her shoulders, I was aware that she wasn't stopping me.

It took maybe ten minutes, and it was pretty great, because who, with kids in the house, ever does it in the morning anymore, with light streaming in and work canceled for the day and the good, expensive clothes cast aside? Teresa murmured something about contraception, but it seemed to me a needless distraction from our more important business. When we were finished, the first thing Teresa said was, "Are we trying to have another baby, Tim?"

I said, "I don't know. Are we?"

"This sort of thing has been happening more often. Do you notice? You keep insisting we don't have to worry."

I tried to count back to other times; then, in what I thought of as a jocular, teasing tone, I asked, "You'd owe me one anyway, wouldn't you?"

"What do you mean?"

"For the last one. The sleeping seduction. Nina."

She was still wearing her small postcoital smile, but it had started to look plastered on.

"So this is you getting back at me?"

"Maybe," I said, trying to keep us in the territory of a joke. "Who knows? Maybe."

Where do fights come from? How do clouds come in seemingly out of nowhere and converge over a given spot and unload?

"I never knew it was such a big thing."

"Well, it was. I mean, at the time."

"Okay." There was dismissal in the way she looked at me before she started to get up.

"Wait. Where are you going?"

"I'm sorry. I don't like the thought of you resenting me all these years for getting pregnant with a child you adore."

"I'm not going around resenting you."

"Tim, we're going to be late."

She went into the bathroom. I lay there for a while, stupidly holding my dick, as if the feel of it could connect me to the blissful moments just past. I could hear her running water in the bathtub, trying to wash out whatever of me she could. When I got up and wandered in, she was reapplying her makeup. She didn't bother to glance my way.

As she examined her face in the mirror, assessing her features, accenting and exaggerating the lines of her eyes and mouth, she seemed to be turning herself into something garish and artificial, something that existed only for other people, for their judgments or their approval.

"You coming, Tim? Or are you going to be naked all day?"

I waited a moment. Without thinking, I said, "Our lives are such bullshit."

A moment of perfect stillness followed. Her face hardened and tightened down to a perfect replica of her father's and stayed in that position for several tense seconds. "Oh, fuck you, Tim," she said. Then she disappeared.

When I left the bathroom, I found her sitting at the top of the steps, staring miserably down at them. Standing over her, I said (though I didn't mean it), "I didn't mean that."

"Oh shut up" was her answer. There seemed nothing to do then but go back into the bedroom and begin dressing. I put back on the silk boxers Teresa had bought me last Christmas, the expensive white shirt whose surface always felt to me like the skin of a soft, exceedingly short-haired animal, and lastly the pants and the shoes I had taken special pains to shine the night before.

"You're going to this funeral alone, I hope you know that," Teresa called from over her shoulder, still on the stairs, where I could see she that had been joined by a roused and mournful (and now seriously aging) Scooter.

It was the sound of her voice, the crude, near-screeching sound she took on in fights that finally got to me. But there was something else, too, something in the brief glimpse I had taken of our backyard, the line of trees, the never quite forgotten presence of the gun out there that always had the power to unsettle me. I had endangered us, and I was never sure why, why I didn't just dig it up and return it. Looking in the mirror, I had to fight the urge, as strong as the erotic one had been before, to bust it. Then, before I knew it, I had done just that, my fist had made a large hole in the center of the mirror, with a nimbus of cracks double the size of it sprouting around it. Even as I'd done it, I'd been saying to myself, Don't do this; this is a stupid thing to do. I watched the shards fall, and then the three or four of them that stuck to the outsides of my fingers brought forth their bright red dots.

Teresa was shouting things like "What are you *do*ing?" and "Are you *crazy*?"—she'd gotten up and come into the bedroom to assess the damage—but I moved past her into the bathroom and began concentrating on running water over my cuts and applying thick balls of cotton to them and trying to keep blood from dripping onto my clothes.

Teresa stood in the doorway, refusing to move on to the place where she had to feel concern for me.

"What is *wrong* with you?"

"Lots, I guess," I said, and stared at her as if I wouldn't accept exorbitant guilt right then and had no true interest in looking inside myself to get the answer. My cuts were just surface ones; the cotton and a few Band-Aids would take care of the problem. Still, as frustrating as my behavior must have been to her, Teresa said, "Tim," as if she was not quite prepared to give up on me. Hearing this, and seeing the accompanying look on her face, I wanted to tell her about the buried gun. I wanted to unload. Instead, I watched her go downstairs and then come back with the broom and dust-pan, and we went to work together on the cleanup, saying nothing.

My mood didn't lighten much until we'd crossed the Tobin Bridge. On that side of the river, though, the air seemed to turn whiter. The wind whipped the flags everyone had started flying that fall, and something started to happen to me. It seemed as if we'd been deposited into a place of openness and latitude after the boxed-in, suffocating greenness of Bradford, and I could remove myself completely from the feelings of the morning. We arrived just as the funeral director was calling out names for the lineup out-side. Freddie, noting our late arrival, lifted his eyebrows and stared mock accusingly at his watch. From out of the thick crowd, my parents offered a surreptitious wave.

It was order itself to drive from Russo's Funeral Home to Sacred Heart, to sit in the seventh row. My parents slipped in quietly be-side us, my father's slight form in an old ash gray suit that was a near match for his skin color, my mother looking comparatively florid at his side. They were at their best at funerals, where they were the social equals, in terms of still being alive, of anyone. My father focused on the gilt splendor of the altar, over which Christ hung resplendent, decked out in robes. Sacred Heart was the Ital-ian church. Our own churchgoing, never entirely regular, had been at the much smaller, simpler, more Protestant-inspired Saint Brigid's across town. Staring up at the figure of Christ, my father leaned in to whisper to me, "It was always my impression that that man was *naked* on the cross, wasn't it yours, Tim?"

Sitting next to me, Teresa had taken on a pose of beautiful wifely reserve. It was as if nothing sordid had happened at home. I wanted now as much as she did to present the image of ourselves as a busy and successful couple, with no edges showing. In a gesture of apology, I reached for her hand, which she abruptly withdrew. My father covered his mouth with his hand as if to study the altar more carefully, but it was clear from the shift in his eyes that he had seen.

Johnny and Carol Lombardi took the pew directly in front of ours. Carol's hair had not yet grown back from her most recent round of chemotherapy; she wore a kerchief over her head, and under it, because I was right behind her, I saw the stubble starting up at the base, a sight that affected me so much I wanted to reach out and touch it. Johnny had taken her coat with a pursed-lip gesture that seemed to sum up the tone of their lives now: he had become fussier, even more recessed, and honorable in a way I knew I couldn't even approach. I touched the Band-Aids on my knuckles and was saved from the gloomy thoughts these brought up only by the sight of everyone turning to see something new coming down the aisle.

It was Mr. Mogavero, flanked by his two sons. The old man's face looked red and buffeted, as though he'd just stepped in from out of a stiff breeze. He was using a walker, and moving fast—too fast, really. The whole congregation seemed on tenterhooks until he was seated. My own worry was that he wouldn't take his seat—his face seemed to contain some other purpose—but would march all the way to the altar, knock the priest aside, stand behind the pulpit, and utter some condemnation of us all. I think even Father Dugas, seated at the altar, might have experienced a moment's fear before Billy guided his father to a seat. Then Billy, with Ronnie just behind him, genuflected and made the sign of the cross.

I watched my father take this in, his eyes narrowing slightly, the way they had when we used to watch sports on TV, when I knew his interest lay less in the eventual outcome of the game than in some tiny, unconscious revelation of character that Rico Petrocelli or Kevin McHale had let slip. Nobody—only the showboaters—did both, genuflected and made the sign of the cross on entering a pew.

Billy took in the surfeit of attention. Even if he gave off only the shade of his former authority, it was still the most potent force in the church. And this in spite of the fact that he looked distinctly shabby. The suit he was wearing was one of his good old expensive ones—dark blue, double-breasted—but it looked as if he hadn't taken care of it, had left it balled up in a chair until he'd put it on this morning.

After the service, we all drove to a cemetery on a hill overlooking Winship—the high ground, heavy with Italians—then on to Kenny's parents' house. Though I enjoyed rubbing shoulders there with the relics of old Winship, I could tell that my father was bothered by the noise. This crowd was too expressive for him.

"Shall we go out, Dad? Do you want a smoke?"

In the hallway, I found my father's coat and helped him into it. It was warm enough now, even in November, for me to stand outside in my suit. My father smoked with the effortless grace of 1950s smokers, when the action of lighting up was an utterly natural part of entering a room. It looked appealing enough that I joined him in one.

"I should point out to you, Tim," he said, "that if you want to kill yourself, it's the wrists that need to be slashed, not the knuckles."

"I busted a mirror." There seemed no point in lying to him. He raised his eyebrows in response, but asked for no further explanation.

I found, though, that I wanted to give him one.

"Marriage troubles," I said, and lifted my own eyebrows, as if we were kids stealing a smoke together, bragging to each other about girls. My father's reaction was to take a long, thoughtful gaze in the direction of my mouth.

"I suppose one of these days we'll have to air out your old bedroom for you," he said.

"Some days I'd like nothing better."

The air of seriousness caught us both by surprise. We were uncharacteristically quiet for several drags. Some long, mild joke had constituted the essence of our relationship for the previous forty years, a joke we were always unconsciously adding to in order to put off the punch line. But lately I'd caught him looking at me in a new way, as if he was about to come out with some mild revelation. It never came. I stopped looking for it. I had come to think of those looks, instead, as reassessments, harking back to the old boardwalk deal he had made with my mother: let me in one more time, let me have a son, and I'll climb the greasy pole for you. He had not climbed the greasy pole, and perhaps some late-life guilt

had caught up with him. Or else—and, I thought, more likely—
the evidence of who I'd turned out to be offered some kind of proof
that he need not, after all, feel such guilt. Her end of the bargain—
me—hadn't proved such a winner after all.

Wherever this might have gone, it was interrupted by Billy
driving up in a shiny, copper-colored new Toyota. Ronnie hopped
out of the backseat and opened the door for his father. The old man
was extruded, his walker placed in front of him, and after gripping
it hard, he began to walk, with Ronnie's help, to the curb. A line of
parked cars prevented Billy from getting any closer.

"Hey, Tim, come help me park!" Billy shouted.

I held up my cigarette and gestured toward my father.

"That's all right, Tim," my father said, and stepped down on the
stub of his cigarette. He put on a big false smile with which to
greet Mr. Mogavero. In the time it took him to focus on us, Mr.
Mogavero's gaze seemed to narrow to a tightly focused rage, the
echo of what I'd seen in the church. Cataracts, I thought. He can't
hate us that much.

Ronnie, I noticed, couldn't meet my eyes.

"Tim!" Billy shouted again, motioning to the empty seat beside him.

My father gestured that I should go, but there was also on his
face evidence of mistrust of Billy, a look of warning.

In the car, I said, "Like you need help parking."

"Oh, keep me company, for Chrissake."

He drove the car with offhand recklessness, as though he might
just plow a parked car out of its spot to usurp a place.

"This is new, isn't it?" I asked.

"The car?"

I touched the material of the Toyota's dash, studied the sound
system. I couldn't remember the amount of Patty's insurance set-
tlement, though I knew it had been substantial. I wiped the
thought away as soon as it came. Nobody killed his wife in order to
buy a Toyota.

"It's for my father, more than anything," he said. "I drive the old
man around. He's suspicious of those old cars I used to drive.

Which is ridiculous, since they're a lot heavier than this thing. The old guys want to feel safe, you know?"

"Sure."

"This *town*'s getting ridiculous, isn't it?" he said. "For parking. Pretty soon we'll be like fucking Cambridge. You'll need a permit to park on the streets."

We were a full two blocks from the DiGiovannis' when he shoehorned the car into a spot, sending the car in back of him and the car in front a couple of inches out of joint. Billy made no move to get out. He leaned back in his seat, rested his hand over the place where his stomach met his thigh on the left side, and grimaced.

"Some days it feels like it's gonna open up all over again," he said, and looked at me. "No scars on your body, huh, Tim?"

"None."

He took the information in without comment.

"Should we go see Kenny?" I asked.

"Not yet. Okay? Couple of minutes. Big crowds make me nervous." He looked down at the fingernails of his right hand, bunching them tight against his palm.

"Why?"

"I'm a celebrity now. Don't you know that?"

"I guess maybe I forget that."

"Yeah, well, I don't forget. I walk into that house, every *eye*—"

"You don't like that?"

"No," he said, and shook his head.

"Looks like you need a girlfriend." I gestured to his hair, which was untrimmed and stuck out over his ears and in the back. "Somebody to help fix you up."

His gaze, though, was riveted on my clothes. "What's that, Tim?" he asked, pointing to my sleeve.

I looked down. I had missed it, a spot of dried blood just past the button on my cuff.

"Oh. Marital scuffle."

"You knocking the wife around?"

"No."

I tried first to hide the spot; then I lifted it to scratch it off.

Billy seemed to be looking at me—at the whole action—with curiosity. "How's your life then, Tim?"

"We should be with Kenny."

"Kenny's surrounded, Tim. He doesn't need us." His stare, fixed straight ahead, had grown sharper and more thoughtful. "I'm thinking of moving back here," he said after a moment's quiet.

"Yeah, I figured you might do that."

"I thought I wanted to go back to Waltham. I guess I didn't realize what it would be like."

"So what'll you, move back with your father?"

"Into the bear's den?" He shook his head and grinned. "We're too fucking masculine in there. It's like testosterone city. You want a woman's touch."

He was still staring ahead, and he looked young for a moment, the way boys in their early twenties do when they're making a plan and they believe all must go well with them. "No. Paula's house is empty now. You remember her son, Ryan? He's off at college."

"Where?"

"Nowhere fancy. Bridgewater State."

He glanced over at me quickly to see if I would scoff at such a place, which had been good enough for us once but which he knew I would consider nowhere good enough for my own children.

"He lives in a dorm. I pay for him."

"That's generous."

"Thing is, in Waltham, all the neighbors—I get gawked at. I get gawked at here, too, but hell, I've always gotten gawked at here."

He leaned back and put one hand on the steering wheel and the other, his right, against the headrest, very near my head. I thought he was going to touch me. Though I could feel myself wanting him to rough up my hair or squeeze my neck, the way he once would have done, I shifted away. Billy noticed and looked at me a second, as if he was wondering at something, and then he let that wonderment go. As I had during the phone conversation with him, I felt him trying to seek out some agreement with me, and then I wondered if that was just me, if I was reading too much into everything these days.

"I guess I'm about ready to face the mob," Billy said after a moment.

He opened the door. Out on the sidewalk he completed the gesture I hadn't allowed in the car. He touched me, adjusted my collar. He smiled down on me as if I were the kid brother he had to watch out for. His step was lively, and by the time we reached Kenny's house, he seemed eager for the crowd. I wanted to call him back, get him back into the car. I'd missed another opportunity, and I hated the feeling that left me with.

The crowd at the DiGiovannis' hadn't thinned out any. The kitchen table had been extended and heaped with pastries. Teresa was huddled with the other wives. My parents had apparently used up all their contacts in the room and were standing off to the side, my father looking as if he was cooling his heels outside the door of a principal who had called him in for a long-delayed and much-resisted meeting about his son's behavior. I touched their elbows and gestured to Billy.

"You remember this guy," I said.

"Mr. and Mrs. O'Kane." Billy spoke politely, but there was still that tiny smile that had started outdoors. I was struck all over again by his immense physical vitality, especially when I saw him next to my father.

"I haven't said much to Kenny," I said as a means of excusing myself, expecting Billy to follow me. But he didn't.

On my way to Kenny, Ronnie and I locked eyes for a second. I wondered how accidental this was, whether he hadn't been waiting, searching me out. There was a weak form of defiance in his eyes, which vanished right away and turned into a look of fear.

Kenny was holding his little boy Benjamin, who seemed moments away from a meltdown.

"Hey, Ken," I said when I finally got close enough to touch his shoulder.

At first I didn't think he'd seen me. He was buffeted by a group of old guys standing around him, and it surprised me when he said, "You want to get out of here, Tim?"

For a moment I thought he was booting me out. He lowered his son, pointed him in the direction of the boy's mother, and faced me with exhausted-looking eyes.

"Go down to the beach, something?" he asked.

"Sure."

"Round up Johnny and Freddie. I need some air. Just for a minute."

It didn't take long, though it did take a bit of convincing to pry Johnny away from his wife. We all walked in silence down to the beach, following Kenny's lead. At the head of the beach, he put his hands in his pockets, surveyed the mostly empty sand.

"A little claustrophobic in there," he said.

Then he started walking down to the waterline, enough ahead of us that we had to walk fast to keep up.

"Listen," Freddie said when we were all stopped, maybe twenty feet away from the water. "It's sacrilegious, I know, but is anybody else thinking about masturbation?"

Kenny just looked at him.

"I'm *remembering*. Your house. The basement."

"Right." Kenny nodded, as if he'd forgotten until that moment the ritual of our adolescence and was not pleased to have it brought up.

"I think that's Freddie's attempt to leaven things," Johnny said.

"Right. Shoot me," Freddie answered. He looked jowly and prosperous, and with the weight he'd put on, very much the oldest of us.

"You get any exercise, Fred?" I asked.

"Why do you ask that?"

I poked a finger into his gut.

"What? Am I fat? You guys don't remember what it's like to have a little one. I'm about ten years behind the rest of you. I'm in Babyland. What's exercise?"

He patted his stomach with both hands. Then he picked up a flat rock from the beach and with a mock-balletic motion sent it skipping six or seven times over the water. The motion had landed him a dozen feet ahead of us, and when he turned back, he was wearing a big, goofy grin. Suddenly his face changed. He looked stricken. He clutched his chest and staggered, and after a half pivot landed on his back on the sand.

"You think that's funny?" Kenny asked.

"It isn't?" Freddie, still on his back, said.

"At my mother's funeral?"

"Get up, Fred," Johnny said.

Freddie stood up and dusted off his suit. We were all wearing big smiles on our faces, and Johnny was laughing. Freddie's had been one of those jokes that is only funny after the fact, when the ridiculousness of it sneaks up on you.

"That fat body," Johnny said.

"All right, so leave me alone. I can't stand *gyms*, is the problem. I can't stand hanging out with a lot of guys whose basic goal is to *sweat*. I never knew that was going to be one of the goals of adulthood, and I categorically reject it."

It was after we'd been silent, and the tittering stopped, that one of us said, with the air of having let enough time lapse before the inevitable had to be spoken, "Mogavero."

And someone else—Johnny—said with an outpouring of breath, "Yeah. He looks like shit."

"*Worse* than shit," Freddie said, bouncing on his heels in the enthusiasm of disgust. "This is the way he shows up for work. We pay him sixty thousand just, basically, to show up. And he can't—you know—go to a *cleaner*. Get a *haircut*." He bounced a couple of more times, as if searching for the perfect criticism. "I can't send him out. I can't introduce him to anybody. We're just waiting for this to have blown over enough so that we can give him his walking papers."

"It's blown over enough," Johnny said.

"No. In certain circles he's still a local hero. Believe me. There's the pity factor." For a couple of seconds Freddie sucked in air so as not to seem overly callous. "We are doing no business, by the way. Seventy layoffs this year. So you can imagine what sixty thousand means to us."

It was then, in the pause after this conversation, that we all became aware, though not at the same time, of Kenny's dense silence.

"You okay?" Freddie asked.

Kenny was gazing out at the water, his skin pale, the vaguely cyborg look of his skin-grafted features at last humanized by the onset of lines.

"They found"—Kenny cleared his throat—"this car. Hey, I'm not supposed to know this." He shook his head and seemed about to turn back toward the house.

Freddie stopped him. "What are you talking about, Ken?"

"Nothing."

We were all silent a moment. Kenny made a couple of vague gestures with his hands, as if he was getting and rejecting ideas.

"I sit in my office, and faxes come in."

"So ignore them," Johnny said, as if he already knew what Kenny was talking about.

"*You* try doing that."

"So what's going on?" Freddie asked, his voice a caricature of subtlety.

"They found this—car had been stolen. From Lynn. And it turned up in Winship. An Escort. Matching the description of the getaway car from the night Patty died." Kenny shook his head and ran one finger under his nose.

"A car was stolen?" Freddie asked. "What are you talking about? "

"This is something that just turned up. A detective, just for the hell of it, did a scan of stolen cars from that night."

"That's—" Freddie said, and appeared to be calculating something, then shook his head in bewilderment.

"This is a warning. I don't know. Nothing may happen, but then again, things may begin to heat up for Billy. They're going to investigate him. That's all I know." Kenny looked at his watch. "I should go back. My father."

"No, no, Ken, wait," Freddie said, his hands out at his sides, as if he would physically stop Kenny from leaving. "You're saying the phantom car, the—what was it?"

"Hatchback with a spoiler," Johnny said in the tone of an afterthought. "An Escort."

"So what the fuck difference does it make if a car like that was stolen from here?"

Kenny didn't answer at first. He shifted his hands in his pockets. "From Lynn. *Returned* here. But you didn't hear that."

"So what does this mean?" Freddie asked.

Kenny didn't answer at first, so Johnny stepped forward. "It means up until now they've been looking for a black guy who owns a car fitting that description. But now maybe it turns out it wasn't some phantom black guy. Maybe it was a setup."

"So things are going to 'heat up' for Billy? I don't get this. Why does some car stolen from Lynn mean it was him?"

"Maybe it's got nothing to do with the killing," I said, and they all turned to me. There was in each of their faces a certain wild hope, as if I might be in possession of a logic that would free them from their new suspicions. It hit me then that in not telling them about Ronnie's Labor Day visit to me, I had betrayed them all.

Kenny was the first to dismiss what I'd said. "It's just too much of a coincidence not to investigate. I mean, that it was *here*—that it was that exact car and it happened *here*. In this town. Listen, I've got to get back."

"So what are you telling us, this is a fait accompli?" Freddie's voice was rising now. He was almost laughing, trying to make it sound ridiculous. "Billy did it? Billy stole a car and shot himself?"

"That's enough," Kenny said. "This is like, a fucking *fax* that came into my office by mistake. I ripped it up, and that is the last question I intend to answer about it." He paused. "But I wanted to tell you guys. They may come and start asking questions." Again his hands shifted in his pockets. He looked at Freddie, a little embarrassed now, as if he were providing important information late in the game. "It may be time to cut him loose."

"Wait," Freddie said, one hand resting with some force against Kenny's chest. "What are you not telling us? You know something more than what you just told us?"

"I didn't say anything," Kenny said.

"Will you stop—listen, all due respect, this is your mother's funeral—but will you stop acting like you've told us nothing?"

"I haven't told you anything but this one thing, okay? And that's all I know, I swear to God. So don't jump to conclusions."

Kenny immediately started up the beach, the rest of us following. We'd gone only a block before we saw Billy in the distance opening the door of his Toyota and easing his father in.

It was one thing to be apart from Billy and hear information about him. Vague as it had been, almost anything seemed enough now to implicate him. But it was entirely another thing to come upon him in the flesh—to witness the easy way he moved, the lightness of his gestures as he settled his father in the car. He stood up and saw us coming and gave us a smile.

Something in the look he sent us made it impossible to believe that this was a murderer. "Pathetic" would be the wrong word to describe him, but there was still something you had to pity in the sight of him. He'd gained nothing by Patty's death, not a flashier car, not a better house, not a younger, sexier, less-encumbered woman. In fact, the opposite. It was as if he'd gone back to what he was before Freddie tried to mold him into something else, and he was happier here.

"You boys having a powwow?" he called. He didn't wait for us to answer, got into the driver's side of the car, started to pull out. As he passed us, Mr. Mogavero stared straight ahead, that Old Testament severity still having not let go of his face. Cataracts, I thought again.

ten

The small white-walled reception area of the Suffolk County District Attorney's Office featured photographs of several of the community outreach programs the office had a hand in supporting. The children, facing the camera, had been posed to look eager and grateful, headed for lives over which crime would hold no sway. The wishfulness seemed embarrassingly naked within these particular confines. With few exceptions, the faces were black or Hispanic.

Kenny and I had a lunch appointment. I was a few minutes early. I had waited a month before calling him, figuring he had enough on his plate. It was just after Christmas when I phoned him at home and suggested lunch. He'd sounded tired, and suspicious. "Lunch" was not something we really did.

Nor had I ever visited him in his office, in the tall, skinny new building located between the Boston Sports Club and a series of other, similarly odd-shaped buildings—lawyer's offices, from the looks of them. This was a premodern section of Boston, with short, stubby streets running every which way—Hancock Street, Bulfinch Place, Bowdoin and Somerset streets. It was still Paul Revere territory, though from the sight of derricks and booms jutting out from a tall, new edifice around the corner, I wondered for how long.

I was wearing a suit, though I'd taken the day off. I didn't know what was code in the D.A.'s office. When the elevator doors opened and Kenny appeared, I was surprised to find him in street clothes—

a blue button-down shirt and chinos. He took in the sight of me and smiled a drawn, slightly crooked smile and invited me into the elevator. The new security was tight. He'd had to come down and get me himself.

"Nice that you dressed," he said, and punched one of the buttons. "I should have told you, on Fridays we only pretend to work around here. Just come up to my office a minute. A couple of things I have to tie up; then we can take a long lunch."

In his office we were immediately interrupted by the entrance of a crew-cut young Irish guy who placed a clipping from that day's *Herald* on Kenny's desk. Kenny scanned it and made a quick motion with his mouth and introduced me to the Irish guy, who was the office's press representative. They had a short discussion as to what effect, if any, this press coverage of new developments in the investigation of a child's murder in Quincy would have on their prosecution of the case, and then the press secretary left and Kenny flipped the article onto a corner of his desk.

"One call," Kenny said, and dialed.

He cradled the phone between his cheek and shoulder and wrote down a couple of things as he spoke. His office faced the Government Center buildings and the expressway; beyond them, a sliver of harbor was visible. I watched him at his desk, not really listening to what he was saying, and remembered how Kenny had once been the smallest of us, the least cool, the most attached to his mother, a boy who had gone through periods of fatness, and now this once chubby, once clueless little boy sat in this office and spoke in the clipped, referent-heavy language—it sounded to me like language that was always tilting down a slope—of the Law. By speaking it, he seemed to master it, and to take this in was both daunting and comforting. It was as though his knowing what he knew kept a certain danger away from all of us.

"That was my brother," he said after lowering the phone and rubbing his eyes.

"He in some kind of trouble?"

"No, no." He looked out the window. He lifted his hand and then lowered it, as if in defense against the light. "These days when a parent dies, Tim, you don't get five minutes to mourn, because you've got to take care of the other. The surviving parent. The crazy one." He sat back heavily in his chair, rocked in it. "My father wants to stay in the house. Of course. They all want to stay in the house. He keeps making up people who want to come and stay with him. He swears to God that a guy named Rookie Santamaria has always wanted to come and live with him."

"So? You check it out?"

He smiled. "Rookie Santamaria is in worse shape than he is. We tell him that, it registers for about thirty seconds; then two minutes later it's 'Did you call Rookie?'" He leaned slightly forward in his chair. "You hungry, Tim?"

"Starved."

"With that suit, I should take you someplace fancy. But I'm fond of this burger joint across the street."

I said burgers were fine with me, so he led me out of the building and down an alley. McHATTIE'S PUB was what was written on the sign outside the restaurant—a green sign, gold lettering, with a foaming stein carved into the sign.

"A lawyer's hangout," Kenny said. "But I think we can be private."

It was dark and not all that warm inside, surprisingly uncrowded for the Friday lunch hour. A waitress passing us as we entered called, "Hey, Ken, two?" and asked us to wait "just a sec." She was wearing shorts—black and tight—in January, and they revealed the thick hams of an old field hockey player at a probably now defunct parochial school. She found us a table in the corner. "You want quiet, right?" She flipped us menus before dashing off.

Kenny asked about my family, and we did that back and forth until we'd ordered. Then he folded his hands on the table, glanced to the side, and said, "Okay. Shoot."

"You knew it was something, right?" I asked.

"I knew it was something." Finally he looked at me, a little warily. "And I had a very mild suspicion as to what it might be about."

I waited before speaking. Our beers arrived. I took a big sip and turned away from him. "Okay," I said. "You know"—I tapped the table a couple of times, as if only some physical release could jog the words out in the right order—"me and Billy—he's shared stuff with me."

"I'm going to stop you, Tim. I can't hear this. I really can't."

"No, I think you've got to."

"Tim, I've gotta tell you. I can't know things. It makes my job impossible." The words were spoken with a hard edge, which he tried to retract. Though he wasn't quite smiling, his mouth made a little allusion to a smile. "If there's information you want to give me, I can direct you to the right person, that's all."

We were both quiet and uncomfortable for a moment.

"That presents me with a difficulty, Ken." I knew I sounded a little arch, as if I was trying too hard to affect the voice of the court.

"How's that?" His hands were folded on the table, and he lifted one and patted it down on the other.

"I don't want to be involved in this." I wondered if some desperation was showing in my words. Just as you check for protruding snot when the person you are talking to looks too closely at your nose, so I checked my body posture for cravenness. "I can't go to some cop, or some lawyer, and tell them what I know."

"It would be a cop. And why not?"

After he'd asked it, Kenny looked at me with what I thought was a kind of calculation, the beginnings of a worked-up defense. "Okay," he said, and leaned forward as if he were about to tell me a world-class piece of gossip—the mayor is fucking Julia Roberts, something on that exalted level. "I'm going to spell it out for you, Tim. Black-and-white. Like we're not even friends, okay? Not that there should be any mystery here. You watch cop shows on television, you know this. Anything you know that could possibly lead to the solution to this thing, that you're holding back—" He rocked one hand back and forth and followed the gesture with a look of extreme concern for me.

I turned away from him—it had been a vaguely insulting look—and surveyed the room. As I did, I thought that this restaurant, with its old booths and leaded windows and thick-hammed, familiar waitresses, was a safer world than the one I lived in. I thought of my days, my lunches, usually eaten quickly in college hangouts where I had no purchase, where I was older than the students but shared no common cause with the professors. It was a floating world I lived in, and I wondered how much the loneliness of my working life affected the choices I made.

Our hamburgers came, but I wasn't hungry anymore.

"Okay, Kenny, listen. This is driving me crazy. So let me tell you something that maybe has nothing to do with this case. I don't want to sit in a room with some cop you sic on me and give up information about Billy. Don't ask me why. I can't do that."

"Why?"

"I said, don't ask me why."

"No. This is what somebody needs to ask you. Why? And what's wrong with your hamburger?"

"Nothing. I'm not hungry. Just let me tell you, all right? Friendship, all right? Because you can advise me in a way your friend—or whoever you want to hook me up with—can't. Or won't."

Kenny sat up and wiped his mouth with a napkin. "How old are your kids now, Tim?"

"What?"

"How old?" With his fingers, he encouraged the answer.

"Eleven and nine."

"Eleven, eight, and four. Me. Mine. Very needy ages, wouldn't you say?"

"I don't know. My older girl has never much needed me."

"Okay, but she's going to want to go to college. Forget college. Braces. Music lessons."

"Music lessons?" I stared at him with a put-on look of skepticism and tried to fake a laugh. "Who the fuck lives their lives so their kids can have music lessons? We never had—"

"We do now. We're those kind of people. We live in those places now. Piano. Violin. You drive down the street, you hear the music coming out of the houses, right? It's very nice. No social life. Carpooling. No extramarital affairs. Too busy carpooling. Our kids' lives become our lives. Don't ask me how it happened. It happened. And let me tell you something, you can dis this world we're living in, but the minute it's threatened, you'd kill for it. Like anybody else. Like our fathers would have. Threaten it, it becomes fucking beautiful."

"I know this."

"So what I'm telling you is, do not do anything that's going to threaten it. Nothing. For Billy. For friendship. Nothing." He speared a french fry and gave it a critical look, as if checking it for flaws, before putting it in his mouth.

I waited for his focus to return to me. "There's something I want you to investigate."

"Jesus Christ. Do I need to walk out?" Kenny started reaching for his wallet.

"There's a woman named Hortense," I said, and watched Kenny shift his head away, as if a dramatic enough movement would prevent his hearing this. He slapped a twenty on the table.

"She was the woman who watched Billy's father, and she had Billy's baby. She was a married woman, Ken."

I had said it quickly, it was heard, and Kenny fingered the twenty as if he couldn't make up his mind about staying.

"I'm sorry to screw up your life. But this is something you could easily know. Don't give me this bullshit about how you can't know anything. You know about the car."

"Yes, Tim, I do." He looked up, his eyes gone a little dead. "And now I know this."

"Well, tell someone to investigate it. If you're going to go hunting down stolen cars, hunt this down, too."

"Hortense Joseph," Kenny said. In the next instant, whatever thought was running through his head seemed to disgust him. "Right?"

"I think her name was Hortense." It felt strange to hear myself backtrack like this.

"Her name is Hortense. Thank you, Tim. It's been investigated. You're not telling us anything new."

"How do you know?" I asked.

His eyes became slits. I knew he hated me now, for what I was forcing him to admit.

"Listen, this investigation has been going on for—what? Seven months now? I was very hands-off for about four of those months. I barely read the papers."

He lifted his hamburger as if he was about to take a big bite, then put it down.

"Then I began to wonder. We are very very concerned—" He stopped and looked as though he was sifting thoughts. "*Concerned*, in the office, about a perception. Look, there are two places in the United States where race relations haven't moved a step forward since the Civil War. One is Mississippi. The other is Boston. Don't ask me why. Don't try and get me to explain to you why we're locked into something here, but we are, and we always have been. So we try very hard"—he tilted his head back and pointed with his chin in the direction of his office—"to offset a perception. That every crime we investigate, we assume the race of the guy who did it. Unfortunately, your gorgeous, juicy white collar crimes occur out in the suburbs. In Woburn. In Reading. We don't have the luxury here of pointing to ten prominent white guys and saying, Look, we prosecuted them, too. We don't have the luxury of hockey dads or suburban wife murders. We get what we get. And then this one comes along—"

He looked at the table a moment, again measuring his words.

"Billy hands us a beaut. Suburban white couple gunned down in *Southie*. Black assailant seen. Well, who the fuck knows if that's true, but it *becomes* true. The narrative appeals. We haven't solved anything, becomes the story. We've got race on the table again. And we love this because it eases things for us. Black guys coming out of the night and gunning for us. Who doesn't believe this? Only very soon—let me tell you this now, since we're so far over the fucking line I don't even remember where the line was—very soon Billy becomes a suspect. Okay? Very early on. Investigating cops, one or two, start saying things aren't adding up. So we have a couple of meetings, and I step away. I've got to. But a couple of months of silence, it becomes unbearable. We pull in two black suspects, both of them wind up clean. We are starting to look bad, and if it turns out to be Billy, we're going to look even worse. Like we kept this thing going because we couldn't bring ourselves to believe a white guy would ever do such a thing. So I ask questions. I follow, at a distance, the investigation. I slip as much to you guys as I can, and at night I chew enough Maalox to kill an ulcer the size of Moby Dick." He stopped, having taken himself to a pitch of red-facedness. "So thank you very much for the tip on Hortense Joseph, but it's been followed."

I sat back, feeling depleted. "What'd you find out?" I asked.

"I think I've said enough."

A group of lawyers came in, guys who obviously knew Kenny. There were waves, and one approached him.

When they left us, I said, "I thought this was important."

Kenny responded by moving his plate a quarter turn. Then he sat back and positioned himself so that he was looking out the window.

"Maalox," I said, to lighten things.

"How do you know it was his baby, Tim?"

He still hadn't looked at me. I shifted in my chair, sat up straighter.

"Are you saying you don't know?" I asked.

"How do you know? How?"

I looked down at the table, slightly embarrassed but still excited that this information was, after all, new.

"He used to take me there."

"Where?"

"To his house. She was the woman who watched his father. You know that."

"Yes."

"We had these nights. Stupid. I regret them. After we'd leave the Branding Iron, after you guys took off, we'd go—the two of us—we'd drive up to Gloucester. Deep conversations, you know?"

"I can imagine." Kenny was looking me now as if I'd revealed more than I had.

"So fuck me. Yes, I went. Don't ask me why I went."

"Maybe I will. Someday. But go on."

"He was trying to decide whether to get married. He carried a little flask."

"The scene is just getting abundantly clear. Where did Teresa think you were?"

"Who the fuck knows?"

I looked at him a moment, asking him to lay off. He didn't. He kept staring at me in that mildly accusatory way.

"Okay," he said finally.

"But afterward, after these talks, he'd drive me to his house, where I usually left my car. And the woman would be there. And he'd indicate all over the place that they were sleeping together."

Kenny had taken one of the pepper shakers and turned it upside down, then right side up again. His eyes were off me. He was seeing something else.

"I went by the house one time. I was with Nina. We stopped, we knocked on the door, there was the woman with the baby. Billy wasn't there; Ronnie was. It was like he was trying to hide it from us. Their little secret."

Kenny looked up. I could see in his eyes now the wish to believe something, at war with his innate skepticism.

"We went out to dinner. Patty was on her umpteenth miscarriage. Billy took me aside. He practically admitted it."

"The kid."

"Yes."

"Said, 'The kid is mine.'"

"Didn't say it."

"Implied."

"Yes."

"Strongly."

Kenny ran his fingers a couple of times up and down the pepper shaker. When I still hadn't said anything after five seconds, he looked up and commanded me to speak.

"I could have sworn."

"Could have."

"What is this, lawyer talk?"

"This is lawyer talk. Yes. Because I don't want to send detectives to hunt down the paternity of this baby based on 'could have.' Hortense Joseph's boyfriend has an alibi."

I stared at him, and he held my look for several seconds before glancing down at his half-masticated hamburger and pushing his plate a couple of inches forward. "He also has an Escort."

I was relieved to the point of irrationality by this last bit of information.

Kenny looked at his watch.

"You gotta get back?"

He nodded. I remembered that he had promised me a long lunch. I noticed that his gaze had gone to my Adam's apple. It was a kind of locker-room look I was getting from him now, as if he was checking me out without wanting me to know that was what he was doing. This had nothing to do with nakedness, of course, but with that other male nakedness, the character spill, the way we become, against our wills, psychically undressed in adulthood.

"Okay," I finished. "I've said what I needed to say."

Kenny looked exhausted now. I could imagine him leaving the office as soon as I was gone, driving home, taking his wife into a room, and demanding that he be held. It was what I wanted half the time now from Teresa, more than sex—just to be mothered, protected, allowed to loiter in the vicinity of a pair of warm breasts.

"You think he was lying to me, Ken?"

He seemed roused from faraway thoughts, but he was right with me.

"About the baby? I don't know, Tim. How long ago did you start having these conversations?"

I shrugged. "Long ago. Years ago."

He had picked up his fork and was holding it the way you hold a slingshot.

"Was he bragging? Did he like to brag to you, Tim?"

"He never needed to brag."

He looked at me: I'd just given him something more, I suspected, for his file on me.

"It doesn't need to be his baby for Hortense's husband to have wanted to kill him," Kenny said, as if this were a minor offshoot of the central problem. He placed his fork down gently and studied it. "But we can investigate it. I guess we can; I guess we should. The boyfriend has an alibi, but maybe it's not such a great one, or maybe he got somebody else to do it. Maybe—hell—maybe he got somebody to steal a car that looked like his and leave it in Winship, to frame Billy. Who the fuck knows?"

I could tell he had no investment in these words. They were all leading to something else.

"Whatever, it's a motivation, so we've got to go ahead." He looked at me now, sadness making indentations in the corners of his eyes. "But I'll tell you the question that won't go away. Shall I tell you, Tim?"

"Tell me."

"Are we going too far to try to help him out?"

I hesitated a moment, didn't say anything.

"I am not the most racially sensitive man in America, Tim. At least, I wasn't until recently. I wasn't, growing up. You will remember with some keenness the level of our sensitivity to things racial."

I moved my chin a small amount, just to let him know I was following him.

"Now I think: Why should a white guy get these kinds of breaks? This is some black husband, he'd be in here, we'd have gone to trial already. But he's the suburban Little League coach. Bend over backward, take it up the ass for him because everybody is half in love with him. Remember Patty's funeral? The fucking governor is there. The columnists. They were living this fairy-tale life, Billy and Patty."

He made a motion with his mouth that was all he needed to say. "God rest her soul."

"God rest her soul," I echoed.

"Now does this mean I think he did it? No. If I had to lay bets, I'd say he didn't. But why should we be making it our business to help the guy when he's perfectly capable of helping himself?" His eyes finally shifted away from me after holding on for a little too long. "But okay, for the sake of our friend we will investigate the paternity of this baby."

He drummed the tabletop, picked up the twenty he had placed there and returned it to his wallet, then slapped down his Visa.

"Which is probably a waste of time, but hell, loyalty to the tribe, huh, Tim?"

Outside, after we had argued about splitting the tab, when I was walking him back to his office, I couldn't get out of my mind the sudden fear of being buttfucked in prison. Maybe it was Kenny's casual words about taking it up the ass for Billy, but I found I couldn't shoo it away. There it was, the thing you fight against all your life. There it was, like an inevitability.

"Maybe this Hortense," Kenny said, "you think she's available? Maybe she can come watch my father."

He didn't turn or stop, but kept walking, and he lifted his hand, still without turning, to say goodbye.

eleven

A string of white Christmas lights—one set hooked into another, a seemingly endless succession of them—lined the pathway linking our yard to the DiNardis' that winter. The idea had come out of a complaint Gabrielle made one Sunday night when we were eating pizza in their kitchen. Gabrielle was studying fossil fuels in her combined science–social studies class at school (Bradford was educationally progressive, always looking for intercurricular connections); her teacher had infused the class with an awareness of consumption and waste. "We drive too much," Gabrielle would say at dinner. "We drive everywhere." And that night at the DiNardis', after the pizzas had arrived from a restaurant three miles away: "Look, we live right through the woods, and we drive here. We have to go all the way into town just to turn around and come back on your road. We use—how many miles is it?"

"Where's she getting this?" Tony, slicing into the pizza, asked.

"Her teacher," Teresa said.

"What is she, a Communist?"

"She's *not* a Communist." But as she said it, Gabrielle's face lit up into a smile of vast tolerance for her grandfather, whose face took on a mirroring glow.

Gabrielle, clear-faced and small-featured and heart-tuggingly lovely, had usurped Teresa's place as favored female in Tony Di-Nardi's constellation. He called her Princess (Nina was Sweetheart, a subtle but telling step down), and he loved to take her shopping at the classier malls—Chestnut Hill, Copley Plaza. To watch them in such scenes was to see how at home he was in the commercial world; he piloted his way through stores, and the corridors outside stores, like a captain guiding his boat through a channel he knew intimately.

That night over the pizza Tony had said, "All right, here's an idea. You're using too much gas to visit, we make it easier for you to walk. We light up the path."

So in January, after he'd taken down his own Christmas lights and plundered the post-Christmas sales for every new set he could lay his hands on, he rigged up a lit path to please Gabrielle, who (and I could have told him this) never used it, at least not at night or on any of the visits she dressed up for. Her teacher's influence would not go so far as to ruin a new, or even a semi-new, pair of shoes.

The path, nine hundred feet from end to end, became a kind of folly, a nutty thing to have done, until the night in February when the DiNardis were hosting for themselves a big party, an enormous party, to celebrate their fiftieth anniversary.

There had been discussions at one point in the planning of the party that it should require formal dress. In the end, the DiNardis stopped just short of that. But caterers were hired, and valets to park the cars, and it became, in anticipation, one of those nights we approached with a kind of dread.

The fear Teresa and I both felt came from experience: one or two cutting remarks had recently come our way when Tony didn't feel our appearance at an "affair" had met his exacting if unspoken standard. The perplexing thing was that I knew this side of him—the easily wounded perfectionist—stood beside another aspect of his old age. The same man who could wound us for ten minutes' lateness still made a game of sidling up next to me at those large parties they insisted we attend with them, to scoff at his cronies' pretensions. Sometime before Christmas, one of his compatriots in the building of Graymore's commercial Italian base had had the gall to write his memoirs and have them privately published and sent out as presents to two hundred of his acquaintances. *The Rewards of Life*, the book was called, and when at one of these parties

Tony sat next to me and caught sight of the tall, stooped, hawk-profiled author, he leaned close and whispered in a low, bitter tone, *"The Rewards of Life.* Jesus Christ, I can tell you some of the rewards that guy ladled out. I could tell you something about those rewards."

Neither side of him could be fully trusted, though, and we never knew which to expect. But for all the social uncertainty of the evening, it was still a sweet scene, starting out. The girls, dressing, had warring songs playing in their rooms. It was Shakira versus *Rent*, and we could hear them trading playful insults. While Teresa and I were getting ready, I looked out the window of our bedroom and experienced one of those moments of perfect, unanticipated contentment that could still come over me regardless of what else was going on. These could never last more than a moment or two. Awareness of the buried gun always came back to me, but sometimes it made the sweetness more intense. That night, the sight of the full moon illuminating the field in front of our house, and Scooter, who'd been let out ten minutes before, sauntering crookedly across the field brought me to that place. I stood at the window, arrested by the stillness of this scene, for several seconds.

I turned around to see that Gabrielle had come into the room to ask Teresa about the earrings she was wearing: Were they the right ones, these studs, or should she go for something droopy? Gabrielle would be twelve in the fall. Her breasts were still just buds, but her skin was wonderfully clear and soft and peach-toned, and it radiated in such a way that it gave her a mature confidence. It is an astonishing moment when you realize that your daughter is becoming the kind of girl who would not have condescended to date you in high school. I had a sense of her body under the pale violet dress. I could sense its life, its perfect ripeness. Without thinking about it at all, I said, "Come here."

She looked at me with a bit of surprise, her chin lowering a fraction of an inch. In truth, I couldn't have said why we'd grown distant from each other in the past few years, but we had.

"Come here," I said again; and quickly, to get something over with, she approached me.

"What?"

I didn't say anything at first. I touched her on the neck and watched her flinch a little. "Can't I tell you you look beautiful?"

Her eyes, though dutifully connecting with mine, made the subtlest side motions. "Sure."

I ran my hand along her neck to the top of her back and rubbed there. Just beyond her, I could sense Teresa's form on the edge of the bed, and I felt the stillness in the room and knew that Teresa was watching.

"Hey, you're acting like this is torture," I said, because I could feel her stiffening under my touch.

"No," she said, and looked down.

"I like the little earrings."

It meant nothing to her. I watched her taking in my words as if she was figuring out how to be polite to me.

"Okay, torture over," I said, and let go. She stood still a moment. Impulse drew her back to her mother. The evening's goal was to look gorgeous, and I could not assist in that. But something kept her there a moment, kept her with me, and I couldn't know what it was, what unspoken thing was in that thirty seconds' hesitation.

She turned around, ran to her mother, and said, "I think droopy," then swiveled back so that she was facing me, her hand over her mouth.

"Sorry, Dad."

She ran out of the room.

Teresa did not immediately comment. I had begun to notice lately the first signs in Teresa of a kind of matronliness. I don't mean that in an insulting way. There is a look a pretty Italian woman gets in her forties, if she is nicely taken care of, a settledness in the body and the face, a kind of falling into the formal posture, a declaration that nothing else is going to happen to this woman, no desperation or unsatisfied hunger will speed the aging process. I was always fighting against the part of myself that wanted to accept this. Tonight I wanted to declare to Teresa that it was all right with me that we were becoming older, duller, with less to look forward to. It seemed *all right*. Maybe ours had never been the great romance I had wanted it to be. Maybe I'd imposed a great deal on it from the beginning. No matter. It *was*. I wanted to convey something to Teresa of what I felt.

"She seemed uncomfortable with me" were the words that came out.

"Well, why do you think that is, Tim?"

I didn't want to speak anymore. In fact, I wanted to amend what I'd just said, to drop the subject.

"I don't know."

"You can't be selective about paying attention to her."

"I'm not." Already I hated where this was going.

"You can't make her think you love her just because she looks beautiful."

"But she is."

It could have gone either way, but when she looked at me, I saw a moment's compassion, and I was ready to shower as much gratitude on her as Scooter showered on us just for existing.

"She is," she said.

That was our moment. It may not have been a deep one, but we shared it. Gabrielle's beauty might just be a lucky mix of genetics and nutrition, but for us then it had the weight of an achievement. We let it stand there, a presence in the room, until, under Teresa's scrutiny, I began to feel shy, and loosened my collar.

"What?" she asked.

"Nothing."

"You look cute," she said, and that made me even shier.

Nina was in the doorway now, not filling the soft green dress she wore in the way Gabrielle had, but with muscled shoulders and heft. She was familiar; she was, to me, the known world. A warmth started in my belly, a deeply satisfying sense of all I had.

"Hey, girl," I said.

"I want to walk there," Nina said, and leaned into the doorway.

"That's a ridiculous suggestion." Teresa had moved to her and started to play with Nina's hair. "We'll get there in these nice dresses and they'll be full of mud."

"I don't care," Nina said, and appealed to me. There was a

gnawing look in her eyes, I didn't know what. "You guys in your pretty dresses can ride. Dad and I can walk."

"Do you want me to put something in your hair?" Teresa said.

Still Nina looked at me.

"I think it's a good idea," I said. "The O'Kanes can walk. There's no snow. The ground is as stiff as a board."

"*No!*" we heard Gabrielle cry from another room. She came in wearing the dangly earrings, which I thought spoiled the perfect effect she'd made before.

"Look," I said, "it's not even that cold. Think of all the oil wells we'll be saving."

When Gabrielle looked at me, it was as if our little moment of connection had never happened. She turned, betrayed, to her mother, who gave herself one last primp in the mirror.

"I don't want to make this decision," Teresa said. "Whatever decision I make, somebody's going to be mad at me. But I think we should go together."

We walked. Gabrielle was ahead of us, at a sufficient distance so she could convince herself she had nothing to do with us. "I want to remind you, young lady," I shouted, "this path wouldn't even be *lit* if it weren't for you."

Gabrielle carried her misery into the DiNardis, and Tony picked up on it immediately.

"What happened?" he asked, accusatory, looking right at me. He was dressed in a beautiful suit, a new suit, gray flannel with blue threading in it, and he looked slick and still tan from the two weeks in Florida he and Katie had taken after Christmas. We had arrived ahead of the earliest of the guests, and Teresa's sisters were due to arrive early, too.

Gabrielle moved past Tony to take a seat on a couch.

"That's the greeting you give your grandfather?" Tony was behind the counter in the kitchen, offering instruction to a woman and her two teenage daughters, the early cadre of the catering force that would arrive a bit later.

"Don't ask. She's mad at us because we made her walk," Teresa said, and approached her father and kissed him on the cheek.

The darkness of his skin, up close, seemed to come less from the residue of the tan than from age. It was as if his native swarthiness, the peasant essence of him, had taken over. I saw how Teresa's kiss meant nothing, how he accepted it as his due, no more. His gaze remained fixed on Gabrielle.

"Princess. You look beautiful. You should forget it," he said, but there was not the tender seductiveness Gabrielle was used to, and I thought I saw her register this—her slight diminishment in importance to him tonight—by the faintest movement of her left shoulder blade.

He waited a moment to see if these offhand words were enough to do the trick; when he saw they weren't, he turned back to me.

In his five-second perusal of my body, I saw the whole tone of the evening ahead. His one good eye had lifted and hardened. He took in my suit (a perfectly decent one) and my grooming, and it was as if he saw the son-in-law who had always been a thorn in his side, who had failed to provide that ineffable something that sons-in-law were meant to provide. Which was what, exactly? His judgment was so harsh as to be impersonal.

He turned to the hired women, looked at his watch, and said, "The cheese puffs go in at six-thirty, right?"

"Daddy, what can we do?" Teresa asked, sensing the difficulty and trying to fix it.

"Nothing, it's all done," he said, and left the room.

In his absence, I could see that Teresa wanted to blame me, but I just shrugged. Teresa, Nina, and I moved to the couch. Gabrielle shifted away from us when we came close.

"Oh, stop it, Gabrielle. You're acting like a baby," Teresa spat out.

I saw the lights of one of Teresa's sisters' cars pull into the driveway just as Katie entered the room.

"What happened? He's in a mood," she said, but Katie DiNardi was too much of a businesswoman of family life to allow much leeway to anyone's emotions, her husband's included. She went directly to the caterers and started to take over from them.

Teresa's sister Pat and her husband, Roland, came in then; there

were the greetings and the masked anxieties and the mildly hyster-
ical intonations between the sisters that let me know how much
was at stake for each of them tonight. Roland and Pat's two daughters, older than ours, with the heavily lipsticked, carefully coiffed
look of high-end Newton teenagers, gave us the once-over in the
way of teenage girls, moving their eyes over our clothes as if they
were operating the most delicate of sensing instruments.

When Tony reappeared, he moved with the distracted air of a
man who had just come from a meeting at which great, risky deci-
sions had been made, though whatever he had been doing upstairs
had to have been of a time-killing nature. He barely greeted Pat
and Roland and the girls, moved instead to the wall of windows to
check outside, drawing his lips back over his teeth as he scanned
the driveway. He glanced once at Gabrielle, to see if there had been
any movement there, before his gaze returned to the window.

"Your sister's late," he said. "Again."

The perpetually "late" Connie and Evan pulled up within a few
minutes of this remark. "Ignore him," Katie said when she saw the
kind of greeting they were getting.

Connie and Evan had produced the only boy among the seven
DiNardi grandchildren, a brawny sixteen-year-old hockey player
named Josh. They lived in Reading, where, to hear Connie tell it,
their lives were spent in a constant rush to get Josh to his next
game or practice, to buy Josh the new equipment he needed, to reserve Josh ice time in the off-season. Josh had attained a certain
fame in the family for having been not quite present but close
enough to the locker room where, a year before, after a scrimmage,
one Reading father had beaten another Reading father to his death.
Proximity to that horror hadn't left much of a mark on Josh. He
had the spiked hair and the large, flushed face of the teenage stud.
His sisters—one older, one younger—did not take their secondary
roles in the household to heart. Dark-skinned and black-haired like
their grandparents, they had the aggressive, no-nonsense manner of
girls who will someday take over a family business and carry it to
its height.

These were the Reading contingent: hockey and an oversize house and an oversize SUV to match. They ought to have been a comfortable fit for Tony, except they weren't. He had an unmistakable disdain for Reading; there was something too overtly commercial about the town, in his view, and he never gave it his full approval.

But then neither did Newton get the highest marks from him. He hated Newton's air of exclusivity and had once confided in me that Newton was a town only a Jew could love. Somehow he managed to convey all this in the way he surveyed his gathered family, as though they had arrived from outposts less civilized than Bradford, the family seat. Though I was convinced that underneath our leafy, genteel Clara's Home-Cooked exterior we were as deeply commercial as Reading, I didn't think he saw that, not yet. Nor did he see how we were as snobbish and attentive to the professional pecking order as Newton was. In his view, these unattractive qualities had been absorbed by an elusive third element, Bradford's seeming allegiance to something older and more durable. During our walks together through the woods we jointly owned, the word Tony used most often was "sure." He said it not as the beginning of a sentence or in answer to a comment of mine, but as a response to the revealed world: to the discovery of a stone wall or an old sheep path. It was as if he wanted to know that these things existed and would go on existing, and took comfort from that knowledge, in opposition or maybe blindness to the fact that a good deal of his worldly energy had been spent in trampling stone walls and sheep paths underfoot, at least metaphorically.

"Let's," he said when he looked up, though the cast of his eye seemed to reach slightly beyond this circle, "let's have a drink, a toast, how about, while it's just us."

The daughters made a roused, happy noise, though it sounded to me like they were forcing things.

Tony reached under the counter and drew out an ancient mandolin-shaped bottle. There was gold webbing around it. "I've been saving this," he said, and began pouring small amounts into brandy snifters and passing it around.

He raised his glass. "Who's making the toast tonight?"

The daughters looked at one another. I knew that no decision had actually been made, but Pat, the eldest, said, "I guess that's me, Daddy."

"Well, say—I don't care what you say—fifty years." As he spoke, he reached out and touched his wife on the shoulder. Katie looked uncertain of where he was going, but not afraid to look him in the eye. "Fifty years is not nothing." His voice had started to break, after a surge upward. "Tell them," he said, and looked down, overcome by emotion.

"Daddy," the girls all seemed to be saying at once, moving forward from their waists.

"My wife," he said, still not lifting his gaze. He nodded a couple of times, biting back on something. "Three beautiful daughters. Seven grandchildren." When he looked up, it seemed he had mastered himself. "I only wish *that* one would come and give me the hug I never got when she came in."

He had gestured with his glass toward Gabrielle, and I was happy to see her rise after a second or two and go to him. He placed a hand against her back and drew her to him. The mothers all let out a sigh, only partially laced with a competitive sense that Gabrielle had been singled out.

"Okay," he said, and lifted his snifter. We were all encouraged to drink.

It was a harsh, unhealthy-tasting cognac he had poured us. It tasted as if it had been closed up too long, but incompletely, so that some combination of cork and bottle and old air had conspired to put a rot at the center of it. Half of us gagged.

"Daddy, what *is* that?" Pat asked, putting her snifter down.

"Aged, that's what it is," Tony said, and smacked his lips. "Special. You kids want a taste?"

Ariana, the younger of the two Newton sisters, said, "Oh yeah, Grandpa, it looks great," and the others laughed. Suddenly the collective DiNardi mood turned to giddiness, as if we couldn't quite get over our delight in one another's company. Tony could do that to us, the relief in the lifting of his dark moods making every other problem in life seem manageable. My brother-in-law Evan clapped me on the back. We were suddenly clubby.

Things began moving swiftly then. The rest of the caterers arrived, bearing trays, shooing us from the kitchen. A band set up in
the oversize family room–den, where the dancing would be. Within
the next half hour the first guests arrived.

Tony's uneasy pre-party mood gave over to benevolence. He
moved from gathering to gathering as the rooms filled, his face lac-
quered with sweat and his dark lips creased in a permanent grin. At
each social port, he reached up and grabbed a friend's shoulders and
squeezed. It appeared as though he loved them all, harbored no ill
feelings even toward the author of *The Rewards of Life*. With each of
the women he executed a little dance step, appropriate to whatever
song happened to be playing. He had opened his suit jacket in reaction to the party's heat. Under his white shirt he appeared to be
showing off his enormous gut, like acreage he had cultivated since
coming here.

The last of the guests to arrive were Chip and Amy Holmes,
whom Tony had surprised us by inviting. Chip was the only one of
the men not wearing a suit. He'd dressed in a black silk shirt and
tight black pants, with a cool little silver bolo tie hanging from his
collar. A recent addition to his face was a small Fu Manchu goatee,
taking the form of a lick of hair under his chin.

Since we were the only people Chip and Amy knew, they tended
to stick by Teresa and me. But every once in a while Tony would
grab Chip by the shoulder and drag him over to meet one of his
friends. "This is *Chip*," Tony would say, coming down hard on the
final consonant, as if the extreme Waspishness of Chip's name required a kind of transcription. "We elected him selectman—he
won by a *landslide*—and he's going to clean up the situation here."

Tony ended this by hitching up his pants, as if to give some
indication of how much he meant business. What the recipient
didn't—couldn't—know was the string of fabrications contained
in this little speech. Though Chip's margin of victory had been
strong, it was hardly a landslide. And there was no particular dirt-
iness in the Bradford situation to be cleaned up. But no matter.
Tony wanted all his old compatriots to believe he had come here
like the sheriff of Dodge City.

"Only thing is, I don't know why he insists on looking like the Cisco Kid." Tony then wet and lifted one large thumb, moving it in the direction of Chip's chin. "Here, lemme clean that up for you."

Chip endured all this, but he seemed glad when Amy pulled him away from one of Tony's groupings and insisted that he dance with her. She had the big hair and enormous breasts of a former porn star (she practiced psychotherapy, very successfully, in Weston), and the two of them attracted attention not simply for their looks but for the skill of their dancing. It wasn't long before several of the guests stopped their own dancing in order to watch. Tony grabbed Katie and tried to imitate Chip's moves, which he did clumsily, though with great enthusiasm. When the song was over, it was Chip, not Katie, who received Tony's hug. I watched Tony's hand reach up to administer one of his painful shoulder squeezes, while Chip moved deftly out of range.

The bandleader interrupted. He announced that everyone should find a glass; there was to be a toast. The caterers made the rounds with champagne. Then he handed the microphone to Pat.

Pat was an older, darker version of Teresa, but where Teresa's Italian features had been planted on her face glancingly, by a light brush, Pat's had been deliberately impressed, stressed almost to the point of coarseness. Like Teresa, she was a teacher, and as I watched her holding the microphone, smiling and reaching for a glass of champagne, I couldn't dodge a moment's depression at thinking that this was Pat's big moment—this toast at a suburban party— that her life contained no moments in the larger world to match it. This was unfair, I knew: she had her class of students, her own family, her Newton social life. But wherever this feeling was coming from, when my glance landed on Josh, I couldn't help sending him a little cheer: *Do* it, man. Fuck all the girls. Grab every bit of glory you can get. Don't live here. Don't *live* here.

"Everyone have a glass?" Pat asked.

There were shouts of assent.

"I wanted to say a few words about my parents—" Pat began.

Tony, as soon as the next of the evening's events had announced itself, had taken a short step away from Chip, and his face had gone, in an instant, from one of wild and happy celebration into a graver, more considering mode. This required him to gaze at the floor and move his foot over it, like a man on a beach scanning sand with a metal detector.

"They brought us up, of course, in—well, you just have to look around. Comfort, is that the word? I mean, it seems like it was more than comfort."

Pat cleared her throat, moved one hand up to brush away her hair, then briefly looked down. Tony mimicked her. He was locked into something now.

"But lots of people grow up comfortably and don't get what I think we got from our parents. We always felt like we were cared about. I mean, *really* cared about." It was one of those speeches in which the speaker seems to be tugging at words, as if to indicate how inadequate they are, and making sounds afterward alluding to some impossible eloquence riding under the surface. "Sometimes too much, I think." Tony looked up, a big grin on his face, as if this were a laugh line, one he was ready to join, though no one else was laughing. "But always from love." She lifted her glass. There was a moment's hesitation on her part. She was deciding, I knew, whether she'd said enough. "I mean, there's so much more I could say, but I'm afraid I'd cry."

"Cry!" someone shouted.

There was laughter, but Pat shook her head. "No, not tonight. This is just—to appreciate them, that's all. To Tony and Katie. Fifty years."

I wondered if I was alone in feeling there had been something deliberately withheld in this speech, some resistance to going as far emotionally as Tony would have liked, as if this were Pat's sly form of rebellion. In Tony's face I thought I caught a shade of disappointment. He licked his lips and glanced downward as the rest of the guests echoed Pat's "fifty years" and drank.

Then there was cheering, until Tony lifted his arm to stop it. He was wearing a big smile now—not a convulsed smile, more a deliberate one. He moved to the microphone, holding his glass high. He gave Pat a kiss on the cheek and said, "Thank you, Sweetheart."

Then he waited out everyone's attention. "That was a beautiful speech, but you know I have to have the last word."

His single eye glistened now. He scanned the crowd and licked his lips and said, "Always," and continued to smile and wait out the laughter.

"No, because here's the truth, and they won't say it, because they're modest kids, but I wanted to tell you something about these kids of mine. You know they insisted on paying for this party. My daughters and their husbands." He tilted his head in an unconvincing show of humility. "And parties like this, let me tell you, don't come cheap."

I had begun my scan of the sisters and their husbands because I wanted to see their faces now and compare their responses to my own. I expected we would catch one another's eyes and share the joke—the old man at it again—which would be the only way to remove ourselves from the humiliation of what he was doing. We hadn't paid for a thing.

But as my gaze landed on each of the faces—Pat, Connie, then Evan and Roland (Teresa's face was hidden from me)—I had the eerie sensation that I was the only one feeling remotely *odd*. Tony was going on, nodding sagely, alerting us all to the gravity involved in paying for things, and what it implied of filial duty and filial love. He was putting into the evening what Pat's speech had left out: a kind of excess. Watching the others, it began to make a kind of unhappy sense to me. Allowing him to put this illusion on display was our way of paying him back, for the gift of Josh's hockey equipment, for help in meeting the financial exigencies of Newton, for our presence, Teresa's and mine, in Bradford itself.

Tony didn't make a long or emotional speech. When it was over, the band took up their instruments and went back into the music. Tony shook a number of hands, his face looking emboldened and newly excited, and Chip Holmes sidled up next to me.

"Must have cost a pretty penny, huh?"

He was making a close assessment of my face, an assault I tried to dodge.

"You'll see me out tomorrow morning," I said, because I had to say something, "pushing a shopping cart, looking for bottles. I need the nickels."

He laughed, though it was the weakest of jokes.

I told him I was heading up to the bathroom, and escaped.

There were three bathrooms on the second floor of the DiNardi house. I chose the farthest one, the one least likely to be sought out by the other guests. I shut the door behind me and for a moment or two didn't even turn on the lights. Then I did.

I sat on the closed cover of the toilet and tried to empty my mind. Three magazines were in a wicker basket next to the toilet. *Boating*, *Modern Maturity*, and *Brides*. I picked up *Brides* (it was the closest) and flipped through the succession of articles on wedding cakes, on dresses and floral arrangements, on gift ideas for the groomsmen. In the photographs, pastels dominated; the light was soft and the sun perpetual. There was a predominance of blondes, and the world seemed exclusively white. Even the very occasional black guests and the single black bride looked as if they had been dipped in the vat of the suburban, so that their color seemed an accident, a clung-to habit from earlier, less-prosperous days. Looking at them, I couldn't help but remember what Kenny had said about the story that the city embraced to explain Billy's and Patty's shootings: our fear of the dark ones appearing out of nowhere, gunning for us. Not these. Not these clever, handsome men and this doe-eyed, full-lipped bride who gazed directly at me, who I wanted to fuck. I wanted to loosen my pants and unleash my already partially swollen dick and imagine those thick black lips parting to receive it. We would go inside this old stone house where her very white wedding was taking place, and I would fuck her blind. Jesus. I would fuck her back into her own blackness.

I dropped the magazine and tried to forcibly close off this line of thought. Already my hand had gone to my dick, already I was holding it, feeling its familiar distended skin. I was forty-one years old, too old for this, but did we ever stop looking for consolation this way? The desire to fuck a beautiful black model could at least remove me for a second or two from the impoverished life of being Tony DiNardi's son-in-law, humiliated at a grand party because this confused, powerful man could not finally decide what he wanted.

But who could? I thought back to my single moment of connection with Gabrielle in the bedroom a few hours before. She had offered me the tiniest of openings to get back to something good between us, and within minutes I had blown it by forcing us to walk. The same thing seemed true of the whole relationship: it had been a thing I did not know how to sustain. This was, after all, the same little girl I had packed into a Snugli and walked into the woods with eleven years ago, ecstatic at every minuscule gas-induced pucker of her lips. Another man would have honored the beauty of those moments by seeing, before him, a single determining goal, and following it. I envied and wanted to be that man. He would have said no to a great deal: to the insistence of Tony DiNardi that a big house must be built, to the belief that the scale of your life need not correspond to your actual accomplishments. A connection would have existed between that man and his wife, that man and his children. Straddling the state, alone in his car, he would have resisted the promise of the radio dial: the promise that one further touch would take him to the land of "Losing My Religion," of "China Girl," where you, above all others, become the one who does not age, who remains adorable—a sleek, burnished figure, suitable for the stage. That man would have resisted, too, the nights with Billy in the car in Gloucester, looking at the water and listening to his low, seductive voice. But I had not been that honorable man.

The further shame of it was that I wanted to get away from these feelings by escaping to my own house and narcotizing myself there. Perfection right now would be popcorn and a stupid action movie, holed up on the couch with Scooter. A little marijuana. A little self-soothing. That scene, so close at hand, still seemed remote, because on the way to it I would have to pass through the house, I would have to accept the false congratulations of the Italians, I would no doubt be seen leaving by Teresa. So I continued to sit there for another five or ten minutes, like a man waiting for a self-induced anesthesia to kick in. I think I actually had my head in my hands, and my effort to numb myself was so successful that I didn't hear—or at least didn't register for several seconds that it had anything to do with me—the knocking at the door, the voice of Teresa shouting, "Tim? Are you in there, Tim? This is important. You better come downstairs."

twelve

The cause of Teresa's distress wasn't evident right away. She looked worried, but the worry seemed more about me than any downstairs tragedy: What had I been doing in the bathroom so long? From this look I knew at least that no one was dead, the children were all right. "He's here," she said, and turned so that I should follow her.

Who "he" was I didn't immediately guess, though I should have. I first saw Billy across the dance area. Teresa had positioned me so that I couldn't miss him. He was wearing a leather jacket that looked new and expensive, but under it his shirt and jeans looked Billy-worn. He was talking to no one. His eyes, even from a distance, seemed to have a glazed, faraway look.

"What's he doing here?" I asked.

Teresa just sent me another look, as though I ought to be closer to the answer to that one than she was.

My first reaction, though, was that I was not responsible for him. Someone else must have invited him. I hadn't spoken to Billy in weeks, and I'd certainly never mentioned anything about Teresa's parents' party. The funny thing was, he didn't look entirely out of place. On the level of absurdity, Billy's presence was not significantly greater than the sight of the white-haired landscape-gardening aristocracy of Graymore dancing to the band's rendition of "Hot Hot Hot."

Teresa pointed to her father, standing at the opposite side of the room in the company of the big, thuggish captain of the valets.

"I had to convince him he was a friend of yours," Teresa said.

"He thought we were being crashed, and he wanted that guy to hustle him out."

"I think 'that guy' might have spent the night in the hospital. If that had happened." I braced myself for something. "Okay."

I moved toward Billy, which required some dodging of the wild elderly dancers. Billy saw me when I was about ten feet away. The only sign of recognition was a slight movement on the right side of his mouth. He was holding a plate of food.

"To what do we owe—" I asked, and stood next to him and folded my arms.

He had something in his mouth, and he pointed up to it, indicating that I should wait.

"This is good," he said after he'd chewed and swallowed. "This chicken, what is it?"

The DiNardi's had gone upscale in their food choices tonight.

"I think it's some sort of Malaysian thing—you want me to ask the caterers for the recipe? What are you *doing* here?"

He reached up to work out a piece of chicken that had gotten stuck between his teeth. He let my question hang a minute. Then he took another bite and, between his first chews, said, "I came looking for you."

"Where? Here?"

With his chin he indicated my house, through the woods, and I knew of course how he had gotten here: he had followed the white lights.

"It's okay for me to be here, isn't it?" he asked, as though there could be no reason why he should be asked to leave. He went on eating, and I couldn't help, in the midst of the discomfort I knew I should be feeling—and *did* feel, though only a little—a faint amusement at his entitledness. It had never been a problem for him at Winerip, not from the beginning: the parties and the Boston caterers and the good poured champagne. He had taken off his coat and thrown it on the couch of commercial Boston, and women had looked at him. There are women who when asked during an introductory conversation if they want to fuck do not blink. Freddie had told me some of those early stories.

From across the room, though, I could sense Tony DiNardi's anger.

"Listen, in a little while we should maybe go over to my house," I said. "Not that you aren't welcome here, Billy, but I think this is freaking my father-in-law out."

Billy licked his fingers. "He's got that *Reservoir Dogs* guy over there at his side. I noticed." He glanced at me as if taking me in for the first time. "Is this embarrassing you, Tim?"

"No."

His look forced another, different answer.

"All right, a little. It's embarrassing me a little."

"Well, I don't want to do that."

"Good."

"These people know who I am?"

"I don't think so. I don't think they remember. And—"

I was about to tell him he looked different, worse.

"And what?"

"Memory is short."

"Right. They've moved on. I was last year's tragedy."

He put his plate down at his feet.

"Maybe we should hand that to one of the—"

"What are you, afraid it'll break?"

"No."

But it was exactly what I'd been afraid of: giving Tony reason for offense. I lifted the plate and held it. It took a full minute before someone came by with a tray.

"Well, now that the dish has been collected, we can relax, huh, Tim?"

I finally took a hard look at him. His eyes were laced with red capillaries. They were—but I knew this already—a stoned man's eyes. I had hesitated until now to really take him in, because to do so was to take in a kind of decay I had no experience with. I thought my fear, my disgust, my sadness might all be showing in my own eyes, but if so, Billy didn't shy away from them.

My eyes lowered to take in his jacket. Up close, I could see it was more than expensive.

"Nice," I said.

"You like it?"

I whistled appreciatively.

"I'll buy you one."

There was a covering impulse in that offer of his. I could see it embarrassed him a little, the sheer beauty of this precious thing he wore on his back. For an instant it flashed across my mind that Billy was spending his money wildly, recklessly—the Toyota, Ryan's room and board, this jacket, and who knew what else?—in order to wear down what he'd gained from Patty's death. He had been a rich man for the past several months, and he didn't like it.

"Jesus, you look stoned," I said.

"Oh, I am."

"Well, let's get you to my house. I'll make you coffee. What'd you come for anyway, Bill?"

Tony was moving across the room toward us, the valet just behind him. The determination in Tony's expression broke just long enough for him to offer smiling greetings to those in his path, though the smile was confined to the bottom half of his face.

"Now listen," he said when he'd come close, lowering his head as if he were making a weapon of it. "I don't believe you were invited here."

"It's all right, Tony. I'm taking him to my house." I touched Tony on the shoulder, and he looked like he was a half step from swatting my hand away. "He was looking for me. He found the path. Listen, this is a guy who lost his wife less than a year ago."

It was like putting a bridle on Tony's one good eye: he held back from whatever the next thing was that he intended to say. As for Billy, he looked beyond this little altercation and seemed to be staring into the face of the valet, who had put on one of those dreamy, above-the-battle looks Italian guys put on an instant before breaking into violence.

"Come on," I said, and tried to pull Billy away with me.

Tony's face, now that he saw that Billy was going to leave, didn't exactly soften, but shifted from anger to a kind of probing. "You're the guy . . . your wife was shot. Mogavero."

Billy, still impassive, shifted his eyes from the valet to Tony.

"I'm sorry for you," Tony said.

There was only the flicker of an apology behind Tony's eyes, but I knew what it had cost him. He turned to the valet and made a swift, hard motion with his chin. "You should direct your men outside," he said. "There may be some early . . . people leaving early."

The valet turned to him without seeming to understand the shift that had taken place here, but he obeyed the command.

Stepping up to take his place, an eager social smile on his face, was Chip Holmes.

"Hey," he said, as though this were a small, exclusive confab at the party, one he felt no compunction about crashing.

Tony wore a look of mild social embarrassment. "This is . . . I'm sorry, I forget your first name."

"Billy," I answered for him.

"Right." Tony nodded and turned to Chip. "Mogavero. You remember, in the newspapers."

"I remember very well. Chip Holmes." He held out his hand, smiling in a way that seemed a little unhinged.

"You'll excuse me," Tony said. "I have guests."

His hesitancy to leave was one of the reasons why I could never give up on Tony. There was a bedrock decency to the man, even if, at times, it may have been at odds with other, more urgent impulses. There was no reason he had to stay and keep Billy company, but somewhere in him was the feeling that he ought to.

"I knew you were a friend of Tim's," Chip said after Tony left us. "I'm awfully sorry."

It took me a couple of seconds to realize that Billy's celebrity was what was making Chip act so weird.

"We're actually heading back to my house," I said quickly, because I didn't trust what Billy's reaction to Chip might be.

"Well, I'll walk you a little, how's that?" Chip asked. "Rumor has it you walked here. Along the famous Path of Lights. I heard all about the little fight."

Billy, beside me, was studying Chip with the identical disbelieving gravity with which he had studied his four former acolytes the day they'd shown up at the paint store where he worked. It was as if he knew all he had to do was keep absolutely still, and the buffoonery of the world would endlessly reveal itself.

"Billy," I said. He looked at me, and I caught the roused smile in his eyes.

I kept my hand on his arm until we reached the back door, where my coat was. Chip was still with us.

When we were outside, heading toward the path, Chip kept prattling on. "It's an ingenious invention, these lights, isn't it? I mean, never mind what it cost Tony. Think of the *time.* And think of the guy out here—he's what? seventy-five?—plugging one set into another." At the start of the path, Chip said, "Hey. Guys. Wait."

He reached into his pocket and removed what looked like a very soft, beautifully embroidered lady's purse. From it he removed a joint and held it up as if to study it in the moonlight. It was an odd kind of display, a way of showing off while still making gentle fun of himself.

"Hmm? Hmm? Gentlemen?"

Billy took a step back so as to study Chip. He looked suddenly more tolerant.

"*Very* nice stuff," Chip said, and reached into his pocket for a lighter. "I didn't think it would go over big at the party, but I've been *dying*—" He lit up and drew in smoke and expanded his chest mock dramatically before handing the joint to Billy. "Because to tell you the truth, Tim," he said on the exhale, "the party is driving me crazy."

"I'm not offended," I said.

Chip watched Billy drawing in smoke with the intensity of a man trying to learn a new skill just by watching. "Where are you guys going, by the way?"

"We have some business," I said.

Billy handed me the joint, but I passed it on to Chip without taking any.

On its next pass around, Billy held on to the joint. Chip stood there waiting, smiling as if to maintain normality, even as Billy took two long tokes and seemed to be preparing for a third. Finally

Chip cleared his throat. "A-hem," he said, followed by a whistling snort of laughter, to let Billy knew he got the joke. By the time Billy stubbed out the spent joint without ever giving it back, the moment had taken on some of the tension of a school showdown.

"Well, I guess you two *do* want to be alone." It was spoken with a certain elegance; it allowed Chip to turn around and go back to the party without serious loss of face. I kept waiting for him to do that. I could apologize to him in the morning, making a quick call to explain Billy's eccentricities. Why I should care so much about this—why my social standing in Bradford should still be a cause of concern—was something I only briefly marveled at, because Billy had spoken. I didn't hear exactly what he said, and neither did Chip.

"Hmm?" Chip asked.

"I said, why do guys wear earrings?"

Chip offered a thin, savvy smile, to let Billy know he was capable of fielding any ball, there were no impossible corners in his green universe.

"I mean it. Why?"

Chip looked at me, half smiling, asking for an assist. Billy reached out and touched one of Chip's ears. He fondled it with a slow, nearly sexual interest. He studied the underside of Chip's ear, where the stud was clasped. Chip endured all this, though something—a planned defense—was going on in his eyes.

"And this," Billy said. He touched Chip's bolo tie. He was like a man in a store, fondling an object he would never buy.

"Hmm?" Billy asked. "I mean it, 'cause I don't know. I'm a simple guy."

Chip's smile widened. "Oh, I don't think that's true at all."

"Tell him, Timmy."

"I think, probably, we should—" I gestured to the path.

"No. I grew up in Winship, you know?" Billy said to Chip. His earnestness was so convincing, I wondered if it wasn't the result of some advanced state of stonedness. "I stayed there mostly. I come to the world, to a place like this, and I don't understand. Earrings. Or those little ponytails guys wear. Why? I mean, you're not wearing one, but you look like the sort of guy who's at least considered it. You look like the sort of asshole who looks at himself in the mirror and thinks, Shit, what would I look like in a ponytail? I bet you have had that thought, Chip. Tell me. Admit it."

Billy was smiling now, and so, marvelously, was Chip. It was like a duel of smiles.

"Good night," Chip said in a high, lilting, self-mocking tone, his intended exit line.

Billy reached out to touch the bolo tie one more time, and Chip's arm lifted to block him—very quickly, impressively—except that it became Billy's excuse to grab the tie with his other, free hand, and then force it upward against Chip's throat, holding Chip for a few seconds so that he went up on his toes. During this—it lasted only seconds—Billy smiled as if it were a teasing gesture on his part, a form of friendly arm wrestling.

"Billy," I said, trying to break it up, but Billy had already released Chip.

"Okay," Chip said, and looked at me. If we'd been boys, this would have been the moment when he'd have spat out the damning accusation that had ridden under us all night, and said something like, I know you didn't pay for this party. You didn't even pay for this house. But it was, after all, the sort of thing boys did. We didn't need to.

"Shit, Billy," I said after Chip had headed back to the house.

"You don't like him."

"How do you know that?"

"Oh, I can tell. I can tell everything. Come on. Take me to your house. Make me that coffee. Sober me up. Though I'm not, strictly speaking, drunk."

Billy put his arm around me. He held me to him, and we walked the path. The close contact—the surprise of it, and the sudden intensity—rolled over whatever feelings I'd had about the scene with Chip. Before us, the long string of lights shone against the hard ground, and we walked, with Billy's arm clutching my shoulder, and the thick, furry presence of his body against me, very warm, very human.

The late February cold—it had deepened since I'd taken this walk with my family a few hours before—made things snap on either side of us. Branches moved in the slight wind. Billy didn't let go. I felt an impulse to ask him to define things—what was this tight holding about, anyway?—but I didn't. Billy lifted the fingers of his free hand to rub his nose, and started to whistle a little. That was the only human sound except his breathing. For those few minutes it took us to walk the path, with his hand never releasing its tension on my shoulder, it was like being caught up, not uncomfortably, in his larger impulses. Like being tucked under the fin of a large fish and carried, its night vision relieving you of the necessity of keeping your eyes open.

"There's your big house," Billy said when it was in sight. He spoke gently.

From this angle, the house looked overlarge, but then it often had. I was aware of a man, me, who had often come out on this path—younger, mostly, and child-laden. I was feeling the old lost pride, keenly sensible of the fact that those old feelings had been nobler things than what I was feeling now.

When Billy let go of me, it was, for the first moment anyway, almost unbearable. I stood there a moment, biting back on this feeling.

"We going in?" he asked.

"Sure."

Up the stairs, Scooter did all he could to press the door open for us. Even in old age he possessed that wide-open neediness that set his tail wagging wildly and his body shivering and buckling at the sight of company. I patted him on the neck and walked Billy to the kitchen, where he made himself comfortable at the counter.

It felt funny that it was my house.

"What can I get you?" I asked.

"Nothing, Tim. I'm fine."

"All right. If you don't want anything, why don't you tell me?"

"Tell you what?"

"What you came for."

Billy looked to the side, distracted and seeming to focus on the furniture. "I understand my brother came and left something with you," he said.

I was too shocked to say anything. He had spoken as though it were some inconsequential thing.

"Must have been a surprise." Billy was wearing the small, kind smile that had started before he spoke, except that now he seemed to want to demonstrate a larger measure of empathy.

"It was. Yes," I said, and felt a small flood in the belly.

"I'd like it back." The smile remained. He was determined to keep this in a minor key.

But for me, no response seemed appropriate. I must have looked frozen there in the kitchen, and Billy laughed lightly. Then he simply waited.

I bunched my chin stupidly, thought of excusing myself, going into another room.

"Tim," he said, tilting his head forward, drawing me back.

"I didn't think you knew" was all I could come up with.

He held back his response; I could see him doing that. After a moment he puffed his cheeks out, got up off the counter stool, and came up behind me. He settled his big hands on my shoulders and began rubbing. I was torn between enjoying it and wanting to shrug him off.

"It's okay," he said quietly.

He stopped rubbing and stood beside me. We both now faced the range.

"You told Kenny about Hortense's baby, Tim."

"Yes."

"Before I told you to. I think I told you I wanted to hold that information."

"I thought it could help you."

As stoned as I knew he was, there was something careful and precise about him now. He was weighing everything he said.

"You know what they did?" He chuckled. "They are so—They took me to a McDonald's. The cops. To question me. And they offered me a straw to drink my Coke. It's no big deal, right? I mean of *course* you drink Coke out of a straw. So I took it. But when I'm finished, they put my straw into a bag to throw it away, and at the last minute I realize it's the only thing in the bag. There's all this other garbage, but they're throwing away this bag—empty except for my straw. And somewhere in this restaurant is another cop. I can't guess who it is, because it's all guys with kids. But maybe one of them is talking to his kid in a way different than guys usually do. More animated, maybe. To look normal. As soon as I'm not looking, that guy is going to carry his tray to the trash, like this is as everyday as you can get, and he's going to take the bag with my straw out of the trash. DNA."

He shook his head. He covered his face with his hand. "They think I'm so *dumb*, Timmy. The cops. Why do they think that?"

"I don't know."

"That's how I knew you told Kenny. When I saw them doing that."

I wasn't looking at him then, but I felt him looking at me. It was like we were just on the other side of something certain, of a group of words that would wipe out any remaining ambiguity, and I prayed they wouldn't be said. I could still free myself—I believed that. All I'd have to do was march out to the backyard, dig up the gun, hand it to him, and say, All right, get out of here. I never saw this gun, and Ronnie never came here and asked me to hide it. He would leave then, and I would rejoin the party. It was the memory of the emasculated faces of Roland and Evan that kept me from doing that. At least that's what I told myself.

"The other thing—I don't *know* this, but I can guess—is that they paid a visit to Hortense. She's a black woman—an *island* black woman, she's got an *accent*—what the fuck do they care? They would have taken one of Charles's toys. One of his—what are those things, those little nipples a kid sucks on?"

"A Nuk."

"Right. They would steal one of those. Compare DNA. They'd think Hortense wouldn't notice. If *I'm* dumb, she's a cretin. That's the thinking. The Boston cops." He shook his head.

"So," I spoke finally. "If they find out he's yours, they have to go back after the husband. Right? That's what you wanted." It felt stupid, weak, to be holding up the story he'd constructed, as if asking him to go back to it.

"Yes. You thought you were helping me."

Billy followed that by taking a breath. Then he touched my hand. My two hands were resting on the range top, and he touched one of them, put his whole hand on top of it and pulled gently, tenderly at the skin.

"Where is it, Tim?" he practically whispered.

"I don't understand why the timing was so important."

"Let's just say it was, Tim."

"I don't understand this. Are you saying you killed her?" Afterward, the only way to deal with having said those words was to look around the kitchen, to pretend to a distraction, to hide the thumping of my heart in anticipation of the answer.

Billy's response was to look at me with a mixture of disappointment and pity, then to go to my refrigerator and open it. He looked over the contents, picked up a couple of things, and rejected them. "I wish I had a little more of that Malaysian chicken," he said. Then he closed the refrigerator door and came to me. I anticipated another of his sexual approaches and was on guard against it. Instead, he just stood there.

"Where is it, Tim?"

"I want to know what I've done."

"Do you?"

"Yes."

"Okay. You did me a favor. Now I want to protect you. I want you to give it back to me, and it never happened. You do this, Tim, and you're free."

I was gripping the handle of the oven door very hard. I felt that.

"Yeah, but I need to know. Still."

"No, I didn't kill her, Tim." He started glancing around the room.

I didn't completely believe him, but I was grateful anyway for his saying it.

"Now do I need to start looking for it?"

"You think I'm such an idiot I'd hide it here?"

Billy looked encouraged by that. "Okay. Good. Tell me. Where?"

"I'll give it to you if you tell me the whole truth."

Billy moved around the adjacent dining room. My question had bothered him; I don't think he actually thought he'd find the gun there. He sat on one of the chairs and went silent for a moment.

"Here's what's going to happen, Tim. They're going to find out about the paternity of this baby, and that's going to make them less interested in Hortense's husband."

"Why?" His hesitation in answering was making me feel stupid, a step or two behind him. "Are you saying the baby's not yours?"

He covered his face in his hands, leaned into his elbows, rubbed his eyes, then released them. "Probably not. No, I don't think so."

"You practically told me, Billy."

He glanced over at me with light amusement. "Yes. You were panting with excitement. Billy fucked a black woman and gave her a baby. That is, like, the white man's fantasy, isn't it? We don't even admit that in our *brains*. It doesn't make it anywhere close to the front of the brain, but it's there. You *loved* what I was telling you. All I had to do was suggest it."

I stared at the range again. It seemed the only safe place to look.

"So probably not, Tim. I mean, I fucked her, but I'm as pristine as anybody. I wear rubbers. I'm as scared as anybody, too, about— you know, about disease. Now that's settled, I can't tell you why I need the gun, but I need it."

"What'll you do with it?"

Billy shrugged. "I told you I can't tell you that."

"Listen, if you killed her, Billy, this is it."

"This is what?"

I just closed my mouth hard.

"Tim, I want to protect you. This DNA shit is going to change everything for the cops, all right? If I'm not the father of this baby, what the fuck excuse would Hortense's boyfriend have for trying to kill me? That's the subtlety of their thinking. So they'll hit up my brother, and who knows what he'll say? And then one night you'll get a visit from the cops and you will have to show them. They will turn your house inside out and dig up your yard until they find it.

And then you will go to jail." He raised his eyebrows. "And in jail they will love your redheaded ass, Tim. And your girls will not live here anymore. Not because they won't be able to afford it—Daddy over there will take care of things—but because the embarrassment will be so intense—"

"It's in the woods," I said, to stop this scenario as much as anything. "I buried it in the woods. I doubt we could find it. The ground's frozen."

"Well, we can try." He stood up, absurdly cheered by this. "Come on."

I hesitated before opening the sliding glass doors that led out onto the deck, but as soon as we were out there, I realized how foolish it was to be going out without a flashlight, without digging tools; as hopeless as the plan was to begin with, this made it more hopeless.

"Wait here, Billy. I've got to get some things."

"Don't be long," he said, and leaned against the deck railing.

I turned on the light in my garage, and in that overbright light, all the things I had neatly hanging against the back wall above my makeshift "workbench"—my hammers and saws, my weekend carpenter's little world—looked like the tools of a criminal. I found a flashlight and picked up a hand rake and walked around the long way out, out the garage door and around the back of the house. The sight of Billy leaning against the porch rail, smoking a cigarette, struck me as the seediest thing I'd ever seen.

I turned on the flashlight and shone it in front of me. He joined me on my way into the woods.

"This'll be impossible," I said.

He didn't answer.

"I mean, I don't know where I went into the woods. It could have been any—"

I didn't finish the sentence. Instead, I shone the flashlight into the first layer of trees as if there were something meaningful, something scientific in that act. We followed the light until we were six or seven feet in.

"I don't remember how far I went in, either."

"What'd you, just bury it somewhere?"

"Yes."

He took the flashlight from me and waved it around. Small patches of snow still lay in here, over a much thicker layer of fallen leaves. I had ceded responsibility to him, as if he'd be more able to find it than I would.

"Jesus, didn't you think to *mark* it, Tim?"

"I wasn't thinking."

"No. Fuck no."

"What was I burying, Billy? How the fuck did I know what I was burying?"

He got down on his knees and began pawing at the ground in various places, uncovering leaves.

"You don't remember how far in you got?"

"I don't."

He made a sigh of profound dismissal of me, as if the last and most important thing he had ever asked me to do, I had fucked up. Standing over him, hearing this, and holding the small rake in my hand, I suddenly felt as if I were holding a dangerous weapon. As if I could lift it and club him. I wanted to throw the rake away, but that would not help things.

"I think it was farther in. I think I was farther in. I didn't want anybody to see me."

He shone the flashlight in my face so I had to turn away.

"You are a dumb shit. You know it?"

"Put the flashlight down."

He kept it right in my face until I pawed at it to push it away, and that started a scuffle. Billy hit me on the side of the face with the flashlight—I didn't think deliberately—and I hit him somewhere on the side with the garden rake, and then, just as quickly as it had started, it was over, and we stood, both of us, breathing hard.

He shone the flashlight in my face again, but this time not in my eyes. "Oh shit, look what I did."

I reached up and felt a bump on my cheek.

"Going to be bad. Going to be a nice bruise there, Tim." He lowered the flashlight and shone it on the ground. "It's hopeless, isn't it?" he said.

I couldn't stop touching the new bruise, which seemed to be growing. A clean swipe with the garden rake would put Billy down, but then what?

"I thought I'd come out in the spring," I said. "That was my plan. When everything melted. I figured there'd be a patch that looked different from all the other patches."

"Oh, that was a smart fucking thing to think."

"I swear to God, if you don't stop insulting me, I'm going to hit you with this thing."

"Are you? Go ahead."

He deliberately turned his back on me and then moved a few feet farther into the woods. I heard him unzipping and then watering a patch of snow, maybe to try to melt it. It was about all I could take.

"Jesus, Billy, you fucking killed your wife, didn't you? You killed Patty—"

I had to fight the urge to cry, which I hated. But the speaking of her name was the first time I'd allowed her to become real again. The girl in the front seat of the car on those nights when we drove together. "Jesus, Billy. Don't you remember *anything*? Don't you remember dancing with her? Jesus Christ."

He zipped himself up and came toward me. "I remember."

That was all. After a moment's silence, in which all he did was look hard at me, he grabbed the back of my neck and pulled me toward him. He wanted me to sob against him—"Go ahead, go ahead," he was saying—but I pushed him away.

"You're a fucking monster."

"You think so? You really think so?" He ducked his head slightly, so that he had to look upward into my downcast eyes. He grabbed one of my hands and pumped his own chest with it. "Remember me, Tim? You think I'm a fucking monster? Really? You really think I did this?"

He released my hand with some anger. "Okay," he said, as if he was waiting for me to come around to some superior logic. "Listen, if you are done asking stupid questions, we can deal with this very real thing, Timothy. Okay? We've got a gun buried here, and I guarantee you that now that no other suspects exist on the horizon, they'll start coming around to my house, talking to my brother. I'm going to give you an assignment, Tim. Find this gun, okay? Find it. Search high and low. Find it, and when you do, call me. I will get rid of it."

"Why don't you just tell Ronnie to shut up about it?"

"Nice. But I'm not there when they question him. My brother is retarded, Tim. We never used that word, growing up. He was almost normal. My father beat me up once for using it. Nice guy, my father. The intellectual. Beat the shit out of me. This is the thing we could never admit. I think it'd be easier for my father to think I was a killer than to admit his son is retarded."

He looked at the ground a moment, then back at me. "If I show Ronnie the gun, I can tell him I've had it all along. That you called me the day after he brought it to you and insisted I take it back. That will be your story. I will fucking save you if you let me."

The plea in his face seemed as honest as anything I'd ever received from him. "Only the deal is, you can't ask me bullshit questions. You can't ask me if I remember my wife. You can't even *enter* those places with me."

He ended this by slapping me against the shoulder, hard.

"Jesus," I said.

"Okay," he said. "I'm going home."

It was, however, too late for Billy to make a clean escape. Just as those words were out of Billy's mouth, we heard a voice calling, "Who's in there? Hey!"

It was unmistakably Tony. His voice came from a distance, from behind my house. The flashlight, which Billy had left on, had given us away.

"Turn it off," I whispered, and Billy did. We remained still, and I prayed he'd go away.

But Tony was already moving toward our spot of woods, shouting, "Who the hell is in there?" and I gestured to Billy that we should meet him. At the last moment I had presence enough of mind to throw the garden rake away.

Tony, with Nina beside him, had covered half the distance between us by the time Billy and I stepped out of the woods. Nina, when she saw it was me, came running to meet us. But before she reached us, she stopped and looked up at us, uncertain.

"I got sick, Dad," she said.

"What's the matter?" I asked.

"I don't know. I felt like throwing up."

Tony was moving slowly out of the dark, nothing but a form, really, large and barreling slowly from side to side in his beautiful suit.

"What were you doing in there?" Tony asked.

"I was just showing him——."

I didn't finish. Tony took in the flashlight in Billy's hand.

"Showing him what? I thought it was kids in here. I thought it was hooligans."

I shrugged and made some kind of noise, something I hoped would suffice as an answer. "Why'd you leave the party, Tony?"

He dismissed the question with a single movement. "What happened to your face?" Enough light existed apparently for him to make out the bruise.

Again I said nothing, and Tony stared up at me with the highly developed probing gaze of the old Graymore warrior. Then, having come to whatever conclusion he had come to, he looked over my shoulder into the woods and put his hand on Nina's shoulder. "Come on, Sweetheart," he said, murmuring, "I've gotta get back," as he began walking her toward the house.

thirteen

It was now late February, and my trips into the woods were only frustrating. The ground was hard, packed leaves covered nearly everything, and I kept looking, apparently, in all the wrong places. On days in early March when it felt like the thaw might be starting, I brought Scooter in with me; he was my excuse for spending so much time in there. I had him sniff my hands, and then I pointed to the ground, but he only looked at me with his ancient trust, his tongue hanging out, panting after the thrilling onset of another spring.

It didn't help that I had so little time. March was the month when we presented our fall list, before the professors could lock in their course book choices for the following year. Endicott was excited that the editors of our long-anticipated gay and lesbian anthology had completed their work. We were planning to bring the book out in August. The salesmen had all been provided with a table of contents and a glossy forty-page sample to be handed out to prospective buyers. At a sales meeting, we'd been pitched the book by our company president and by the well-muscled young Brit who was one of the book's editors. The shades were pulled down in the Endicott conference room, and we watched a video presentation that began with images of naked gymnasts training under the grainy black-and-white light of 1920s film stock while the piano of Erik Satie played. We were to make the videotape available to the interested.

I took to the road with this material, but where once upon a time the earnest young salesman would have pored through the forty-page sample looking for specific examples to cite in my meetings with professors, I found myself resisting it now, hoping against hope it would just sell itself.

This became my life for a while. Weekends I searched for the gun; weekdays I drove to Hanover and Northampton and Middletown, or else to New Haven or Williamstown, and kept my distance from the *Endicott Anthology of Gay and Lesbian Literature*. On the nights when I had to stay over in motels, I distracted myself with pay-per-view, settling usually on one of those dark thrillers in which men like me, middle-aged white men with families, found themselves in deep trouble. The only stories that could engage me now were ones in which Michael Douglas or Bruce Willis sweated and came close to death or to losing a child, before being saved in the nick of time.

In my solo moments—there were many—I constructed a way in which my situation might still work out decently. Billy, upon receiving the gun from me, would turn himself in. The murder would be shown to be unpremeditated, a lover's quarrel. Passion had taken over. There were holes in this, of course, ones only a desperate man wouldn't see right away: If passion had taken over, why was Billy carrying a loaded gun at the time? It always ended like that, in that sort of quagmire, and then I would turn in the other direction and begin constructing scenarios in which Billy turned out to be telling the truth, not having done it at all.

In the meantime I had started to fail as a book salesman. The book would not sell itself, at least not to my usual clients, the men (and some women) who had come to depend on my regular presence. Most of them wore perplexed looks when I presented them with the sample pages. "This is not what I do," one of them said bluntly, as though I'd come selling a prosthetic device to a man with all his limbs intact. So it became clear that if I was to succeed (and Endicott made it very clear that we were all to succeed, a substantial investment had been made in this book), I was going to have to broaden my network. I was going to have to knock on the doors of professors I had up to this point avoided.

I always knew who they were. Every campus had its share of them. You could tell sometimes what kind of mind occupied each office by what was posted on their doors. If the main image from *Eraserhead*—the nimbus of overgrown hair and under it the doughy, poorly shaped face—was posted on a door, you pretty much knew who was going to answer it if you knocked. And if a simple blue square of index card with posted office hours was all that was there, you knew something else: someone wanted to be approached, was looking for company whether he knew it or not.

There were two images posted to Helen Fallows's door at Smith the day I knocked there. One was Joan Crawford and Mercedes Mc-Cambridge squaring off against each other, holding six-shooters in *Johnny Guitar.* The other was an excessively pierced, indeterminately gendered face sulking in close-up. But I'd been told by someone I trusted that Helen Fallows was the reigning queer theorist at Smith, the one most likely to be interested in the book I was hawking, so one day at two o'clock, the precise start of her office hours, I waited outside her door.

I had little hope for this encounter, but also little choice. The raw salesman's despair I hadn't really known since the beginning of my career had come back. I was newly aware that for years I had been selling not a book, but a life to my clients—at least the agreement behind such a life. In our conversations I could sometimes feel the actual force of that agreement: worldly ambition, academic excellence—these gave way to something else, to the shared memory of the first indescribably good sip of beer on a Saturday night, as the light fell and the coals glowed and you waited, staring into your thick woods, with a plate of salmon steaks to be grilled. To support such a moment, I had always been able to suggest, you didn't need anything cutting edge: John Cheever would always do, or Hawthorne or Melville, or any of the men ranging through the pages of "White Guys." Whatever the darkness in their stories, you always had the feeling that Cheever and Hawthorne and Melville knew the beer-and-woods-and-salmon moment, and that they secretly, guiltily affirmed it.

No such scent of the agreed-upon life wafted out from under

Helen Fallows's door. She was already with a student, and while I waited, three others lined up. I tried to smile at them, but the foolishness of my smile turned back on itself. When Helen Fallows finally dismissed the student she was with and came to the door, she seemed surprised to find me there. "What can I do for you?" she asked, more polite than I'd expected. She was a short, heavy woman with an eye problem even glasses couldn't correct; behind one of the lenses, the left eye veered off under a milky film. For a moment I thought of her as Tony DiNardi's lesbian double. I lifted the glossy cover of the forty-page sample and told her I was from Endicott. She stared at the title and asked if I might wait until she'd seen all her students. Twenty minutes later, there were still two waiting, but she told me to step in.

Helen Fallows's desk was covered, as were her walls, with announcements, invitations to conferences, memories of previous conferences. But her look was not unwelcoming, and as she flipped through the sample, she stopped to read in a couple of places with evident interest. I wondered, for a thrilling instant, whether my luck wasn't going to hold and this woman—this tough sell—was going to say yes to Timmy O'Kane.

Finally she looked up. I thought I saw the trace of a smile on her lips. In my younger days I'd had an instinct for this turn in the conversation. I'd known brilliantly how to offer up the nakedness of the young salesman asking for help as he gazed across the field of the wounded that Literature represented.

Tell me who you are, Helen Fallows might as well have been saying.

I could feel a part of myself ready to leap at this. But something felt lodged in the way of pure instinct. I felt slow, less than brave, too willing to take the long way around when the quick lunge was what was called for. I found myself hiding behind the editors' names, the contributors' names, knowing right off that it was the wrong choice.

"Sure, the people are good. Everybody's good. We're *all* good." She shrugged and laughed. "But there are a million of these books. Why this one? What's special?"

I reached into my briefcase to take out the video.

"We have something here for you to watch."

She shook her head and pushed the offered thing away with one hand. "Promotional material. I'm up to my neck in it. That's what you're here for, right? To cut through the crap."

"Yes." I smiled, understanding from a look in her eye why she had so readily invited me in. She wanted to know how a man who looked like I did would possibly sell such a book. With a short movement of her chin she alluded to students waiting in the hallway: please, I don't have all day.

I moved the video from hand to hand, wishing it were a ball of some sort, something I could sink my fingers into. In spite of the fact that I thought I was being very subtly played with, the challenge kindled something in me. I remembered the feeling that had come over me when Billy put his arm around me and held me on our walk along the path of lights. Whatever wish to succeed I had in me was speaking: Tell her about that feeling. Show her how all her assumptions were wrong—how a guy like you, a straight guy in a suit, lover of the beer-and-salmon moment, tell her how even *you* can feel such a thing. And tell her further—make up a moving story—about how in reading this book, you realized it was not just for the committed deviant (but *never* use that word), how it spoke to people like you. *Tell her that.*

I was ready to, but somehow I didn't know how to begin, and in gathering my thoughts together rather than plunging forward, I lost her.

"Well, I'll look at it," she said. "I'll consider it. You come back on your rounds, I assume?"

And that was that. I went outside on this late March day where there was everywhere the promise of spring, early dogwood bulbs, lime laid down in lines along the low grass. I found a bench and sat. I hated this sinking feeling I carried with me, the feeling that I had come close to success. What a coup that would have been, to sell a book to Helen Fallows! How it would have sent me into all the other offices I needed to storm with a rush of confidence. For a moment I believed that being able to sell this book would solve all my other problems in life. Then that moment fell out, and an opposite feeling took its place. Sitting on that bench, I had an irresistible conviction that things—all things, all the parts of my life—were about to turn very bad.

The police arrived, as I'd been warned by Kenny they would, late one Friday afternoon. I was returning from New Haven, another fruitless trip. On the long drive, I'd tried to listen to an Erik Satie tape I'd taken out of the Bradford Library (as if some form of osmosis would help me sell; I was not about to give up), then turned it off and made a sweep of the oldies stations. On Friday afternoons the deejays cater to secretaries getting out of work. The songs are uniformly joyous and stupid (it is the time of the week you are most likely to have to endure "Sugar Sugar"). I turned the radio off and rode in silence the last forty miles, thinking it was actually time to rake the leaves out of the flower beds surrounding the house. I'd neglected this early spring duty, one I'd always enjoyed.

The car I found sitting at the top of our driveway was nondescript, one of those Dodges or Buicks built to look like Jaguars. I could not place its owner, but when I went in and found Teresa at the dining-room table with the two investigating officers, I knew right away who they were. Their suits, in any case, would have given them away; there ought to be a rack in Filene's that says COPS. One of them was Irish and graying, though only in his late thirties, with the rangy look of the brilliant weekend softballer. He was Officer Cahillane. The other, Officer Medina, was shorter, with the slight hunchback and the rodenty face of the British actor who plays Mr. Bean.

There was coffee and, of course, expensive cookies. You don't seal your fate with Chips Ahoy, but with something more elegant, something from the faux-British import store that had recently opened in one of Bradford's mini-malls. I shook hands, then sat and didn't even try to look nonchalant. There seemed no point to that, or to holding my cards close to the vest, either. I knew that any attempt I made to whitewash Billy would probably backfire.

"Kenny told me you guys would be coming," I said.

The Irish guy—Cahillane—made a little grimace. Were we all supposed to pretend Kenny wasn't keeping his friends informed?

The Italian guy made polite chitchat about Kenny, how well liked he was by the department, what a prince.

Yes, sure. I nodded.

"We understand you used to double-date with Bill and Patty Mogavero," the Irish guy cut through.

"They've been asking me about those dates," Teresa said, smiling.

"Oh, really?" Still I didn't smile or put on a face to try to pretend those dates had been conventionally innocent, and I noticed the cops noticing this about me.

"Did you see him alone?" the Italian one asked. "As friends, I mean. I understand there used to be a kind of club. At the Branding Iron restaurant, in Allston."

"Sure," I said. "It wasn't a club. We used to eat there, that's all."

"And sometimes you and he—Bill Mogavero—would talk alone."

"Billy," I corrected him. "Yes, we'd talk alone."

"Did he ever talk about his wife? His marriage?"

There was something about this Medina that was overly proud of his own shrewdness. I was pleased with myself that I could peg him as a BC grad. I'd known enough guys from BC or Holy Cross to be able to pick up what was Jesuitical in their manners. It came down to a slight shivering in the way they held their heads—intellectual reserve coursing through the body like a low fever.

"His marriage? Yeah. He talked about it."

Then, because I had no intention of talking deeply and truly about Billy's marriage and also because I was tired from the long drive, I went to the refrigerator and found a beer. I opened it and returned to the table without offering one to either of them. They reacted to everything I did as if it was some kind of fodder for them, the outrageousness of my rudeness intensely revealing of *something*.

"Tim, aren't you going to offer them any?" Teresa asked, not as if she was shocked, but as if she wanted to act shocked for these cops. "Can I get you guys one?"

They both shook their heads.

"Where are the kids?" I asked her.

"Nina's upstairs being a hermit. Gabrielle's at Molly's. I've got to pick her up."

"We thank you, Mrs. O'Kane. We can talk to your husband," Medina said.

I drank the beer, loving my own elusiveness, without any clue as to where I was finding it in myself to play so fast and loose with them.

"Oh, I don't have to leave for a while," Teresa said.

"So what kind of conversations were these?" Cahillane, the blunter of the two, asked.

Medina sent him a look, subtly chastising him for his directness.

"What we mean is," Medina said, "we know this is private territory. No one's accusing your friend of anything." He lifted his hand, a gesture I understood from growing up among Italians. It was an attempt to state the seriousness of a situation while removing it from threat. "I don't know how much your friend Ken Di-Giovanni has told you."

"Nothing, basically."

"Except that we were coming."

It was the first time he'd caught me at anything, and his eyes registered it. The sides of his mouth went up in appreciation of his own smoothness.

"Except that you were coming," I echoed him. "Look, I think I know where you guys are driving. There's no point in pretending this wasn't a guy who went into marriage with a deep ambivalence. Which makes him part of—what?—ninety-nine percent of guys who get married?"

They both offered nonplussed looks.

I turned to Teresa to pretend to apologize. "I'm part of the other one percent, of course."

It was such an odd performance I was giving that Teresa raised her eyebrows slightly. But I found I couldn't stop.

"He had a long history—lots of dating, lots of women. But I think he loved her. I don't think he felt any compulsion to get married just for the sake of getting married."

Unlike me, I might have added.

"I mean, the *places* they used to take us." I turned to Teresa. "Remember?"

She nodded. Some kind of warning I couldn't read was in her eyes.

"What kind of places were those?" Medina asked.

"These old Italian places. Ten Acres, out in Hudson. Pier 4."

Medina glanced at Teresa. Apparently this checked out with what she'd told him, because I caught the look between them. He was waiting for a slip from me.

"I'll tell you something. This is something I'm sure Teresa didn't tell you, because she doesn't know. Billy had a row of apple trees in his backyard in Waltham. And the branches hung down too low for a decent game of catch. Two weeks before the shootings, he had some tree guys come and clip the branches. This is still like months— what? two months?—before his kid would have been born."

I smiled at them, as if this said everything, and I watched Medina make a note of this.

"Do you know the name of the tree company?"

"I don't. What are you—"

I couldn't believe he would go to them, and as I wrestled with this, it occurred to me that Billy had been lying.

"Did you ever see the trees?" Medina asked.

"No. I didn't go over there much. At first, but not later."

"He had a girlfriend living with him pretty recently after his wife was killed. Did you think that was strange?"

"No." I hadn't had to put on a face. "Not if you knew Billy."

They both simply stared at me. For the first time, I noticed that Cahillane was chewing gum, though slowly.

"Who else have you guys talked to?"

Medina thought a moment, then consulted a list he took out of his inside jacket pocket.

"Fred Tortolla. You know him, right? He's another member of this club."

"It's not a club."

"Right. He told us Mogavero had girlfriends—apparently, while he was married. Did you know about this?"

"Freddie told you that?"

"He also told us about a fire that was set when you were all— still in Winship. High school. High jinks, I guess."

"Yes."

He paused a second, studying me.

"But you stayed behind. The others ran off; you stayed. Your friend took the heat on that one. Assaulting a police officer. A little jail sentence. But you were there."

"Yes."

He gestured with his chin, as if I'd implied a lot with that yes.

"He protected you; is that how it worked?"

"I didn't have anything to do with setting that fire. I never touched the cop."

"Right. But in the transcript of your friend's hearing, he said everybody took off."

It began to feel like a scene I'd watched a hundred times, the slow breaking down of a guy like me. I ran one finger around the lip of my beer bottle and for a moment felt out of control. I looked out the window, at the woods. Let them follow my gaze.

"We'd just like to know—" Medina spoke. "Lots of guys seem happy in their marriages. We all put on an act for one another, let's face it. But did he ever let you see—something else? Like maybe he wasn't so blissfully happy?"

"We were jealous of them," Teresa answered, though the question had been meant for me. "Weren't we, Tim?" She reached over and touched my forearm. "We used to come home from dates with them, and well, it was kind of overwhelming. That much passion between two people."

I wondered if she was covering for me, sensing my loss of control.

"Losing the babies was hard, though," Teresa said. "You could see it taking its toll on both of them. We went out—there was one dinner in particular, just before this last pregnancy. Billy was drinking a little heavily. It was understandable, though. I mean, you could understand it."

I was sitting there, remaining silent, and I could see both cops were waiting for me to throw in my two cents.

"But this one looked hopeful," Teresa said.

Without any warning, she started crying. Medina looked bug-eyed and astonished, but Cahillane took a handkerchief out of his pocket and offered it to her. Teresa shook her head, reached for some tissues on the counter.

"Sorry."

"It's all right," Medina said. I knew from his reaction to her outburst that he was unmarried, or else had a hopeless marriage.

I put my arm around Teresa, knowing as I did so that we must look stiff, that this was an unconvincing picture to offer these guys. I suspected they had already pegged me as someone they would want to talk to again later, alone.

"It's an upsetting business, Mrs. O'Kane," Medina said. "We regret it, but it's our job to look at every possibility."

"He didn't kill her," Teresa said, at the end of her tears now. "I mean, somebody else, I could believe it. But you should have seen the way he looked at her. There was this incredible—" She looked toward me, as if to secure my agreement. "I just think he needed her so much. He was this big, bluff guy, and I'd have no trouble believing other things about him—that he cheated on her, I mean. If I was married to a guy like him, I think that's what I'd expect."

The two cops' eyes shifted to me for the briefest moment.

"And she *knew*—I mean, she confided to me once. Sometimes, with a certain type of guy, you expect that. It's almost like they do it *because* they feel such need." She blew her nose and then looked around herself, as if a little startled by what she'd just said. "Pardon my *Redbook* magazine school of psychology. There are certain things women are smart about, that's all."

"No doubt," Medina said.

Teresa looked at him, a little insulted, red-faced from the crying.

"Is that how you saw it, Mr. O'Kane?"

"I don't read *Redbook*," I said, and smiled, I wasn't sure why. The urge to defend Billy had dropped out of me entirely. So I shook my head. "If he needed her, I think he fought hard against it. I guess you're not going to get a glowing picture of their marriage from us." I took a sip from my beer and watched them.

"Did he ever *say* anything?" Medina asked.

"Like what? 'I want to kill my wife'? No."

"Men have been known to say it, believe me."

"He never did."

"And—" Medina leaned forward now, and his mouth twisted into a funny little knot. "This is delicate. We know you spent time with him in the hospital when he was coming out of surgery. Can you tell us, as he was coming out, you know, regaining conscious-ness, did he ask about his wife?"

It was a harder, more surprising question than I'd anticipated, though the answer was not hard to find. In defense of Billy, he'd been only half conscious. Besides, there'd been the infant there. I'd assumed someone had already told him about Patty. But no, he hadn't asked.

"I can't remember."

Medina looked patiently at me, but I saw him making a mental note.

Nina had entered the kitchen. She went to the refrigerator, though it was unclear that she wanted anything there. Both officers watched her every move, as if the analysis of our lives here, as much as clues about Billy, were what they had come for.

"Honey, these are police officers. This is our daughter Nina."

Cahillane nodded to her—a father for certain. Medina, who I was coming to believe lived under a rock somewhere, only went on staring.

Nina was in one of her moods. They had increased of late: strange illnesses, quickly on her and just as quickly off, depressions that had Teresa worried. I offered her an inviting gesture, and she came and sat on my lap. I touched her hair and she lowered her head to my shoulder and I offered this scene—this core of my existence—to the officers as if to say, Take this, fuckers. Everything you think you know about us, add this to it.

"Well, I think maybe we've asked our questions." Medina stood. "No need to see us out, Mrs. O'Kane. But I'm going to—" He removed a card from his wallet and placed it on our table. "Anything you want to add."

Teresa saw them out.

Nina remained in my lap, affectionate in the near-sexual way that, within a couple of years, I knew she would no longer find it possible to be.

"Take me to the batting cage," she said.

"It's not open yet. Remember? They open it to coincide with opening day at Fenway."

"Then take me to the store. I need an Ace bandage."

"Ankle still sore?"

"Mm hmm."

Her warm body snuggled in deeper. There was ecstasy in this. But when Teresa returned after seeing the cops out, I knew she was annoyed with me. She gathered their cups and put them in the sink.

"What?" I asked.

"Nothing." But her refusal to open up lasted only seconds. "I hope you're as loyal to me as you are to your supposed friend. Practically telling them he's a murderer."

"Who?" Nina asked.

"Nobody," I said. "Listen, go put your sneakers on. We'll go buy the bandage."

"Who's a murderer?"

Teresa looked at her. "Nobody's a murderer, Nina. Those policemen were just here to talk with us about Billy. You know Billy, right?"

Nina hesitated. "The one you were out in the woods with?" she asked me.

"That's the one," I answered quickly. It was not a question I thought Teresa should be invited to dwell on. "His wife died, remember? She was shot. It's the policemen's job to explore everything, every angle. Your mother's upset because Billy's not the sweetest guy in the world, and I didn't think there was any point in not saying that. It doesn't mean he's a murderer."

Nina looked at me with a glassy expression, then slid off my lap, went to get her sneakers.

"What's this about the woods?" Teresa asked.

"Your father never told you? The night Billy came to your parents' party, we were out there."

"Doing what?"

"What do you think? Smoking dope. Your father the narc spotted us. We had to make up a quick story."

"God, things are getting awfully sordid around here, aren't they, Tim? The police coming to our house. You and your friend sneaking into the woods for dope. This is like some advanced stage of teenagerhood, isn't it?"

I turned away from her. Unconsciously, or maybe more than that, I reached up to where I'd received a bump from Billy's flashlight that night. Teresa had of course noticed it, and I'd made up some excuse. Now I prayed she wouldn't put two and two together.

"The least you could do is paint a rosier picture of him," she said, going blessedly back to her original gripe.

"Why?"

"I don't know." She leaned forward and covered her eyes. "Because of what he's been through, maybe. Does he need this?"

I thought she might cry again, but I remained in my chair.

"Hasn't it ever occurred to you for even a second that he might have done it?"

Teresa looked at me with a film over her eyes (I hadn't been wrong that she'd been about to cry) that her offended sense cut right through.

"*No,*" she said, and after a moment's still-astonished pause: "*Tim.* A black man pulled up to that house and got out and *shot* them. Everybody saw that."

"Right."

"It was *seen*, Tim. What are you *saying*?"

I stared at the floor. If ever the moment had come to tell her, it was now. The phone had started to ring. I could have said, Don't pick it up. On the fourth ring, just before the machine would have gone into action, she reached for it.

It was her father. I could tell immediately by her tone. Servile in a daughterly way, falsely glad to hear from him. He called two or three times a day.

I drove Nina into town for the bandage. It was one of the strangest rides, because I kept expecting to see the cops. The result, no doubt, of having seen too many movies: I had them following me, scouting my every move.

When we got home, I told Teresa I wanted to do the garden beds, changed into work clothes, and, hoping she wouldn't notice, slipped into the woods. It was an exceedingly warm afternoon, one of those freakish April days in Massachusetts that makes you think, against the evidence of all previous years, that spring will actually arrive on time and not make you beg for it all the way into June. I tried to follow some remembered line from the night Ronnie had come, turning back toward the house to try to navigate that way: how big, exactly, had the windows been when I'd tried to look up after the burial? I remembered now. In September the trees would have been loaded down. That I could see the house at all meant I could not have been more than ten or so feet in. Using that distance, I made a traverse of fifty feet parallel to the house, studying the ground. The burial spot would have been small, not even a foot in diameter. If ever I was to find it, it would be now, while the growth was still low. And it had to be now. The presence of the cops left me feeling slightly desperate.

Scooter came and joined me, uninvited, and as it turned out, it was Scooter who found it. He started sniffing at a certain spot. I went and looked. Nothing would have given this away as the place to dig. A covering of moss had grown already, and there was a tiny oak sapling pushing up. I shooed Scooter away and started digging with the hand rake I'd brought. Four or five inches down, I felt something hard. It might only have been a rock, except when I uncovered it, I scratched something papery and brown, wet and seriously decayed. I dug a circle, nearly big enough to lift it out, and at the last instant realized Scooter was no longer with me. When I looked up, I saw Tony in the woods, fifty or so feet away.

Scooter had gone to join him. I didn't believe he'd seen me yet, so I dropped the hand rake, stood up, wiped my hands on the sides of my khakis. I stepped forward about six feet and called, "Dad!"

No smile of greeting appeared on his face. If anything, he looked suspicious. He was wearing a pair of pants not unlike mine, though more expensive and worn old-man style, where the dick is completely hidden and the seat tucks into weird fissures in the aging male ass. His powder blue jacket looked sort of lovely against the faint dusting of new green in the woods.

I started to move toward him.

"You spend a lot of time in here," he said, having waited until I was close enough so that he wouldn't have to raise his voice.

I glanced around, as if my answer required an appraisal of the woods.

"You know what I'm looking for," I answered, trying to work up a little smile, "is stones. I want to do something with the gardens this year. Something different."

"Stones."

"Yes."

He gazed at the ground, the liver spots on his face standing out a bit more than normal. "I was thinking you might be thinking of selling your half of the woods." He reached down and picked up a deadfall branch and tried to break it in two, but couldn't. "I know there are people snooping. The economy stinks, but the price of land goes up. Figure that one, huh?"

"No. I wasn't thinking of selling."

He met my eyes finally. From the look of his, I wondered how much he actually knew.

"Because it would be a terrible thing to break this up. It becomes like every other town then." He took from one of the buttoned side pockets of his jacket a roll of LifeSavers and offered me one, which I refused. "You know; you see them; it's easier for them to chop down all the trees, so you see these little treeless lots. Why people want to live there, I don't know." He shrugged and sucked on his LifeSaver. "Though you could get three or four hundred thousand for what you've got here."

"I wouldn't do that, Tony."

He chewed in an exaggerated, unattractive way, then bit down hard on the candy in his mouth. "So, stones," he said.

"Yes."

Now his face seemed to fall into an older posture, one I remembered from the early days, when I was a suitor turning up at his door, about whom he'd been deeply unsure.

"What the hell are you hiding in here, Tim?"

I hesitated before saying, "Nothing."

"Bullshit."

Then I said nothing.

"I find you in here with your friend last month. Middle of the night. What are you two doing in here? I ask myself. Maybe nothing. But then I notice you keep going in. I call Teresa. Where's Tim? She says the cops have been to your house and now you're in the woods again." He shrugged, a performance of bafflement.

"Dad, I told you."

"*Stones?*" He chuckled, and afterward wore a mirthless smile. "Listen, let me tell you something, Tim. When my daughters were young, sometimes boys would call up. And I guess I must have had this reputation as a hard guy. They were afraid of me. One time this boy called up, I answered the phone. He pretended to be a girl. He made his voice go high. Like this." He raised his voice into a falsetto to demonstrate. "And I wanted to crush this kid's head. So help me God. For lying to me. Be a man, I'd say. Say your name. Take your punishment, whatever it is. *Stones.*"

I just went on staring at him, knowing any words I could say right now would be wrong. He looked over my shoulder to see if anything was visible. We were at least far enough away so that he couldn't see the hole I'd dug.

"Your friend ask you to hide something for him?" He asked it gently, solicitously.

"No."

"*No?* So what were you two doing in the woods that night?"

"We were smoking pot, Tony. All right?"

His eyes widened slightly, then narrowed again.

"Marijuana? Something stronger?"

"Marijuana."

"Teresa know?"

"Yes. Sure."

He thought about that a second. "Tell me. How do you get a bruise on the side of your face from smoking marijuana?"

"I tripped."

He looked at me with absolute hatred then. His finger went out, pointed so hard that it shook. "Don't you fucking lie to me, Tim. You're out here smoking marijuana, you say." He had started past me, and he began looking around. "*I* say how do you get a bump on the side of the face from smoking that stuff?" He scoffed, made a false laugh. "Jesus, that's a good one. You think I'm *stupid*?"

"No, Tony."

He was moving in the right direction. He would come upon it, a certainty.

"You think I'm an idiot? I don't know what goes around? What are you two, boyfriends? What are you doing out here, woods, middle of the night? He comes looking for you at my anniversary party?"

"Tony. This is stupid."

"I get lies from you, Tim. I get nothing but lies. What am I supposed to think?"

Scooter was walking just ahead of Tony, looking up at him. I could only pray that Tony's direction moved slightly to the left. But Scooter was leading him in a direct line to the burial spot.

"Tony, I've been meaning to talk to you."

He stopped, turned back to me.

"About what?"

"I need help."

After a moment of staring, he allowed the glimmer of a smile to appear.

"You know what? You might as well say, You're hot, Tim. You know that game? You hide something. You're cold. You're hot. You just said, 'You're hot.'"

"But I do. I need help."

"What kind of help?"

Already he had started forward. Within ten steps he would be there.

"I'm in trouble," I half shouted.

There might as easily have been an arrow pointing to it. Tony zeroed in on the spot. Scooter, having led him there, looked back at me, tongue protruding: Did I do good? The old man bent down. The formidable left cheek of his ass pulled hard against the material of his slacks. He reached down into the hole with difficulty and turned to look back at me.

"What the hell's in here, Tim?"

He was having trouble getting it out. I wasn't in any hurry to help, but I was also fresh out of excuses. There are moments when it is foolish to do anything but submit.

I didn't like the look of him huffing and puffing as he dug, so I went forward, got the rake, made a circle wide enough to pull the gun out. The bag fell apart on its way to the air. The gun looked smaller and snubber now. Its silver was duller. There was rust on the barrel and on the handle.

"There," I said, laying it down between us.

Tony didn't say anything. He was on his knees, and he rocked forward a bit, looking at the gun. It was as if someone had presented him with awful financial news; he could barely take it in without trying to alter the figures before him.

Then he stood with some difficulty and studied the knees of his trousers, soiled from the ground. He hadn't looked at me since I'd placed the gun down.

"Put it back in," he said finally, an immense sadness in his tone. Finally his eyes met mine. "That's the gun he did it with?"

"I couldn't tell you that," I said. "His brother brought it to me." I wanted to go on with the story, but I'd decided that making excuses for myself was the wrong way to go.

"Is it—still loaded?"

"I haven't checked."

"It's a dangerous thing to have around the kids." He was breathing hard now.

"I never thought the kids would come in here looking."

He made a quick check of the house to be sure we weren't being watched, but in the moment afterward I caught sight of some deeper sense of exposure working its way through him. It was as if he wanted to hide from the eye of whatever local god lingered here in these woods.

"Put it back. Bury it."

"I can't do that."

"Why not?"

"I've got to return it."

Carefully, as though it might still have some active agent in it, he turned and stared down at the gun.

"First thing, check to see that it's not loaded."

"Tony, I don't know how to do that. I've never handled a gun."

After a pause he said, "Neither have I," and we stared at each other, acknowledging our mutual helplessness.

"Return it where?" he asked.

He had mumbled. I had to ask him to repeat it.

"You said you had to return it. Where?" Now he was annoyed.

"I can't tell you that. But I'll take care of it."

I had tried to speak with authority. Tony had recovered sufficiently to gaze upon this put-on authority with some of his old skepticism. I saw in his face, though, his realization that he had no choice but to give power to me now.

"You'll get rid of it. Hold the trigger—don't touch the trigger when you pick it up. Hold it away from you. You could shoot yourself."

"Right."

I picked it up by the handle, which was encrusted with dirt from its winter residence. I held it down and away from me. "You've got to cover for me, Tony."

He looked as if he didn't know what I meant.

"Distract Teresa."

He gazed up at the house. "She's gone. Gone to pick up Gaby. I talked to her just before she left. Nina's the only one home."

"Okay," I said. "Go in and distract her. Take her to the other side of the house. Just let me get this to the car."

"You don't have to get it all the way to the car. Take it to the back deck; find something to cover it with." He kept staring at the gun as if the sight of it hurt him physically. "Where you bringing it back to? Your friend?"

"I told you, I can't tell you that. But this'll be the end, I promise."

"How long's it been in there?"

"Since September."

"You've been covering for him since September?" He looked at me, astonished, maybe even a little impressed.

"Tony, we shouldn't talk. Teresa could be home any minute."

"You never told her?"

"No."

He stared at the ground, trying to decide whether this was good or not.

"Give me five minutes," he said.

He started out of the woods, walking slowly. There was no question that holding the gun, even holding it as I was doing, in the least threatening way, gave me a charge, as if I'd risen a little higher, for just this moment, from all the tiny domestic arrangements involving Tony, involving Teresa. Tony would go into the house and distract Nina, and for those few minutes he'd be acting at my command. I wanted to turn away from my own indulgence in this, except that it was so weirdly satisfying to see Tony moving over the lawn as if caved in by some claim on his territory other than the one he himself had always made.

Once he was inside, I counted off a couple of minutes and followed his footsteps. This was the most vulnerable part of the plan because these were the moments when I was most exposed. I carried the gun away from my body the way I might carry a snake I'd killed. I could have hidden it in my pants, but Tony was right, I'd be sure to shoot myself. But this degree of exposure meant that at the point where I crested the hill and still had twenty or so feet to go to reach my back deck, I was visible not only to the driveway but even to the patch of road that ran by the house. The cops, realizing they'd left something behind, might be driving up at that moment. Or Teresa and Gabrielle. But no one drove by. I reached the deck and laid the gun on the table and went in to find a bag.

I chose the heftiest one I could find, a white lined plastic bag from an electronics store. The house was silent. I imagined Tony sitting in Nina's room, his big, morose face she must be wondering about: Why did he come and sit? Why did he remain so silent, so dark? I slipped outside, placed the gun in the bag, and brought it around to the front. Teresa had taken the Explorer, so I folded it into the glove compartment of the Lexus, careful not to touch the trigger.

Then I went upstairs to tell Tony and Nina I was leaving. In her room, Tony was leaning over Nina while she wrapped her ankle with the bandage. He tried to hold it for her, but she was expert in doing it herself.

He looked up, a little helpless in this domestic sphere. Sports injuries were not something his own daughters had prepared him for.

"You've got to watch this ankle," he said to me, exaggerating some imagined danger. "What do they play in the spring for, anyway?" he said, and stood. "Spring's for baseball."

"Soccer's all year round, Tony. Relax. She'll be good at it. It'll help her get into college."

I could see how desperate he was for authority right now. For an instant, there appeared in his eyes a look of fear, as if the whole notion of college, of a future for Nina, had been jeopardized by what I'd done. He looked out the window and announced, "The rest of the family's home."

I found Teresa in the kitchen, unloading a bag of groceries.

"I've got to go and see Billy," I said.

She looked astonished. "Why?"

"He called. Kenny must have told him about the cops. Your father's upstairs."

She frowned. *"Why?"*

"He came over. I don't know. Listen, where's Gaby?"

"She thought she left a CD in the Lexus."

I moved so quickly through the house that the sight of things became literally a blur. I expected at any moment to hear the shot. When I reached the porch and saw her in the car, I flung my arms out wildly and called her name. She was slumped in the front seat. In one leap I made it to the bottom of the steps and pulled the car door open and grabbed her. She nearly fell into my arms.

She didn't understand, but it was not important that she understand. I pressed myself against her cheek, and when she pulled away from me, I saw the bag containing the gun, fallen to the car floor as she'd opened the glove compartment in her search for the CD. Some luck I hadn't deserved had held. In pulling it out, she'd failed to set off the trigger.

When I looked back to the porch, I saw Teresa and Tony there, both watching. Tony's face had closed down to a small dark hole.

Beside him, Teresa understood nothing at all, but she had enough awareness to look deeply concerned.

Gabrielle separated from me, looked at her mother, said to the assembled, "What?" as if some accusation lay in our staring at her.

"Nothing," I said, and looked down again at the bag on the floor of the car. I had been lucky beyond dreams, and there was nothing to do now but get rid of it.

"I'll be back, I hope in about an hour."

"Why do you have to go to Winship, Tim?"

Teresa held on to the question a second or two before turning to her father, whose tight, cold, fist-bunching stance must have told her that he knew.

"Come here, Princess," Tony said.

"I'm still looking for it, Mom," Gabrielle said.

"Nobody goes in this car," I announced self-importantly, and I caught Teresa's look again. Wisely, she refrained from saying anything. I shut the passenger door.

Gabrielle made some little exclamation of disappointment and brushed past her grandfather into the house. I moved to the driver's side door and looked up again. Whenever I had imagined doing this, digging up the gun and returning it to Winship, I'd imagined deep secrecy and stealth. But here the early April light had still not fallen, and it seemed to say everything about my life that this act was so thoroughly exposed.

I got in and closed the door. Teresa did not have to call after me. She and Tony would both be waiting when I got home. I rolled down the long gravel driveway into the light reflected on the high new leaves—just buds, really—of the birches. As at many such moments of my life, I could not help noticing how incredibly beautiful Bradford was.

fourteen

The dark arrived somewhere between the Tobin Bridge and Winship. On Billy's street, in window after window, televisions were on, people watching the early news. The television was on in Billy's house. I'd tried calling him on his cell phone and been told it was out of service. Ronnie answered the door, his boy's face like some half-thawed thing, still sharply frozen at the crest—nose, eyes— while the edges had started to melt into fat.

He did not greet me at first, only stared, as if there could be nothing between us but the one thing. He forced himself to put on his version of social ease.

"Tim, what can I do for you?" It sounded false, a young man's attempt at an older, more-settled male heartiness.

"Is Billy home?" I asked.

Ronnie shook his head and went on scouring my face for some sense of what I might have come for.

"You know what time he's coming home, Ron?"

He was trying hard not to look scared. He turned, to check, I knew, with his father, and I pushed myself into the house to see the old man sitting before the TV.

"Mr. Mogavero," I said, and lifted my hand.

Behind the thick glasses he looked ancient and blind, with that stoicism that can pass for deep wisdom in old Italian faces. I wondered if he, too, knew what I had come for.

"Billy's with Paula," he said, as lucidly as a sixty-year-old. "He stays with her most of the time."

I had to marvel at the word choice. Not "lives with," not "sleeps with," but "stays with."

"You think I could find him there?" I asked.

He shrugged, a gesture that barely qualified as movement. "He's got no schedule anymore. He's not working."

This hardly came as a surprise.

"Fine. I'll try there," I said. "What's the number?" They gave it to me, but I decided it would be better to show up in person. "You guys know the address? I've only been there once."

Ronnie was who I'd turned to, but the answer came from Mr. Mogavero.

"Clement Street. Number sixty-seven."

"Thanks. Listen, Billy's cell phone says it's out of service."

The look from both of them this time was blank.

"He usually checks in at night," Mr. Mogavero said.

"Okay, if I don't reach him, when he calls, will you tell him I'm looking for him? He has my cell phone number, but let me leave it anyway."

Neither of them rushed to offer me pen and paper, so I went to the nearest table, found an old pencil and an envelope, a bill from the oil company. "Can I?" I asked, holding up the bill. "Write on the back of this?"

Since they neither confirmed nor denied, I wrote down my number. When I put the envelope down, I touched the scarred wood of the old table and felt a moment's rush of appreciation for this house, which I hadn't seen the inside of for years, the air of it so thick and unchanged, an accumulation of day after day of habit. I glanced around, hungry for something that still existed here, then went outside.

I vaguely remembered the way to Paula's. After a couple of wrong turns I found Clement Street and stopped at number 67. There were no lights on inside. Still, I knocked, rang the bell. A man from one of the neighboring houses took a bag of garbage out to the can in front of his house, glanced at me, and lit a cigarette. I sat on Paula's step and allowed him to cast his suspicion on me.

"You looking for Bill?" he asked.

"Yes."

He shrugged, puffed in that emphysemic way of old guys. The wait might be long. I considered visiting my parents, but how could I explain my presence here? Instead, I sat and waited. Eventually the smoking man went inside, though not before giving my Lexus a long, appraising look. He carried with him so much of this town I knew so well—its low, tightly packed expectations—that in his absence I missed him. And then I couldn't help it, things from the past started to come back to me. For reasons I couldn't have begun to explain to myself, I found myself thinking of a night with Maureen Feeney, a night when I came to her directly from work and took a shower in her apartment and then didn't want to change back into my work clothes, which had gotten sweaty during the day. She was cooking at her stove, and I came into the kitchen in a towel and said, "I don't want to change." Her reply was, "Fine. Eat naked. I don't care." So I'd taken off the towel, but the mere suggestion in this was too much, I was excited, and Maureen was at first amused and then bothered by the sight of me walking around with a hard-on, so after a while she sighed, turned down the heat under whatever she was cooking, removed her apron, said, "Oh, listen," and drew me to a chair and had me sit down and then efficiently blew me, less out of lust than just so she could get on with the cooking. I could still remember looking up while she was doing that, so full of the sense of being at the *beginning* of things, and was all of life going to be like this?

I stood up then, to force the thought out of my mind. I had nearly gotten my daughter killed. It was unacceptable to be descending into the bog of sexual memory. I drove to my parents' street and slowed down, crawled, really, until I was in front of the house. I could see into the living room, the overhead light on and my father standing with his hand on the back of the chair where he usually sat to watch TV, his head tilted, talking to my mother in the next room. He turned away from that conversation, and if he lifted his eyes even a little bit, he would have seen me. But he did not look up. He patted his pockets, and I knew what he was looking for, and then he disappeared from the frame and came back a few minutes later with the cigarettes. He put one in his mouth but didn't light it. Instead, he stepped forward and put his hand on top of the TV and tapped his fingers against it and scratched the back of his head and only then lit up. My mother entered the room, wiping her hands on a towel, and gestured toward the TV. My father leaned forward to turn it on and then stepped back, as if there was something wrong with the picture. My mother watched this, enduring yet another of the petty irritations that had marked their life together, but then the screen must have cleared, my father stepped back and sat, and my mother, after a moment, sat beside him. She brushed away smoke from his cigarette, and he looked at her, and even from this distance I could tell that his look was amused, even teasing, and her response had some humor in it. The two of them were laughing at something, something coming not from the TV but from each other, and I could see then, as much as you can ever see, what was the invisible glue between them, this amusement with each other they'd shared probably from the beginning.

At that point my cell phone started ringing.

"Tim, you're looking for me," Billy said.

"Where are you?" I was whispering. I wanted to go on looking at my parents, to follow the adventure of their night together, and I thought, foolishly of course, that my loud voice would spoil everything.

"We just got home. To Paula's." He paused. "You got something for me?"

"I do."

There was silence on the other end of the line.

"Well bring it over, okay?" Billy said finally.

"Listen, you want to meet me in the car?"

"What is this, *Spy vs. Spy*?" Billy was exaggerating my whispering.

"No. I just don't know. I figured you might want to keep this a secret from Paula."

He went silent a moment.

"All right, listen. You know where the boardwalk meets Auburn

Street? That's the turnoff to Paula's house. I'll meet you there.
What are you driving?"

"The Lexus."

"That piece of shit. All right. Park there. I'll meet you. Five
minutes. Where are you now?"

"I'm on my street. Looking at my parents."

He let that pass. "Five minutes."

It was hard to tear myself away, but I thought I'd seen the moment I'd come to see. They'd settled into something else now,
something duller. Soon one or the other of them would close their
eyes. There would be no superfluous kindness from the other, no
tucking of a blanket over the sleeping form. When it was time to
go to bed, there would be a prod, none too gentle.

I drove to the place Billy had suggested, and I waited. This was
a more raucous stretch of the boardwalk. Teenagers congregated
here, and it seemed that every car that passed them honked and
shouted. The kids were not all black, but even among the white
kids there was the adolescent wish to borrow from blackness some
of its thrust. Their music was uniformly rap and hip-hop, played
loud. I found myself staring at the young girls' asses. Their skirts
and jeans had gotten tighter, and they all showed off their navels
now, but there was nothing particularly erotic in my staring. It felt
clinical, as if I was studying "youth." Billy must have been watching me for a while before he got into the car, because the first thing
he said was, "The *chicas*. You getting your fill, Tim?"

Immediately he changed the air in the car with that particular
wasted density of his.

"It's in the glove compartment," I said.

He opened the glove compartment, looked at the bag, then
shut it.

"Why don't you take it?"

"How'd you find it?"

"My dog."

He nodded: of course.

"You want to come over, say hello to Paula?"

"Billy, this isn't a social visit." There was a little shock after I'd said it, both of us registering the harshness of my tone. "I want you to take it, that's all."

He seemed less eager to comply than to try to figure me out— *this* me, the one who had come with the gun.

"Go ahead, Billy. Come on."

"It's not a good idea, Tim. Not with all these people standing around watching." He went on staring at me in a close, careful way that made me uncomfortable.

"So what do we do?"

He made a slight shrugging motion with his lips. "We drive somewhere. Separate cars. Somewhere nobody can see us."

"Where's that?"

"Not in this town."

"Billy, I haven't got time to go anywhere with you. I've got a family waiting at home."

"They know where you are?"

"Teresa does."

"She know why you're here?"

"No."

"Tim."

"She doesn't, Billy. I swear. Two cops came to my house today, asking questions." I turned to see if he was surprised by this. He didn't appear to be; only interested. "I told her I had to go see you."

"What'd they ask? The cops?"

"About your marriage, mostly."

That made him smile. "Like, were we *happy*?" he asked, and chuckled, though it was his way of chuckling, not like anybody else's.

In the silence afterward I tried to listen to what was beyond the teenagers' laughter and the rappers' voices. I tried to hear the sound of the surf.

"What'd you tell them?" he asked.

"I thought you were," I said, and looked away from him. "Shouldn't I be telling them that, Billy? That you were a stand-up guy, devoted to his wife?" Then I turned back to him, searching for some crack, waiting for him to finally admit something. "What am I helping you do, Billy?"

He wrapped his left hand around his right wrist and turned it, as if there were soreness there he needed to work out. Then he looked outside. "All you're doing, Tim, is returning something that was given to you by my brother. End of story."

He seemed patient and quiet then, as if his fugitive life—if that's what it was—had strangely matured him. I started to ask another question, then stopped myself. The appeal of what he'd said was strong. Leave it at this. Go home to your family. Your daughter has been spared, and that is enough. Once this gun is out of your hands, it is not important to you whether or not Billy did it. At least not for the moment.

"Where would I drive?" I asked.

He shrugged. "Gloucester."

"Not that far."

"Swampscott. Lynn. You name it."

I thought a moment.

"Nahant," I said. "That little beach we used to go to. I could go that far."

He nodded. "Okay." Then, without any formalizing of our agreement, he got out of the car and went, presumably, to his own. I couldn't see him. I pulled out past the party of teenagers. Within a quarter mile, traffic thinned out, as had the boardwalk life. The houses facing the water along this stretch had been the houses of wealthy girls. "Class," we had called it, but those girls were exactly like us in most ways. They sat beside us in Winship High, they allowed us to unhook their bras on the Naugahyde sofas in their finished basements. "Class" had meant only money, nothing else, and money itself hadn't created any real separation. I looked behind me for Billy's car, but there were only indistinguishable headlights. Because I had so little choice, I trusted.

At the end of the beach was the place where the Blue Grotto once was. It was now condos. I shut off memory. There'd been enough memory. It seemed foolish now to see Billy as anything but a killer. Something in his manner in the car had confirmed it for me and made all the past, all the ways I had ever made excuses for him, a place of willful belief I'd lingered in too long. So end it here.

Think of Gabrielle in that first moment when I'd seen her slumped in the front seat of the car and expected to find her dead. Solder yourself to that moment. I made the turn onto the causeway and crossed over the water that separated Winship from Lynn, then drove along the long spit of Lynn Beach, the oildrum city of Lynn in the distance, a city redeemed only by the touch of water on its shore. High on mescaline, teenagers, we'd all taken off our clothes and plunged into the water here. Billy had suggested we search for packs of girls, but we found none. Forget all that, forget who he'd once been and what you once considered his glory. I pulled into the parking lot at the end of Long Beach, pulled far enough away so that I was out of sight of the restaurant and the coffee shop, and waited for him.

Something had delayed him. When five minutes had gone by, I got out of the car, half shivering, just to get away from the gun, the continuing implication of the gun, which I'd held on to so long, but which now seemed intolerable. Where was Billy? That was when the paranoia kicked in: Billy had called the cops; they would come and find me here; it had all been a trap. I thought of chucking the gun into the water, throwing it as far as I could. There was no one else in the parking lot, and though the lights were on in the Dunkin' Donuts above the lot, it, too, looked empty. I thought if he wasn't here in five minutes, I would do it.

Five minutes went by, then six, seven, and I went back to the car and sat in the passenger seat and stared at the glove compartment. I pushed the button that opened it and gazed at the gun. The beach here was shallow. To throw it out, even far, would mean nothing, because at low tide it would lie uncovered. What I would have to do was drive up to Nahant, past these houses that dotted the shore here, up to the rocks that jutted out into the deeper water.

But right away, having thought that, I became aware of a taboo. This was "class," these rocks at Nahant. The houses on top of these rocks were the houses of people whose wealth hadn't come from construction or from brokering insurance, but from some other, mysterious place. Here was the opposite of Winship, an incomprehensible wealth we'd known not to intrude upon. Whether the people here were really different from us hadn't mattered. We made them different. We insisted on "class."

I hesitated even now from going up there. Tony DiNardi had lost his eye on those rocks. The story had always been told in a shadowy manner, a fishing mishap involving a distant relation—a stupid, untrustworthy relative. Tony survived, but he had not scaled these heights, though in moving to Bradford, he had tried to. Thinking this, I had a moment's clear perception of why I had done what I'd done, and how I had justified to myself hiding the gun for Billy. Then the thought, or the clarity of the thought, fragmented. I was left feeling as if I were holding a line from which some enormous fish had managed to free itself. The slack contained the memory of weight.

Headlights appeared behind me at the entrance to the lot. I could not be absolutely sure. But then the lights went off; the door slammed. I saw the white shirt and the bulk that was Billy's. I took the bag from the glove compartment and got out of the car to meet him.

He accepted it as though doubt had assailed him at the last minute. He smiled against that doubt (if that was what it was), took the bag from me.

"Nobody followed me," he said. "That was good."

He brought the bag to his own car, opened the trunk, put it under the cover of the trunk bottom near the spare tire. He thought more clearly than I did. Gabrielle would never have been in danger if I'd done that. Still, there was something sordid about thinking so clearly about things like this, about guns.

"We should take off now," Billy said, as if that would be the end. "Before somebody finds us."

Foolishly, I was waiting for Billy to explain. When he didn't, I asked the question. "What was it, was it a fight, Billy?"

He looked curiously at me, his eyes widening.

"Passion, something like that?" I asked.

Billy stared at me as if he'd come upon me in some compromising posture. In the next instant it was as if he was deciding not to embarrass me by acknowledging this.

Then he got into his car, turned it on, and shone the headlights in my face. I lifted my hand against them, knowing I appeared weak doing that, yet wondering how he saw me, if he saw in me something besides weakness. He pulled away, and then I was alone there.

They were all waiting, though it was nearly ten by the time I got home. At the dining-room table, within the pool of light, with coffee and the cookies left over from our visit with Officers Cahillane and Medina.

Katie was the first to look up, her formerly beautiful face caught somewhere between the affection she'd always felt for me and the new fear and confusion caused by this latest turn of events. At her cue, Tony canted his body toward me, wearing a look of grave concern that looked rehearsed.

Only Teresa had not looked up.

In fact, Scooter was the one who seemed happiest to see me, so I reached down and made a big show of scratching him.

"Pour him a cup of coffee," Katie instructed Teresa.

"Do you want coffee?" Teresa asked, still not looking up.

"No. Uh-uh," I said.

Then there was a silence, in which Katie pushed the plate of cookies forward and then thought better of the gesture.

"So tell us," Tony said.

"Tell you what? What do you want to know?"

I was still standing away from them, not only because I was uncertain of my welcome but because I could feel Tony holding back just this side of his urge to break me.

"We want to know what happened with the gun."

At the mention of the word "gun," Katie's eyes traveled up to the ceiling.

"I returned it," I said, as if that should end it.

"You know she could have died," Tony said, and ran one finger along the table.

"Right. I think Scooter needs a walk."

"Don't you dare, don't you dare, mister!" Tony had already started out of his seat.

"*Mister?* What is this *mister?* If Teresa had come home two minutes later, none of this would have happened."

I had spoken less to justify myself than to bring out that violence that was simmering in him. And it worked. He was now fully out of his chair, his movement accompanied by some inarticulate grumbling with the word "sonofabitch" somewhere in it, checked only by his wife's hand on his sleeve and Teresa uttering the words, "Daddy, don't."

Even then he did not sit down, but asserted his bull-like, heavy-breathing presence, his way of letting me know that whatever authority I believed I had brought into this room had been usurped. Having made his point, he sat.

"I think the only one of you I owe an apology to is Teresa," I said, though I could see it would take much more than this just to get her to look at me.

"You owe it to all of us," Tony grumbled. "You owe it to your daughter."

"Okay, yes, and I will make it to her."

From his position, hands folded, at the table, Tony glanced up at his own daughter, as if to remind her of the wisdom of something he had once said to her, something that had evidently been spoken out of my hearing.

"In the meantime, Tim, we'd all like to know what that gun was doing out there in the first place."

I looked quickly at Teresa, and it was to her I spoke, trying to keep as little as possible of what I said from seeming to be aimed in Tony's direction.

"Last Labor Day, you remember, we had Chip and Amy over for a barbecue?"

"I remember," Tony said, his lips retreating to that pose of annoyance that seemed to have become his idling speed tonight.

"After they left, Billy's brother, Ronnie, showed up. He was scared. He was carrying a bag."

"You knew what was in it?" Tony asked.

"Yes. I knew a gun was in it. But I thought I knew something else."

They all waited. Katie's eyes appeared red-rimmed and ferocious in their desire that something adhere to this story to make it normal, an acceptable part of our world.

"I knew that Billy had had an affair with his father's nurse. A woman from Trinidad. She'd had a baby. She was a married woman, but I thought that baby was Billy's." I paused a moment, more for dramatic effect than because I needed to gather any thoughts. "In the hospital room, when Billy was recovering, they made me think, him and his brother both, that they knew who had done this. That it was the nurse's husband, looking for revenge. I thought—I believed—that Billy had bought a gun and Ronnie wanted me to hide it from him."

I could almost feel their mental activity like a buzz in the room, their will to try to see me as something other than a villain. Tony's hand was making wide circles on the polished table.

"Why didn't you tell me?" Teresa asked. It wasn't much, but it felt huge to me.

"I didn't tell you because—what? Maybe I wanted to protect you."

She looked as though she was rejecting that.

Tony cut through. "This is all well and good. But the point is, you gave it back tonight. Yes? What'd he say? It doesn't make sense. You hide the gun, this guy can buy another one. Did he confess to you?"

I watched Teresa close her eyes.

"No, he hasn't confessed," I said.

"Well, you asked him?"

"Yes."

"And what'd he say?"

"He didn't say anything, Tony. He won't confess to me."

At that, Tony threw up his hands, but it was only a momentary loss of direction.

"Listen, from what you've told us, you're in the clear. You go to the police, you explain what you did, what your understanding was, that's it. Nobody can come after you."

"And if he did it, Tony—you know what I am then? I've looked this up. I'm an accessory after the fact. You know what you get for that? Two to five years in the state pen."

This was all an invention. I'd never actually had the courage to look it up. This time Tony made no attempt to curb his frustration. When he looked at Teresa, I thought I could read the whole past, going all the way back to the night she had rejected Peter Graceffa, that solid citizen, in favor of something Tony could never be expected to understand.

Katie put her hand on her husband's sleeve and said, "He's a good boy, Tony."

The "good boy" moved past them, went to the windows, and said, "Now if you don't mind, I'd like you guys to leave so I can talk to my wife."

Tony looked up at his daughter to see if she was going to go along with this. Katie said, "Ya, we should go. It's late. We can talk about this tomorrow." She lifted up a couple of dishes and headed to the kitchen.

"Leave them, Ma," Teresa said. By now I had turned away, with my back to them. I was staring out the glass doors into the backyard, but in the reflection I could see Teresa cover her father's hand on the table. She said, "He doesn't mean to be rude, Daddy."

I knew then—of course I knew—that I needed only to be quiet now. They would go, and I would have the scene I wanted with Teresa. But I couldn't resist—or maybe I didn't really want that scene. I repeated the word "Daddy," in just the fawning way she'd said it.

Teresa turned to me as though she wanted to be sure she'd heard me right.

"Daddy," I repeated. "When are we going to grow up? When are we going to stop treating him like the guy who's going to save us all?" And then, because it didn't seem quite enough: "Nice trick at your party. Nice trick telling everybody we paid for it."

I don't suppose it's true that there was even a moment before it happened, a moment of stillness such as I remember, with Katie poised at the sink, running water over the dishes, and Tony staring at me. I'm sure it happened more quickly than I remember it, but what I see in my memory is Tony rising in increments, his face masked and boxlike, sculpted into something from a comic book, a figure of rage rising from the table and coming at me, and his hair—this is how I know I am remembering it in slow motion—his hair rising off his head in the shape of the slicked-up wave he'd been wearing since the 1940s, rising in its own shape before settling. His hand lifted and then was on me, ripping the collar of my sweatshirt, so that I felt a rush of air toward the place the sweatshirt usually protected, and then I felt his gnarly hands on either side of my neck, and I tried to push them away with my forearms until I realized, with a terrible mid-violence awareness, that I couldn't, that I was weaker than he was, that at seventy-five he could still beat me in a fight.

Teresa was shouting, and that brought him back from the place he'd gone. He lowered his eyes, collecting himself, and looked at his hands, which were still raised, as if he was surprised at their size or their shape or the condition they were in.

The girls arrived in the kitchen, alerted by the noise, just as Katie crossed the room and took her husband's hands and pushed them down. The girls didn't know what to make of this, so they stood in the doorway, all character wiped from their faces, as though they were being asked to comprehend a reality that, five minutes before, would have seemed beyond the sphere of our lives. Tony appeared more bothered by their witness than I was. He managed an eerie smile, as if to tell them they should ignore this, this was nothing, distancing himself from what he had just done, asking them not to believe the evidence of their eyes.

"Come on," Katie said, "we're going home. We'll see youse all tomorrow."

On his way out, Tony touched Gabrielle on the shoulder.

"What happened?" Nina asked when they were gone.

"It's okay, honey. We're going up to bed," Teresa said.

Nina stood her ground a moment or two, looking up at me and waiting.

"Go up to bed," I said. "Go ahead. Grandpa got mad at me. It's nothing. We'll talk about it tomorrow."

It was Teresa's insistence more than my words that made it possible for them to leave. After they were gone, I busied myself with
the sorts of order-making things I always do after a scene of chaos,
putting the napkin holder in its place, washing the coffee cups
Katie had left in the sink. Then I took Scooter out and watched him
take a mournful shit at the edge of the woods. As I stared into the
woods, I realized it was the first time in months that they didn't
contain a thing only I knew about, a hidden gun.

I didn't know what I would find when I got upstairs. The doors
to both girls' rooms were shut. I found Teresa in the bathroom off
of our bedroom, in front of the piles of lotions that constituted
a nightly ritual for her. She was applying them to her face,
which stretched toward the mirror and didn't shift at all to take
me in. There was something predictable in this as an opening
strategy, so I leaned against the wall and crossed my arms and
waited a few moments. Then I fingered my ripped sweatshirt and
said, "Nice guy."

"Is that what this is going to be about, Tim? Your sweatshirt?"

"No, it doesn't have to be. What do you want it to be about?"

She replied by rubbing lotion hard into her neck and then trying so hard to screw the top back on a tube that she sent it flying
across the room.

"I don't want it to be about anything. I have spent the week
with an extremely demanding class of second graders, and I *hate* it
that I am finishing it by learning that my husband has been lying
to me—for *months*—with a gun buried in our backyard."

I hadn't come in here to make excuses for myself, and when she
saw that, it seemed to make her angrier.

"Do you have any idea how this affects us all? Is that in any part
of your brain? What would have happened if she died?"

"I'm not going to go there, Teresa. That was just a crazy thing."

"Right. And how do kids die, Tim? From logical things? You
do something like that, you endanger us all. My father doesn't do
things like that. You can make fun of my relationship with him all
you like, but he protects us."

"Sure. He protects us by squeezing all the life out of us."

"Is that the issue here? Is that why you hid the gun? Because he was squeezing the life out of us?"

"Teresa, keep your voice down. The girls—" I halted there, feeling cowardly for bringing this up, and feeling her looking at me as if we were both acknowledging this. She ran some water and washed her face, and she was as careful about this as she'd have been if she were alone in the room.

When she was done, she said in a quieter tone, "I want to know why you lied to me."

But having said that, she didn't wait for an answer. She dried herself and moved past me into the bedroom, where I followed her and watched her take off the nightgown she'd been wearing, so she was briefly naked. I wondered if she was doing this so she could torture me: look what you can't have tonight. But it didn't work.

She got into another, different nightgown, a move that made me even more certain she'd done the naked thing for effect. Then she got under the covers.

"Aren't you going to turn the light out?" I asked.

She didn't answer, but turned and stared at me, expecting something.

"You want to know why I lied to you? All right, that's fair. Those things that happened in the hospital, when Billy was recovering, they made me think I knew the story." I paused. "I believed I knew the story."

I wondered how much of what I was telling her was a lie. Yes, I had believed those things at first, but when exactly had doubt come in, and how had I managed to ignore it?

"I never would have let you hide a gun here. No matter what the story was."

"Maybe I knew that."

"Maybe you did. Maybe it was part of your relationship with Billy that I couldn't have a part of. Was that it?"

"Teresa, let's not do this."

"Why? Let's have the rules, Tim, of what we can and cannot do. Is that why you did it? So that you could go on having this ridiculous relationship with him?"

"No."

"Guys like you two, it can't be sex, so it's got to be something else. Did he do it, Tim?"

It stopped me, the clarity of what she was asking and how she was asking it.

"And you can't say 'I don't know.'"

I thought for only a second before answering. "Yeah, I think he did." I paused after I spoke, trying to gauge how she was taking it. "I didn't think it for a while, but now I do."

"But you haven't asked him."

"I did ask him. You know Billy. The words 'Yes, Tim, I did it' are not in his vocabulary. He slides all over the place."

For the first time, I saw her taking it in. The energy in her eyes seemed to retreat.

The admission—the humiliation built into it—had exhausted me as well. I felt as if I might fall asleep on my feet, so I started to undress. As I did, she turned halfway toward me, looking at me and, I thought, not looking at me at the same time. As I peeled my clothes off and left them at my feet on the floor, I wondered if the same thing was happening to her as had happened to me before, that we had reached the point where our nakedness didn't have an effect on each other anymore.

I got into bed and turned out the light, and she said, in a way that sounded drugged or half asleep, "What are we doing?"

"Going to sleep," I said.

There was a pause, and then she asked, "When did you know, Tim?"

"I don't know. Over time. Slowly. I figured it out. The night he came to your parents' party, I knew that night."

"And you didn't tell me. You knew, and you didn't tell me."

"How was I going to tell you? Billy did it. Is that what I was going to say? Today after the cops were here, I tried to tell you."

Her hand lifted up to her forehead. "Jesus, I forgot that. I completely forgot that. That they were here."

After a long moment in this uncomfortable presleep silence, I turned to her on the bed. My nakedness and the thinness of her nightgown made something seem possible that I wouldn't have thought possible five minutes before. Or maybe it was a form of avoidance. But so what? Why not avoid?

"Tim, no."

"Why?"

"Just no."

"It'll keep me awake. It seems like what we should do."

"What was it like being married to me, holding this tremendous secret? Tell me what you think the point is of being married? So you can fuck somebody and then have your real life be your secret life with Billy?"

"Stop it."

"Why? Your real life is with a murderer. Do you realize that? You check in here, I'm good enough to fuck, but I'm not important enough to tell this major secret to?"

"My secret life isn't with Billy. Not anymore. I'm not going to see him anymore."

"Is that true?"

"It's true, yes. I've given him back the gun. Now this is it." I paused for a few seconds. "That doesn't mean there aren't things wrong here, with our lives. But I'm not going to see him anymore. That part of things is over."

Teresa held back a moment, quiet in the dark.

"What things?" When I didn't answer right away, she said, "What things are wrong with our lives?"

"Your father. You know." I was leaving something out. I wondered if she sensed it. But her silence seemed like a form of agreement. Encouraged, I tried to touch her again.

Sometimes, if you've been married a long time, you can begin to think of your wife as this enormous being, taking up immense space in the universe, but as I touched her, I realized how untrue this was, how little space she actually took up. How she was separate from me—astonishing, she was *separate*—and it was just going to be us now, me and this separate being. We were going to drive our children to their events and go to our jobs and occasionally look at each other and not know what to say, and this was going to be *it*, the whole deal.

Although I had an erection, I didn't think I could make love now. Teresa wouldn't understand that. Women could never see how the blunt thing didn't always mean what they thought it meant. "I don't want to make love. Don't think that," I said. That seemed to make it all right. She let me hold her and lose myself there in her softness, without thinking anything, without thinking, Teresa, but only that this was it now, this, here, this was my life.

fifteen

Two weeks later, driving home from Middletown, Connecticut, on a Tuesday afternoon, I heard Robert Siegel on NPR utter the words "an unsolved murder in Boston" and immediately sat forward and turned the radio louder. "A new lead in an unsolved murder in Boston" were the actual words, followed by "an investigation that has bedeviled the Boston Police Department for nearly a year," and then Robert Siegel turned the report over to a Boston feed.

It was an unusual voice for NPR, this thick-necked Boston reporter's. "Robert, investigators believe what might be the literal smoking gun in the long and frustrating murder investigation of a six-months' pregnant woman shot with her husband a year ago has been found in the trunk of a car in Mattapan. Acting on what was apparently an anonymous tip, police broke into the car of a T worker named Kevin Sammy and found the gun that seems to be the one that killed Patty Mogavero and her unborn child." There was, in the reporter's breathing, the feel of a sports bar, like a group of hearties stood just behind him ready to throw up a cheer. His mood was a little overripe for NPR, and Siegel came in to nuance things.

"Now, this has been a source of considerable racial tension in Boston, hasn't it, this investigation?" he asked, sticking on the words "racial tension" as if he had to pry them off the roof of his mouth.

"Yes, it has, Robert. Classic stuff. The white couple from the suburbs gunned down in the South Boston projects while the victim, Patty Mogavero, was visiting her mother. And the irony, of course, is that we're talking about a predominantly white section of Boston."

"But there have been charges, have there not, against the police, that they leaped toward the assumption that the perpetrator was a black man?"

The Boston guy hesitated, aware that the standard neighborhood response—Who the fuck else were they supposed to suspect, Robert?—was maybe not appropriate for NPR.

"That's right, Robert. And the BPD took a lot of heat early in the investigation when all their initial suspects proved."

"Proved," Siegel murmured, pausing as if to translate for the NPR listening audience. "That means they had alibis."

By this time I had pulled over to the side of the road, my heart pumping wildly.

"That's right, Robert. Which is why the investigation, almost for want of any other lead, had started to focus on the husband. So if this turns out to be it, it's going to be a major vindication for the Boston police."

"Or maybe we should say, for the assumptions of the Boston police."

"Yes," the reporter said, obviously holding himself back. They were tripping over the invisible line, each of them, and the effort seemed to be for each of them to try to ignore the fact that the line existed.

"But either way, I would imagine," Siegel announced with the air of bringing this to a close, "a tragedy for the city of Boston."

"That's true, Robert."

There was something not quite false in the reporter's last words, or maybe only false if you knew where he was coming from.

A report on immigration followed. I turned the radio off. A T worker in Mattapan seemed, at first, to have so little to do with the facts as I knew them that I experienced a wild surge of hope. I resisted the urge to call Kenny on my cell phone. If he knew anything that would cut into this sweet belief, I didn't want to hear it.

By the time I got home, Teresa and the girls still hadn't arrived.

I paced, listened to the radio (nothing about Billy, and nothing on CNN either), walked Scooter, and kept a lookout for the car. As soon as I saw it, I ran to the driveway and practically pounced on Teresa.

"Did you listen to the news? Did you hear?"

She wore her characteristic end-of-the-day look: of having been asked to do too many things and of possibly harboring some burdensome secret about the girls that I, being male, would never be asked to carry. No, she hadn't heard.

"They found the gun," I said, as overexcited now as the Boston reporter had been. "Some guy in Mattapan. Had it hidden in his car."

Teresa looked confused, then briefly hopeful. But it took her all of three seconds to see through this. She turned her attention to the girls in the backseat, who were both staring at me in some dreamy, half-absent way. The word "gun" had to have some power for them, but they couldn't as yet know what to make of it.

Inside the house, the girls stuck close to Teresa. There would be no talking about it until after dinner. I was sent to get takeout. The local stations were covering the story, but there was nothing new. On line at Clara's Home-Cooked, I had no patience with quiet, middle-of-the-road Bradford. The steadiness, the caution that pervaded the town, that air of PTO virtue.

I bolted dinner. Teresa wanted to talk with the girls about the state-mandated skills tests they were taking at school, but I couldn't force myself to pay attention. On the six-thirty news I got my first glimpse of Kevin Sammy being walked, handcuffed, into a Boston police station. Long-faced, wispy-bearded, the picture of guilt. Let it be him, I found myself thinking. From the police station, the TV cut to a shot of the projects where Patty had been shot, then to Billy's house, in front of which a group of neighborhood kids had congregated. One of the kids looked directly into the camera. Young Winship, redheaded like me. On the verge, and excited.

I called Johnny, but he wasn't home yet. Then Freddie, and I left a message. I still hesitated to call Kenny. Finally the girls went upstairs and I stood in the kitchen watching Teresa. She looked tired, throwing away the aluminum trays from Clara's Home-Cooked, saving leftovers.

"So, do you think this is it?" she asked, as though this were an event that had happened to me at work, one she had to pretend to an interest in.

"I don't know," I said. After all this waiting, all this tension, there didn't seem anything to say. I was trying to read her face.

"Don't hope too hard, Tim." She went to her shoulder bag, where she kept her students' papers, and started laying them out on the empty table.

"You have papers to correct?"

"I always have papers to correct."

"You think he planted it there?" I asked, just to show her I wasn't completely an idiot, that the thought had at least occurred to me. "I mean, the timing is pretty incredible."

"Tim, I can't think about this right now."

"Are you all right?" I wasn't sure why I'd asked her. Something in her pallor, an exhaustion.

"I'm fine," she said. "Just two weeks late, as it happens."

"What?" I sat across from her. And because she didn't answer, didn't look up, I asked it again.

"Two weeks late. I've been two weeks late before."

"You were going to tell me . . ."

"Eventually. If I needed to."

She began grading papers. I wanted to grasp her wrist, force something from her.

"Teresa."

"Tim, don't get excited."

"We're forty-two."

"There's no statute of limitations, is there? And it's not exactly like we've been super careful."

"Why are you being cold about it?"

She put down her pen, stared at the page in front of her. Beside it was a roll of smiley stickers.

"I can't think about this," she said. "I don't want to be pregnant, and I don't think I am. But if I am, I'll deal with it then."

"What does that mean?"

As she looked at me, I could feel her censoring herself. I spoke before she could say anything.

"What, have you given up on me, Teresa?"

"No."

She had answered too quickly.

"Because I hid that gun, that means I don't get a say in what happens to my own kid?"

She couldn't hold my gaze, made a mark on a paper that I knew was not a necessary mark.

"Teresa."

"You want this guy to be it so you're off the hook, Tim? You're not off the hook." She shook her head, but couldn't look at me. "I don't trust you anymore, that's all."

The phone had started ringing. I considered ignoring it, but then thought whoever it was would be a relief from the intensity of this moment. It was Johnny. We chatted a little bit, though he didn't have much to say. Freddie called immediately after, and he was far more eager to schmooze, to sort out the possibilities.

"Listen," he said, "Kenny doesn't come right out and say it, but he's known for months that Billy did this. I'm convinced of it. Remember his mother's funeral? He knew then; he was telling us then."

"Is that why you fired him?"

"I didn't fire him. I let Billy excise himself. Billy just walked out to the end of the employability branch, and the branch snapped."

"Okay," I said. "So what is this? This guy in Mattapan?"

"Well, I guess we all have to sit back, watch, and wait, don't we?"

The conversation was depressing me, so I made a move to get off the phone.

"Listen, it's been too long since the four of us have gotten together," Freddie said. I was used to this; he said it every time we talked, and nothing ever came of it.

"Right," I answered. "Let's go back to the Branding Iron. We can show them our AARP cards, get a discount."

"Very funny. You'll see. I'm going to make it happen. What's your schedule?"

I told him, then was glad to get off the phone. In the aftermath, I went back to Teresa, stood behind her, hovering a bit while she graded papers and affixed smiley stickers to them.

"Tim, are you going to stand there all night?"

"Yes. Probably."

She looked up. "What do you want?"

I got down so I was close to her. It couldn't be said, really. To have her trust back? A new baby? Billy revealed to be not a killer, just a classic fuckup? All of the above? But from the look she gave me before she turned away, I saw that she would give me hope for none of them.

True to his word, Freddie set up a meeting of the four of us in the Branding Iron, though it was two weeks before we were all free. In those two weeks, nothing new surfaced about Kevin Sammy. It became one of those news stories that went under, bubbling up on page 4 or 6 of the paper, with details added. I clung to every one: the gun verified as the one used to shoot Patty, the date of an arraignment in early June.

Kenny was the one I was least eager to see, and he arrived first, of course. I was already waiting.

"We have a table?" he asked.

"As soon as we're all here."

"You still drink?"

"A little."

"I'm off it. This is going to be a weird night for me."

He seemed not to want to talk to me. I asked him about his kids, his dad, who'd been moved into assisted care. The words "We're here to talk about Billy" refused to surface.

Johnny was next, his manner as dull as Kenny's, though he was much better dressed, as if he was at least making some sartorial nod to our past here.

We all visibly relaxed when Freddie arrived, though we were a

little surprised to see his big face graced—if that's the word—by a
slim, shaggy beard, the kind that lines the jaw like a fringe of
clinging moss.

"Jesus," Kenny said, "when's your audition for ZZ Top?"

Freddie gestured to the girl at the podium, and she led us to
a lousy table near the kitchen. We accepted it, though Freddie
looked as if he was on the verge of complaining.

"We made this place," he said. "Do they not know that?"

Our former, regular booth was occupied by a mixed group,
women with frosted hair and black suits accompanied by a pair of
gay-looking men. Things had changed here, though they were hard
to put your finger on and seemed indistinguishable from the way
the city itself had changed. The lack of cigar smoke was a big, obvious thing to notice. The other changes seemed matters of tone.
The ways in which money had become ever more important
couldn't be traced to any one detail, but to the edge even a restaurant like this had taken on, a baseline of nervousness. To me, the
change was most evident in the way a defining Irishness was grad-
ually being rubbed out of the city by a corporate slickness, the way
corporate logos like Fleet and Tweeter were taking over the names
of everything. It was as if Boston was making an enormous effort to
stop being local.

When the waitress came around, Freddie made a lame attempt
at flirtation, but the big-breasted mothers of three who had warmed
our evenings a decade before had been replaced by what looked like
very skinny young MBAs in training.

"So, John, any news about Carol?" Freddie asked, breaking the
ice in a somewhat self-conscious manner.

Johnny shook his head, playing it close to the vest.

"Kids okay? How's everybody's kids?" Freddie's tone was that of
a man pushing an agenda. He told us he was on the verge of leaving Winerip, a surprise. Boston development had apparently peaked,
and it was either relocate to Atlanta or Cincinnati or else seek new
employment. Freddie told us this matter-of-factly, gulped down
half his drink, and said, "So how else can we avoid talking about
the big subject?"

"What big subject?" Kenny asked.

Freddie sat back, took another sip of his drink, and spilled some Scotch on his tie. "Oh, I think we know what the big subject is." He started to dab water on his tie. "Is our ex-friend a killer or not?"

After a short, awkward silence Kenny said, "I don't think I know that any better than you."

"Come on, there's no *gossip*? What does your office make of this?"

Freddie was leaning forward, looking as though this would be fun, an attitude that seemed to tire Kenny.

"If there was gossip, Fred—*if*—I don't think I could tell you what it was."

"Who's this guy they brought in?"

"You read the papers."

"I do. Yes."

"Okay. We don't bring somebody in unless there's a reason to. That was the gun. In the trunk of his car. End of story. Or middle of story, as far as I know. I can't tell you, because I'm out of it."

"And that story you told us at your mother's funeral? Car found in Winship—Escort, wasn't it?"

The waitress interrupted us, and we all ordered quickly, none of us, I sensed, choosing what we wanted, too excited to get back to this.

When she was gone, Kenny sat back in his seat, hiked his pants, clearly trying to douse our interest. "Escort, yes. The world's full of coincidences."

"Bullshit."

"We all have to wait and see. If he's got no alibi, if the gun is found in his trunk . . . If he happens to have some connection."

"What connection?"

"If. I said, if."

"Oh fuck, Kenny. Come on."

Kenny angled his body slightly away from us and looked in the direction of the far windows.

"Just say this," Freddie said. "Is there one?"

Still Kenny wouldn't budge. "A couple of months ago my stomach started bothering me," he said. "That's why I gave up the booze."

"Fascinating," Freddie said.

"You guys don't believe me when I tell you I don't know any more than you do. Is that why we got together tonight, so you could pump me?"

Freddie sat back and rested his drink on his paunch, waiting him out.

"I gave you some information so you could protect yourselves. That's all. Maybe it turned out to be untrue information. The investigation appeared to be going one way. Now it appears to be going another."

"Did I fire Billy for nothing?" Freddie asked. "That's all I want to know."

"I don't know. Did you? Is that what you're pining about here, Fred? Were there other reasons to fire him, or was that the main one?"

Freddie's eyes looked slightly glazed now. "I think you panicked, Ken."

"Maybe I did." Kenny looked quickly at me, but long enough for Freddie to notice. "I don't know."

"What is this voodoo look you guys just sent each other?" Freddie asked.

"Shall we tell them?" Kenny surprised me. He hadn't missed a beat. His eyes were steadily on me now.

"What are you two, engaged?" Freddie asked.

"Our friend here," Kenny said, "came up with a theory a few months ago and passed it on to me. Seems there was a nurse. Watching Billy's father. Who Billy was shtupping. And there was a baby. So Sherlock Holmes here came up with the theory that the nurse's husband had a motive for killing Billy."

Johnny looked at me in a shaded, superior way. He already knew this; Kenny had told him.

"So I passed the information along. When that didn't work out—when it was seen that I might be trying to influence the investigation so as to protect my friend—I was shut out. An uncomfortable moment, to say the least. And it's essentially why I can't tell you guys anything." He opened his palms, smiling. "I've got nothing to tell."

"I apologize," I said.

"Oh good. Thank you. I've been waiting for that."

"I thought I could save us all a lot of embarrassment."

"Right. Good."

Freddie had been taking all this in, a grin creeping onto his face. Now he leaned forward. "Wait wait wait. What is this?"

"You heard it," I said.

"What's this about a baby? Billy knocked up his father's nurse?"

"Except he didn't, as it turned out," I said.

Kenny looked at me, his features sharpened a bit. "How do you know that?"

I didn't answer right away, just shrugged. "We still saw each other for a while."

"And he knew all this was going on? The testing?"

I nodded, and Kenny took it in. "What else do you know?"

"Nothing. That's all. I stopped seeing him."

I was holding my glass a little too tight. I wondered if the others noticed.

"Since he left Winerip, you went on seeing him?" Freddie asked.

"Sometimes."

"*Why?*"

"I don't know. I'm not as smart as you guys. I didn't know how to cut loose."

All their suppositions gathered on the table in that moment. I tried to loosen my hold on the glass, but it seemed too conscious, too potentially self-revealing an effort.

"He ever say anything about me?" Freddie asked.

"A little."

"What'd he say?" Freddie continued to grin, but his eyes looked vigilant.

"Nothing substantive."

Without knowing it, Kenny came in and saved him from what I believed was an excruciating moment. "I think the police would very much have liked to get their hands on some evidence to point this thing to Billy. I think they'd have loved that. They never could find any. That is, as far as I can tell."

"Shit. Did he do it?" Freddie asked. He banged his fist on the table lightly.

"If he did, he's smarter than any of us ever gave him credit for." Kenny seemed as if he was being honest now, one of us. "If he did, he's a genius. Because who drove that car? His brother? His brother was home with the father. The father swore to that. What, old man Mogavero's gonna lie to cover his son's murder? Besides, we know they'd never leave the old guy alone. So who else? Did Billy hire somebody? You know this is a very loose town. Word gets out. Criminals are not, fundamentally, a very bright class of people."

"Maybe it was Tim," Freddie said.

"Oh, cut it out."

"The one of us who went on hanging out with him."

Kenny stared at me a moment as if considering this. Then his eyes narrowed in amusement. "Tim in blackface. The witnesses were all certain it was a black man."

"A person of color," Freddie said.

"Right. Like Billy would hire a black guy to drive off with the gun. Does Billy *know* a black guy? Would he ever trust a black guy to keep his secret?" There was something in Kenny's tone that suddenly gave me pause, a subtle sense of pushing an argument. I didn't like it.

"So who is this guy?" Freddie leaned toward Kenny, simultaneously hungry and hugely amused. "You said there's a connection. What's the connection?"

Kenny, aware that he might already have offered us too much, sat back. "He's nobody. Now stop asking questions, Fred, or I have to leave."

Freddie put his drink down hard, spilling a little. "Fuck. This is torture. You tease us and then you pull back. Why bring it up at all?"

"Look." Kenny glanced at him, and a strange little moment followed where I saw him making up his mind. He was so used to keeping things to himself that this next moment—his decision to open up to us—seemed almost cagey. "There's a big movement to get to the end of this story. That's all I can tell you. The city's getting sick of it. It's gone on too long." He stretched his fingers out on the table, to be sure we were following this. "You understand what I'm saying here? The wind is blowing in a certain direction. Like people are saying, Enough. End it. Let it be the black guy." He looked at each of us. "The cops all came and interviewed you guys?"

There was a general nodding.

"What stories did you tell them?"

"I can tell you what Freddie told them," I said. "That I stayed around the night of the fire. Winship Beach 1978. Thank you, Fred."

"I was speaking of many general subjects," Freddie said, and he sounded so pompous I had to laugh.

"We all told them, basically, the worst we could tell them. We held nothing back, right?" Kenny said.

Again, nodding.

"And with all this, they still have nothing on Billy. So let the thing go where it's going to go."

"Which is this guy behind bars."

"Don't break your heart over this guy, Fred." Kenny had spoken too quickly. Now he tried to slow himself down, to affect a court-room cynicism that lifted him above us. "You know the cliché. Not guilty of one thing, guilty of another."

Freddie only smiled. "You still think Billy did it, don't you?"

Kenny looked at him, hating this, I could see. He didn't speak right away. "It doesn't matter what I think. I am tired of the whole thing, and I have nothing to offer." He lifted his hand as if to brush away something. "Let them do what they're going to do."

"Kenny's looking for closure," Johnny said.

"Closure," Freddie repeated, spinning the word for all the irony it was worth.

Then we were silent. It was my time to speak, if ever I was going to. But Kenny had given me an out: let the state do its work. I didn't like what this was doing to him, the exhaustion in his face. All of this held me back. It was just that there was something maybe even more troubling than his look of exhaustion: another look I was picking up from him, there in his willingness to go along with the city's desire for an acceptable fabrication. Leaving it uncorrected was like leaving untouched the first taint of spoilage in wood.

I lingered near Kenny's car in the parking lot after the others had gone. He'd moved up from his old compacts to a Subaru Legacy.

"Nice," I said.

He didn't answer, didn't seem to want to joke.

"You don't have to get home, Tim?" he asked, fingering his keys, not looking at me.

"What are you, still mad at me?"

"Why would I be mad?"

"Don't bullshit me."

"You had information; you should have let me direct you somewhere else with it, Tim. I'm mad at myself."

"You wanted it not to be him as much as anybody."

Kenny paused, pretended to look thoughtful—mocking me, I knew—and leaned against his car.

"What's Kevin Sammy's connection?" I asked.

Kenny stared up at the surrounding buildings, pretending great interest in the architecture of Allston.

"Hmm?"

"This is some high-pressure job you've got, Tim. I'm dropping on my feet, you want to stay here and *chat*."

"I know you're tired. I apologize for keeping you up. Just tell me, what's the connection?"

"Well, you can guess, Tim. If you're smart. But I can't tell you."

"Sometimes I'm not. Smart. But let me guess. Is this guy connected to the nurse? To the nurse's husband?"

Kenny made a slight motion with his mouth, as much as I needed to know I'd gotten it right.

"Yes?"

"I'm not saying anything."

"Kenny, you're not out of this investigation at all."

"I'm out of it. That doesn't mean information doesn't filter down to me. But I haven't said a word to you. It'll be in the papers any day, and you can read it there."

"Ken, about the thing with the nurse. You know they'd have gotten that information on their own."

"On their own. Exactly. Without my help. Only I don't think they would have suspected the paternity of that baby. That was a Tim O'Kane special, bought and paid for by Kenneth DiGiovanni."

"How many times do I have to apologize?"

"The thing is, why should we have cared, Tim? Whether it was him? We weren't friends with him anymore. *I* wasn't."

"He fucked with me," I said, and looked down at the ground between us.

"How's that?" Kenny looked at his watch.

"He wanted me to know. He knew the investigation would get around to him. He knew that. He wanted me to believe he was the father of that baby. I don't know why."

Kenny looked at me a moment as if he did know why, but to say it aloud would insult me.

"You know what, Tim? I don't really care anymore." He looked at his car keys, as if he were just remembering them, and went to the driver's side door of his car.

"So what am I picking up, Kenny? That this is all a setup? Him planting this information, then, miracle of miracles, the gun shows up in the car of this nurse's husband's friend? Where Billy maybe planted it, figuring, hey, people might believe the nurse's husband got his friend to do it. He knew the city would be sick of it by now, ready to believe some trumped-up story. For *closure.*"

He hated that, I could see. "You think I'm going along with it, Tim? You think there's something I know that I'm holding back? Based on what? Based on your theories? You got something else for me, Tim? Something concrete?" His fatigue was so deep it brought out the contours of his old plastic surgery.

"No," I said.

"Then we're spectators, aren't we? Like everybody else."

There was a new quiet in the parking lot. A car had just taken off, leaving that silent wake behind it.

"Where are you going on vacation this year, Tim?"

I could read the effort behind the question, his attempt to return us to neutral territory.

"We always go to the same place. One of Teresa's father's houses."

"Nice."

It just then occurred to me we couldn't this year, not unless I offered an apology.

"You?"

He shrugged. "I dream of islands. Far away. Mai tais. Jimmy Buffet."

We laughed uneasily.

"It'll probably be a week at the Cape. Rain. The outlets. The kids."

"What are you always saying, Ken? It's not perfect, but we've got to love it. These lives. Music lessons."

"Music lessons. Right."

"My kids don't . . ."

"No, mine either."

We looked at each other. It was impossible to hold back any longer.

"If I did have something, Ken . . ."

"Something more to clear Billy? I don't think he needs it."

"Maybe it goes the other way, Ken."

His eyes widened just slightly before narrowing again. "Oh, Jesus Christ," he said, and turning away from me, he unlocked the door of his car.

"Okay," I said. "Go home. Forget I said anything."

Kenny got into his car, started it up. I backed up a couple of steps to clear a space for him. The car wasn't moving. I saw the back of Kenny's head in the dim light inside the car. In another moment he was outside of it, tapping his keys on the roof.

"I don't want to know what you've got, Tim." He tapped his keys on the roof again. "I forbid you to tell me, understand? Don't send me a fax, don't send me an e-mail, nothing. Okay?"

"Okay."

"If you've *got* something . . ." He bit down on the word. For an instant I thought he was going to cry, but it was only the difficulty he was having getting the words out. "I can give you a name. I'm not going to send you to one of my buddies in the office, because I'm already in too deep. I'm going to give you the name of a lawyer. If you call this guy, he will ask you who gave you his name. You can tell him it was me, but that the conversation ended there. I will not allow you to fuck me up any further."

"Right. Okay."

"You got that?"

"Yes."

Then he went silent again.

"This may not change anything, Kenny. It's just something I've got to get off my chest."

"You've got a lot on that chest of yours, Tim. You gonna let it dribble out piece by piece or all at once?"

"No, this is the last thing."

He was silent again, hesitating, fighting a war inside himself. He wanted it to be over. The rain and the outlets on the Cape waited, and there would be a kind of balm in that, if he could only get to it.

But finally Kenny took a business card out of his wallet, wrote quickly on the back of it, flicked it across the car roof until it was close enough that I could pick it up. I noted the name, then turned the card over. It was Kenny's frequent customer card at Moldoff's Cleaners: ten punches and you got a ten-dollar cleaning free.

"You've got two to go," I said. "Two punches. You sure you want to give this to me?"

Kenny was just looking at me.

It was, after all was said and done, maybe too easy to figure out, easy in a way that shamed me. On the drive home, down Storrow Drive, onto Route 2, through Fresh Pond, I could almost read Billy's mind. All the way back to the night when he'd insisted I come into the house to meet Hortense, to let me know he was fuck-ing her. And after that, after the baby, the birth of Charles, the not-so-veiled hints that the boy was his, knowing I'd buy into it, the myth of Billy, Mr. Potency. It was as if Billy had been planning forever to get away with something this big.

But in the hospital they had been so convincing—Billy and Ronnie both—the assailant was known! Billy had to hush Ronnie from saying the name; there was no prompting necessary then. Ronnie was not smart enough to be such a good actor.

However it was achieved, Billy had meant all this to have an effect. He had needed to plant the suspicion of Hortense's husband as Patty's killer. And though he'd asked me to hold the information back until he was ready to release it, he might have known, too, that I couldn't hold it, that it would be investigated, the paternity proved false, but still, something suggested, a potential story laid out.

At which point he needed the gun back.

I was stopped at a red light in Fresh Pond. Once, there had been a drive-in movie here, a long, flat, dreamy landscape like the old Winship landscape. Now it was massively built up. I couldn't help staring at the great commercial structures, which seemed to close in on a driver so oppressively, and thinking that this was part of what Billy hated. If I was ever to understand why he'd done what he'd done, I'd have to try to understand as well his sense that this commercial riot all around me represented some darker ruin. Even now I couldn't help but reach back to some pure, discarded part of him.

He'd needed the gun (the light had changed, I was on my way again) because, the story having been planted, he required another protagonist, someone without an alibi. Kevin Sammy. The husband's friend. The paternity of Charles mattered less than the fucking itself. People would believe that a man would murder another man because that man was fucking his wife. It happened all the time; it needed no explanation. But they would also believe that a smart man would not do it himself, but get another man to do it, someone no one would guess to look for, until an "anonymous tip" pointed the police in the right direction. I had no real knowledge of how the world worked, but like everybody else, I'd been to the movies, and the movies provided an endless supply of stories like this. Billy had counted on the city to be tired. It hadn't let him down.

But underlying all of this, there was still the large question. How could Billy know absolutely that Kevin Sammy had no alibi for the night of Patty's murder? If Kevin Sammy was somewhere else—if Billy's planting of the gun fell through—suspicion would automatically fall back on him. He must know that. It was this little opening, this tiny crack in what otherwise seemed to me such an obvious scenario, that kept me fingering the card in my pocket that Kenny had given me, running my finger along the creases, reminding myself that I didn't yet have enough to go on.

sixteen

In the lot of the Star Market, I parked within sight of the door. I had no idea what time Ronnie got out. It was a Tuesday, and I should have been at work. But for days now, I hadn't been able to let go of an idea. I needed to see Ronnie. Teresa didn't even know I was here. I had dressed for work and left at the normal time, but at the last minute I'd decided that this was what I had to do.

I had had to kill most of the day, walking on the beach, eating pizza on the seawall, visiting old haunts. None of this was difficult. The earliest I figured Ronnie would get out would be three o'clock, but I kept checking to make sure he was there, bagging and moving down the rows of aisles as if he ran the place. The employees all seemed to enter and leave through the front door, so that was where I positioned myself, and at four I saw him moving toward the doors, his apron untied and slung over his shoulder, stopping to rack up some of the pushcarts—good proprietorial Ronnie, indispensable Ronnie—before leaving.

He saw me standing there in my suit, and his eyes did what I knew they would do: became scared and shaded, then falsely confident, as if he was determined not to be knocked off stride. He found an errant pushcart in the lot and pushed it into the rack they kept outside.

"Ronnie," I called, and as I walked toward him, I thought of touching him, but didn't.

"Tim." All his life, his effort had gone into trying to act like a man. That was what he was doing now, squaring his shoulders and trying to meet me on some imagined terms.

"Can we talk, Ronnie? I need to talk to you."

He gazed suspiciously at the collar of my shirt. "What about?"

I shrugged, not wanting to appear threatening. "Can I take you out for coffee?"

He shook his head and looked at his watch. It was an expensive one. Billy must have given it to him. "I'm supposed to get home."

"What, you have to take care of your father?"

"Yeah."

"This'll take five minutes, Ronnie."

He focused a moment on my suit, seemed to be gauging my intention from the fabric of it. He suddenly looked amused by it—or by something—a hint of a smile playing on his features.

"We can sit in my car, all right? Over there. That black one."

"The Lexus?"

"Yes. Did you ever sit in one?"

It had always been impossible to tell exactly how slow Ronnie was. But right away I saw that I'd insulted him by calling into question the level of his sophistication.

"Never mind that. That was a stupid question. Something's been bothering me, and you're the only person that can help me with it."

"Okay," he said. He looked more confident now, as if my misjudging him had given him some psychic heft.

"Ronnie, when I came to see your brother in the hospital after he was shot—I was practically sleeping over, remember?"

He nodded.

"I love your brother. You know that, don't you?"

"Sure."

"And I don't want to hurt him."

He didn't agree quite so readily to this.

"Okay. You two were talking in the hospital, and you already knew who shot him, right?"

He rubbed his nose, resistant to this.

"Remember? You said 'the bitch,' something like that?"

He nodded his head.

"How'd you know, Ron?"

He looked at me as if I was the slow one now.

"'Cause you knew. You knew right away. You seemed to. How'd you know?"

When he next shrugged, it was like the answer should have been obvious.

"Ronnie, you know they've arrested this guy, right?"

"Sure."

"So what was the gun you brought me that night?"

With his whole face he seemed to be pushing something unpleasant away. It was as though, in spite of all the warnings, he was surprised at where this conversation had led.

"Tim, come on, you want to know these things, you should talk to Billy."

"No, *you* brought me the gun, Ron."

I had prodded him on the breastplate with one outstretched finger. That became our subject then, him looking at my finger. That I had assaulted him gave him a momentary advantage.

"Ronnie, was it you who drove the car that night?"

He looked unsurprised by the question. "Police asked me that, Tim. We don't leave our father alone. I was with my father. You find me anybody else who was with my father. We don't leave him. It couldn't have been me."

He seemed to be talking about himself not as a flesh-and-blood being, but as a concept, a figure on a chessboard.

"So it was somebody else? Somebody you know?"

"Sure. It was the nigger." He moved back a half step, aware that this was not the right word. "The black guy. The one they arrested."

"He drove the car for your brother?"

He looked at me as though I'd gotten it completely wrong, in a way that was so off-base it became offensive to him. But it was clear to me now that there was a story inside him, something that could explain it all.

"What was the gun you asked me to hide that night, Ronnie?"

"It was just some gun. I don't know. You didn't have to hide it."

"No? You show up at my house, Labor Day. You won't talk. What am I supposed to do?"

His look was blank. But it jogged something in my memory.

"How'd you find my house, Ron?"

He looked as though he didn't remember at all. He started to move away from me.

"You remember? The Internet?" I was following him now. "That little mapping thing they have? That's what you told me. You want to come with me and show me how to use it? We can go to the library. You want to show me how to use the Internet? If you can do that, I'll believe you."

"I know how to use it."

"Good. Show me."

He was clearly scared by the challenge, in a way that made him aggressive.

"I don't have to do that, Tim. I don't have to do a fucking thing."

He had reached his car by now, opened the door, got inside. I tapped on the window.

"Ronnie."

I tapped louder, practically banged, as if something was coming unhinged in me. I shouted his name until he rolled down the window. His face looked surly. Within his town, he was certain I couldn't get to him.

"Did your brother kill Patty?" I asked, directing the words sharply enough to try to penetrate that aura of safety around him. "Just tell me, okay? Tell me the story."

The look he sent me was remarkable. He studied my face as though I'd said something so beyond his capacity for belief that it rendered me insane. I understood then that whatever story Ronnie had inside him, it didn't necessarily correspond to the truth. The evidence of Patty's body at Billy's feet, and his brother holding the smoking gun, even this would not have convinced him that such a thing was possible.

"You're crazy," he said, and started the car, but the words weren't used as insults. They contained in them a kind of awe, a perverse care for me. But not enough to keep him there. He took off.

Leaving me there in my suit in the Star Market parking lot. When I looked up and around me, I noticed that we—or maybe I—had attracted attention. Shoppers—women—had stopped. They held their carts in suspended animation. How loud had I been? In another moment they turned away from me and carried on.

I brooded over this meeting for days, but I still did not make the call to the lawyer. I kept expecting Billy to call me. I knew he'd have heard about what had happened with Ronnie.

It was in the midst of this short brooding period that I received an unexpected visit. Sunday night, the early May dusk, the girls doing their homework (they both loathed Sunday nights and disappeared upstairs into their separate miseries), Teresa getting ready for the next day, me looking over my schedule for the week while we discussed what the girls would need for their lunches—could I make a late run into town for turkey breast? The doorbell rang.

My father was standing on the porch in a light jacket. It was still warm, but he seemed hunched against an imaginary chill.

"Dad, what are you doing here?" I stepped out onto the porch rather than inviting him in, because I suspected he'd come to bring me bad news. "Is Mom okay?"

"She's fine, Tim."

He had his hands in his jacket pockets. He needed a haircut so badly it was all I could do to keep from smoothing his wild gray hair behind his ears.

"She in the car?"

"No. I came alone, Tim."

I waited for the explanation. He peered inside the door. "Why don't I—" With one hand he gestured that I should let him in.

"Say hello to Teresa and the girls? Sure. Come on."

He clapped his hands when he saw Teresa, who looked shocked to see him.

"Well, here's my lovely daughter-in-law," he said. Just the sound of those words unsettled us both. He liked Teresa, but the words "lovely daughter-in-law" belonged to another, more conventional man.

"Dad, what are you—" she said, and then came and kissed him. "Is Mom—"

"I'm alone. And I didn't come to eat, so don't bother."

He was offering no clues as to how to proceed. "The girls are where? Upstairs?"

Teresa called them. Seeing him, Gabrielle's expression did not change at all—she had never quite gotten him—but I hoped he'd get a warmer greeting from Nina, who had been my companion on many visits and who had developed, I thought, a certain affection for his eccentricity, his refusal to lard his grandchildren with gifts, his take-it-or-leave-it attitude toward himself.

"Well, girls," he said, and everything he did compounded the strangeness, so that I was convinced he had come to tell us he was going to die, and as that thought locked around my heart, I found it difficult to stand, and I wanted to get him away from this forced cheerfulness, to take him back to Winship and sit him in his chair and light a cigarette for him and then watch him survey his beloved television screen with his old, beautiful skepticism.

"Dad, are you sure we can't get you anything?" Teresa asked.

"No, no. I wanted to take Tim out, actually. I took a drive—" He pointed out to his car, as if we might not otherwise understand the concept of "a drive."

"You want to take a walk, Dad?" I asked. "Or better yet, I've got to take a trip into town. You mind coming?"

He nodded, still masking his intention, and we wandered out to the Lexus. He was slow, and he surveyed the field.

"You haven't been here for a while," I said.

"No." He shook his head. "I'm happy to see it's just as baronial as ever."

Once I got him settled in the car, after insisting he put on a seat belt, I watched him take in the dashboard lights, the smoothness of the leather. He settled into the luxury of the Lexus as if yes, he'd enjoy having such a thing, in another world, though he couldn't imagine why anyone would lift a finger to have it in this one.

"You don't mind helping me with the chores?"

"Oh, I don't mind, no."

"We like to get the girls' lunches settled for the week," I said.

"Sensible."

As we were pulling down the long driveway, he said, "Baloney."

I turned to him, thinking he'd meant it as a criticism.

"That's what you liked to eat. As I recall. As a boy. People in those days used to buy a lot of baloney."

I laughed quietly in relief, and he went on. "Nobody does anymore, I don't suppose. Or at least, not here." We rode under the trees. "Pretty, pretty town." He whistled after a while.

In the market, as I ordered meat for the girls, he picked up and studied the delicacies the store displayed by the deli counter, the imported crackers and cookies. Wine pretzels, biscotti. He studied them as if trying to decipher their use, then checked the prices and put them down as if they'd become radioactive. When we were back in the car, he said, "Why don't we stop somewhere?"

"It's a Sunday night, Dad. Not much is open."

"Oh, I imagine there'll be a place."

I headed to one of our mini-malls, but all the lights were out.

"Ellen's Java," my father said, his voice sliding into that familiar tone of effortless disdain. "Four and Twenty Blackbirds Bakery. Triton Fish Market. Why bother with these places, Tim, when we have good old Dunkin' Donuts across the way."

"I thought I'd take you someplace fancy."

He smiled, but I saw in it his impatience, his need to *get* somewhere with me tonight.

"Why don't we make it my treat, Tim?"

We both ordered coffee, and my father took a couple of minutes to make his doughnut selection. He tried to be friendly and chatty with the girl behind the counter, but she didn't seem to understand his old-school style at all.

When we were seated at a little table, my father looked absurdly satisfied, as though having found this place in Bradford and forcing me to patronize it was a triumph.

"It's nice they have scones here." He broke his powdery filled doughnut in two.

"Yes."

"It's becoming a scones world, have you noticed?"

I detected, a little late, the critical tone in his voice.

"Even in Winship we have a Starbucks now. We have a latte crowd. But you know what I've noticed? The old plain coffee is not as good in those places. Here, well, this place is quite reliable."

"And you came all the way from Winship to tell me this. To sing the praises of Dunkin' Donuts."

He was on the verge of laughter.

"Yes, I've always been a great lecturer."

"Well, lecture me."

A small pile of sugar had fallen off his doughnut. After looking into my eyes, he carefully condensed it and flicked it into his hand, then into a bag, a neat cleaning up after himself.

"I don't suppose they'll let me smoke in here."

"No, Dad. We're smoke free."

"All right then." He was looking past my shoulder with distaste for the next thing he would have to say.

"It seems you were seen, Tim. Not much gossip comes to me, you understand, but your mother gets out. Her Beano nights, and such. You were seen in the parking lot of the Star Market the other day, browbeating the Mogavero boy."

This was not what I'd expected. I took a small sip of coffee.

"Yes," I said finally.

"Well, it's none of my business, of course. You could say your mother put me up to this." He took a long, slow slurp. "What I'm really upset about is that you didn't come visit."

"I apologize for that. It was the middle of a weekday."

He lifted his eyebrows. "Work took you near to Winship, did it?"

"You know, the home office."

He nodded, clearly not believing me. "Just left long enough to go to the Star Market and browbeat the Mogavero boy. That's the word used, anyway. Reported to your mother. At some Beano affair or another."

"I'm sorry to embarrass you."

"It doesn't embarrass me in the least. It embarrasses your mother, but I daresay she'll survive."

"So this is . . ."

"Call it curiosity, Tim."

He took another long slurp, eyeing me as he did. "I have nothing much to occupy me. Though I do enjoy that divorce show. People airing their dirty laundry on television. Sex and such."

"Yes," I said. "Sex and such."

Then he looked at me as seriously as he'd ever done. "Well, it's a puzzle, isn't it? Why my son should be doing that sort of thing. In the middle of the day."

"Dad, what's the talk in Winship about this whole thing? This whole murder."

"Talk? I wouldn't hear much talk. Are you sure you don't want a doughnut?"

"I'm sure. Mom hasn't heard anything?"

"If she has, she hasn't told me. They were always a strange family. You know that. The father, the butcher. Held himself a little apart. The mother was a nice enough woman, I suppose. And the younger son, the one you were supposedly browbeating, I see him in the Star Market. I say hello."

"So there's no rumors?"

"Well, if there are—well, I suppose everyone must have thought from time to time that he must have done it himself. He, your friend—"

"Billy."

"You could hardly help but suspect, given that they were finding no one else. But now they've arrested this fellow, I suppose that ties it up. Your friend was keeping company with the hired woman."

I loved the phrase. "Keeping company." How had Mr. Mogavero

framed it? "Billy stays with Paula." This beautiful generation, with their resistance to speaking the word aloud.

"Yes. He was."

"Well, there you have it. The stuff of *Divorce Court*. The dirty laundry. I wouldn't give it another thought if this story hadn't come my way."

"Me browbeating."

"That's right. I rack my brain, I can't put a story to that one. Why don't you illuminate me, Tim?"

I looked down into my cup, perhaps a long time.

"Oh, I don't like this, Tim. I don't like this one bit. I was hoping for a quick, easy answer."

"Which you could have gotten over the phone."

"I thought a drive wouldn't be such a bad idea." He glanced up at me, a little shy but clearly asking.

"I've been involved with them, Dad. I've been . . . involved." I sat back, as if this might take the place of further words.

"Involved how?"

"You know I was there the night it all happened. There with them in the hospital. I mean, I knew the whole story, from the beginning."

"What story?"

"About him 'keeping company' with this woman."

"I see."

We were silent. He moved his mouth in a tight, indecipherable way.

"Look, Tim, if you don't want to tell me, I'll just go home to your mother and inform her that it's none of our business."

"This is what it takes to get you to come here?"

He stopped in the middle of a chew. His eyes looked red and a little runny. He dipped the last of his doughnut into his coffee and then thought better of it. "Should I apologize for that?"

"I don't know." I shook my head. "Should you?"

"You want me to be like one of those fathers on television? Constantly *there*. Constantly *wise*." He smiled slightly. "God, I don't like this modern world."

"Why? Because you don't want to be like one of those fathers on television?"

"No. Because they don't let you *smoke*."

He fidgeted.

"We can go out."

"No. I should be able to stand it for ten minutes without one. It's a form of discipline."

He looked angry now, unsettled by the demand the world had placed on him, which I knew had only partly to do with the no-smoking laws. We both hesitated from moving the conversation forward. I knew it could easily end there. It always had. He would accept what little I offered him. But something was pushing me forward, maybe the new demand for honesty in his parched-looking, cagey eyes. Or maybe it was something else, something from the past: a simple notion that he was owed this much.

"Okay, Dad, I'll tell you."

When he looked up in response, it was with an eagerness that surprised me, as if all this time he'd only been hiding his worry. I considered a lie for about three seconds, but looking into his eyes, I couldn't go through with it.

"I hid a gun for them for almost a year. I thought I was doing something else. I mean, I wouldn't have done it if it was clear it was the murder weapon."

He stared at me the way he once would have stared at a customer at the bank, one whose cash deposit didn't match the amount noted on the slip.

"I'm sick of that story, actually," I said, and held myself back a moment, as if trying to figure out how to physically release the words. "I knew it was the murder weapon."

A breath of air, of release, came with those words. In response, he only stared at me, with no visible reaction at all save for a slight tightening of his jaw.

"Well, now I think we should step out, Tim. Now I think I need that cigarette."

As he cleaned up after himself, I could see that he was shaking.

On the sidewalk in front of Dunkin' Donuts, a boy was making a cursory sweep. We sat on one of the large pots holding shrubs, and my father took out a cigarette. We watched the boy sweep until he went inside.

"Very . . . serious," my father said after he'd lit up and taken a long drag. His hands were still shaking when he'd struck the match.

I placed my hand against his back. He looked surprised by this, then annoyed, until finally he accepted it.

"I'm afraid I'm a little slow, Tim."

"It's nothing, Dad."

"Nothing? He's a killer, then?"

"Yes, I think so."

He let that sit, uncommented on, until it felt very heavy, inexcusable.

"I'm going to go to the police, Dad."

He nearly dropped the cigarette, then recovered it.

"I've been fighting that for a while. I think I need to just do it."

He stared into the middle distance. It felt like I had lost him, failed to hold his interest.

"If this is the murder weapon, Tim," he said, with just the tiniest movement of his chin to indicate that his words were directed toward me, "and you hid it for him, won't that . . . I mean, won't it mean you'll go to jail?"

"I don't know."

His face shook for a moment. He ground his cigarette out. He looked in my direction, but only glancingly, as if the sight of me was too difficult for him to take in.

"What?" I asked.

"This is beyond me, Tim. I have to confess that. Beyond me." Again he made the Parkinson's-like nodding of his head, as if he'd said much more. "I don't know what to say to you."

"It's okay."

"Are you ready to go to jail? Is it worth it?"

"I don't think it'll be so bad."

"No? No?" His head was moving in that unstoppable way. He gripped my knee. "Ah, God."

"Dad, it'll be all right. I'll tell the truth. It'll be all right."

That didn't seem to calm him down any.

"You want me to lie, Dad?"

He looked as if he might be considering it. "I always said this life was wrong."

"Don't lecture me, all right? You never said this life was wrong. You just loved to make fun of it."

He looked at the ground.

"Lots of people know how to live this life," I said. "They do it well. Just not me."

"You'd come home, you'd make fun of my life, too. You'd want to—paint the siding. It wasn't good enough for you."

"Yeah, stop."

"No, I took note. And here you are."

"Yeah."

"And who's going to jail now? Which one of us is going to jail now?"

With a sudden, lunging, indescribable sound he laid his hand on my shoulder and pulled me to him. The sound he made wasn't crying. It had come from somewhere else, from some core belief I'd offended. We were so close I smelled the old man's smell of his skin, and loved it, and wanted to stay inside it.

"Dad, it's okay."

"No."

"Dad."

I thought he wasn't going to let me go. When he finally did, he was staring downward and his face looked thinner. I touched his hair, smoothed it.

"Everything's a lie unless I do this. Do you understand?"

"No."

"Well, understand, okay? My life here. Everything's a lie."

He did not nod his head in agreement, though I wanted him to. He continued to stare at some point between us. I couldn't know what it was, but he remained fixed there, and when he looked up, I saw the red capillaries in his eyes. He was looking at me as if I'd woken him from a dream.

"Let's go home," he said, and though I didn't know exactly which home he was referring to, I helped him up and kept my hand against his back as we moved toward the car.

One night when we were both brushing our teeth, I told Teresa what I was doing. She listened as though she was not surprised. I told her it was eating me alive, the evidence was too strong, that I couldn't go through the rest of my life knowing I might have helped Billy get away with murder. She had no response. We went about our business as though we were talking about something that would have little effect. But lying in bed afterward, Teresa was unusually quiet. I asked her what she was thinking.

She waited a moment. "There are ways to protect yourself, right? I mean, this doesn't mean, Tim—"

I looked past her, out the window, and thought how whatever fate you imagine for yourself always has a certain melodrama to it. Teresa was probably thinking about visiting me in jail wearing a kerchief over her head, the way pathetic women did in the movies. And I couldn't stop thinking about gang rape. When, for a moment, I could see past these things, I imagined something good might follow from this action of mine, and I believed, once I got past the high-flown reasons I had for turning Billy in, that this was the real reason I was doing it—to purify our lives. Her period still hadn't come, and she was suffering a slight bloatedness that worried even her. She'd told me, in an offhand way, that she had made an appointment with her gynecologist. I was convinced that she was pregnant and that she thought me unworthy of becoming a father again. I was convinced, too, that these various parts of my life—the need to free myself of Billy, the child who might or might not be born as a result of it—were coming together for a reason.

The lawyer whose name Kenny had given me was Tommy Newman, and he was willing to see me right away. It was me who put the meeting off for a week. That week, though, filled with my thinking about what I was about to do, became agonizingly slow. It happened to be a week full of soccer. Nina was having a good spring season. On the sidelines, Teresa and I cheered, and accepted the congratulations of other parents, and did a particularly good imitation of a couple who had no great pressing concerns other than to bask in the thrill of raising a daughter with splendid opportunities before her, the sort of girl for whom the new Bradford existed.

Chip Holmes was at some of those games. He moved from couple to couple, making conversation, and I always marveled at how easy it was for him to chat with me and never allude to what had happened between us. But I knew that the softball coaching assignments had been made for the new season, and I had not been asked to join him.

It turned out that Teresa's appointment with her gynecologist had been made for the same day that I was meeting Tommy Newman.

His office was in one of the new buildings near the D.A.'s office, high up over Charles Street. He was balding, his rusty hair combed over the bald spot, and under it a crinkly boy's face. As eager as he'd seemed on the phone to hear my story, in person he seemed to be backing away from his own interest. He listened with a look that I read as forced gravity. Once or twice his face broke into a thin smile that did not seem occasioned by anything I'd said.

"Let me ask you something," he said when I was finished. "*Why* do you want to do this?"

It was not a question I'd expected.

"I'm worried about what happens when they trace this back to me."

His face made a kind of tic, indicating that a thought was going through his head, one he didn't necessarily intend to share.

"It's almost better if they do trace it back to you," he said. "Makes it neater for them. This way you're forcing them to make a case."

"Yes. I know that."

"*Do* you?"

He picked up a rubber band and began playing with it, sitting back in his chair, that half smile still on his face. He seemed to enjoy watching me there in my discomfort.

"They've got a case, and now you're forcing them to make a new one. Based on a phantom gun. Which they didn't even know was hidden. They're going to hate you."

"I know that."

"*Do* you?"

"Look, I've watched this thing happen. I've watched how he's been playing the city. Now I can't anymore."

He nodded, as if I'd said something inconsequential. He got up and went to the cooling unit by his window and adjusted it. Then he looked out the window with his hands in his pockets, so I had to look at his back.

"Is that your son?" I asked, referring to a picture of a boy in a football uniform he kept on his credenza. He looked where I'd directed him, but didn't respond, as though he wanted to have no traffic with the personal.

"Look, I'm going to lay out some options for you. But I've gotta say, I think this is very tricky." He glanced at me as if he had just chosen to notice my clothes, the shape of my chin. "You're certain the police arrested the wrong guy."

"I'm ninety-nine percent certain."

"That's ninety-nine percent. All you know is you were asked to hide a gun, by the brother, and you had no suspicion—"

"How could I help but have a suspicion?"

"Okay, if this is such a terrible burden to you, why didn't you call the cops then? When you still had the gun?" Again he was smiling, and I hated it. He seemed to be smiling at my stupidity. "Because they're going to ask that."

"I wanted to see how it played out."

"Oh, bright. But I don't believe you. I think you couldn't believe it was your friend."

"True."

"Okay. But now, because there's the coincidence of the returned gun and the gun found in this guy's car, *now* you're convinced."

"I've been convinced a long time."

He paused, staring at me, playing with the rubber band. His buzzer went off. He ignored it.

"Tell me about your friend. Tell me about this guy."

"What do you want to know?"

"What the whole town wants to know." He shrugged, as if this would be a good story I could share with him. "What's the appeal of this guy?"

In a law office—this world governed by purposefulness, rules, and order—it was not an easy question to answer.

"I mean, is this spurned love?"

"What?"

"I'm asking questions you're going to be asked. They'll want to know why now. They'll want to know whether you've got any reason to want to frame this guy."

"It's not spurned love."

"All right." His smile was wide, but I could see, behind it, that he was doing a covert scan of my face. "Only kidding. Maybe. It's a question. Is the brother going to corroborate what you're telling me?"

I thought about Ronnie in the parking lot. I didn't want this anymore.

"The brother's holding to a story. That he was home that night. They don't leave the father. They're his caretakers, and he's like eighty-nine years old. But I'm sure it was the brother who drove the car."

"You know this."

"Look, everybody said the guy who ran off and got into the car was a black man. Well, the brother's dark. He could be mistaken, in the dark, for being black."

Tommy Newman continued to sit there, unimpressed.

"You *know* this."

This time I said nothing.

"Or is it a story you've made up?"

"I didn't make it up. *You* put it together. What was the gun they asked me to hide?"

"I don't know. Not my business to know. My business is, before I turn you over to these guys, do you have some protection? Do you know what I charge an hour?"

I nodded.

"Do you want to keep talking?"

"Yes."

But for the moment, he didn't ask any more questions. He put his hands together with his elbows on his desk and looked out the window. He didn't need to tell me to be quiet. I hated this, hated the feeling of his being able to see three or four steps beyond what I could see, while I had to sit passively by.

"You comfortable helping them go after the brother?" Tommy Newman asked. "Because if they believe you, that's what they're going to have to do."

I slunk down a little in my chair.

"There's nothing here without the brother breaking down. It's a story; that's all it is. And then, you're implicating him. Have you thought about that?"

Miserably, I nodded.

"Sending two people to jail. Three, if the father's in on it."

"The father's not in on it."

"No? You seem to have a very good, very thorough sense of the case. Congratulations. The girlfriend? What about her?"

"I don't know any of this."

I just looked at him. He seemed to be loving this, the spinning of the widest web.

"All right," he said. "I'll stop. But they won't. That's my promise. Because your friend Ken DiGiovanni won't tell you this, but I will. They're desperate for this to be the black guy. You know why? Because if it's the white guy, they screwed up. What took them so long? Remorse requires that they get everybody." He made a slicing motion with his hand. "Everybody. To say to the city: *See? We're not racists.*"

"So what are you advising me? What's the advice?"

"No advice. I'm not going to do that. I'm only going to lay out a series of likelihoods so that you can make an informed decision.

You will devastate a town, and you will be seen as the bad guy. Your parents live in this town. You ready to take them in? Because they will not want to live in Winship anymore. We've got the parents now, living upstairs in your house. You like this so far?"

"Go on."

"I don't know where to go. I can only respond to what you've told me. Are there other people involved?"

I shook my head. I thought of my mother's Beano nights, and I shook my head again. Surely he was exaggerating.

"And if I don't do this," I said, "I'm a guy who's protecting a killer."

"Potentially."

"Right. Potentially."

He deliberately allowed the next silence, forced it.

"But let me do my job thoroughly, because that's you in your own eyes. The harboring a killer part. In the eyes of the law, you're something else."

"What's that?"

He smiled, liking what he was about to say.

"In the eyes of the law, you're a man with a hole in his back-yard."

His advice, which he would not dignify with the name of advice, was to "think it over." I had expected something simpler, that merely by appearing in his office I would set the wheels of justice in motion. But it would take more. If I wanted, he would set up a meeting with the D.A.'s people. He could not promise anything beyond what he called an "informal proffer"; it was up to me to look this up afterward. Was I looking at jail? I wanted to know. He smiled. "Jail time? For what? Illegal possession of a gun?"

As soon as I was outside the building, I tried calling Teresa but could not reach her. I drove home, knowing I'd be ahead of every-one, and waited with Scooter on the porch. Both girls had after-school activities, and I knew that Teresa was planning to pick up one if not both of them on her way back from the gynecologist. But it was at least possible that she might arrive alone, and we could have a few minutes together.

Not many cars ever passed our house, so when I saw one approaching, I became as alerted, as point-nosed as Scooter. The car was still in the distance, and it took me a moment to discern color and shape. Teresa had the Explorer, and as this car approached, I could see it was a different car, one I didn't recognize. It slowed and stopped at the end of the driveway.

Something told me to go into the house. I lifted the phone, so if someone got out of the car, I could call 911. Then I would run into the woods. That was my plan. But the car, after parking there for several moments, continued down the road. Through the window I could see an old man at the wheel, completely befuddled. Still shaking, I put down the phone.

The detectives, when I finally got to them, treated me like someone beneath contempt. I was seated in a chair in a small, closed room, Tommy Newman beside me, and the detectives were standing, jacketless, constantly turning their asses toward us, as if this were an accepted part of the ritual. Tommy Newman adjusted his glasses, patient and even a little amused by the mistreatment we were getting. I was intensely aware of the clock ticking, the three hundred dollars an hour he charged. He did not say, Relax. He did not say, This is the usual thing. Instead, I detected a residual annoyance with me under his calm exterior.

At a certain point, maybe twenty minutes after we'd gotten there, Officer Medina came in, as if he'd been called out of something much more important and had very little time for us. He carried a notebook and directed his first questions to Tommy Newman.

"Is Dennis going to join us?" Tommy Newman asked.

"Dennis apologizes. He's on his way."

Officer Medina clicked his pen a couple of times on the table before turning his attention to me. It seemed part of the game the others had been playing. He had only come in here, like them, to study me.

"How's your wife?" he asked.

"My wife is fine."

That seemed the extent of his questions. Teresa had come home from the doctor with a diagnosed case of hypothyroid. The diagnosis wasn't a happy one, but it did relieve us of the pressure of a difficult decision. Still, I felt something lingering from that decision, some residue, as though Teresa had already made it without me.

"Can you describe this gun you hid?" Medina said, and flipped his notebook up and down on his crossed knee.

Tommy Newman touched his own lips, as if he was patiently waiting something out, but when he turned to me, it was to prod me to answer.

"I don't know anything about guns," I said. "It was snub."

"Snub," Medina repeated, and glanced at Tommy Newman, as if later, when they were alone, they would laugh hysterically at this.

"So it wasn't a Luger. Or a Walther. It wasn't a James Bond–type gun."

I didn't answer. I thought this was all in the manner of a ritual humiliation.

"You can answer that," Tommy Newman said.

"No, it wasn't."

"It was 'snub.' Do you know what a Colt .45 looks like?"

"No, I don't."

"He doesn't know guns," Medina said, and opened his hands to Tommy Newman.

"If you showed it to me, I could recognize it," I said.

Medina raised his eyebrows, as if he wanted to compliment me: he had not thought of such an obvious, brilliant solution.

"It had rust on it, from being buried so long."

But this did, indeed, seem to suggest something to him. His eyelids lowered, and he wrote, with an air of unwillingness, something in his notebook that looked like nothing, like a squib.

"Rust can come from a lot of places, Mr. O'Kane."

"There might be dirt on it."

"Okay, there's an idea. You had it buried how long?"

I had to think a moment, to count all over again. "Seven months."

"Seven months." Medina wrote it down. "In the dirt outside your house." He nodded by bunching his chin. "You think we can come match the dirt outside your house with the dirt on this gun? You think we can bring the FBI in on this one, Tom? I think maybe your client watches too much television."

Before he could say anything more, the door opened and another man came in, slightly better dressed, with prematurely gray hair and the bulk and a hint of the lumpy good looks of the basketball player Bill Walton. Medina deferred to him, got up, left him the chair. This large man nodded to Tommy Newman and then to me and said, "I'm Dennis McBride." I recognized the name of the man I'd been waiting for, the assistant D.A.

"Okay, from what I understand from my conversation with Tom, you hid a gun you're claiming was given to you by Ron Mogavero. This right?"

"Yes."

"And he told you he wanted to hide it."

"I'm not saying that. The kid was very helpless."

"Kid?" Dennis McBride looked slightly confused.

"Right. He's not a kid. He's in his mid-thirties. But he's borderline retarded."

Dennis McBride looked as though he was trying to remember whether he knew that. "I don't recall anything like that."

"No. There wouldn't be anything like that. Anywhere. They never went for a diagnosis on this kid. They were—embarrassed."

Dennis McBride peered at me through the sort of translucent blue eyes I associated with surfers, druggies.

"If you're going to prosecute this case, you've got to understand Winship," I said.

"I think we can dispense with sociology," Tommy Newman said.

There was a silence, until Dennis McBride tipped his head forward. "Well, I might as well know."

"You grew up there, in the sixties anyway, the seventies, you've got a kid—a son, a brother—who's retarded, there's nothing you can do about it except figure out how he fits in. You don't—I mean, they weren't trying to get this kid into Harvard."

Dennis McBride cocked his head, as if trying to gauge the potential weight of this argument. "There's nothing in the books."

"You should go and talk to people who know him. Before, I mean, before you go prosecuting him."

"Okay," Tommy Newman said. "This is not what we're here for, to establish the mental retardation of Ron Mogavero."

"No, but it's interesting," Dennis McBride said, and I couldn't tell whether he was trashing me with those words.

Medina remained in the corner the whole time, looking increasingly impatient with this line of questioning.

"So take me through this." McBride eased back in his chair. "Ron Mogavero—kid, retarded, whatever—he comes to you. When?"

"Last Labor Day."

"And what happens?"

"He looked helpless," I said. "He never *asked* me to do anything. The thing is, he claimed he found my house through the Internet. I don't think this kid could even use the Internet. I think he was sent."

McBride looked at Tommy Newman. Something brief and subtle passed between them. Tommy Newman had advised me that if I wanted leniency from the court, I should not try to save Ronnie.

"So without being asked, you hid the gun for him."

"Not *for* him. He didn't know what to do with it."

Dennis McBride, all genial gym-shorts affability, ball carried high under the shoulder, revealed for an instant some depth of hardness that, brought to bear, would have crushed me in an instant. He lifted one hand, stretched it in front of his forehead, and scratched around the area of his left eyebrow, a deliberately prolonged gesture.

"I don't see this. Failure of the imagination, I guess. This guy comes to your house—what?—the gun is exposed?"

"It's in a bag."

"Okay."

"He drops the bag on my table, that's all. He can't deal with it anymore."

After studying me in silence for about twenty seconds, Dennis McBride turned to Tommy Newman.

"I'm sorry. I'm having a little trouble with this scenario." He looked at his watch. "Your client didn't ask him anything. He wasn't told anything." He turned to me with that look of lingering distaste. "This is true?" McBride asked me.

"Yes."

"So let's say we want to get you in front of a grand jury. What you'll say in court is that the brother came to you, dropped a gun helplessly on your kitchen table."

"Dining room."

"Excuse me. Dining-room table. Ran out. End of story."

"That's all I'll testify. But look—"

McBride seemed to be waiting, assessing my capabilities like a coach on the first day of practice, not hopeful.

"It's obvious his brother had given him the gun."

"Is it?" McBride leaned forward now. "It's not obvious to me. How do we know this gun wasn't dropped at the murder scene, uncovered by Bill Mogavero, hidden from the hospital authorities—"

"Jesus, he was bleeding to death."

"Exactly. How do we know we aren't bringing in an innocent man because you, Mr. Fucknuts, seem not to have asked any questions?"

I stopped a second, registered it, turned to Tommy Newman. "I didn't know I was going to be called Mr. Fucknuts here."

"Yes, well, you've just been called Mr. Fucknuts." He paused. "You want me to ask for an apology?"

"No."

Dennis McBride stood. "You might tell your client, Tom, that if somebody else comes up with this story, we can't protect him from prosecution."

"If you'd stay here one minute, Dennis."

Dennis McBride tucked the folder he carried in close to his chest, crossed his arms.

Tommy Newman leaned toward me. "That, what he just said, is

not Aramaic, Tim. I assume you understand it. We're assuming the only people who know what happened that night are you and the brother." He did that funny breathing thing lawyers do, as if to assert that the air they breathe has more heft, more nuanced truth in it than the air the rest of us breathe. "If it comes out some other way, from somebody else, there's a limit to how much you can be protected unless you're willing to help."

I took it in.

"I'm not going to say something's true that isn't true. And I'm not going to say anything to help put Ronnie away. This, what I've told you, this is the whole story."

Dennis McBride got up to leave. "We'll get back to you, Mr. O'Kane."

Medina followed him.

"Oh good," Tommy said when we were alone. "What a jolly afternoon we're having. They don't believe a word you've said."

He started to put his things away.

"If this involves making a case against Ronnie, I can't go through with it."

"Look, let me point out something. First of all, you don't decide whether you'll testify. This information you've given them is out. They'll tell *you* whether you testify. Unless you want to say no, in which case you're in contempt, and we'll go to jail. We'll see if we can get you a short sentence out in Concord. You must be familiar with that facility, living out in the sticks where you do."

"If there's a trial, I'll just say what I told you. I'll tell them Ronnie was retarded. I'll just tell them the simple story."

"Look, forget Ronnie for a minute, okay? If you want immunity, you've got to cooperate with these guys. At least if you want to protect your family. Which I was under the impression you were."

"Right," I said, and couldn't look at him.

"And while we're on the subject, let me illuminate one little thing for you. We don't have trials so you can tell nice stories. The commonwealth isn't going to spend a small fortune bringing this to trial so you can get up and tell your story about what a good guy you are, wanting to help the sweet retarded kid, and what a model of pre–safety net America Winship, Massachusetts, is. Fuck all that."

He smiled widely now. "They will have a trial so they can punish everyone in sight. They are *embarrassed*, all right? They will get the brother anyway. Everybody loses. Congratulations."

"Just shut up, okay?"

"Fine."

"I'm sorry. Just give me a minute."

In silence, his pen went back into his pocket. "Sure. Yes. How old are your kids?"

"I told you, I just want to think about this a minute."

"Think. Go ahead."

"Nobody ever said anything definite. Nobody ever said to me, here's what happened. I had to figure it out for myself."

"Exactly," he said, and he waited.

seventeen

A threat hung over me for the next couple of weeks. Tommy Newman told me the police would indeed get back in touch with me, most likely to identify the gun. After that, he assured me, a no-man's-land opened.

I waited for Billy to call me. Whatever the relative uselessness of the information I'd given the cops, I couldn't believe they'd be sitting on it. They'd have to be questioning Ronnie, and Billy would hear about it. In the meantime, a silence seemed to hang over the prosecution of Kevin Sammy.

One night we gave a dinner party. It was not the sort of thing we usually went in for, but Teresa had warmed to a couple—the Fletchers—who had recently moved to Bradford and whose daughter played soccer with Nina. I had balked at the idea of inviting them over, but Teresa insisted.

"What, are we just going to wait until you go to jail, Tim? Is that our lives now? The girls aren't supposed to have friends? Everything's got to shut down while you act out your little drama?"

Lying beneath us now was my memory of the way Teresa had dealt with the phantom pregnancy, how she'd shut me out.

The evening with the Fletchers had that pleasantness I'd come to despise in our social arrangements. Teresa was, I was always surprised to be reminded, a brilliant actress. We were a sterling couple. She joked about us, things we did, as if to put us on display. We hadn't made love in weeks, and I wondered if some subverted sexual energy wasn't stoking this performance of hers. Peter Fletcher had an awful bald spot I couldn't bear to look at. His wife had the unimpeachable complexion and the short, well-tended hair of a woman who came from money and was now making every effort to hide that fact. Our conversation was all about soccer. This was how we'd be expected to live now, I thought. An endless succession of evenings like this.

I was washing dishes after the Fletchers had gone, when I saw the figure in the backyard. I looked away from him, then back, as if I were seeing something that wasn't there. His white shirt was worn outside his pants. He looked like a man who had gotten lost in the woods, arrived in a brightly lit backyard, and was using it as a coordinate. I carried the dish towel with me out onto the deck and didn't speak at first.

His back was to me as he stared into the woods. After I'd been out there a few moments, he turned to me.

I was aware that I should have felt a chill, but I didn't. There was something quietly defusing in the sight of Billy's large body.

"Hey," I said.

He didn't answer.

"Some people come to the front door," I said. When he still didn't answer, my words came back to me like a mocking of our old joking relationship. "What are you doing here?"

He just went on looking at me. That was when I started to get scared. I couldn't see his left hand, because that side of him was turned away from me, and I started to worry what might be in that hand. But when he turned fully toward me, I saw that it was empty.

I thought he would just walk off. He seemed to be deciding whether or not to do that. Then he started moving toward me.

Before he got to the porch, he stopped again.

"I thought I'd wait until your guests were gone," he said finally.

"Yeah. Thanks."

"The bald guy. The guy with the designer bald spot."

I waited for more.

"They drive an Audi. You notice that?"

"No."

"Well, yes. Shit, it was an Audi. Can I come in?"

"Of course."

When he got close to me on the deck, I smelled something on him, not liquor, some advanced state of sweat. His forehead was red and sweaty, too, and his hair stuck up in the front. His shirt looked soiled, but it was a good shirt. His face was impossible to read. The thrust of his body suggested he wanted to do something to me, but his words, when they came out, had a perverse gentleness.

"You have a good time tonight, Tim?"

"No. Not really."

"Teresa make something good?"

I didn't answer.

"What'd she make?"

"Shrimp."

He nodded. "There any left?"

Surprised, I hesitated a moment. "There might be a few."

"Can I have some?"

"Yes. Of course."

I opened the door. I was going to follow him, not the opposite.

He stood in the kitchen as if he were too large for it, a simple movement coming from him would break something. All his complex physical grace was gone. I opened the refrigerator, took out the shrimp I'd put in a Tupperware container, transferred it to a dish, and popped it into the microwave.

"Ah, I don't care if it's hot."

"No, have it hot."

He stared at the microwave the whole time the plate was turning, even after the beeper went off.

"Things give you cancer, don't they?"

"Come on, Billy, don't you have one?"

"Not at home. My father refuses. Paula's got one, but I won't eat anything out of it."

He took the plate, though, and started scarfing the shrimp down. He was ravenous.

We both looked up at the same time when we heard Teresa gasp. She was standing in the doorway. She'd changed into a bathrobe. Her makeup was off her face. She reached up to touch her face, as if that was the most important thing. Billy looked at her, noting this, then went on shoveling in the food. It made his cheeks bulge. Some of the rice stuck to the side of his lips.

"What are you doing here?" Teresa asked.

He looked up, and his eyes, like his clothes, looked soiled. They were too wide for the moment.

"I'm eating your food," he said. "Which is delicious."

She finally turned to me: What was I going to do about this? I shook my head to warn her against her impulse to throw him out. Billy put his plate down. With one finger he made a circle of the plate and then sucked his finger, which had collected the last of the sauce. He made an elaborate show of looking for a napkin until finally I handed him one. He wiped his mouth and went on staring at Teresa.

"You don't want me to be here?" he asked with a slight air of pretend offense.

She paused and said, "No." Then: "Please get out."

Billy turned to me, and again I gave Teresa what I thought was a reassuring look, a look that said, Let me take care of this.

"Oh, what, Tim? What's he going to ask you to do this time?"

"Teresa, I need to talk to him."

"I never . . ." Billy held one hand out and looked for a moment like he wasn't certain he should enter this marital spat. "Let's get one thing clear: I never asked Tim to do anything for me."

"Oh no," she said. "Oh no, no you didn't."

She was breathing hard suddenly. "Ask him to leave."

"Billy, maybe you and I should go somewhere else."

He looked at me. I was not sure whether he was about to agree or disagree. Then he took a step toward Teresa. He moved so he was between us, closer to her than to me. I saw only the back of his head. I could not tell what his face was doing, but I saw Teresa looking at him as if there were two things going on in her at the same time. One was repulsion and the other, well, the other was like a revelation of the hugest mystery about her. It was like seeing the erotic life she lived when she wasn't with me. I didn't think

Billy was doing anything on purpose to make her feel that. It was something he couldn't help. Women always touched things, if only briefly, when they were with him; it might be a part of themselves they never let out otherwise.

She pulled her stare away from him, focused on the floor, as if she couldn't bear it another second. Billy just went on looking at her.

"Billy, come on," I said.

He turned back to me, and it was as if I was the least important person in the room. He didn't say anything.

"Leave her alone. Let's go somewhere."

There was still that uncertainty in his face, as though he couldn't imagine what I was talking about or why I didn't leave myself. A thought went through me: with him it wouldn't have been hypothyroid, with him it would have been a baby. Having that thought angered me so much I put my hand on his shoulder to pull him away.

He knocked my hand away. "Fuck off," he said.

"All right, out," I said.

His eyes widened slightly.

"Get out. I was going to talk to you. I was going to treat you like a reasonable person. I see that's fucked."

He looked only mildly amused by this, not the least bit threatened.

"Are you two going to have a fight?" Teresa asked. "If you're going to have a fight, go outside and do it. I don't want you breaking things. I don't want my daughters woken up."

"Your daughters," Billy repeated, and scratched the hair at the base of his neck. For an instant he just looked tired, and Teresa, sensing something—maybe some weakness in him—locked into him.

"Why don't you turn yourself in and keep my husband from going to jail?"

He took that in as if he had superior information. He held it a second.

"Don't smile like that. Don't give me that stupid smile."

She took a step back from him. He seemed to be marveling at her every move.

"Why don't you do that?"

"Maybe I will. Where's the phone?"

"Billy, we should talk first."

Teresa looked at me as if she was more scared by my stupidity than by anything Billy might do.

"Talk?" Billy asked. "What are we going to talk about? Where is it?"

"It's over there," Teresa said, and pointed.

He went to it. He picked it up. Then he held the receiver against his chest.

"Who am I calling?"

Teresa briefly closed her eyes. "The police."

"And telling them what?"

As if she couldn't stand it any longer, she picked up Billy's plate and brought it to the sink and seemed about to wash it, but instead she broke it. She threw it down into the sink and covered her face.

"Whoa," Billy said.

"I can't stand it," Teresa said. "I want this awful thing over. I don't know what I walked into with you two, but I want it over."

She was not quite crying. She seemed too angry to cry.

"I'll do it. I'll fucking do it, Teresa," Billy said, and you had to have known him forever to know he was mocking her. He had the attitude of a man who knows where all the secret compartments in a desk are and thus can sit there, knowing you will not find the hidden thing.

"He's making fun of you, Teresa."

"No, I'm not," Billy said.

"Go to bed. Go up to bed, and I'll deal with this."

"Like you've been dealing with it so far? You've been doing a terrific job so far, Tim. We're on the verge of losing everything."

"How's that?" Billy asked with a stab at innocence that an outsider might believe. "How is it you're on the verge of losing everything?"

At the sink, we both turned to him, and I realized we were not going to get rid of him. The thought of doing violence to him came over me, and then the thought of Teresa seeing me do that violence. I believed it might be good for her to see me do that, but I couldn't do anything to Billy. I didn't have that rage against him.

"Teresa, go up to bed, and I will make sure he leaves."

"You think I could lie in bed knowing he's in this house?"

"God, I am feeling major waves of hatred coming from both of you," Billy said.

"Billy, what did you come for?" I asked.

He loosened his grip on the phone. "Shrimp. I was hungry."

He sat at the counter. For the moment he was only our lost, derelict friend, a romantically hapless bachelor who looked in on his settled married friends after a disappointing night in which his only other option was to go home alone.

I went and sat across from him.

"Okay, Teresa's not leaving, and I have some questions for you, Bill."

"Shoot. Go ahead. Shoot."

"You know I've gone to the police and told them Ronnie asked me to hide a gun here."

"How would I know that, Tim?"

"I don't know. But I know you know it."

He looked at me the way I imagine a man must look at his accountant after he's been told he's made a large miscalculation and is going to have to pay a hefty penalty. He was not happy, but neither was it the end of the world.

"You did that," he said.

"Yes."

"And thank God," Teresa said. "Because otherwise you'd have gotten away with this."

He turned to her, unaffected by what she said but mildly interested in her nonetheless. He put his hand on a small olive oil plate on our counter and spun it, then pushed it forward.

"Tell me you're surprised by this," I said.

When he looked at me, I saw that he was. Against all the odds, he hadn't known.

"Then what did you come here for?" I asked.

"To see you." He spoke with a simplicity that had nothing under it, no mocking of us. I knew him that well.

So I was stopped in my tracks. Teresa made a snickering noise behind me.

He looked up at her. "You think I'm a killer, don't you?"

She raised her eyebrows. "Oh, why would I think that? I can't imagine."

"Why?"

He turned back to me, and it was like looking at Ronnie, like coming into contact with an innocence so deep it has lost the capacity to be penetrated. Just as Ronnie was incapable of believing his brother could do the worst, it was as if Billy could not believe it of himself. The murder existed in some other sphere, having nothing to do with our world, this kitchen. I knew that in his own mind he fully believed he deserved to be here.

"Tim, I'm starting to think this is not a good idea," Teresa said. "Being alone with him like this. I'm thinking we should call the police."

Billy just turned to the side, not doing anything to stop her.

"I've got nothing in my pockets. You can look in my pockets," he said.

"Because you hid the gun in that man's car," she said.

He went on looking at her but chose not to speak the words that were in him.

"I wouldn't hurt you guys," was what he finally said. He stood. "You want me to go, I'll go. I ate your shrimp. I'm sorry." He reached into his pocket, pulled out his wallet, slapped a twenty on the table. "That should cover it."

"Put that back," I said.

"Why?" Teresa said. "We should keep it."

"Yeah, keep it. You know I put your daughters into my will." He looked from one to the other of us. "I made a lot of money. Patty's insurance. My brother and I'll inherit the house when my father dies." He reached up and loosened his collar. "Not a lot. I didn't leave them a lot. Most of it I have to leave to Ronnie." He nodded and went to the door.

"What are their names, Billy?" Teresa had her arms crossed. "Our daughters' names. That you put in your will?"

He just looked at her as if he was honestly trying to remember. He opened the door and went outside.

In the aftermath we didn't quite know what to do with ourselves. Teresa went about cleaning up the broken dish.

"I'll do that," I said.

"No," she said harshly. She looked out the window over the sink to see if she could see Billy. "Just make sure he leaves," she said.

"You can see he's not going to do anything," I said.

She didn't dignify it with a response, but had a response in silence.

"In his will," she said, and shook her head.

I went out onto the deck. Billy was lying in a ball at the edge of it.

"Jesus," I said, and went over and prodded him.

"Let me sleep here," he said.

"Why do you need to sleep here?"

"Maybe I've been thrown out."

I crouched over him. "Paula threw you out."

"Maybe that's what I came to talk to you about. Maybe that's why I was so upset."

"I thought you two were good together."

Billy lay back, nearly smiling as he stared up at the sky. "Oh, I'm real good, Tim. I got a wife dead, a kid dead. I'm a *catch*."

He was silent a moment. "Let me sleep here."

"I can't do that. Teresa's upset with you. She'd never allow it."

"And you? You said I asked you to hide a gun."

"Yes. That's what I said."

"I never did. I never asked you anything."

I didn't respond, just to see where he might go with this.

"How'd Ronnie get that gun, Bill?"

He didn't answer, looked as if he was on the verge of sleep.

"I'm doing this so I can protect your brother."

He opened his eyes, as if to call me on the lie. He didn't have to say anything.

"All right, maybe that's not true, but you can still save him."

"How?"

"Turn yourself in."

I was encouraged when he didn't answer.

"Come on, I'll drive you right now. We can go into Boston. You can make a statement."

"Let me sleep."

"Billy, I can't let you sleep here. It's time to end this."

He kept his eyes closed. "End what?"

"Billy. Just say it. Please. Just say it. Admit you killed Patty."

He was silent. Eyes closed. I thought he might slip into sleep, so I shook him, my hand on his chest. He grabbed my hand by the wrist and held it hard.

"Jesus, Billy."

He wouldn't let go. I tried to pull it away, and he wound up on top of me. He pinned me down, the whole enormous weight of him on my chest, my hands clamped down above my head.

"What'd you do? What'd you do, Tim?"

"I turned you in," I said.

He was looking at me as though he wanted to hate me more than he did. There was violence in him, and there was something that was fighting against the violence. He banged my held fists against the wood of the deck and let go. But then, as a kind of afterthought, he took my head in both hands and banged it against the deck.

"Jesus Christ, why?" he asked.

At that point the door opened. Teresa must have been watching, because she came out with the empty wine bottle we'd drunk with the Fletchers, holding it as a weapon.

Seeing this, Billy laughed, though he hadn't let go of his anger.

"Oh, Jesus, look. She's gonna hit me. She's gonna bean me with that."

"Teresa, go inside."

"And let him kill you?"

"Get the fuck *inside*," Billy shouted, so loud the neighbors might hear us, as far away as that was. "Get the fuck inside. This isn't about you. This was *never* about you."

Teresa lowered the bottle but otherwise didn't move.

"Go inside," Billy said more gently. "I'm not going to hurt your pansy husband."

Billy got off me and stood to the side, held out his hands. "See?"

"I'm not going anywhere."

He seemed to be marveling at her. "This is some woman you've got here," he said. "Ready to defend you, Tim."

He shook his hands out, as if he was shaking out the violence in himself.

"You're going, or I'm calling the cops. In fact, I'm calling them anyway. I'm calling them now. You hurt him, I swear I'll kill you."

She went inside.

Billy looked at his watch, then at me. "How's your head?"

It was as close to an apology as I thought I'd get.

"Okay."

He looked down at the slats of the deck, leaned down on his haunches, and tried to pull a sliver of wood up.

"You better go before the cops come." I slid up so I was sitting. My head hurt. "I mean it. If you want to go in and make a statement, I'll go with you. Otherwise, Bill, Ronnie gets caught up in this. You understand that?"

"Oh, I understand it."

He looked at me with a measure of sadness in his face. There was something else I couldn't read. Then he straightened up with his hands in his pockets and took the two steps off the deck. He looked up at the house. For a second or two, it was like being with the old Billy, the Billy of before the murder, the Billy who marveled at things and stayed clear of them. For a moment he seemed to be acknowledging my triumph.

"Where you going? Where are you going to sleep?" I asked.

"What the fuck do you care, Tim?"

I put my hand over my eyes.

"You go inside. Okay? Your daughters. Upstairs. Your wife, she wants to take care of you."

It was as if he were slipping into shadows as he spoke, though I didn't think he was moving. Maybe the blow to my head was affecting me late, altering my vision. I was watching Billy slip into another place, and whatever he'd done, I didn't want him to go there.

Maybe I spoke his name. Maybe I closed my eyes for longer than I thought, but when I opened them, he was gone.

It took the city of Boston a few days to notice Billy's disappearance. I first read about it on page 14 of the *Globe*: the husband of the woman murdered a year ago in South Boston had disappeared. His family had not heard from him in days. He was last seen heading out to what his father had been told was a job interview.

It was Freddie who told me what happened, Freddie assisted by a few reluctant words from Kenny: the police had come looking for Billy and found him gone. Freddie found it irresistible to add a little piece of gossip then floating around, that two of Patty's brothers, having finally put two and two together, had come after Billy.

"They'll find him floating somewhere," Freddie said.

"No, I don't think so" was my answer.

The *Herald* broke the story that Billy had at last become the named suspect. They printed the least attractive of his pictures, one taken later, in his post-Patty decline, where his cheeks looked bulgy and his hair unkempt and his eyes had a sly, I've-gotten-away-with-something look. In the headlines and the accompanying articles Billy was transformed, as though the city had blotted out overnight all memory of its previous romance with him as suburban husband and Little League coach. The hard-boiled female *Herald* columnist who had written the hugely influential "They Killed One of Their Own" wrote an equally influential front-page editorial called "Anatomy of a Fast One," in which the new Billy emerged. "He slept with his father's Trinidadian caretaker, and possibly fathered a baby with her," the columnist wrote, in defiance of the DNA tests. "All this while living the life of suburban do-gooder, good son and good dad-to-be. His Waltham neighbors (it's enough to make you barf) reported the tender care he took of his apple trees."

Upon Kevin Sammy's release from custody, the Boston Police

Department issued a painfully worded apology to the black and Hispanic communities of greater Boston. The department insisted it would spare no effort in finding the missing man.

All this broke—Billy's picture everywhere, in newspapers and tabloid magazine covers, flashed up next to the face of Greta Van Susteren on Fox News—during that dreamy, lilac-scented time, late spring in the suburbs. It was the busiest time of the year for us. The schedules of the girls bulked up uncontrollably. The science fair had to be attended, and the end-of-the-year chorus concert. Soccer play-offs began. There was no possibility of freedom on a Saturday for weeks.

I started a running ritual at night. Usually my running was sporadic, squeezed in where I could find the time, but in those first weeks after Billy's disappearance I became religious about it, running when I got home, no matter how late. It was time I set aside to think about him, but it didn't work. Not exactly. I found it was hard in that season, even with all the publicity he got, to keep Billy at center.

If I was lucky, I got to run while it was still light, and I usually ran as far as the softball grounds, where I stayed and watched an inning or two, sweating nicely in my expensive running clothes. I stayed until the lights came on, because there was something so appealing to me in the sight of the young players under the lights, the green and the brown of the playing field, the chalk lines. I wondered then, if I thought about him at all, what Billy had really been to me, what my long fascination had been about, and how it really compared with a scene such as this, so orderly, so perfect. The police called me in shortly after Billy's disappearance. I was asked to identify the gun, which had been cleaned but which I could see right away was the same gun. Tommy Newman told me I would almost certainly be asked to play a part in the prosecution of Billy after he was caught—they were planning to indict him in absentia—but the most that this could cause me would be some social embarrassment. I'd be known for a day or two as the man who'd hid a gun, believing, in so doing, that he was keeping his friend from seeking revenge. Tommy Newman could use the words "social embarrassment" lightly, as if he were telling me about a surgery that would cause me a couple of days of soreness, but I knew, standing there under those lights, that it would be more than that, that it would cause me isolation, that rather than be just a man, a runner who had stopped to watch a game, I would become a man to be pointed out. But that had not happened yet, and under those lights I could almost will it away.

Then I would run home, walking the last quarter mile. I could see the lights in our windows, and I would feel then as much as I ever had as a young man that feeling of wanting passionately to live within the reduced life, to be merely what I looked like to cars passing by: a guy who lived here in expensive luxury, a manner of the baked-goods table at the soccer games, a partaker of the general feast. I would climb the lawn to my porch and sit there watching the last of the light going over the trees and run my hands over the red hairs on my legs, and it was possible to feel like a guy who, whatever the penance to come, had fundamentally escaped.

But I wondered if I had. Teresa and I had experienced a sexual thaw after the night of Billy's visit. She'd been a she-bear that night and needed to be rewarded. So the sounds of lovemaking rang out again in the O'Kane home. But after that lovemaking, and sometimes during it, I felt a little embarrassed, a little reticent, as though she knew things about me—had witnessed things on the night of Billy's visit—that made me want to hide from her. An air of unreality hung over us, the way you feel after you go on with an activity even after you have admitted to yourself that the reason for it has disappeared. It was as though we were making love in order to avoid the conversation we should be having.

Even Tony DiNardi thawed somewhat toward me. Teresa must have told him what Tommy Newman had said—that legally I was pretty much in the clear—because he started to show up again at the house. Things between us were still tense, but we could at least manage to talk civilly to one another. Our weeks at Sebago and Good Harbor were blocked out and anticipated.

Weeks went by like this, eerily normal. Word on the manhunt for Billy came at us sideways: on the news, in chance remarks, in the repetition of certain images of him on the covers of those magazines I sometimes bought and sometimes left untouched on the supermarket racks. As the days passed, I expected to hear that he was dead. One day Freddie told me that Billy's father had suffered a stroke and been hospitalized. Should we visit him? No, we agreed almost at the same time. Better not.

It was a night in June, a month after Billy's disappearance, that this illusory time ended. I was standing in the kitchen, trying to repair a drawer that had gotten stuck. Teresa was at the dining-room table working on end-of-the-year school business. It was just dark enough that she needed the overhead light on. The girls were outside, chasing each other in the backyard, celebrating their release from school.

My cell phone rang, and I knew. The screen revealed a 617 area code and a number I didn't recognize. It could have been literally anyone. But I knew. The moment—the simple, spring-lit perfection of the moment—made me know it had to be disturbed.

"Tim," the voice said after holding back a moment, and I thought, the way you do at such times, *of course.* I had always known somehow I wasn't going to get away with this.

Teresa looked up. I always remembered, afterward, how odd that was, that she should know, too. It gave me a little flicker of hope that we were connected in some way. I didn't say his name, though. I stepped outside onto the deck.

"Where are you?" I asked.

"What, you got the police there, Tim? They camped out at your house?"

He was speaking slowly, in a tired manner. I didn't answer.

"They tapping your phone, Tim?"

His voice sounded husky. Not drunk, but like a voice that had gone underground.

"Billy, come on, where are you?"

It was the only thing I could think to ask.

"Tim, I want to go see my father."

I could see, in the distance, by the tree line, that the girls' play had erupted into something else, the beginning of a fight. Gabrielle's shoulders had lifted. I stepped down onto the grass, as if at any moment they'd need me as referee.

"Did you hear me?" he asked.

"Billy." I couldn't come up with the first thing to say. "Billy, do you know there's a manhunt out for you?"

He allowed a brief silence.

"No shit. No kidding. What are you doing, Tim? Right now. What are you doing that you're so busy you can't take me to the hospital to see my father?"

I didn't answer. But I could hear, in that last, a note of desperation I wasn't used to in Billy. I started moving toward the girls. At the same time, Gabrielle started walking toward me.

"What's the matter?" I asked Gabrielle. It had become very important in that instant to assert a fatherly presence, as much for Billy's benefit as my own. To let him know I was needed here, that I had a life. Gabrielle moved past me without saying a word. I watched her go into the house, and after a moment I saw Teresa's outline at the glass door. She was watching me.

"Billy?"

"Here."

"I can't take you to your father, Billy. The cops are not here, I haven't been talking to the cops, and so far as I know, my phone is not tapped."

I heard the glass door open, and Teresa stepped out onto the deck.

"Tim?" she called.

I dropped the phone to my side, as if to hide it.

"Where's Nina?" she asked.

"I don't know. She was here a minute ago."

"Find her, will you?"

She hesitated before going inside, as if she wanted to allow me the chance to undo something or to get off the phone.

"Billy, I've got to look for my daughter," I said, and I stepped into the woods.

It was quiet in there, monumentally hushed, and I knew right away I had come into the woods not to find Nina—why would she have come in here?—so much as to get away from the pressures that had built between Billy on the one hand and Teresa on the other. I held the phone tight to my ear and whispered, as though I were talking to him in a closed room.

"Billy, where have you been hiding?"

"Around. Not very far," he answered.

"Why haven't they caught you?"

"I guess because they're stupid. That's my guess, anyway."

He was speaking nearly as low as I was, and this, combined with the silence of the woods, created an intimacy between the two of us. But I was not so deep into the woods that I couldn't see what was going on in the yard, and when I saw Teresa bolt out the back door, I stepped out and called to her.

"Where are you going?"

"I'm going to find her. I don't like her out in the woods when it's dark."

She sounded strident in a way that was overplayed. Nina was not in any great danger. Yet it was impossible for her to say what she really wanted to say—to ask, That's him, isn't it?

"Teresa, I'll go look for her. You go back in the house."

She waited to see what I would do. I started toward the path leading to the DiNardis'. I was far enough from her that she couldn't hear what I said into the phone.

"I've got a domestic situation here, Bill."

"I can hear. Jesus. Kid lost. Better go find her. Fuck me."

"What do you want?" I asked.

"Tim, tell her to come home right away!" Teresa shouted.

"Oh, that hurt," Billy said, referring, I was certain, to the sound of Teresa's voice.

"I asked you a question."

"Right. What I want is to go see my father. In the fucking hospital. Anybody can understand that. Guy's dying. Jesus."

I tried to pierce what he was telling me through his tone, but it was difficult. The telephone wasn't our medium. You needed all of Billy—his body, his eyes—in order to hear him.

"You're close by, is that where you are, Billy?"

"I'm close."

"You know, if I take you to the hospital, they're going to get you. You know that, right? Is that what you want?"

"Tim, I'm ready to face the music."

In everything—words and tone both—it was too offhand. I didn't trust it.

"Why am I having trouble believing this, Billy?"

"I don't know. You want me to be sincere?"

"You're ready to go to jail? Because I will—I will testify against you, Billy."

It sounded odd even to me. Like I was talking not to him, but to Teresa. To someone else, anyway.

After several seconds of silence I said, "Tell me where you are." As if that could ease what I'd just said. I was approaching the Di-Nardis'. I had to get him off before I got there.

"Billy?"

"I don't feel comfortable speaking it, Tim. This is your cell phone, right?"

"Right."

"Okay, so you've got my number. The number I'm calling from. Call when you're in the car, okay? Head up one twenty-eight and call me."

"Billy, what's the point of that?"

"Just—let's do it this way. And don't leave me alone here, Tim."

That I heard distinctly. The fear in it.

"Okay, Billy."

"Promise?"

"Promise."

I switched off the call.

I could see Nina now. Tony had built a flagstone patio, terraced into his backyard, a splendid thing, with wrought-iron furniture and thick padding on the chairs. Nina was sitting in one of those chairs, her hands under her legs, head forward, looking down, while Tony hovered above her as if trying to coerce something from her. His hands were in his pockets. He was wearing a white pair of shorts. His ass looked enormous, a kind of weight he might throw around for leverage.

"Nina!" I shouted.

They both turned toward me.

"Nina, you scared us half to death. Come on home."

Neither of them moved. In the light over the patio I thought I could see Tony's lips purse.

"Trouble at home, Tim?" Tony asked as I approached.

The door into their house opened, and Katie came out with a tray of what looked like iced tea.

"Look who's here!" she said, trying to affect ease and pleasure. "Come, sit down."

"There's no trouble," I said to Tony. "The girls got into a fight, that's all."

"Tell him what you told me," Tony said to Nina.

She shook her head.

"Here, have some of this," Katie said, and rested her tray on one of the wrought-iron tables.

"Go ahead, tell him," Tony said.

He reached into his mouth with the nail of one thumb to work at a tooth. He gazed around his yard with a sudden interest in something. I followed his gaze. I expected to see Billy in the woods, Billy close by. For the first time, I felt scared, not because I might see him now, but because I *would* see him before the night was over.

"Speak up, Sweetheart," Tony said.

Nina drank her iced tea, silent.

"What's this about?" I asked.

"She says there's tension in the house. That's not the word she used. What was the word?"

Nina had no visible response. In spite of my fear, I was beginning to hate this, to want only to escape.

Katie said, "I'll pour you some of this, Tim."

"No, I don't want anything. What's the word, Nina? I want to hear it."

Tony turned ceremoniously toward her. "She asked if she could stay here tonight."

"I don't want her staying here," I said.

Tony's dark face darkened further. He had his hands in his pockets, shifted back and forth on the balls of his feet.

"What are we going to do, Sweetheart?" he asked. "Your father doesn't want you staying here."

"It's vacation," Nina said.

I went forward and grabbed her hand. Tony's hand was very quickly on my wrist. I yanked it away before he could get a grip. Nina was looking up at me. She had a little of Tony's darkness in her. It shone out of her Irishness like a negative charge.

"She's right," Katie said, watching our hands—Tony's and mine—carefully. "It's her vacation now. Nobody needs to get up early. Everybody can use a break."

"Her mother wants her to come home."

Tony looked at me a moment, reached down and scratched at some of the loose cement holding the flagstones together, shook his head against the shoddiness of the work. Then he went and sat with his wife and sipped his iced tea.

"Nina, come on."

The cell phone in my pocket vibrated, indicating I had a message. I must have been out of range on the end of the path. I nearly reached for it. Both Tony and Katie took note of this, and I realized then that they knew, of course they knew, Teresa had called them and told them who I'd been talking to.

"Katie's right, Tim," Tony said. "We could all use a break here. You take care of things at home. We'll take care of Nina."

I no longer knew how to fight for her, or even if I wanted to. Part of me wanted to just let them have her so I could get to Billy. I was desperate to know where he was. But Nina was asking for something. I could tell by her posture, her face. She had sensed that I'd slipped away, and she wanted me back. Wanted to come running into me, as after soccer, and be carried to the car. Wanted the bliss of our silent rides home.

It occurred to me then that I could ignore Billy's message.

"Let me get you a glass," Katie said.

They seemed expectant, watching me carefully. Tony ran his hand along his wife's thigh, the gesture of the impossibly long marriage, the uneroticized familiarity of those who mate for life. Nina seemed to be timing me, waiting, clocking the stillness.

On the path back to my house, having given Nina permission to stay, I was aware that I had done something very wrong. But I had to know.

Billy's message said, "Okay, Tim, I'm at the Wingaersheek Motel, room seven. Don't bother calling. I'm guessing you know where that is." A surprise, but then, what wouldn't be? It was barely thirty miles north.

I snuck around the house without Teresa's seeing me, and I deliberately did not look up at the house as I backed down the driveway, wanting to avoid, if at all possible, the sight of her calling me back. *"Just this,"* I said aloud, with the urgency of someone trying to convince himself of something.

As soon as I was on the highway, the eeriness of what I was doing hit me, and the uncertainty. Route 128 was deserted. The weather changed as I drove north; it became cloudy, with a little rain around Woburn, lasting into Lynnfield, then a post-rain fogginess as I hit the marshy country around Peabody. The rain was moving south.

The lights of the great Peabody malls sparkled and seemed to go on for miles. They promised warmth and company and made some other promise that went beyond those things. I smelled low tide and wondered if anyone who didn't grow up by the sea would know the meaning of that smell of uncovered muck. It was a moment of buffeting myself, asserting the specialness of knowing things. Teresa hadn't called, even though she would have spoken to her parents and found out I'd been there. It made me feel unimportant, as if the results of this trip would matter to no one but me.

But they did, after all, matter to me. And maybe it would go just as Billy had seemed to promise: the trip to the hospital, his being apprehended by the police, a last smile offered as they took him away. It felt like a movie scene as I imagined it. But maybe he was tired of running, and I could do this. I could deliver him.

I wanted the drive to last longer than it did. The exit to the motel appeared before I was quite ready. I knew it from a thousand drives to Gloucester, knew exactly where the motel sat at the end of the exit ramp. I parked away from the motel, under an overhanging vine. Then I sat in the car a moment, listening to its ticking. The beautiful, quiet dependability of my Lexus. I smelled the good car scent, looked with a small, nostalgic smile at my box of CDs. It seemed, at this moment, a cozy life I lived.

I opened the car door and glanced across at the small motel, the nondescript door marked 7. In the office, a teenage boy was playing video games at the computer, his mouth half open. The shades were drawn in room 7. I knew the door would be unlocked, and I hesitated a moment before opening it.

The TV was on. Otherwise the room was dark. Billy's form was laid out, I thought asleep, in his underwear. I could see right away that he'd shaved his head, which looked enormous and rough in the gray light. I went to the bedside table, but before I'd even turned on the light, he let me know he was awake. He sat up and turned off the TV.

"Tim." He was wearing a gold earring in one ear.

"What's that?" I asked.

"What?"

"In your ear."

He reached for it as if he'd forgotten what was there. But even after he'd touched it, he didn't acknowledge my small joke. Around him, on the table, were the remains of vending machine food: Jax Snax, a Diet Coke. Billy was skinny. It took a moment to notice that, the way his underwear hung on him, the way his face sagged.

"Sit down," he said. "I've got a wicked headache."

"Maybe it's this diet of yours."

He glanced at the wrappers on the dresser. This joke went no better than the first. I was having trouble getting the tone for this meeting right.

He got up and went into the bathroom but didn't close the door while he used it. Then he stood in the bathroom doorway and studied me in that reserved, quietly critical manner he managed to summon on those occasions when time had passed between our meetings and he wanted to absorb the changes that had come over Timmy O'Kane. But it was over in seconds; he couldn't maintain his focus on me. He seemed too self-enclosed to take in anyone else.

"You haven't been here all this time, in this motel, have you?" I asked.

"Does it look that way?" He sat on the edge of the bed, as if he was hurting. "You have any water, Tim?"

"Water?"

"Yeah. You know, the kind you pay for."

He was annoyed, as though he expected things of me and I hadn't come prepared.

"No, I don't."

He got up, went into the bathroom again, filled a glass with tap water, and downed two aspirin. I could see his image in the bathroom mirror. With the shaved head and thinner face, he looked extraordinarily ugly. But I thought he appreciated even that about himself. He studied himself and ran his hand over the stubble on his head.

"So? You ready?" he asked, as if I could have no needs tonight more pressing than to chauffeur him around.

"What hospital is your father in?"

"They took him to Mass General."

I nodded, but there must have been some look on my face, because he seemed arrested by it. For the first time, we each seemed to be acknowledging the invisible ball we kept tossing to each other.

"What's the matter, Tim? The room stink or something?"

"It does, yeah."

"I've let my hygiene go."

He ran his tongue along his top row of teeth, then turned back to the sink and started brushing vigorously. When he was done, he stepped out of the bathroom and pulled on a pair of jeans and a polo shirt.

"You gonna pack?" I asked.

He looked at me as if he had to pull my words apart in order to understand them. In place of an answer, he put on underarm deodorant. Then a baseball cap.

In this guise, I saw how he'd eluded capture. He looked like anyone. It was only his size and his undisguisable swagger that marked him out, and then only if you knew him. Otherwise he was anonymous. We could have been two suburban guys heading off to Fenway.

"Ready," he said. "Let's get out of here."

I opened the door.

An immediate sound outside alerted Billy. He took a step back in. Looking at him, I caught a whiff of his suspicion of me: Had I set him up? The boy from the office was taking out garbage.

"It's the kid," I said to Billy, and he stepped outside again.

The boy, seeing Billy, smiled.

"Mark," Billy greeted him.

"Hey, Brian," the boy said, and dragged the garbage to a Dumpster at the edge of the lot.

Outdoors, Billy seemed to become smaller, or maybe I was just picking up, from his manner, his quiet, and his uncertainty, a hint of how he'd lived these past few weeks.

In the car, I asked, "What's the story you've been telling that kid, Billy?"

"I want you to take the scenic route," he said, not responding.

"What scenic route?"

"One twenty-seven," he said.

"Fuck, Billy, I'm taking you to your father. No scenic route. I'm taking one twenty-eight."

"Shh."

He tapped the side window gently. Behind us, the boy, Mark, was making his way back to the office, wiping his soiled hands on the ass of his jeans.

"You're not gonna make me happy, huh, Tim?"

As I pulled out, Billy lifted my box of CDs. The first one he chose was Lionel Richie. I saw the smile take over his face.

"Don't make fun. I go on long drives," I said.

"Sure. I like Lionel Richie, too. Who doesn't?"

He quickly dropped whatever teasing he'd started, as if he couldn't sustain his own interest in it, and after a while he seemed to be only looking at the scenery. He didn't speak until we were past Manchester.

"You hungry?" he asked.

"No."

"I feel like some fried clams. Shit. I should have had you go to Ipswich."

"I'm taking you to your father. That's the deal. That's the whole deal."

He said nothing.

"Tell me, if you haven't been hiding in Gloucester all this time, where have you been hiding?"

"If you were smart, you could look at me and figure that out."

"Well, maybe I'm not smart."

"Tim, take me to Lynn. I want to run on the beach a little."

"We're going straight to the hospital."

I knew he was looking at me, though I kept my eyes on the road ahead of me.

"You know where I'm going, Tim?"

After a moment I said, "Yeah, I know where you're going."

He didn't say anything more; he knew he didn't have to. Before we got to Lynn, he nudged me.

"How about that little place in Swampscott we used to swim?"

I knew the place he meant. It was a private beach we'd liked to crash.

"Take me there."

It took a while to find it again. The street was clearly marked with NO PARKING signs, and there were lights on in some of the surrounding houses. Billy lowered his window all the way and looked out.

"Not much room to run around here, Bill."

He opened the door, got out, then leaned in to speak to me.

"Why don't you come, Tim?"

"I don't want to."

But after he left, it seemed silly to be alone in the car. I watched him cross the little green separating the street from the water. You had to go down a set of steps to get to the beach. I caught up with him at the low-tide line, far down the beach. He found a couple of flat rocks and skipped them in the water.

"Contest," he said, challenging me.

"No contest."

He looked disappointed in me.

"We couldn't even count the skips in the dark."

"Right."

He seemed to be smiling as he looked out at the water. It was a pretty cove, and I knew Billy liked the fact that we were transgressors here. Egg Rock and the coast of Nahant were visible in the moonlight.

"I think I'll go in."

"Billy, come on."

He was already taking his clothes off.

"Shit, Billy."

"You think they have swimming pools where I'm going, Tim?"

I watched him go in. His body was different now: skinnier and older. I remembered what it was like to see him naked when he was young, that image we had all measured ourselves against. It made no sense, but I wanted to undo things, wanted this night to reveal things opposite from what they were revealing. I still wanted him to tell me he didn't do it.

He was far out—I could see the disturbance he made in the water—when I took a couple of steps up to where I could see the car. The lights of another car were just behind it. Of course it would be a police car. I couldn't shout "Billy," so I shouted "Brian," the name the boy in the parking lot had called him.

I had to shout it several times before he called back, "What is it?"

"It's the cops, Brian."

I wondered if he would swim away then. For a moment I hoped so. *Go,* I almost said. I would have to answer for him, make an excuse, but that would be all right. I could see the cops' flashlights shining into my car. Billy had left nothing there, I knew, to give away his identity.

The police flashlight shone on the stretch leading to the beach. I could see it approaching and then heard the words, "Who's down there?"

For a second I considered saying nothing.

"Here," I said finally.

The cop was invisible, only the orb of his flashlight shining. "What are you doing?" His voice sounded familiar, characteristically north shore.

"I just wanted to look at the water, Officer," I said.

There were two cops. I could hear them talking to each other. One of them seemed to laugh.

I held up my hands. "Sorry," I said.

Behind me, Billy was coming out of the water. I reached down and handed him his hat, thinking it would serve as some kind of disguise. Billy just held it. I heard the two cops still talking.

"What are you two doing?" one of them said as he got close.

"My friend wanted to go for a swim," I said.

They shone the flashlight against us. Billy put on his hat. I lifted my arm against the light. For a long moment they studied us.

"You wanted to go for a swim?" the one with the flashlight asked. It was clear what they thought.

"My friend just wanted to swim," I said.

I knew in the next few seconds that their local character, their thickness, and the way sex blocks out everything else would save Billy.

"You want to put on your clothes," the one with the flashlight said, weirdly polite.

"Officer," Billy said, and I couldn't help but think, as I watched the awkwardness with which he dressed, of Charlie Porto, the burning of the sign, the physical command Billy had shown that night.

"Back to your car," the first cop said. "Okay? There's no parking here at night."

When we were at the car, under the streetlamps, I could see the cops more clearly. They were classics: one of them tall and thin, the other tall and stocky, steaming in their own parochial wisdom, boys who had grown up on the beach and decided this was all they ever needed to know.

"You stay dressed now," the one who had spoken said. It was a joke between them.

Billy looked at him but said nothing.

After that, the cops seemed to want to talk only to each other.

"Lexus," the one who had been silent said to his partner.

"Where you from?" the other asked us.

"Bradford," I answered. "We live in Bradford."

"The two of you?"

"Yes." Let them think what they wanted. It was safer for them to think that.

Something came over the squawk box in their car. One of them went in to answer it.

"We're going to wait until you go," the first one said.

Billy and I got into the car. He brought the saltwater smell in with him. We pulled out, and when we were out of sight, Billy started to laugh, though it didn't sound strong and confident.

"Okay, more adventures like that?" I was trying to help him by pretending I hadn't sensed his fear.

He shook his head.

"You had your good swim. We go to the hospital now."

It had begun to seem, even then, unreal, the hospital as destination.

"Just drive through Winship, okay? Just—lemme see Nahant. Sentimental journey. I won't swim, I promise."

We took the long drive down the spit of Lynn in silence. Billy's mood seemed to have shifted again. He held his hands between his knees, pensive. He pointed ahead. When we reached Nahant, I turned around. I didn't believe he was seeing anything; his nostalgia, if that was what it was, felt rote. We both knew the next stop was Winship, past the Lynnway, over the channel; then it was close, and though he wasn't saying anything, I thought Billy probably wanted me to approach the long way, starting at the end, the big houses that seemed to announce the dates they'd been built—the sixties, with its gaudy, proud Italianness. They were houses that matched the spreading waistlines of their owners. There was a lot we both could have said, but we said nothing. Billy was just looking ahead, his head swiveling. His concentration seemed fixed on some absent thing. There was traffic as we approached the town center.

We were near the place where Maureen Feeney had lived, and I said, surprising myself, "You know she died."

"Who?"

"Maureen Feeney. Remember, from the bank?"

Billy didn't remember.

"She was older. She was the one I was fucking, that summer." I didn't like the word "fucking." It was disrespectful. But I still didn't know how to shape the story for Billy.

"What summer, Tim?"

"I never told you. The summer Carol Casella was pregnant."

There it was. The summer of Maureen Feeney set against the other event of that summer, and thereby diminished. For a moment I wanted to have been another person, or else I wanted to invest the person I had been—that boy—with a self-respect he never had.

"And she died? No shit."

He was hardly paying attention. I said nothing more. Out of instinct, I drove down his street and stopped in front of his house. Enough lights were on so that we knew someone was home. Billy scratched his finger against the material of the Lexus seat. He seemed not to want to linger. I was the one who was forcing him to do that.

"Who's taking care of Ronnie, Bill?"

"Fuck if I know."

He lifted his head, as if to gesture me on. But I didn't move.

"Just tell me, okay? It was him who drove the car that night?"

Billy held his head very still for a moment. Then he turned to me, a little smile on his face, as if I was being clever, that was all. He wasn't going to answer.

"The big myth in your family is you never leave your father alone. But you left him alone."

His look said he was just being patient with me now, as if I was stuck on an old theme, one he'd grown bored with.

"Just maybe keep going, Tim," he said after a few moments of silence. His face, without doing much, let me know he wasn't going to release anything.

I negotiated the bottleneck. Behind us were the great stores, lit up. The movies. I wondered what ever happened to the museum that had been announced years ago, the Fantasia Museum, another civic impulse forgotten. The sign that had once been so important was locked away somewhere. Billy had not needed, after all, to destroy it.

We had crossed the Tobin Bridge, the city laid out before us, when Billy told me he wanted me to stop.

"What's the matter? We're near Mass General."

"Just stop, Tim. Get off the bridge and stop."

"You think that's easy?"

"Find a way to do it, okay?"

It took me to Storrow Drive before I could pull off.

"I want you to turn around," he said when we were parked. We were near the jogging path, and a couple of guys passed us, Harvard guys or MIT guys or brokers who lived on Beacon Hill. The water of the Charles glistened on the other side of the jogging path.

"Billy, we're almost there. Mass General is right here."

"He's not at Mass General, Tim."

I was quiet a moment. "Well, where the fuck is he, Bill?"

"You think they bring somebody like him to Mass General? You think this is some important old guy? He's in some derelict hospital on the other side of the river. I want to take a look at something."

"What?"

"Just—go back over the bridge, okay?"

"Billy, this is starting to feel—"

"What? What's it starting to feel?"

"I want it over, okay? I got a family. I *left*—I want it over."

"Okay," he said, and looked at me, and there was something in his eyes I didn't like then. "Okay, it'll be over. You can go back to your family."

The way he said it had the force, for me, of a tiny revelation. I had always heard him making fun of the word when he'd said it before. But he seemed incapable of that now, as if, in spite of the fact of what he'd done, there was an awful respect for the word in him.

I restarted the car, turned around at the next exit, and headed back.

"You don't know what hospital he's in, do you?" I asked.

"I know what hospital he's in. Just stop on the bridge. I just want to look, okay?"

"Okay, but this is it, Bill. Five minutes, I drive you to this hospital, I'm going home."

"Sure," he said after a moment.

We were on the bridge, and he was alert. He pointed to a place, then rejected it, but at another place, where the lane veered to the left and abruptly stopped, a pocket maybe reserved for police cars, he said, "There, Tim, there," and grabbed the wheel so we wouldn't miss it. I came to a stop. Cars passed us at intervals, traffic very slow at this hour.

"Why here?"

He shook his head, bit his lip, then one of the fingernails of his left hand. He lifted his baseball cap for a moment and put it back.

"We have—how long would you say, Tim?"

"For what?"

"Until someone asks us why we're here."

"I don't know. It's late. Go ahead. Take your fill. Last look at the city of Boston."

He looked at me as if to tell me something else. I didn't like what I was picking up from him.

"You know, if you tell me, Billy, maybe I can *help*—"

His eyes softened a moment, looking at me, but he couldn't stay there. His face looked secretive, not a little scared, slightly belligerent, as though he was withdrawing deeper and deeper into himself.

"What?" I asked.

He opened the door. He went to the guardrail and leaned forward. He lifted one foot and propped it on the guardrail.

Beyond him lay the city—not the new buildings, but the old,

oily heart that stretched and bled over the surrounding area for miles. With the window down, a strong breeze came into the car. It had that mashy, male weight, the city, that fierce macho clamor of chain-link fences and hot dogs at the old Boston Garden, that grand old structure that had been refurbished and renamed for a bank. It seemed to me now like a city built for hockey, no more gentle sport, yet it had tried in recent years to learn some more modern, genteel game. Maybe I was looking at it the way I imagined Billy was looking at it, hungry and wishing it had had balls enough to hold on to what it had been, to not have sold itself to the highest bidder.

"Had enough?" I called. "Seen the water?"

He didn't budge.

"Billy?"

He still didn't move. I got out of the car. I stood next to him and watched him staring down into the swirling water, the currents meeting and forming dark, circular pockets far below us. I wondered if he knew I was there. I wondered how long ago he'd left me. I touched him on the shoulder. It alerted him, but it was as though someone else, not me, had grabbed him. When he saw it was just me, he went back to staring at the water.

"Come on," I said as gently as I could. "Your father."

He turned to me. His lower lip formed a kind of beckoning pout, and I knew this must have been the way Billy had once looked at girls, women. It was why they gave in, even knowing the danger in him. It was because he knew how to want you. That was what he was doing now. Though he wasn't moving, I could feel him pushing the whole force of himself against me with his mouth and lips. His hand went out and touched my shirt and grabbed it. I was about to say something. But then, all of a sudden, I understood the specific nature of his request.

"No, Billy" was what I said.

He looked as if he would not accept the answer, would demand another. The instinct of violence was in him, and I stepped back.

"No, Billy," I said again.

He wanted me to come with him. The whole long-standing

danger of him was in front of me, without filter, without disguise. It was like seeing God after all the talk of God, an amazing density to the presence, a size beyond what you'd ever imagined. This was what he had always been, this being onto whom I had painted another, more thoughtful, more reasonable face. This before me was the actual size of desire.

"You won't come," he said, though they didn't sound like actual words, more like sounds I translated into those words.

His face looked heavy. He took off his hat and flung it over the bridge. He didn't even watch it go. The last thing I saw clearly was his head, the thickness of the scalp, and I wanted some intimacy with it—with its brute humanness—that would restore him and keep him from doing the next thing I knew he would do. I wanted to forgive him.

I grabbed at his body while he tried to climb over the railing. I grabbed hard, but he kicked at me, so that I was on the ground, the wind knocked out of me, when he disappeared. By the time I got up, I was too late even to see him fall, or to know for certain which of the fissures in the water had been made by him.

eighteen

It was impossible not to have conversations about Billy for weeks, even months afterward. People wanted to talk about him, strangers even, and when they found out I knew him—those whom I chose to tell—they didn't want to let me go. The murder of a wife, a pregnant wife, hits a live nerve; it takes a long time for the shocks to wear off. Of course, I'm not saying anything profound when I say that.

In some of those conversations, especially in the early weeks and especially among those who knew how close to Billy I had been, I found I had to check an impulse in myself to defend him, to come up with an argument that made what he'd done less grisly, less entirely reprehensible than it was. The words that came to define Billy in the weeks after his death—"sleazeball," "sociopath," "monster"—became the operative words. Nothing could soften or alter them, and what, anyway, would I say in his defense? That at the end I had seen just how helpless he was, and how limited?

After Billy jumped into the water that night, and after I'd taken God knows how long to recover my wits, I called Kenny and told him I was going to call the cops. I had no intention of holding back my identity.

But Kenny cautioned me not to do that, and he told me where to drive my car. He said he would meet me on the other side of the bridge after he'd gone with the cops to the site I'd described to him. That was how I managed to keep my name out of the papers. When the story was reported, it stated only that an "unidentified motorist" had reported seeing Billy jump. I waited for weeks for the cops in Swampscott to put two and two together and report the license plate of the Lexus from Bradford, but either they never did or Kenny managed to keep that from the reporters, too.

Kenny finally met me and had me follow him to the D.A.'s office. There was work for him to do, and I was not to get off the hook completely. The police needed to thoroughly grill me: Why had Billy called me, and when? What had the plan been? If we were headed to the hospital to see his father, why were we coming from the direction of Boston? When this was all over, we ended up in Kenny's office. He asked me if I wanted to call Teresa, and I told him no, not yet, but then I thought better of it. We had a brief conversation (I'd woken her). I told her she would hear about Billy's death in the morning, but I was all right. She didn't probe (there was the sense that the probing would be intense, but could wait). I also told her I was going to sleep in Kenny's office, and that was what I did. He offered me his couch. He watched over me. I must have slept a couple of hours, and when I awoke in that first murky light, Kenny was at his desk, fingering his chin, staring out at the city.

When he became aware of me waking up, he gazed at me for several seconds and then smiled a little before the grimness returned to his face.

"In the old days," Kenny said, "night like this, guy like me would keep a bottle in his desk. All night long, that's what I've wanted. A drink."

"I thought you gave it up."

He ignored my question.

"I've been sitting here wondering who in this office might keep a bottle. I can't think of anyone. That's how pathetic we've become."

"Kenny," I said, not sure what I even meant, something in the way of thanks.

"This'll be a big one, town waking up to this. Big story." He opened and closed his hands. Something came over his face briefly, a kind of pretense that the story had nothing to do with us.

"Kenny, I appreciate this."

He glanced down at the rug at his feet, kicked at something there. Then he looked up at me. "How'd he get you to drive him?"

"He called me."

"Out of the blue?"

"Yes."

"You knew where he was?"

"It was a total surprise."

Kenny shook his head, some combination of disgust and sadness in his features, and before I knew it, he was crying. He wiped his eyes with his hands. It was one of those messy, intimate moments between men that make you want to forget it even while it is happening.

"I'm sorry. Jesus. Sorry." He made an effort to control himself. "While you've been sleeping, I've been sitting here thinking. Remembering. As much as the guy's a fucking monster, I'm sorry he's dead."

Kenny asked me if I wanted to come and watch them drag the river for Billy's body. I didn't, though I did later see the images, endlessly repeated on TV, of his wet body being hoisted up over the side of the boat, his jeans and polo shirt clinging to his body. When I watched those images, I kept expecting him to shake off the water, to put on that surly expression of his and stand up.

I drove home. Teresa had not waited for me; she'd gone to work. I took the longest shower of my life. The house, empty and light-filled, did not feel particularly welcoming. I walked with Scooter into the woods. I searched for the place where the gun had been hidden, though until I was near it, I hadn't known that was what I was doing. When I found the unfilled hole, I kicked dirt into it until it was half full. Scooter looked at me curiously. The night came back to me in a wave, my last sight of Billy, Kenny crying in his office. I got down on my knees and scratched at the earth until I'd filled the hole completely.

For a time afterward the world seemed to me entirely strange, a thing of covenants that seemed both blessed and tenuous. Everything that had happened with Billy took on the aura of a bad dream, especially when I compared it with what was daily before me: the box I held in my hand from Clara's Home-Cooked, the sparkling look in the eye of the high school girl who had handed it to me, her boyfriend waiting in the corner of the store, a decent boy waiting to lay her as soon as her shift was over, and from under the lid of the box the smell of dill and fresh batter, the smell of lightly fried scallops I was bringing home to my family. The invitation, I understood, is always to allow yourself to be absorbed, and there are these textures so powerful they become agreements. Bradford was waiting, after Billy's death, flawless in late June, children in bathing suits, mothers buying them ice cream, the red and green of traffic lights in the summery dusk. If something made me still slightly too willing to follow the line that connected that boy in the corner of Clara's Home-Cooked to the clean and sparkling girl at the counter, to want to follow imaginatively the destination of that line, to see them in a car at night or on a bed, to imagine the moment when the boy stopped being a decent boy but something else, something closer to what Billy had revealed himself to be at the end, that does not mean I did not do my duty. Stop at the red light. Drive the food home. Joke with the girls. Wait for the night to come, watch Charlie Rose, the sports wrap-ups, anything, really, until I could be sure Teresa was asleep.

Though this part was difficult—Teresa did not want to probe, as I'd anticipated; instead, she seemed to want to punish me—I did not believe that even this would last forever. We live in a world of illimitable second chances. I knew that, however cold to each other we were now, eventually a moment would come when we would begin to mend things. We would make love again. A moment would come, catching us by surprise, when we would find ourselves laughing at something together. Of course we wouldn't leave it at that. A therapist would be suggested. We would "talk things through," though I couldn't imagine ever being truly honest or Teresa really wanting to hear. A good enough approximation of the truth would be arrived at. Then there would be Sebago, Good Harbor, and another truth would become more important: the truth of breasts and dicks, of habit and children. We would find these things again irresistible. We would live pleasantly enough in the fuller, thinner world.

Though I could see that the natural course of events would be to forget Billy, he kept coming back. Several weeks after his death, the *Globe* ran an interview with Paula, in which she revealed that in his early days at Winerip, Billy had attempted to educate himself. She described him studying the dictionary at night, as soon as he'd been told he had the job. "He wanted to make a real good impression," she was quoted as saying.

I remember the photograph of her. Not that it's all that hard to remember; I kept clippings for a while. I still have them somewhere, unfiled. Paula was at her kitchen table, while all around her on the tabletop, obviously set up by the photographer, were pictures of Billy in his days as a coach. Paula looked slightly ratty, but with something of the soiled dignity of old rockers, that Marianne Faithful look of having loved hard and making no apologies for it. I kept hoping that that story about Billy would make people think better of him, but I knew the picture really did all the work: here was the tramp he had gone after—after rejecting, in the most sordid and violent way possible, the pretty, hardworking girl who had wanted only to bear his child. I might have been the only one who took away from that article the image of Billy staying up late with the dictionary, believing that in his work in marketing it might be helpful to know the word "aspidistra." Believing, too, if only at the beginning, that the Winerip Company and the great world it represented might demand something from him other than what Winship had always demanded.

There was a movement, in the aftermath of the shock of Billy's death, for the four of us to get together at the Branding Iron, but I don't think any of us really had much desire for it. In any case, it never happened. Freddie, after a discouraging foray into the job market, accepted Edwin Winerip's offer to relocate to Cincinnati, where the Winerip Company was going to be involved in the expansion of the airport.

In one of our later conversations, Kenny told me that though the district attorney's office believed that Ronnie was the driver of the car on the night of Patty's murder, no one was pushing hard to prosecute. "There's some doubt," Kenny said. "I mean, how do you say what Ronnie *is?*" At the end of that conversation Kenny allowed himself a moment's quiet musing. "We're never going to know why he did it, are we?" It was a simple question, but it sounded less like a question than a request that whatever I knew, I would keep quiet and shrouded. I might have told him he needn't ask. We were never going to know, none of us, not even me. Billy had gone over the bridge with a secret, and though I believed in the moment before he dropped that he'd been trying to reveal himself to me, I had turned away, frightened at the last of the depths of hunger Billy wanted to expose.

Nina played in a summer soccer league, and we usually attended her games, Tony and Katie joining us most nights as well. One night after Nina's team had scored a big victory, Teresa and Katie wanted to take her out for ice cream. I was tired, and Tony, uncharacteristically, was, too, so it was decided that Teresa would take our car and Tony would drop me off at home in the Lincoln.

It was just dark as we took to the streets. Traffic in Bradford had thickened considerably in the years we'd been there, to the point where there were small traffic jams in the middle of town. Under his breath, Tony cursed these.

We passed the long woods where the lights of houses were coming on. Tony seemed to notice each one, each house, as if they were individuals with distinct characteristics that pleased or bothered him. Tonight, as I watched him doing this, I sensed that something was eating at him. I decided to speak, a great risk in that car.

"You remember when we first came here?" I asked.

At first he didn't answer, glanced at me sideways, his hands lightly atop the wheel, like a man steering a boat.

"Sure," he said finally.

"Lots of new houses since then," I said. "Lots of new building."

He allowed that, didn't comment. It was as if I were his child, distracting him from the great, many-spronged world of business with idle talk.

"Sure, everybody wants to come here, Tim," he said.

We drove in silence awhile. I wondered where it had come from, my supposition that he was ready again to be my confidant.

"You remember the lady who showed us around?" I asked. "In her jacket?"

It seemed I was being relentless in my search for common ground.

"We were very impressed," Tony said. His smile was the formal grimace he wore at parties, the social mask he put on to hide the frequently savage opinions he held of the men he'd come up with. "We thought we were moving somewhere," he said, and tapped the wheel, and it felt like something was riding under that "somewhere." "The woods," he said.

"Well, we were," I said, marveling briefly at the fact that we were having a conversation. "It was the new world," I said. "It was . . . empty."

His next glance at me was full of something, I didn't know what, the bubbles that rise over simmering rice when the lid is on the pot.

"Right," he said. "And now it's getting full."

We didn't know where to go with this. He gazed out to the side, as if I had coerced something out of him and he wasn't sure he liked it.

"Something comes," he said.

"What?" I asked. I genuinely wanted to know what he thought "comes."

He shook his head, self-disparaging in his inarticulateness. "I don't know, Tim. I don't know. Everything gets bought, and then, when they build . . ."

He let it trail off. I thought awhile before I spoke again.

"Listen, I know you're disappointed. I know you feel like I

screwed things up between you and Chip Holmes. You wanted to have influence."

He didn't answer. He stared ahead, thoughtful, a half smile on his face. He shook his head. "No, that's not it," he said.

"But I screwed up."

"Yes. You did. No way around that one. But that's a separate thing from what I'm talking about."

"Well then, what is it?"

"I'm not a college man; I can't put it into words."

"We used to take walks, remember? With the dog. You used to see a stone wall. It would do something to you."

"Yes." He said nothing more for a minute or so. It was as if he was embarrassed by what he was feeling. "There's not a respect for something here. I thought there was. At the beginning. Another class of people, they'd have respect. They'd want to leave it like it is. Leave it wild, empty. Leave a little of what was here before."

Without saying anything more, he was managing to convey something, though I was surprised he didn't realize that the class of people he'd been referring to had been replaced by him, by me, by all those who followed in our wake. The new houses that had been built all made unsubtle gestures to the past: in lanterns over their doors, in the style of fences. Bradford was beginning to look like a museum of an idea of the past. I remembered an old phrase of Billy's: "a hit of the real." What people would do, he'd wondered, for a hit of the real. But here it seemed a separate impulse existed: Bradford wanted a hit of the fake. Over and over again. In the mini-malls, in the houses we passed. Bradford had torn down Elijah Grierson's house and then put up another, more cheerful version of the past. I was surprised Tony had noticed, though I shouldn't have been.

Then, whether because I hadn't responded quickly enough or because he was embarrassed at having voiced these sentiments, he shook his head. "But it's beautiful. Can't anybody tell you it's not beautiful."

We had nearly reached my house. It appeared over its bank, its lights out. He made the turn, and we cruised lightly up the drive, gravel crunching under us. It was like cresting small waves.

I didn't want to go, didn't want to leave him. I sensed he had come out briefly and now was retreating, remembering my sin, going back under his hard shell.

"Look, it doesn't matter what we think, does it?" he asked.

"What do you mean?"

"There's the kids. Your kids. My grandchildren."

He covered his face with one hand, tired, then looked at my house. "When will you give it a new stain?"

"I don't know. You think it needs it?"

"I think it needs it. Yes."

Our old conversation was sinking—I could see it just under the water—but it would be impolitic to drag it up.

"Well, maybe this fall," I said.

"I can give you the name of a guy." He studied my face in the falling dark, as if going over a checklist: chimneys, roof, gutters. "Can you afford it?"

"Jesus, Tony."

"Can you?"

"Yes."

He sat behind the wheel studying his nails. It was like he was punishing me for opening him up before. "Well, if you can't, we can talk."

"Okay. Thanks for the ride."

I stepped out of the car, closed the door behind me. He wasn't moving. He stared ahead, as if I'd already gone inside.

"You all right?" I looked in.

"Fine."

He shifted into reverse with great fanfare, as if he were about to ride herd on a fleet of foot-dragging salesmen, as if the world still waited for him to whip it into shape. He backed up hugely and dramatically and drove down the slope and disappeared.

I waited a few moments. The house, unlit, arose before me. I could hear Scooter, aware of my return, scratching at the door, begging to be let out. I walked up the steps and opened the door and received his huge, wet welcome. Then I turned on the switch and watched the porch receive its light. I took Scooter down into the dark field until I was far enough in so that I could lose myself in that moment I have always treasured, to be standing in the dark looking up at a lit place, knowing that I can return to it but that I don't have to, not just yet.

In January 1990, I was driving home when I heard on the radio that Charles Stuart, the man who'd been shot along with his pregnant wife in the Mission Hill section of Boston a year before, had jumped to his death from the Tobin Bridge. My immediate assumption was that Stuart had done it out of grief; both his wife and infant son had died as a result of the attack. I, like the entire city of Boston—like the nation as a whole—had been taken in by Stuart, by the moving letter he'd written his dying son from his hospital bed, by the story of a black man charging out of the night into Stuart's car, robbing him of what was most dear to him. In my own car, driving home that night, I remember being overcome by a wave of pity.

What makes novels, as opposed to newspaper stories, is what came next. As the truth came out (or as much truth as we'll ever know about Charles Stuart), as the city and the nation came to learn that it was all a ruse—the gun-toting black man, the grief over the dying son—that Stuart had done it all himself, some part of me refused to let go of the pity. I liked the story I had come up with on my own better than the one being reported in the papers. I liked the Charles Stuart I had created over the past year or so, since the incident of the shooting had first been reported, better than the amended Charles Stuart, about whom we now knew certain facts. Those facts were being used to put the story into a tight, familiar, and unthreatening shape. I much preferred the more ambiguous story I had come to believe.

Within the next year, a raft of instant books were published, and there was a made-for-TV movie about the Stuart case. I ignored them, and the public got its fill of another gruesome true-crime story.

That is, much of the public did. As the novel I wanted to write began to gestate, I kept finding people who wanted to talk about Stuart. Some part of his effect had not been completely absorbed by all the media coverage. When I got into the real research, talking to people in law enforcement, it seemed that every other person I spoke to wanted to get me in touch with someone who really "knew" the Stuart story: acquaintances of Stuart or his brother. I resisted these tips. By the time I got around to writing this book, it was no longer about Charles Stuart. It was about that man I'd created over the months of Stuart's "grief," the man who was with me in the car as I heard the news about Stuart's suicide. We participate in the stories we care about, however distant from us they may be, and as much as this novel is a record of the participation of my narrator, Timmy O'Kane, in his friend Billy Mogavero's Stuart-like story, so is it a record of my own participation with a murderer whom I have never been able to believe was quite as simple as the recorded story would ask us to accept.

acknowledgments

A number of people provided invaluable assistance—with factual information, with encouragement, and sometimes with simple listening—during the writing of this book.

I would like to thank first the group of writers to whom I read the manuscript from beginning to end—Joann Kobin, Marisa Labozzetta, Roger King, Betsy Hartmann, and Mordicai Gerstein—all of whom were smart about the book, and about Billy, from the very start. Michael Gorra and David Hoose read the manuscript and provided excellent literary and legal advice, respectively. Charles Sennott and Kevin Cullen of *The Boston Globe* gave me useful insights into South Boston.

I am indebted to Dr. Steven Eipper for medical advice, to Jonathan Smylie for filling me in on the details of the life of the textbook salesman, and to Tom Gilmore for doing the same with the inner workings of a developer not unlike the one Billy comes to work for. Steve Brackett and Clarence Joseph provided important details concerning things automotive and Trinidadian, respectively. When it came time to explore the workings of the criminal justice system, Martha Coakley, District Attorney for Middlesex County, opened her doors to me. Her press representative, Emily LaGrassa, was extremely generous in setting up a meeting with David Procopio, her counterpart at the Suffolk County D.A.'s office, where David Meier, the Chief of Homicide, and Dennis Collins were both very helpful in providing information.

My childhood friend Barry Kennedy, to whom this book is in part dedicated, gave me access to parts of Dorchester and South Boston I'd never have gotten to on my own. Aside from being the funniest person I have ever known, Barry had become a knowledgeable guide to a world far from the cozy suburb where we grew up. His death in the midst of my writing this novel haunts both it and me, but I will not forget the help he gave me or the friend he remained to the end.

The other part of the dedication goes to Sloan Harris, who as an agent has spoiled me beyond reason, acting as friend, coach, and drill sergeant; most importantly, he has forced me to think beyond my very Italian American sense of my own limitations. For this, as for everything else, he has a hallowed place in my life. His assistant, Katherine Cluverius, performed yeoman service. Together, they are a team worthy of a Howard Hawks pairing.

It was my great fortune to work with Jonathan Galassi. He is of course everyone's dream editor. The surprise and delight I found in working with him was how direct and unfancy his responses were. We were two Massachusetts boys who both knew the familiar world I was trying to re-create; his great gift to me was in asking me to render it truly, and allow the literary to take care of itself. Lorin Stein came in to line edit, brilliantly, in a way we are all told doesn't happen anymore. I am indebted to both of them.

Finally, there are those people who don't read the manuscript until the very end, but who have to live with the writer. My daughter Nicola has been out of the house for a few years, but her insights into racial and generational issues have permanently affected the way I think about those things. My younger daughter, Sophia, holds me to a standard I don't dare fail to meet; any day now, she will surpass me. My wife, Eileen, in addition to offering technical assistance born of her sixteen years as a labor and delivery nurse, had the good sense to ask me very few questions about what I was writing, knowing as she did that if the past was any sort of guide, I was cooking up another "dark" view of marriage. In the long education that our married lives have been, I have learned a great many things from her. The one thing I hope she has learned from me is that even someone so flagrantly self-revealing as a writer knows that there are things too precious to be exposed. If my own marriage ever creeps into one of my books, it will be because I have forgotten that important lesson.